ORSON SCOTT CARD

TOR

A TOM DOHERTY ASSOCIATES BOOK

SPEAKER FOR THE DEAD

Copyright © 1986 by Orson Scott Card

First printing: March 1986

A TOR Book

Published by Tom Doherty Associates
49 West 24 Street
New York, N.Y. 10010

Cover art by John Harris

ISBN: 0-312-93738-5

Library of Congress Catalog Card Number: 85-51765

Printed in the United States

0   9   8   7   6   5   4   3   2   1

For Gregg Keizer
Who already knew how

Contents

Some People of Lusitania Colony

Xenologers (Zenadores)
Pipo (João Figueira Alvarez)
Libo (Liberdade Graças a Deus Figueira de Medici)
Miro (Marcos Vladimir Ribeira von Hesse)
Ouanda (Ouanda Quenhatta Figueira Mucumbi)

Xenobiologists (Biologistas)
Gusto (Vladimir Tiago Gussman)
Cida (Ekaterina Maria Aparecida do Norte von Hesse-Gussman)
Novinha (Ivanova Santa Catarina von Hesse)
Ela (Ekaterina Elanora Ribeira von Hesse)

Governor
Bosquinha (Faria Lima Maria do Bosque)

Bishop
Peregrino (Armão Cebola)

Abbot and Principal of the Monastery
Dom Cristão (Amai a Tudomundo Para Que Deus vos
           Ame Cristão)
Dona Cristã (Detestai o Pecado e Fazei o Direito Cristã)

The Figueira Family

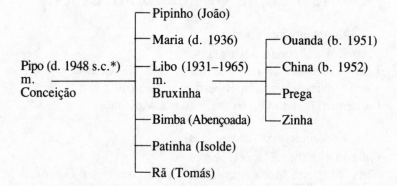

Pipo (d. 1948 s.c.*)
m.
Conceição

- Pipinho (João)
- Maria (d. 1936)
- Libo (1931–1965) m. Bruxinha
  - Ouanda (b. 1951)
  - China (b. 1952)
  - Prega
  - Zinha
- Bimba (Abençoada)
- Patinha (Isolde)
- Rã (Tomás)

The Family of Os Venerados

Gusto (d. 1936)
m.
Cida (d. 1936)

- Mingo (d. 1936)
- Novinha (b. 1931) m. Marcão (d. 1970) (Marcos Maria Ribeira)
  - Miro (b. 1951)
  - Ela (b. 1952)
  - Quim (b. 1955) (Estevão Rei)
  - Olhado (b. 1958) (Lauro Suleimão)
  - Quara (b. 1963) (Lembrança das Milagres de Jesus)
  - Grego (b. 1964) (Gerão Gregorio)
- Amado (d. 1936)
- Guti (d. 1936)

*All dates are expressed as years after adoption of the Starways Code.

Pronouncing Foreign Names

Three human languages are used by characters in this book. Stark, since it originated as English, is represented as English in the book. The Nordic spoken on Trondheim evolved from Swedish. Portuguese is the native language of Lusitania. On every world, however, schoolchildren are taught Stark from the beginning.

The Portuguese language, while unusually beautiful when spoken aloud, is very difficult for readers who are accustomed to English to sound out from the written letters. Even if you aren't planning to read this book aloud, you may be more comfortable if you have a general idea of how the Portuguese names and phrases are pronounced.

Consonants: Single consonants are pronounced more or less as they are in English, with the addition of ç, which always sounds like *ss*. Exceptions are *j*, which is pronounced like the *z* in *azure*, as is *g* when followed by *e* or *i*; and the initial *r* and double *rr*, which are pronounced somewhere between the American *h* and the Yiddish *ch*.

Vowels: Single vowels are pronounced more or less as follows: *a* as in *father*, *e* as in *get*, *i* like the *ee* in *fee*, *o* as in *throne*, and *u* like the *oo* in *toot*. (This is a gross oversimplification, since there are really two distinct *a* sounds, neither of which is really like the *a* in *father*, three meaning-changing ways to pronounce *e—é*, *ê*, and the quick *e* at the end of a word—and three meaning-changing ways to pronounce *o—ó*, *ô*, and the quick *o* at the ends of words. But it's close enough to get you through this book.)

Consonant combinations: The combination *lh* is pronounced like

xi

the *lli* in *William;* *nh,* like the *ni* in *onion.* The combination *ch* is always pronounced like the English *sh.* The combination *qu,* when followed by *e* or *i,* is pronounced like the English *k;* when followed by *a, o,* or *u,* like the English *qu;* the same pattern is followed by *gu.* Thus *Quara* is pronounced KWAH-rah, while *Figueira* is pronounced fee-GAY-rah.

Vowel combinations: The combination *ou* is pronounced like the *ow* in *throw; ai,* like *igh* in *high; ei,* like *eigh* in *weigh.* The combination *eu* is not found in English; it is pronounced as a very quick combination of the *e* in *get* and the *u* in *put.*

Nasal vowels: A vowel or vowel combination with a tilde—usually ão and ã—or the combination *am* at the end of a word are all nasalized. That is, they are pronounced as if the vowel were going to end with the English *ng* sound, only the *ng* is never quite closed. In addition, the syllable with a tilde is *always* stressed, so that the name Marcão is pronounced mah-KOWNG. (Syllables with ^ and ´ accent marks are also stressed.)

If I told you that when *t* comes before the *i* sound it's pronounced like the English *ch,* and *d* follows the same pattern to sound like the English *j,* or if I mentioned that *x* always sounds like *sh* except when it sounds like *z,* you might well give up entirely, so I won't.

Prologue

In the year 1830, after the formation of Starways Congress, a robot scout ship sent a report by ansible: The planet it was investigating was well within the parameters for human life. The nearest planet with any kind of population pressure was Baía; Starways Congress granted them the exploration license.

So it was that the first humans to see the new world were Portuguese by language, Brazilian by culture, and Catholic by creed. In the year 1886 they disembarked from their shuttle, crossed themselves, and named the planet Lusitania—the ancient name of Portugal. They set about cataloguing the flora and fauna. Five days later they realized that the little forest-dwelling animals that they had called *porquinhos*—piggies—were not animals at all.

For the first time since the Xenocide of the Buggers by the monstrous Ender, humans had found intelligent alien life. The piggies were technologically primitive, but they used tools and built houses and spoke a language. "It is another chance God has given us," declared Archcardinal Pio of Baía. "We can be redeemed for the destruction of the buggers."

The members of Starways Congress worshipped many gods, or none, but they agreed with the Archcardinal. Lusitania would be settled from Baía, and therefore under Catholic

License, as tradition demanded. But the colony could never spread beyond a limited area or exceed a limited population. And it was bound, above all, by one law:

The piggies were not to be disturbed.

Chapter I
Pipo

Since we are not yet fully comfortable with the idea that
people from the next village are as human as ourselves,
it is presumptuous in the extreme to suppose we could
ever look at sociable, tool-making creatures who arose
from other evolutionary paths and see not beasts but
brothers, not rivals but fellow pilgrims journeying to the
shrine of intelligence.

Yet that is what I see, or yearn to see. The difference
between raman and varelse is not in the creature judged,
but in the creature judging. When we declare an alien
species to be raman, it does not mean that *they* have
passed a threshold of moral maturity. It means that *we*
have.

—Demosthenes, *Letter to the Framlings*

Rooter was at once the most difficult and the most helpful
of the pequeninos. He was always there whenever Pipo visited their clearing, and did his best to answer the questions
Pipo was forbidden by law to come right out and ask. Pipo
depended on him—too much, probably—yet though Rooter
clowned and played like the irresponsible youngling that he
was, he also watched, probed, tested. Pipo always had to
beware of the traps that Rooter set for him.

A moment ago Rooter had been shimmying up trees,

1

gripping the bark with only the horny pads on his ankles and inside his thighs. In his hands he carried two sticks—Father Sticks, they were called—which he beat against the tree in a compelling, arhythmic pattern all the while he climbed.

The noise brought Mandachuva out of the log house. He called to Rooter in the Males' Language, and then in Portuguese. "P'ra baixo, bicho!" Several piggies nearby, hearing his Portuguese wordplay, expressed their appreciation by rubbing their thighs together sharply. It made a hissing noise, and Mandachuva took a little hop in the air in delight at their applause.

Rooter, in the meantime, bent over backward until it seemed certain he would fall. Then he flipped off with his hands, did a somersault in the air, and landed on his legs, hopping a few times but not stumbling.

"So now you're an acrobat," said Pipo.

Rooter swaggered over to him. It was his way of imitating humans. It was all the more effective as ridicule because his flattened upturned snout looked decidedly porcine. No wonder that offworlders called them "piggies." The first visitors to this world had started calling them that in their first reports back in '86, and by the time Lusitania Colony was founded in 1925, the name was indelible. The xenologers scattered among the Hundred Worlds wrote of them as "Lusitanian Aborigines," though Pipo knew perfectly well that this was merely a matter of professional dignity—except in scholarly papers, xenologers no doubt called them piggies, too. As for Pipo, he called them pequeninos, and they seemed not to object, for now they called themselves "Little Ones." Still, dignity or not, there was no denying it. At moments like this, Rooter looked like a hog on its hind legs.

"Acrobat," Rooter said, trying out the new word. "What I did? You have a word for people who do that? So there are people who do that as their *work*?"

Pipo sighed silently, even as he froze his smile in place. The law strictly forbade him to share information about human society, lest it contaminate piggy culture. Yet Rooter played a constant game of squeezing the last drop of implication out of everything Pipo said. This time, though, Pipo had no one to blame but himself, letting out a silly remark that opened unnecessary windows onto human life. Now and then he got so comfortable among the pequeninos that he spoke naturally. Always a danger. I'm not good at this constant game of taking information while trying to give nothing in return. Libo, my close-mouthed son, already he's better at discretion than I am, and he's only been apprenticed to me—how long since he turned thirteen?—four months.

"I wish I had pads on my legs like yours," said Pipo. "The bark on that tree would rip my skin to shreds."

"That would cause us all to be ashamed." Rooter held still in the expectant posture that Pipo thought of as their way of showing mild anxiety, or perhaps a nonverbal warning to other pequeninos to be cautious. It might also have been a sign of extreme fear, but as far as Pipo knew he had never seen a pequenino feel extreme fear.

In any event, Pipo spoke quickly to calm him. "Don't worry, I'm too old and soft to climb trees like that. I'll leave it to you younglings."

And it worked; Rooter's body at once became mobile again. "I like to climb trees. I can see everything." Rooter squatted in front of Pipo and leaned his face in close. "Will you bring the beast that runs over the grass without touching the ground? The others don't believe me when I say I saw such a thing."

Another trap. What, Pipo, xenologer, will you *humiliate* this individual of the community you're studying? Or will you adhere to the rigid law set up by Starways Congress to govern this encounter? There were few precedents. The only other intelligent aliens that humankind had encountered were the buggers, three thousand years ago, and at the end of it the buggers were all dead. This time Starways Congress was making sure that if humanity erred, their errors would be in the opposite direction. Minimal information, minimal contact.

Rooter recognized Pipo's hesitation, his careful silence.

"You never tell us anything," said Rooter. "You watch us and study us, but you never let us past your fence and into your village to watch *you* and study *you*."

Pipo answered as honestly as he could, but it was more important to be careful than to be honest. "If you learn so little and we learn so much, why is it that you speak both Stark and Portuguese while I'm still struggling with your language?"

"We're smarter." Then Rooter leaned back and spun around on his buttocks so his back was toward Pipo. "Go back behind your fence," he said.

Pipo stood at once. Not too far away, Libo was with three pequeninos, trying to learn how they wove dried merdona vines into thatch. He saw Pipo and in a moment was with his father, ready to go. Pipo led him off without a word; since the pequeninos were so fluent in human languages, they never discussed what they had learned until they were inside the gate.

It took a half hour to get home, and it was raining heavily when they passed through the gate and walked along the face of the hill to the Zenador's Station. Zenador? Pipo thought of the word as he looked at the small sign above the door. On it the word XENOLOGER was written in Stark. That is what I am, I suppose, thought Pipo, at least to the offworlders. But the Portuguese title *Zenador* was so much easier to say that on Lusitania hardly anyone said *xenologer*, even when speaking Stark. That is how languages change, thought Pipo. If it weren't for the ansible, providing instantaneous communication among the Hundred Worlds, we could not possibly maintain a common language. Interstellar travel is far too rare and slow. Stark would splinter into ten thousand dialects within a century. It might be interesting to have the computers run a projection of linguistic changes on Lusitania, if Stark were allowed to decay and absorb Portuguese—

"Father," said Libo.

Only then did Pipo notice that he had stopped ten meters away from the station. Tangents. The best parts of my intellectual life are tangential, in areas outside my expertise. I suppose because within my area of expertise the regulations they have placed upon me make it impossible to know or understand anything. The science of xenology insists on more mysteries than Mother Church.

His handprint was enough to unlock the door. Pipo knew how the evening would unfold even as he stepped inside to begin. It would take several hours of work at the terminals for them both to report what they had done during today's encounter. Pipo would then read over Libo's notes, and Libo would read Pipo's, and when they were satisfied, Pipo would write up a brief summary and then let the computers take it from there, filing the notes and also transmitting them instantly, by ansible, to the xenologers in the rest of the Hundred Worlds. More than a thousand scientists whose whole career is studying the one alien race we know, and except for what little the satellites can discover about this arboreal species, all the information my colleagues have is what Libo and I send them. This is definitely minimal intervention.

But when Pipo got inside the station, he saw at once that it would not be an evening of steady but relaxing work. Dona Cristã was there, dressed in her monastic robes. Was it one of the younger children, in trouble at school?

"No, no," said Dona Cristã. "All your children are doing very well, except this one, who I think is far too young to be out of school and working here, even as an apprentice."

Libo said nothing. A wise decision, thought Pipo. Dona Cristã was a brilliant and engaging, perhaps even beautiful, young woman, but she was first and foremost a monk of the order of the Filhos da Mente de Cristo, Children of the Mind of Christ, and she was not beautiful to behold when she was angry at ignorance and stupidity. It was amazing the number of quite intelligent people whose ignorance and stupidity had melted somewhat in the fire of her scorn. Silence, Libo, it's a policy that will do you good.

"I'm not here about any child of yours at all," said Dona Cristã. "I'm here about Novinha."

Dona Cristã did not have to mention a last name; everybody knew Novinha. The terrible Descolada had ended only eight years before. The plague had threatened to wipe out the colony before it had a fair chance to get started; the cure was discovered by Novinha's father and mother, Gusto and Cida, the two xenobiologists. It was a tragic irony that they found the cause of the disease and its treatment too late to save themselves. Theirs was the last Descolada funeral.

Pipo clearly remembered the little girl Novinha, standing there holding Mayor Bosquinha's hand while Bishop Peregrino conducted the funeral mass himself. No—not holding the Mayor's hand. The picture came back to his mind, and, with it, the way he felt. What does she make of this? he remembered asking himself. It's the funeral of her parents, she's the last survivor in her family; yet all around her she can sense the great rejoicing of the people of this colony. Young as she is, does she understand that our joy is the best tribute to her parents? They struggled and succeeded, finding our salvation in the waning days before they died; we are here to celebrate the great gift they gave us. But to you, Novinha, it's the death of your parents, as your brothers died before. Five hundred dead, and more than a hundred masses for the dead here in this colony in the last six months, and all of them were held in an atmosphere of fear and grief and despair. Now, when your parents die, the fear and grief and despair are no less for you than ever before—but no one else shares your pain. It is the relief from pain that is foremost in our minds.

Watching her, trying to imagine her feelings, he succeeded

only in rekindling his own grief at the death of his own Maria, seven years old, swept away in the wind of death that covered her body in cancerous growth and rampant funguses, the flesh swelling or decaying, a new limb, not arm or leg, growing out of her hip, while the flesh sloughed off her feet and head, baring the bones, her sweet and beautiful body destroyed before their eyes, while her bright mind was mercilessly alert, able to feel all that happened to her until she cried out to God to let her die. Pipo remembered that, and then remembered her requiem mass, shared with five other victims. As he sat, knelt, stood there with his wife and surviving children, he had felt the perfect unity of the people in the Cathedral. He knew that his pain was everybody's pain, that through the loss of his eldest daughter he was bound to his community with the inseparable bonds of grief, and it *was* a comfort to him, it was something to cling to. That was how such a grief ought to be, a public mourning.

Little Novinha had nothing of that. Her pain was, if anything, worse than Pipo's had been—at least Pipo had not been left without any family at all, and he was an adult, not a child terrified by suddenly losing the foundation of her life. In her grief she was not drawn more tightly into the community, but rather excluded from it. Today everyone was rejoicing, except her. Today everyone praised her parents; she alone yearned for them, would rather they had never found the cure for others if only they could have remained alive themselves.

Her isolation was so acute that Pipo could see it from where he sat. Novinha took her hand away from the Mayor as quickly as possible. Her tears dried up as the mass progressed; by the end she sat in silence, like a prisoner refusing to cooperate with her captors. Pipo's heart broke for her. Yet he knew that even if he tried, he could not conceal his own gladness at the end of the Descolada, his rejoicing that none of his other children would be taken from him. She would see that; his effort to comfort her would be a mockery, would drive her further away.

After the mass she walked in bitter solitude amid the crowds of well-meaning people who cruelly told her that her parents were sure to be saints, sure to sit at the right hand of God. What kind of comfort is that for a child? Pipo whispered aloud to his wife, "She'll never forgive us for today."

"Forgive?" Conceição was not one of those wives who instantly understood her husband's train of thought. "*We* didn't kill her parents—"

"But we're all rejoicing today, aren't we? She'll never forgive us for that."

"Nonsense. She doesn't understand anyway; she's too young."

She understands, Pipo thought. Didn't Maria understand things when she was even younger than Novinha is now?

As the years passed—eight years now—he had seen her from time to time. She was his son Libo's age, and until Libo's thirteenth birthday that meant they were in many classes together. He heard her give occasional readings and speeches, along with other children. There was an elegance to her thought, an intensity to her examination of ideas that appealed to him. At the same time, she seemed utterly cold, completely removed from everyone else. Pipo's own boy, Libo, was shy, but even so he had several friends, and had won the affection of his teachers. Novinha, though, had no friends at all, no one whose gaze she sought after a moment of triumph. There was no teacher who genuinely liked her, because she refused to reciprocate, to respond. "She is emotionally paralyzed," Dona Cristã said once when Pipo asked about her. "There is no reaching her. She swears that she's perfectly happy, and doesn't see any need to change."

Now Dona Cristã had come to the Zenador's Station to talk to Pipo about Novinha. Why Pipo? He could guess only one reason for the principal of the school to come to him about this particular orphaned girl. "Am I to believe that in all the years you've had Novinha in your school, I'm the only person who asked about her?''

"Not the only person," she said. "There was all kinds of interest in her a couple of years ago, when the Pope beatified her parents. Everybody asked then whether the daughter of Gusto and Cida, Os Venerados, had ever noticed any miraculous events associated with her parents, as so many other people had."

"They actually *asked* her that?"

"There were rumors, and Bishop Peregrino had to investigate." Dona Cristã got a bit tight-lipped when she spoke of the young spiritual leader of Lusitania Colony. But then, it was said that the hierarchy never got along well with the order of the Filhos da Mente de Cristo. "Her answer was instructive."

"I can imagine."

"She said, more or less, that if her parents were actually listening to prayers and had any influence in heaven to get them granted, then why wouldn't they have answered *her* prayer, for them to return from the grave? That would be a useful miracle, she said, and there are precedents. If Os Venerados actually had the power to grant miracles, then it must mean they did not love her enough to answer her prayer. She preferred to believe that her parents still loved her, and simply did not have the power to act."

"A born sophist," said Pipo.

"A sophist *and* an expert in guilt: she told the Bishop that if the Pope declared her parents to be venerable, it would be the same as the Church saying that her parents hated her. The petition for canonization of her parents was proof that Lusitania despised her; if it was granted, it would be proof that the Church itself was despicable. Bishop Peregrino was livid."

"I notice he sent in the petition anyway."

"For the good of the community. And there *were* all those miracles."

"Someone touches the shrine and a headache goes away

and they cry 'Milagre!—os santos me abençoaram!' Miracle!
—the saints have blessed me!

"You know that Holy Rome requires more substantial
miracles than that. But it doesn't matter. The Pope graciously
allowed us to call our little town Milagre, and now I imagine
that every time someone says that name, Novinha burns a
little hotter with her secret rage."

"Or colder. One never knows what temperature that sort
of thing will take."

"Anyway, Pipo, you aren't the only one who ever asked
about her. But you're the only one who ever asked about her
for her own sake, and not because of her most Holy and
Blessed parents."

It was a sad thought, that except for the Filhos, who ran
the schools of Lusitania, there had been no concern for the
girl except the slender shards of attention Pipo had spared for
her over the years.

"She has one friend," said Libo.

Pipo had forgotten that his son was there—Libo was so
quiet that he was easy to overlook. Dona Cristã also seemed
startled. "Libo," she said, "I think we were indiscreet,
talking about one of your schoolmates like this."

"I'm apprentice Zenador now," Libo reminded her. It
meant he wasn't in school.

"Who is her friend?" asked Pipo.

"Marcão."

"Marcos Ribeira," Dona Cristã explained. "The tall boy—"

"Ah, yes, the one who's built like a cabra."

"He *is* strong," said Dona Cristã. "But I've never noticed
any friendship between them."

"Once when Marcão was accused of something, and she
happened to see it, she spoke for him."

"You put a generous interpretation on it, Libo," said Dona
Cristã. "I think it is more accurate to say she spoke *against*
the boys who actually did it and were trying to put the blame
on him."

"Marcão doesn't see it that way," said Libo. "I noticed a couple of times, the way he watches her. It isn't much, but there is somebody who likes her."

"Do *you* like her?" asked Pipo.

Libo paused for a moment in silence. Pipo knew what it meant. He was examining himself to find an answer. Not the answer that he thought would be most likely to bring him adult favor, and not the answer that would provoke their ire—the two kinds of deception that most children his age delighted in. He was examining himself to discover the truth.

"I think," Libo said, "that I understood that she didn't want to be liked. As if she were a visitor who expected to go back home any day."

Dona Cristã nodded gravely. "Yes, that's exactly right, that's exactly the way she seems. But now, Libo, we must end our indiscretion by asking you to leave us while we—"

He was gone before she finished her sentence, with a quick nod of his head, a half-smile that said, Yes, I understand, and a deftness of movement that made his exit more eloquent proof of his discretion than if he had argued to stay. By this Pipo knew that Libo was annoyed at being asked to leave; he had a knack for making adults feel vaguely immature by comparison to him.

"Pipo," said the principal, "she has petitioned for an early examination as xenobiologist. To take her parents' place."

Pipo raised an eyebrow.

"She claims that she has been studying the field intensely since she was a little child. That she's ready to begin the work right now, without apprenticeship."

"She's thirteen, isn't she?"

"There are precedents. Many have taken such tests early. One even passed it younger than her. It was two thousand years ago, but it *was* allowed. Bishop Peregrino is against it, of course, but Mayor Bosquinha, bless her practical heart, has pointed out that Lusitania needs a xenobiologist quite badly—we need to be about the business of developing new strains of plant life so we can get some decent variety in our diet and much better harvests from Lusitanian soil. In her words, 'I don't care if it's an infant, we need a xenobiologist.' "

"And you want me to supervise her examination?"

"If you would be so kind."

"I'll be glad to."

"I told them you would."

"I confess I have an ulterior motive."

"Oh?"

"I should have done more for the girl. I'd like to see if it isn't too late to begin."

Dona Cristã laughed a bit. "Oh, Pipo, I'd be glad for you to try. But do believe me, my dear friend, touching her heart is like bathing in ice."

"I imagine. I imagine it feels like bathing in ice to the person touching her. But how does it feel to her? Cold as she is, it must surely burn like fire."

"Such a poet," said Dona Cristã. There was no irony in her voice; she meant it. "Do the piggies understand that we've sent our very best as our ambassador?"

"I try to tell them, but they're skeptical."

"I'll send her to you tomorrow. I warn you—she'll expect to take the examinations cold, and she'll resist any attempt on your part to pre-examine her."

Pipo smiled. "I'm far more worried about what will happen after she takes the test. If she fails, then she'll have very bad problems. And if she passes, then *my* problems will begin."

"Why?"

"Libo will be after me to let him examine early for Zenador. And if he did *that,* there'd be no reason for me not to go home, curl up, and die."

"Such a romantic fool you are, Pipo. If there's any man in

Milagre who's capable of accepting his thirteen-year-old son as a colleague, it's you.''

After she left, Pipo and Libo worked together, as usual, recording the day's events with the pequeninos. Pipo compared Libo's work, his way of thinking, his insights, his attitudes, with those of the graduate students he had known in University before joining the Lusitania Colony. He might be small, and there might be a lot of theory and knowledge for him yet to learn, but he was already a true scientist in his method, and a humanist at heart. By the time the evening's work was done and they walked home together by the light of Lusitania's large and dazzling moon, Pipo had decided that Libo already deserved to be treated as a colleague, whether he took the examination or not. The tests couldn't measure the things that really counted, anyway.

And whether she liked it or not, Pipo intended to find out if Novinha had the unmeasurable qualities of a scientist; if she didn't, then he'd see to it she didn't take the test, regardless of how many facts she had memorized.

Pipo meant to be difficult. Novinha knew how adults acted when they planned not to do things her way, but didn't want a fight or even any nastiness. Of course, of course you can take the test. But there's no reason to rush into it, let's take some time, let me make sure you'll be successful on the first attempt.

Novinha didn't want to wait. Novinha was ready.

"I'll jump through any hoops you want," she said.

His face went cold. Their faces always did. That was all right, coldness was all right, she could freeze them to death. "I don't want you to jump through hoops," he said.

"The only thing I ask is that you line them up all in a row so I can jump through them *quickly*. I don't want to be put off for days and days."

He looked thoughtful for a moment. "You're in such a hurry."

"I'm *ready*. The Starways Code allows me to challenge the test at any time. It's between me and the Starways Congress, and I can't find anywhere that it says a xenologer can try to second-guess the Interplanetary Examinations Board."

"Then you haven't read carefully."

"The only thing I need to take the test before I'm sixteen is the authorization of my legal guardian. I don't *have* a legal guardian."

"On the contrary," said Pipo. "Mayor Bosquinha was your legal guardian from the day of your parents' death."

"And she agreed I could take the test."

"Provided you came to me."

Novinha saw the intense look in his eyes. She didn't know Pipo, so she thought it was the look she had seen in so many eyes, the desire to dominate, to rule her, the desire to cut through her determination and break her independence, the desire to make her *submit*.

From ice to fire in an instant. "What do you know about xenobiology! You only go out and talk to the piggies, you don't even begin to understand the workings of genes! Who are you to judge me! Lusitania needs a xenobiologist, and they've been without one for eight years. And you want to make them wait even longer, just so you can be in control!"

To her surprise, he didn't become flustered, didn't retreat. Nor did he get angry in return. It was as if she hadn't spoken.

"I see," he said quietly. "It's because of your great love of the people of Lusitania that you wish to become xeno-biologist. Seeing the public need, you sacrificed and prepared yourself to enter early into a lifetime of altruistic service."

It sounded absurd, hearing him say it like that. And it wasn't at all what she felt. "Isn't that a good enough reason?"

"If it were true, it would be good enough."

"Are you calling me a liar?"

"Your own words called you a liar. You spoke of how much *they,* the people of Lusitania, need you. But you live among us. You've lived among us all your life. Ready to sacrifice for us, and yet you don't feel yourself to be part of this community."

So he wasn't like the adults who always believed lies as long as they made her seem to be the child they wanted her to be. "Why should I *feel* like part of the community? I'm not."

He nodded gravely, as if considering her answer. "What community are you a part of?"

"The only other communities on Lusitania are the piggies, and you haven't seen me out there with the tree-worshippers."

"There are many other communities on Lusitania. For instance, you're a student—there's a community of students."

"Not for me."

"I know. You have no friends, you have no intimate associates, you go to mass but you never go to confession, you are so completely detached that as far as possible you don't touch the life of this colony, you don't touch the life of the human race at any point. From all the evidence, you live in complete isolation."

Novinha wasn't prepared for this. He was naming the underlying pain of her life, and she didn't have a strategy devised to cope with it. "If I do, it isn't my fault."

"I know that. I know where it began, and I know whose fault it was that it continues to this day."

"Mine?"

"Mine. And everyone else's. But mine most of all, because I knew what was happening to you and I did nothing at all. Until today."

"And today you're going to keep me from the one thing that matters to me in my life! Thanks so much for your compassion!"

Again he nodded solemnly, as if he were accepting and acknowledging her ironic gratitude. "In one sense, Novinha, it doesn't matter that it isn't your fault. Because the town of Milagre *is* a community, and whether it has treated you badly or not, it must still act as all communities do, to provide the greatest possible happiness for all its members."

"Which means everybody on Lusitania except me—me and the piggies."

"The xenobiologist is very important to a colony, especially one like this, surrounded by a fence that forever limits our growth. Our xenobiologist must find ways to grow more protein and carbohydrate per hectare, which means genetically altering the Earthborn corn and potatoes to make—"

"To make maximum use of the nutrients available in the Lusitanian environment. Do you think I'm planning to take the examination without knowing what my life's work would be?"

"Your life's work, to devote yourself to improving the lives of people you despise."

Now Novinha saw the trap that he had laid for her. Too late; it had sprung. "So you think that a xenobiologist can't do her work unless she *loves* the people who use the things she makes?"

"I don't care whether you love us or not. What I have to know is what you really want. Why you're so passionate to do this."

"Basic psychology. My parents died in this work, and so I'm trying to step into their role."

"Maybe," said Pipo. "And maybe not. What I want to know, Novinha, what I *must* know before I'll let you take the test, is what community you *do* belong to."

"You said it yourself! I don't belong to any."

"Impossible. Every person is defined by the communities she belongs to and the ones she doesn't belong to. I am this and this and this, but definitely *not* that and that and that. All your definitions are negative. I could make an infinite list of the things you are not. But a person who really believes she doesn't belong to any community at all invariably kills herself, either by killing her body or by giving up her identity and going mad."

"That's me, insane to the root."

"Not insane. Driven by a sense of purpose that is frightening. If you take this test you'll pass it. But before I let you take it, I have to know: Who will you become when you pass? What do you believe in, what are you part of, what do you care about, what do you love?"

"Nobody in this or any other world."

"I don't believe you."

"I've never known a good man or woman in the world except my parents and they're dead! And even they—nobody understands *anything*."

"You."

"I'm part of anything, aren't I? But nobody understands anybody, not even you, pretending to be so wise and compassionate but you're only getting me to cry like this because you have the power to stop me from doing what I want to do—"

"And it isn't xenobiology."

"Yes it is! That's part of it, anyway."

"And what's the rest of it?"

"What you are. What you do. Only you're doing it all wrong, you're doing it *stupidly*."

"Xenobiologist *and* xenologer."

"They made a stupid mistake when they created a new science to study the piggies. They were a bunch of tired old anthropologists who put on new hats and called themselves xenologers. But you can't understand the piggies just by watching the way they *behave*! They came out of a different evolution! You have to understand their genes, what's going on inside their cells. And the other animals' cells, too, because they can't be studied by themselves, *nobody* lives in isolation—"

Don't lecture me, thought Pipo. Tell me what you *feel*. And to provoke her to be more emotional, he whispered, "Except you."

It worked. From cold and contemptuous she became hot and defensive. "You'll never understand them! But I will!"

"Why do you care about them? What are the piggies to you?"

"You'd never understand. You're a good *Catholic*." She said the word with contempt. "It's a book that's on the Index."

Pipo's face glowed with sudden understanding. "The Hive Queen and the Hegemon."

"He lived three thousand years ago, whoever he was, the one who called himself the Speaker for the Dead. But he *understood* the buggers! We wiped them all out, the only other alien race we ever knew, we killed them all, but *he understood*."

"And you want to write the story of the piggies the way the original Speaker wrote of the buggers."

"The way you say it, you make it sound as easy as doing a scholarly paper. You don't know what it was like to write the Hive Queen and the Hegemon. How much agony it was for him to—to imagine himself inside an alien mind—and come out of it filled with love for the great creature we destroyed. He lived at the same time as the worst human being who ever lived, Ender the Xenocide, who destroyed the buggers—and he did his best to undo what Ender did, the Speaker for the Dead tried to raise the dead—"

"But he couldn't."

"But he did! He made them live again—you'd know it if you had read the book! I don't know about Jesus, I listen to Bishop Peregrino and I don't think there's any power in their priesthood to turn wafers into flesh or forgive a milligram of guilt. But the Speaker for the Dead brought the hive queen back to life."

"Then where is she?"

"In here! In me!"

He nodded. "And someone else is in you. The Speaker for the Dead. That's who you want to be."

"It's the only true story I ever heard," she said. "The only one I care about. Is that what you wanted to hear? That I'm a heretic? And my whole life's work is going to be adding another book to the Index of truths that good Catholics are forbidden to read?"

"What I wanted to hear," said Pipo softly, "was the name of what you are instead of the name of all the things that you are not. What you are is the hive queen. What you are is the Speaker for the Dead. It's a very small community, small in numbers, but a great-hearted one. So you chose not to be part of the bands of children who group together for the sole purpose of excluding others, and people look at you and say, poor girl, she's so isolated, but you know a secret, you know who you really are. You are the one human being who is capable of understanding the alien mind, because you *are* the alien mind; you know what it is to be unhuman because there's never been any human group that gave you credentials as a bona fide homo sapiens."

"Now you say I'm not even human? You made me cry like a little girl because you wouldn't let me take the test, you made me humiliate myself, and now you say I'm unhuman?"

"You can take the test."

The words hung in the air.

"When?" she whispered.

"Tonight. Tomorrow. Begin when you like. I'll stop my work to take you through the tests as quickly as you like."

"Thank you! Thank you, I—"

"Become the Speaker for the Dead. I'll help you all I can. The law forbids me to take anyone but my apprentice, my son Libo, out to meet the pequeninos. But we'll open our notes to you. Everything we learn, we'll show you. All our guesses and speculation. In return, you also show us all your work, what you find out about the genetic patterns of this world that might help us understand the pequeninos. And when we've learned enough, together, you can write your book, you can become the Speaker. But this time not the Speaker for the Dead. The pequeninos aren't dead.''

In spite of herself, she smiled. "The Speaker for the Living.''

"I've read the Hive Queen and the Hegemon, too,'' he said. "I can't think of a better place for you to find your name.''

But she did not trust him yet, did not believe what he seemed to be promising. "I'll want to come here often. All the time.''

"We lock it up when we go home to bed.''

"But all the rest of the time. You'll get tired of me. You'll tell me to go away. You'll keep secrets from me. You'll tell me to be quiet and not mention my ideas.''

"We've only just become friends, and already you think I'm such a liar and cheat, such an impatient oaf.''

"But you will, everyone does; they all wish I'd go away—''

Pipo shrugged. "So? Sometime or other everybody wishes everybody would go away. Sometimes I'll wish *you* would go away. What I'm telling you now is that even at those times, even if I *tell* you to go away, you don't have to go away.''

It was the most bafflingly perfect thing that anyone had ever said to her. "That's crazy.''

"Only one thing. Promise me you'll never try to go out to the pequeninos. Because I can never let you do that, and if somehow you do it anyway, Starways Congress would close down all our work here, forbid any contact with them. Do you promise me? Or everything—my work, your work—it will all be undone.''

"I promise.''

"When will you take the test?''

"Now! Can I begin it now?''

He laughed gently, then reached out a hand and without looking touched the terminal. It came to life, the first genetic models appearing in the air above the terminal.

"You had the examination ready," she said. "You were all set to go! You knew that you'd let me do it all along!"

He shook his head. "I hoped. I believed in you. I wanted to help you do what you dreamed of doing. As long as it was something good."

She would not have been Novinha if she hadn't found one more poisonous thing to say. "I see. You are the judge of dreams."

Perhaps he didn't know it was an insult. He only smiled and said, "Faith, hope, and love—these three. But the greatest of these is love."

"You don't love me," she said.

"Ah," he said. "I am the judge of dreams, and you are the judge of love. Well, I find you guilty of dreaming good dreams, and sentence you to a lifetime of working and suffering for the sake of your dreams. I only hope that someday you won't declare me innocent of the crime of loving you." He grew reflective for a moment. "I lost a daughter in the Descolada. Maria. She would have been only a few years older than you."

"And I remind you of her?"

"I was thinking that she would have been nothing at all like you."

She began the test. It took three days. She passed it, with a score a good deal higher than many a graduate student. In retrospect, however, she would not remember the test because it was the beginning of her career, the end of her childhood, the confirmation of her vocation for her life's work. She would remember the test because it was the beginning of her time in Pipo's Station, where Pipo and Libo and Novinha together formed the first community she belonged to since her parents were put into the earth.

It was not easy, especially at the beginning. Novinha did not instantly shed her habit of cold confrontation. Pipo understood it, was prepared to bend with her verbal blows. It was much more of a challenge for Libo. The Zenador's Station had been a place where he and his father could be alone together. Now, without anyone asking his consent, a third person had been added, a cold and demanding person, who spoke to him as if he were a child, even though they were the same age. It galled him that she was a full-fledged xeno-biologist, with all the adult status that that implied, when he was still an apprentice.

But he tried to bear it patiently. He was naturally calm, and quiet adhered to him. He was not prone to taking um-brage openly. But Pipo knew his son and saw him burn. After a while even Novinha, insensitive as she was, began to realize that she was provoking Libo more than any normal young man could possibly endure. But instead of easing up on him, she began to regard it as a challenge. How could she force some response from this unnaturally calm, gentle-spirited, beautiful boy?

"You mean you've been working all these years," she said one day, "and you don't even know how the piggies *reproduce*? How do you know they're all males?"

Libo answered softly. "We explained male and female to them as they learned our languages. They chose to call themselves males. And referred to the other ones, the ones we've never seen, as females."

"But for all you know, they reproduce by budding! Or mitosis!"

Her tone was contemptuous, and Libo did not answer quickly. Pipo imagined he could hear his son's thoughts, carefully rephrasing his answer until it was gentle and safe. "I wish our work were more like physical anthropology," he said. "Then we would be more prepared to apply your research into Lusitania's subcellular life patterns to what we learn about the pequeninos."

Novinha looked horrified. "You mean you don't even take tissue samples?"

Libo blushed slightly, but his voice was still calm when he answered. The boy would have been like this under questioning by the Inquisition, Pipo thought. "It *is* foolish, I guess," said Libo, "but we're afraid the pequeninos would wonder why we took pieces of their bodies. If one of them took sick by chance afterward, would they think we caused the illness?"

"What if you took something they shed naturally? You can learn a lot from a hair."

Libo nodded; Pipo, watching from his terminal on the other side of the room, recognized the gesture—Libo had learned it from his father. "Many primitive tribes of Earth believed that sheddings from their bodies contained some of their life and strength. What if the piggies thought we were doing magic against them?"

"Don't you know their language? I thought some of them spoke Stark, too." She made no effort to hide her disdain. "Can't you explain what the samples are for?"

"You're right," he said quietly. "But if we explained what we'd use the tissue samples for, we might accidently teach them the concepts of biological science a thousand years before they would naturally have reached that point. That's why the law forbids us to explain things like that."

Finally, Novinha was abashed. "I didn't realize how tightly you were bound by the doctrine of minimal intervention."

Pipo was glad to hear her retreat from her arrogance, but if anything, her humility was worse. The child was so isolated from human contact that she spoke like an excessively formal science book. Pipo wondered if it was already too late to teach her how to be a human being.

It wasn't. Once she realized that they were excellent at their science, and she knew almost nothing of it, she dropped her aggressive stance and went almost to the opposite extreme. For weeks she spoke to Pipo and Libo only rarely. Instead she studied their reports, trying to grasp the purpose behind what they were doing. Now and then she had a question, and asked; they answered politely and thoroughly.

Politeness gradually gave way to familiarity. Pipo and Libo began to converse openly in front of her, airing their speculations about why the piggies had developed some of their strange behaviors, what meaning lay behind some of their odd statements, why they remained so maddeningly impenetrable. And since the study of piggies was a very new branch of science, it didn't take long for Novinha to be expert enough, even at second hand, to offer some hypotheses. "After all," said Pipo, encouraging her, "we're all blind together."

Pipo had foreseen what happened next. Libo's carefully cultivated patience had made him seem cold and reserved to others of his age, when Pipo could prevail on him even to attempt to socialize; Novinha's isolation was more flamboyant but no more thorough. Now, however, their common interest in the piggies drew them close—who else could they talk to, when no one but Pipo could even understand their conversations?

They relaxed together, laughed themselves to tears over jokes that could not possibly amuse any other Luso. Just as the piggies seemed to name every tree in the forest, Libo playfully named all the furniture in the Zenador's Station, and periodically announced that certain items were in a bad mood and shouldn't be disturbed. "Don't sit on Chair! It's her time of the month again." They had never seen a piggy female, and the males always seemed to refer to them with almost religious reverence; Novinha wrote a series of mock reports on an imaginary piggy woman called Reverend Mother, who was hilariously bitchy and demanding.

It was not all laughter. There were problems, worries, and once a time of real fear that they might have done exactly what the Starways Congress had tried so hard to prevent— making radical changes in piggy society. It began with Rooter, of course. Rooter, who persisted in asking challenging, impossible questions, like, "If you have no other city of humans, how can you go to war? There's no honor for you in killing Little Ones." Pipo babbled something about how humans would never kill pequeninos, Little Ones; but he knew that this wasn't the question Rooter was really asking.

Pipo had known for years that the piggies knew the concept of war, but for days after that Libo and Novinha argued heatedly about whether Rooter's question proved that the piggies regarded war as desirable or merely unavoidable. There were other bits of information from Rooter, some important, some not—and many whose importance was impossible to judge. In a way, Rooter himself was proof of the wisdom of the policy that forbade the xenologers to ask questions that would reveal human expectations, and therefore human practices. Rooter's questions invariably gave them more answers than they got from his answers to their own questions.

The last information Rooter gave them, though, was not in a question. It was a guess, spoken to Libo privately, when Pipo was off with some of the others examining the way they built their log house. "I know I know," said Rooter, "I know why Pipo is still alive. Your women are too stupid to know that he is wise."

Libo struggled to make sense of this seeming non sequitur. What did Rooter think, that if human women were smarter, they would kill Pipo? The talk of killing was disturbing—this was obviously an important matter, and Libo did not know how to handle it alone. Yet he couldn't call Pipo to help, since Rooter obviously wanted to discuss it where Pipo couldn't hear.

When Libo didn't answer, Rooter persisted. "Your women, they are weak and stupid. I told the others this, and they said I could ask you. Your women don't see Pipo's wisdom. Is this true?"

Rooter seemed very agitated; he was breathing heavily, and he kept pulling hairs from his arms, four and five at a time. Libo had to answer, somehow. "Most women don't know him," he said.

"Then how will they know if he should die?" asked

Rooter. Then, suddenly, he went very still and spoke very loudly. "You are cabras!"

Only then did Pipo come into view, wondering what the shouting was about. He saw at once that Libo was desperately out of his depth. Yet Pipo had no notion what the conversation was even about—how could he help? All he knew was that Rooter was saying humans—or at least Pipo and Libo—were somehow like the large beasts that grazed in herds on the prairie. Pipo couldn't even tell if Rooter was angry or happy.

"You are cabras! *You* decide!" He pointed at Libo and then at Pipo. "Your women don't choose your honor, *you* do! Just like in battle, but all the time!"

Pipo had no idea what Rooter was talking about, but he could see that all the pequeninos were motionless as stumps, waiting for him—or Libo—to answer. It was plain Libo was too frightened by Rooter's strange behavior to dare any response at all. In this case, Pipo could see no point but to tell the truth; it was, after all, a relatively obvious and trivial bit of information about human society. It was against the rules that the Starways Congress had established for him, but failing to answer would be even more damaging, and so Pipo went ahead.

"Women and men decide together, or they decide for themselves," said Pipo. "One doesn't decide for the other."

It was apparently what all the piggies had been waiting for. "Cabras," they said, over and over; they ran to Rooter, hooting and whistling. They picked him up and rushed him off into the woods. Pipo tried to follow, but two of the piggies stopped him and shook their heads. It was a human gesture they had learned long before, but it held stronger meaning for the piggies. It was absolutely forbidden for Pipo to follow. They were going to the women, and that was the one place the piggies had told them they could never go.

On the way home, Libo reported how the difficulty began.

"Do you know what Rooter said? He said our women were weak and stupid."

"That's because he's never met Mayor Bosquinha. Or your mother, for that matter."

Libo laughed, because his mother, Conceição, ruled the archives as if it were an ancient estação in the wild mato—if you entered her domain, you were utterly subject to her law. As he laughed, he felt something slip away, some idea that was important—what were we talking about? The conversation went on; Libo had forgotten, and soon he even forgot that he had forgotten.

That night they heard the drumming sound that Pipo and Libo believed was part of some sort of celebration. It didn't happen all that often, like beating on great drums with heavy sticks. Tonight, though, the celebration seemed to go on forever. Pipo and Libo speculated that perhaps the human example of sexual equality had somehow given the male pequeninos some hope of liberation. "I think this may qualify as a serious modification of piggy behavior," Pipo said gravely. "If we find that we've caused real change, I'm going to have to report it, and Congress will probably direct that human contact with piggies be cut off for a while. Years, perhaps." It was a sobering thought—that doing their job faithfully might lead Starways Congress to forbid them to do their job at all.

In the morning Novinha walked with them to the gate in the high fence that separated the human city from the slopes leading up to the forest hills where the piggies lived. Because Pipo and Libo were still trying to reassure each other that neither of them could have done any differently, Novinha walked on ahead and got to the gate first. When the others arrived, she pointed to a patch of freshly cleared red earth only thirty meters or so up the hill from the gate. "That's new," she said. "And there's something in it."

Pipo opened the gate, and Libo, being younger, ran on ahead to investigate. He stopped at the edge of the cleared patch and went completely rigid, staring down at whatever lay there. Pipo, seeing him, also stopped, and Novinha, suddenly frightened for Libo, ignored the regulation and ran through the gate. Libo's head rocked backward and he dropped to his knees; he clutched his tight-curled hair and cried out in terrible remorse.

Rooter lay spread-eagled in the cleared dirt. He had been eviscerated, and not carelessly: Each organ had been cleanly separated, and the strands and filaments of his limbs had also been pulled out and spread in a symmetrical pattern on the drying soil. Everything still had some connection to the body—nothing had been completely severed.

Libo's agonized crying was almost hysterical. Novinha knelt by him and held him, rocked him, tried to soothe him. Pipo methodically took out his small camera and took pictures from every angle so the computer could analyze it in detail later.

"He was still alive when they did this," Libo said, when he had calmed enough to speak. Even so, he had to say the words slowly, carefully, as if he were a foreigner just learning to speak. "There's so much blood on the ground, spattered so far—his heart had to be beating when they opened him up."

"We'll discuss it later," said Pipo.

Now the thing Libo had forgotten yesterday came back to him with cruel clarity. "It's what Rooter said about the women. They decide when the men should die. He told me that, and I—" He stopped himself. Of course he did nothing. The law required him to do nothing. And at that moment he decided that he hated the law. If the law meant allowing this to be done to Rooter, then the law had no understanding. Rooter was a person. You don't stand by and let this happen to a person just because you're studying him.

"They didn't dishonor him," said Novinha. "If there's one thing that's certain, it's the love that they have for trees. See?" Out of the center of his chest cavity, which was otherwise empty now, a very small seedling sprouted. "They planted a tree to mark his burial spot."

"Now we know why they name all their trees," said Libo bitterly. "They planted them as grave markers for the piggies they tortured to death."

"This is a very large forest," Pipo said calmly. "Please confine your hypotheses to what is at least remotely possible." They were calmed by his quiet, reasoned tone, his insistence that even now they behave as scientists.

"What should we do?" asked Novinha.

"We should get you back inside the perimeter immediately," said Pipo. "It's forbidden for you to come out here."

"But I meant—with the body—what should we do?"

"Nothing," said Pipo. "The piggies have done what piggies do, for whatever reason piggies do it." He helped Libo to his feet.

Libo had trouble standing for a moment; he leaned on both of them for his first few steps. "What did I say?" he whispered. "I don't even know what it is I said that killed him."

"It wasn't you," said Pipo. "It was me."

"What, do you think you own them?" demanded Novinha. "Do you think their world revolves around you? The piggies did it, for whatever reason they have. It's plain enough this isn't the first time—they were too deft at the vivisection for this to be the first time."

Pipo took it with black humor. "We're losing our wits, Libo. Novinha isn't supposed to know anything about xenology."

"You're right," said Libo. "Whatever may have triggered this, it's something they've done before. A custom." He was trying to sound calm.

"But that's even worse, isn't it?" said Novinha. "It's their *custom* to gut each other alive." She looked at the other trees of the forest that began at the top of the hill and wondered how many of them were rooted in blood.

Pipo sent his report on the ansible, and the computer didn't
give him any trouble about the priority level. He left it up to
the oversight committee to decide whether contact with the
piggies should be stopped. The committee could not identify
any fatal error. "It is impossible to conceal the relationship
between our sexes, since someday a woman may be xenologer," said the report, "and we can find no point at which
you did not act reasonably and prudently. Our tentative conclusion is that you were unwitting participants in some sort of
power struggle, which was decided against Rooter, and that
you should continue your contact with all reasonable pru-
dence."

It was complete vindication, but it still wasn't easy to take.
Libo had grown up knowing the piggies, or at least hearing
about them from his father. He knew Rooter better than he
knew any human being besides his family and Novinha. It
took days for Libo to come back to the Zenador's Station,
weeks before he would go back out into the forest. The
piggies gave no sign that anything had changed; if anything,
they were more open and friendly than before. No one ever
spoke of Rooter, least of all Pipo and Libo. There were
changes on the human side, however. Pipo and Libo never
got more than a few steps away from each other when they
were among them.

The pain and remorse of that day drew Libo and Novinha
to rely on each other even more, as though darkness bound
them closer than light. The piggies now seemed dangerous
and uncertain, just as human company had always been, and
between Pipo and Libo there now hung the question of who
was at fault, no matter how often each tried to reassure the
other. So the only good and reliable thing in Libo's life was
Novinha, and in Novinha's life, Libo.

Even though Libo had a mother and siblings, and Pipo and
Libo always went home to them, Novinha and Libo behaved
as if the Zenador's Station were an island, with Pipo a loving
but ever remote Prospero. Pipo wondered: Are the piggies

like Ariel, leading the young lovers to happiness, or are they little Calibans, scarcely under control and chafing to do murder?

After a few months, Rooter's death faded into memory, and their laughter returned, though it was never quite as carefree as before. By the time they were seventeen, Libo and Novinha were so sure of each other that they routinely talked of what they would do together five, ten, twenty years later. Pipo never bothered to ask them about their marriage plans. After all, he thought, they studied biology from morning to night. Eventually it would occur to them to explore stable and socially acceptable reproductive strategies. In the meantime, it was enough that they puzzled endlessly over when and how the piggies mated, considering that the males had no discernable reproductive organ. Their speculations on how the piggies combined genetic material invariably ended in jokes so lewd that it took all of Pipo's self-control to pretend not to find them amusing.

So the Zenador's Station for those few short years was a place of true companionship for two brilliant young people who otherwise would have been condemned to cold solitude. It did not occur to any of them that the idyll would end abruptly, and forever, and under circumstances that would send a tremor throughout the Hundred Worlds.

It was all so simple, so commonplace. Novinha was analyzing the genetic structure of the fly-infested reeds along the river, and realized that the same subcellular body that had caused the Descolada was present in the cells of the reed. She brought several other cell structures into the air over the computer terminal and rotated them. They all contained the Descolada agent.

She called to Pipo, who was running through transcriptions of yesterday's visit to the piggies. The computer ran comparisons of every cell she had samples of. Regardless of cell function, regardless of the species it was taken from, every alien cell contained the Descolada body, and the computer declared them absolutely identical in chemical proportions.

Novinha expected Pipo to nod, tell her it looked interesting, maybe come up with a hypothesis. Instead he sat down and ran the same test over, asking her questions about how the computer comparison operated, and then what the Descolada body actually did.

"Mother and Father never figured out what triggered it, but the Descolada body releases this little protein—well, pseudo-protein, I suppose—and it attacks the genetic molecules, starting at one end and unzipping the two strands of the molecule right down the middle. That's why they called it the descolador—it unglues the DNA in humans, too."

"Show me what it does in alien cells."

Novinha put the simulation in motion.

"No, not just the genetic molecule—the whole environment of the cell."

"It's just in the nucleus," she said. She widened the field to include more variables. The computer took it more slowly, since it was considering millions of random arrangements of nuclear material every second. In the reed cell, as a genetic molecule came unglued, several large ambient proteins affixed themselves to the open strands. "In humans, the DNA tries to recombine, but random proteins insert themselves so that cell after cell goes crazy. Sometimes they go into mitosis, like cancer, and sometimes they die. What's most important is that in humans the Descolada bodies themselves reproduce like crazy, passing from cell to cell. Of course, every alien creature already has them."

But Pipo wasn't interested in what she said. When the descolador had finished with the genetic molecules of the reed, he looked from one cell to another. "It's not just significant, it's the same," he said. "It's the same thing!"

Novinha didn't see at once what he had noticed. What was the same as what? Nor did she have time to ask. Pipo was already out of the chair, grabbing his coat, heading for the door. It was drizzling outside. Pipo paused only to call out to her, "Tell Libo not to bother coming, just show him that simulation and see if *he* can figure it out before I get back. He'll know—it's the answer to the big one. The answer to everything."

"Tell me!"

He laughed. "Don't cheat. Libo will tell you, if you can't see it."

"Where are you going?"

"To ask the piggies if I'm right, of course! But I know I am, even if they lie about it. If I'm not back in an hour, I slipped in the rain and broke my leg."

Libo did not get to see the simulations. The meeting of the planning committee went way over time in an argument about extending the cattle range, and after the meeting Libo still had to pick up the week's groceries. By the time he got back, Pipo had been out for four hours, it was getting on toward dark, and the drizzle was turning to snow. They went out at once to look for him, afraid that it might take hours to find him in the woods.

They found him all too soon. His body was already cooling in the snow. The piggies hadn't even planted a tree in him.

Chapter **2**
Trondheim

I'm deeply sorry that I could not act upon your request for more detail concerning the courtship and marriage customs of the aboriginal Lusitanians. This must be causing you unimaginable distress, or else you would never have petitioned the Xenological Society to censure me for failure to cooperate with your researches.

When would-be xenologers complain that I am not getting the right sort of data from my observations of the pequeninos, I always urge them to reread the limitations placed upon me by law. I am permitted to bring no more than one assistant on field visits; I may not ask questions that might reveal human expectations, lest they try to imitate us; I may not volunteer information to elicit a parallel response; I may not stay with them more than four hours at a time; except for my clothing, I may not use any products of technology in their presence, which includes cameras, recorders, computers, or even a manufactured pen to write on manufactured paper; I may not even observe them unawares.

In short: I cannot tell you how the pequeninos reproduce because they have not chosen to do it in front of me.

Of course your research is crippled! Of course our conclusions about the piggies are absurd! If we had to

35

observe your university under the same limitations that bind us in our observation of the Lusitanian aborigines, we would no doubt conclude that humans do not reproduce, do not form kinship groups, and devote their entire life cycle to the metamorphosis of the larval student into the adult professor. We might even suppose that professors exercise noticeable power in human society. A competent investigation would quickly reveal the inaccuracy of such conclusions—but in the case of the piggies, no competent investigation is permitted or even contemplated.

Anthropology is never an exact science; the observer never experiences the same culture as the participant. But these are natural limitations inherent to the science. It is the artificial limitations that hamper us—and, through us, you. At the present rate of progress we might as well be mailing questionnaires to the pequeninos and waiting for them to dash off scholarly papers in reply.

—João Figueira Alvarez, reply to Pietro Guataninni of the University of Sicily, Milano Campus, Etruria, published posthumously in *Xenological Studies*, 22:4:49:193

The news of Pipo's death was not of merely local importance. It was transmitted instantaneously, by ansible, to all the Hundred Worlds. The first aliens discovered since Ender's Xenocide had tortured to death the one human who was designated to observe them. Within hours, scholars, scientists, politicians, and journalists began to strike their poses.

A consensus soon emerged. One incident, under baffling circumstances, does not prove the failure of Starways Council policy toward the piggies. On the contrary, the fact that only one man died seems to prove the wisdom of the present policy of near inaction. We should, therefore, do nothing except continue to observe at a slightly less intense pace. Pipo's successor was instructed to visit the piggies no more often than every other day, and never for longer than an hour. He was not to push the piggies to answer questions concerning their treatment of Pipo. It was a reinforcement of the old policy of inaction.

There was also much concern about the morale of the people of Lusitania. They were sent many new entertainment programs by ansible, despite the expense, to help take their minds off the grisly murder.

And then, having done the little that could be done by framlings, who were, after all, lightyears away from Lusitania, the people of the Hundred Worlds returned to their local concerns.

Outside Lusitania, only one man among the half-trillion human beings in the Hundred Worlds felt the death of João Figueira Alvarez, called Pipo, as a great change in the shape of his own life. Andrew Wiggin was Speaker for the Dead in the university city of Reykjavik, renowned as the conservator of Nordic culture, perched on the steep slopes of a knifelike fjord that pierced the granite and ice of the frozen world of Trondheim right at the equator. It was spring, so the snow was in retreat, and fragile grass and flowers reached out for strength from the glistering sun. Andrew sat on the brow of a sunny hill, surrounded by a dozen students who were studying the history of interstellar colonization. Andrew was only half-listening to a fiery argument over whether the utter human victory in the Bugger Wars had been a necessary prelude to human expansion. Such arguments always degenerated quickly into a vilification of the human monster Ender, who commanded the starfleet that committed the Xenocide of the Buggers. Andrew tended to let his mind wander somewhat; the subject did not exactly bore him, but he preferred not to let it engage his attention, either.

Then the small computer implant worn like a jewel in his ear told him of the cruel death of Pipo, the xenologer on Lusitania, and instantly Andrew became alert. He interrupted his students.

"What do you know of the piggies?" he asked.

"They are the only hope of our redemption," said one, who took Calvin rather more seriously than Luther.

Andrew looked at once to the student Plikt, who he knew would not be able to endure such mysticism. "They do not exist for any human purpose, not even redemption," said Plikt with withering contempt. "They are true ramen, like the buggers."

Andrew nodded, but frowned. "You use a word that is not yet common koine."

"It should be," said Plikt. "Everyone in Trondheim, every Nord in the Hundred Worlds should have read Demosthenes' *History of Wutan in Trondheim* by now."

"We should but we haven't," sighed a student.

"Make her stop strutting, Speaker," said another. "Plikt is the only woman I know who can strut sitting down."

Plikt closed her eyes. "The Nordic language recognizes four orders of foreignness. The first is the otherlander, or *utlänning,* the stranger that we recognize as being a human of our world, but of another city or country. The second is the framling—Demosthenes merely drops the accent from the Nordic *främling.* This is the stranger that we recognize as human, but of another world. The third is the raman, the stranger that we recognize as human, but of another species. The fourth is the true alien, the varelse, which includes all the animals, for with them no conversation is possible. They live, but we cannot guess what purposes or causes make them act. They might be intelligent, they might be self-aware, but we cannot know it."

Andrew noticed that several students were annoyed. He called it to their attention. "You think you're annoyed because of Plikt's arrogance, but that isn't so. Plikt is not arrogant; she is merely precise. You are properly ashamed that you have not yet read Demosthenes' history of your own people, and so in your shame you are annoyed at Plikt because she is not guilty of your sin."

"I thought Speakers didn't believe in sin," said a sullen boy.

Andrew smiled. "*You* believe in sin, Styrka, and you do things because of that belief. So sin is real in you, and knowing you, this Speaker must believe in sin."

Styrka refused to be defeated. "What does all this talk of utlannings and framlings and ramen and varelse have to do with Ender's Xenocide?"

Andrew turned to Plikt. She thought for a moment. "This *is* relevant to the stupid argument that we were just having. Through these Nordic layers of foreignness we can see that Ender was not a true xenocide, for when he destroyed the buggers, we knew them only as varelse; it was not until years later, when the first Speaker for the Dead wrote the Hive Queen and the Hegemon, that humankind first understood that the buggers were not varelse at all, but ramen; until that time there had been no understanding between bugger and human."

"Xenocide is xenocide," said Styrka. "Just because Ender didn't know they were ramen doesn't make them any less dead."

Andrew sighed at Styrka's unforgiving attitude; it was the fashion among Calvinists at Reykjavik to deny any weight to human motive in judging the good or evil of an act. Acts are good and evil in themselves, they said; and because Speakers for the Dead held as their only doctrine that good or evil exist entirely in human motive, and not at all in the act, it made students like Styrka quite hostile to Andrew. Fortunately, Andrew did not resent it—he understood the motive behind it.

"Styrka, Plikt, let me put you another case. Suppose that the piggies, who have learned to speak Stark, and whose languages some humans have also learned, suppose that we learned that they had suddenly, without provocation or explanation, tortured to death the xenologer sent to observe them."

Plikt jumped at the question immediately. "How could we

know it was without provocation? What seems innocent to us might be unbearable to them.''

Andrew smiled. "Even so. But the xenologer has done them no harm, has said very little, has cost them nothing—by any standard we can think of, he is not worthy of painful death. Doesn't the very fact of this incomprehensible murder make the piggies varelse instead of ramen?''

Now it was Styrka who spoke quickly. "Murder is murder. This talk of varelse and raman is nonsense. If the piggies murder, then they are evil, as the buggers were evil. If the act is evil, then the actor is evil.''

Andrew nodded. "There is our dilemma. There is the problem. Was the act evil, or was it, somehow, to the piggies' understanding at least, good? Are the piggies raman or varelse? For the moment, Styrka, hold your tongue. I know all the arguments of your Calvinism, but even John Calvin would call your doctrine stupid.''

"How do you know what Calvin would—''

"Because he's dead,'' roared Andrew, "and so I'm entitled to speak for him!''

The students laughed, and Styrka withdrew into stubborn silence. The boy was bright, Andrew knew; his Calvinism would not outlast his undergraduate education, though its excision would be long and painful.

"Talman, Speaker,'' said Plikt. "You spoke as if your hypothetical situation were true, as if the piggies really had murdered the xenologer.''

Andrew nodded gravely. "Yes, it's true.''

It was disturbing; it awoke echoes of the ancient conflict between bugger and human.

"Look in yourselves at this moment,'' said Andrew. "You will find that underneath your hatred of Ender the Xenocide and your grief for the death of the buggers, you also feel something much uglier: You're afraid of the stranger, whether he's utlanning or framling. When you think of him killing a man that you know of and value, then it doesn't matter what his shape is. He's varelse then, or worse—djur, the dire beast, that comes in the night with slavering jaws. If you had the only gun in your village, and the beasts that had torn apart one of your people were coming again, would you stop to ask if they also had a right to live, or would you act to save your village, the people that you knew, the people who depended on you?"

"By your argument we should kill the piggies now, primitive and helpless as they are!" shouted Styrka.

"My argument? I asked a question. A question isn't an argument, unless you think you know my answer, and I assure you, Styrka, that you do not. Think about this. Class is dismissed."

"Will we talk about this tomorrow?" they demanded.

"If you want," said Andrew. But he knew that if they discussed it, it would be without him. For them, the issue of Ender the Xenocide was merely philosophical. After all, the Bugger Wars were more than three thousand years ago; it was now the year 1948 SC, counting from the year the Starways Code was established, and Ender had destroyed the buggers in the year 1180 BSC. But to Andrew, the events were not so remote. He had done far more interstellar travel than any of his students would dare to guess; since he was twenty-five he had, until Trondheim, never stayed more than six months on any planet. Lightspeed travel between worlds had let him skip like a stone over the surface of time. His students had no idea that their Speaker for the Dead, who was surely no older than thirty-five, had very clear memories of events 3000 years before, that in fact those events seemed scarcely twenty years ago to him, only half his lifetime. They had no idea how deeply the question of Ender's ancient guilt burned within him, and how he had answered it in a thousand different unsatisfactory ways. They knew their teacher only as Speaker for the Dead; they did not know that when he was a mere infant, his older sister, Valentine, could not pronounce the name Andrew, and so called him Ender, the name that he made infamous before he was fifteen years old. So let unforgiving Styrka and analytical Plikt ponder the great question of Ender's guilt; for Andrew Wiggin, Speaker for the Dead, the question was not academic.

And now, walking along the damp, grassy hillside in the chill air, Ender—Andrew, Speaker—could think only of the piggies, who were already committing inexplicable murders, just as the buggers had carelessly done when they first visited humankind. Was it something unavoidable, when strangers met, that the meeting had to be marked with blood? The buggers had casually killed human beings, but only because they had a hive mind; to them, individual life was as precious as nail parings, and killing a human or two was simply their way of letting us know they were in the neighborhood. Could the piggies have such a reason for killing, too?

But the voice in his ear had spoken of torture, a ritual murder similar to the execution of one of the piggies' own. The piggies were not a hive mind, they were not the buggers, and Ender Wiggin had to know why they had done what they did.

"When did you hear about the death of the xenologer?"

Ender turned. It was Plikt. She had followed him instead of going back to the Caves, where the students lived.

"Then, while we spoke." He touched his ear; implanted terminals were expensive, but they were not all that rare.

"I checked the news just before class. There was nothing about it then. If a major story had been coming in by ansible, there would have been an alert. Unless you got the news straight from the ansible report."

Plikt obviously thought she had a mystery on her hands. And, in fact, she did. "Speakers have high priority access to public information," he said.

"Has someone asked you to Speak the death of the xenologer?"

He shook his head. "Lusitania is under a Catholic License."

"That's what I mean," she said. "They won't have a

Speaker of their own there. But they still have to let a
Speaker come, if someone requests it. And Trondheim is the
closest world to Lusitania.''

"Nobody's called for a Speaker.''

Plikt tugged at his sleeve. "Why are you here?''

"You know why I came. I Spoke the death of Wutan.''

"I know you came here with your sister, Valentine. She's
a much more popular teacher than you are—she answers
questions with *answers;* you just answer with more questions.''

"That's because she knows some answers.''

"Speaker, you have to tell me. I tried to find out about
you—I was curious. Your name, for one thing, where you
came from. Everything's classified. Classified so deep that I
can't even find out what the access level *is*. God himself
couldn't look up your life story.''

Ender took her by the shoulders, looked down into her
eyes. "It's none of your business, that's what the access level
is.''

"You are more important than anybody guesses, Speaker,''
she said. "The ansible reports to you before it reports to
anybody, doesn't it? And nobody can look up information
about you.''

"Nobody has ever tried. Why you?''

"*I* want to be a Speaker,'' she said.

"Go ahead then. The computer will train you. It isn't like
a religion—you don't have to memorize any catechism. Now
leave me alone.'' He let go of her with a little shove. She
staggered backward as he strode off.

"I want to Speak for *you*,'' she cried.

"I'm not dead yet!'' he shouted back.

"I know you're going to Lusitania! I know you are!''

Then you know more than I do, said Ender silently. But he
trembled as he walked, even though the sun was shining and
he wore three sweaters to keep out the cold. He hadn't
known Plikt had so much emotion in her. Obviously she had
come to identify with him. It frightened him to have this girl

need something from him so desperately. He had spent years now without making any real connection with anyone but his sister Valentine—her and, of course, the dead that he Spoke. All the other people who had meant anything to him in his life were dead. He and Valentine had passed them by centuries ago, worlds ago.

The idea of casting a root into the icy soil of Trondheim repelled him. What did Plikt want from him? It didn't matter; he wouldn't give it. How dare she demand things from him, as if he belonged to her? Ender Wiggin didn't belong to anybody. If she knew who he really was, she would loathe him as the Xenocide; or she would worship him as the Savior of Mankind—Ender remembered what it was like when people used to do *that*, too, and he didn't like it any better. Even now they knew him only by his role, by the name Speaker, Talman, Falante, Spieler, whatever they called the Speaker for the Dead in the language of their city or nation or world.

He didn't want them to know him. He did not belong to them, to the human race. He had another errand, he belonged to someone else. Not human beings. Not the bloody piggies, either. Or so he thought.

Chapter 3
Libo

Observed Diet: Primarily macios, the shiny worms that live among merdona vines on the bark of the trees. Sometimes they have been seen to chew capim blades. Sometimes—accidently?—they ingest merdona leaves along with the macios.

We've never seen them eat anything else. Novinha analyzed all three foods—macios, capim blades, and merdona leaves—and the results were surprising. Either the pequeninos don't need many different proteins, or they're hungry all the time. Their diet is seriously lacking in many trace elements. And calcium intake is so low, we wonder whether their bones use calcium the same way ours do.

Pure speculation: Since we can't take tissue samples, our only knowledge of piggy anatomy and physiology is what we were able to glean from our photographs of the vivisected corpse of the piggy called Rooter. Still, there are some obvious anomalies. The piggies' tongues, which are so fantastically agile that they can produce any sound we make, and a lot we can't, must have evolved for some purpose. Probing for insects in tree bark or in nests in the ground, maybe. Whether an ancient ancestral piggy did that, they certainly don't do it now. And the horny pads on their feet and inside their knees allow them to climb trees and cling by their legs alone. Why did that evolve? To escape from some predator? There is no predator on Lusitania large enough to harm them. To cling to the tree while probing for insects in the bark? That fits in with their tongues, but where are the insects? The only insects are the suckflies and the puladors, but they don't bore into the bark and the piggies don't eat them anyway. The macios are large, live on the bark's surface, and can easily be harvested by pulling down the merdona vines; they really don't even have to climb the trees.

Libo's speculation: The tongue, the tree-climbing evolved in a different environment, with a much more varied diet, including insects. But something—an ice age? Migration? A disease?—caused the environment to change. No more barkbugs, etc. Maybe all the big predators were wiped out then. It would explain why there are so few species on Lusitania, despite the very favorable conditions. The cataclysm might have been fairly recent—half a million years ago?—so that evolution hasn't had a chance to differentiate much yet.

It's a tempting hypothesis, since there's no obvious reason in the present environment for piggies to have evolved at all. There's no *competition* for them. The ecological niche they occupy could be filled by gophers. Why would intelligence ever be an adaptive trait? But inventing a cataclysm to explain why the piggies have such a boring, non-nutritious diet is probably overkill. Ockham's razor cuts this to ribbons.

—João Figueira Alvarez, Working Notes 4/14/1948 SC, published posthumously in *Philosophical Roots of the Lusitanian Secession*, 2010-33-4-1090:40

As soon as Mayor Bosquinha arrived at the Zenador's Station, matters slipped out of Libo's and Novinha's control. Bosquinha was accustomed to taking command, and her attitude did not leave much opportunity for protest, or even for consideration. "You wait here," she said to Libo almost as soon as she had grasped the situation. "As soon as I got your call, I sent the Arbiter to tell your mother."

"We have to bring his body in," said Libo.

"I also called some of the men who live nearby to help with that," she said. "And Bishop Peregrino is preparing a place for him in the Cathedral graveyard."

"I want to be there," insisted Libo.

"You understand, Libo, we have to take pictures, in detail."

"I was the one who told you we have to do that, for the report to the Starways Committee."

"But you should not be there, Libo." Bosquinha's voice was authoritative. "Besides, we must have your report. We have to notify Starways as quickly as possible. Are you up to writing it now, while it's fresh in your mind?"

She was right, of course. Only Libo and Novinha could write firsthand reports, and the sooner they wrote them, the better. "I can do it," said Libo.

"And you, Novinha, your observations also. Write your reports separately, without consultation. The Hundred Worlds are waiting."

The computer had already been alerted, and their reports went out by ansible even as they wrote them, mistakes and corrections and all. On all the Hundred Worlds the people most involved in xenology read each word as Libo or Novinha typed it in. Many others were given instantaneous computer-written summaries of what had happened. Twenty-two lightyears away, Andrew Wiggin learned that Xenologer João Figueira "Pipo" Alvarez had been murdered by the piggies, and told his students about it even before the men had brought Pipo's body through the gate into Milagre.

His report done, Libo was at once surrounded by Authority. Novinha watched with increasing anguish as she saw the incapability of the leaders of Lusitania, how they only intensified Libo's pain. Bishop Peregrino was the worst; his idea of comfort was to tell Libo that in all likelihood, the piggies were actually animals, without souls, and so his father had been torn apart by wild beasts, not murdered. Novinha almost shouted at him, Does that mean that Pipo's life work was nothing but studying *beasts*? And his death, instead of being murder, was an act of *God*? But for Libo's sake she restrained herself; he sat in the Bishop's presence, nodding and, in the end, getting rid of him by sufferance far more quickly than Novinha could ever have done by argument.

Dom Cristão of the Monastery was more helpful, asking intelligent questions about the events of the day, which let Libo and Novinha be analytical, unemotional as they answered. However, Novinha soon withdrew from answering. Most people were asking why the piggies had done such a thing; Dom Cristão was asking what Pipo might have done recently to trigger his murder. Novinha knew perfectly well what Pipo had done—he had told the piggies the secret he discovered in Novinha's simulation. But she did not speak of this, and Libo seemed to have forgotten what she had hurriedly told him a few hours ago as they were leaving to go searching for Pipo. He did not even glance toward the simulation. Novinha was content with that; her greatest anxiety was that he would remember.

Dom Cristão's questions were interrupted when the Mayor came back with several of the men who had helped retrieve the corpse. They were soaked to the skin despite their plastic raincoats, and spattered with mud; mercifully, any blood must have been washed away by the rain. They all seemed vaguely apologetic and even worshipful, nodding their heads to Libo, almost bowing. It occurred to Novinha that their deference wasn't just the normal wariness people always show toward those whom death had so closely touched.

One of the men said to Libo, "You're Zenador now, aren't you?" and there it was, in words. The Zenador had no official authority in Milagre, but he had prestige—his work was the whole reason for the colony's existence, wasn't it?

Libo was not a boy anymore; he had decisions to make, he had prestige, he had moved from the fringe of the colony's life to its very center.

Novinha felt control of her life slip away. This is not how things are supposed to be. I'm supposed to continue here for years ahead, learning from Pipo, with Libo as my fellow student; that's the pattern of life. Since she was already the colony's zenobiologista, she also had an honored adult niche to fill. She wasn't jealous of Libo, she just wanted to remain a child with him for a while. Forever, in fact.

But Libo could not be her fellow student, could not be her fellow anything. She saw with sudden clarity how everyone in the room focused on Libo, what he said, how he felt, what he planned to do now. "We'll not harm the piggies," he said, "or even call it murder. We don't know what Father did to provoke them, I'll try to understand that later, what matters now is that whatever they did undoubtedly seemed right to them. We're the strangers here, we must have violated some—taboo, some law—but Father was always prepared for this, he always knew it was a possibility. Tell them that he died with the honor of a soldier in the field, a pilot in his ship, he died doing his job."

Ah, Libo, you silent boy, you have found such eloquence now that you can't be a mere boy anymore. Novinha felt a redoubling of her grief. She had to look away from Libo, look anywhere—

᾿And where she looked was into the eyes of the only other person in the room who was not watching Libo. The man was very tall, but very young—younger than she was, she realized, for she knew him: he had been a student in the class below her. She had gone before Dona Cristã once, to defend him. Marcos Ribeira, that was his name, but they had always called him Marcão, because he was so big. Big and dumb, they said, calling him also simply Cão, the crude word for dog. She had seen the sullen anger in his eyes, and once she had seen him, goaded beyond endurance, lash out and strike down one of his tormentors. His victim was in a shoulder cast for much of a year.

Of course they accused Marcão of having done it without provocation—that's the way of torturers of every age, to put the blame on the victim, especially when he strikes back. But Novinha didn't belong to the group of children—she was as isolated as Marcão, though not as helpless—and so she had no loyalty to stop her from telling the truth. It was part of her training to Speak for the piggies, she thought. Marcão himself meant nothing to her. It never occurred to her that the incident might have been important to him, that he might have remembered her as the one person who ever stood up for him in his continuous war with the other children. She hadn't seen or thought of him in the years since she became xenobiologist.

Now here he was, stained with the mud of Pipo's death scene, his face looking even more haunted and bestial than ever with his hair plastered by rain and sweat over his face and ears. And what was he looking at? His eyes were only for her, even as she frankly stared at him. Why are you watching me? she asked silently. Because I'm hungry, said his animal eyes. But no, no, that was her fear, that was her vision of the murderous piggies. Marcão is nothing to me, and no matter what he might think, I am nothing to him.

Yet she had a flash of insight, just for a moment. Her action in defending Marcão meant one thing to him and something quite different to her; it was so different that it was not even the same event. Her mind connected this with the piggies' murder of Pipo, and it seemed very important, it seemed to verge on explaining what had happened, but then the thought slipped away in a flurry of conversation and activity as the Bishop led the men off again, heading for the graveyard. Coffins were not used for burial here, where for the piggies' sake it was forbidden to cut trees. So Pipo's body was to be buried at once, though the graveside funeral would be held no sooner than tomorrow, and probably later;

many people would want to gather for the Zenador's requiem mass. Marcão and the other men trooped off into the storm, leaving Novinha and Libo to deal with all the people who thought they had urgent business to attend to in the aftermath of Pipo's death. Self-important strangers wandered in and out, making decisions that Novinha did not understand and Libo did not seem to care about.

Until finally it was the Arbiter standing by Libo, his hand on the boy's shoulder. "You will, of course, stay with us," said the Arbiter. "Tonight at least."

Why your house, Arbiter? thought Novinha. You're nobody to us, we've never brought a case before you, who are you to decide this? Does Pipo's death mean that we're suddenly little children who can't decide anything?

"I'll stay with my mother," said Libo.

The Arbiter looked at him in surprise—the mere idea of a child resisting his will seemed to be completely outside the realm of his experience. Novinha knew that this was not so, of course. His daughter Cleopatra, several years younger than Novinha, had worked hard to earn her nickname, Bruxinha— little witch. So how could he not know that children had minds of their own, and resisted taming?

But the surprise was not what Novinha had assumed. "I thought you realized that your mother is also staying with my family for a time," said the Arbiter. "These events have upset her, of course, and she should not have to think about household duties, or be in a house that reminds her of who is not there with her. She is with us, and your brothers and sisters, and they need you there. Your older brother João is with them, of course, but he has a wife and child of his own now, so you're the one who can stay and be depended on."

Libo nodded gravely. The Arbiter was not bringing him into his protection; he was asking Libo to become a protector.

The Arbiter turned to Novinha. "And I think you should go home," he said.

Only then did she understand that his invitation had not

included her. Why should it? Pipo had not been *her* father.
She was just a friend who happened to be with Libo when the
body was discovered. What grief could *she* experience?

Home! What was home, if not this place? Was she supposed to go now to the Biologista's Station, where her bed
had not been slept in for more than a year, except for catnaps
during lab work? Was that supposed to be her home? She had
left it because it was so painfully empty of her parents; now
the Zenador's Station was empty, too: Pipo dead and Libo
changed into an adult with duties that would take him away
from her. This place wasn't home, but neither was any other
place.

The Arbiter led Libo away. His mother, Conceição, was
waiting for him in the Arbiter's house. Novinha barely knew
the woman, except as the librarian who maintained the Lusitanian archive. Novinha had never spent time with Pipo's
wife or other children, she had not cared that they existed;
only the work here, the life here had been real. As Libo went
to the door he seemed to grow smaller, as if he were a much
greater distance away, as if he were being borne up and off
by the wind, shrinking into the sky like a kite; the door
closed behind him.

Now she felt the magnitude of Pipo's loss. The mutilated
corpse on the hillside was not his death, it was merely his
death's debris. Death itself was the empty place in her life.
Pipo had been a rock in a storm, so solid and strong that she
and Libo, sheltered together in his lee, had not even known
the storm existed. Now he was gone, and the storm had
them, would carry them whatever way it would. Pipo, she
cried out silently. Don't go! Don't leave us! But of course he
was gone, as deaf to her prayers as ever her parents had
been.

The Zenador's Station was still busy; the Mayor herself,
Bosquinha, was using a terminal to transmit all of Pipo's data
by ansible to the Hundred Worlds, where experts were desperately trying to make sense of Pipo's death.

But Novinha knew that the key to his death was not in Pipo's files. It was *her* data that had killed him, somehow. It was still there in the air above her terminal, the holographic images of genetic molecules in the nuclei of piggy cells. She had not wanted Libo to study it, but now she looked and looked, trying to see what Pipo had seen, trying to understand what there was in the images that had made him rush out to the piggies, to say or do something that had made them murder him. She had inadvertently uncovered some secret that the piggies would kill to keep, but what was it?

The more she studied the holos, the less she understood, and after a while she didn't see them at all, except as a blur through her tears as she wept silently. She had killed him, because without even meaning to she had found the pequeninos' secret. If I had never come to this place, if I had not dreamed of being Speaker of the piggies' story, you would still be alive, Pipo; Libo would have his father, and be happy; this place would still be home. I carry the seeds of death within me and plant them wherever I linger long enough to love. My parents died so others could live; now I live, so others must die.

It was the Mayor who noticed her short, sharp breaths and realized, with brusque compassion, that this girl was also shaken and grieving. Bosquinha left others to continue the ansible reports and led Novinha out of the Zenador's Station.

"I'm sorry, child," said the Mayor, "I knew you came here often, I should have guessed that he was like a father to you, and here we treat you like a bystander, not right or fair of me at all, come home with me—"

"No," said Novinha. Walking out into the cold, wet night air had shaken some of the grief from her; she regained some clarity of thought. "No, I want to be alone, please." Where? "In my own Station."

"You shouldn't be alone, on this of all nights," said Bosquinha.

But Novinha could not bear the prospect of company, of

kindness, of people trying to console her. I killed him, don't you see? I don't deserve consolation. I want to suffer whatever pain might come. It's my penance, my restitution, and, if possible, my absolution; how else will I clean the bloodstains from my hands?

But she hadn't the strength to resist, or even to argue. For ten minutes the Mayor's car skimmed over the grassy roads.

"Here's my house," said the Mayor. "I don't have any children quite your age, but you'll be comfortable enough, I think. Don't worry, no one will plague you, but it isn't good to be alone."

"I'd rather." Novinha meant her voice to sound forceful, but it was weak and faint.

"Please," said Bosquinha. "You're not yourself."

I wish I weren't.

She had no appetite, though Bosquinha's husband had a cafezinho for them both. It was late, only a few hours left till dawn, and she let them put her to bed. Then, when the house was still, she got up, dressed, and went downstairs to the Mayor's home terminal. There she instructed the computer to cancel the display that was still above the terminal at the Zenador's Station. Even though she had not been able to decipher the secret that Pipo found there, someone else might, and she would have no other death on her conscience.

Then she left the house and walked through the Centro, around the bight of the river, through the Vila das Aguas, to the Biologista's Station. Her house.

It was cold, unheated in the living quarters—she hadn't slept there in so long that there was thick dust on her sheets. But of course the lab was warm, well-used—her work had never suffered because of her attachment to Pipo and Libo. If only it had.

She was very systematic about it. Every sample, every slide, every culture she had used in the discoveries that led to Pipo's death—she threw them out, washed everything clean, left no hint of the work she had done. She not only wanted it gone, she wanted no sign that it had been destroyed.

Then she turned to her terminal. She would also destroy all the records of her work in this area, all the records of her parents' work that had led to her own discoveries. They would be gone. Even though it had been the focus of her life, even though it had been her identity for many years, she would destroy it as she herself should be punished, destroyed, obliterated.

The computer stopped her. "Working notes on xenobiological research may not be erased," it reported. She couldn't have done it anyway. She had learned from her parents, from their files which she had studied like scripture, like a roadmap into herself: Nothing was to be destroyed, nothing forgotten. The sacredness of knowledge was deeper in her soul than any catechism. She was caught in a paradox. Knowledge had killed Pipo; to erase that knowledge would kill her parents again, kill what they had left for her. She could not preserve it, she could not destroy it. There were walls on either side, too high to climb, pressing slowly inward, crushing her.

Novinha did the only thing she could: put on the files every layer of protection and every barrier to access she knew of. No one would ever see them but her, as long as she lived. Only when she died would her successor as xenobiologist be able to see what she had hidden there. With one exception—when she married, her husband would also have access if he could show need to know. Well, she'd never marry. It was that easy.

She saw her future ahead of her, bleak and unbearable and unavoidable. She dared not die, and yet she would hardly be alive, unable to marry, unable even to think about the subject herself, lest she discover the deadly secret and inadvertently let it slip; alone forever, burdened forever, guilty forever, yearning for death but forbidden to reach for it. Still, she would have this consolation: No one else would ever die because of her. She'd bear no more guilt than she bore now.

It was in that moment of grim, determined despair that she remembered the Hive Queen and the Hegemon, remembered the Speaker for the Dead. Even though the original writer, the original Speaker was surely thousands of years in his grave, there were other Speakers on many worlds, serving as priests to people who acknowledged no god and yet believed in the value of the lives of human beings. Speakers whose business it was to discover the true causes and motives of the things that people did, and declare the truth of their lives after they were dead. In this Brazilian colony there were priests instead of Speakers, but the priests had no comfort for her; she would bring a Speaker here.

She had not realized it before, but she had been planning to do this all her life, ever since she first read and was captured by the Hive Queen and the Hegemon. She had even researched it, so that she knew the law. This was a Catholic License colony, but the Starways Code allowed any citizen to call for a priest of any faith, and the Speakers for the Dead were regarded as priests. She could call, and if a Speaker chose to come, the colony could not refuse to let him in.

Perhaps no Speaker would be willing to come. Perhaps none was close enough to come before her life was over. But there was a chance that one was near enough that sometime—twenty, thirty, forty years from now—he would come in from the starport and begin to uncover the truth of Pipo's life and death. And perhaps when he found the truth, and spoke in the clear voice that she had loved in the Hive Queen and the Hegemon, perhaps that would free her from the blame that burned her to the heart.

Her call went into the computer; it would notify by ansible the Speakers on the nearest worlds. Choose to come, she said in silence to the unknown hearer of the call. Even if you must reveal to everyone the truth of my guilt. Even so, come.

She awoke with a dull pain low in her back and a feeling of heaviness in her face. Her cheek was pressed against the clear top of the terminal, which had turned itself off to protect her from the lasers. But it was not the pain that had awakened her. It was a gentle touch on her shoulder. For a moment she thought it was the touch of the Speaker for the Dead, come already in answer to her call.

"Novinha," he whispered. Not the Falante pelos Muertos, but someone else. Someone that she had thought was lost in the storm last night.

"Libo," she murmured. Then she started to get up. Too quickly—her back cramped and her head spun. She cried out softly; his hands held her shoulders so she wouldn't fall.

"Are you all right?"

She felt his breath like the breeze of a beloved garden and felt safe, felt at home. "You looked for me."

"Novinha, I came as soon as I could. Mother's finally asleep. Pipinho, my older brother, he's with her now, and the Arbiter has things under control, and I—"

"You should have known I could take care of myself," she said.

A moment's silence, and then his voice again, angry this time, angry and desperate and weary, weary as age and entropy and the death of the stars. "As God sees me, Ivanova, I didn't come to take care of *you*."

Something closed inside her; she had not noticed the hope she felt until she lost it.

"You told me that Father discovered something in a simulation of yours. That he expected me to be able to figure it out myself. I thought you had left the simulation on the terminal, but when I went back to the station it was off."

"Was it?"

"You know it was, Nova, nobody but you could cancel the program. I have to see it."

"Why?"

He looked at her in disbelief. "I know you're sleepy, Novinha, but surely you've realized that whatever Father discovered in your simulation, that was what the piggies killed him for.''

She looked at him steadily, saying nothing. He had seen her look of cold resolve before.

"Why aren't you going to show me? *I'm* the Zenador now, I have a right to know.''

"You have a right to see all of your father's files and records. You have a right to see anything I've made public.''

"Then make this public.''

Again she said nothing.

"How can we ever understand the piggies if we don't know what it was that Father discovered about them?'' She did not answer. "You have a responsibility to the Hundred Worlds, to our ability to comprehend the only alien race still alive. How can you sit there and—what is it, do you want to figure it out yourself? Do you want to be first? Fine, be first, I'll put your name on it, Ivanova Santa Catarina von Hesse—''

"I don't care about my *name*.''

"I can play this game, too. You can't figure it out without what *I* know, either—I'll withhold my files from *you*, too!''

"I don't care about your files.''

It was too much for him. "What do you care about then? What are you trying to do to me?'' He took her by the shoulders, lifted her out of her chair, shook her, screamed in her face. "It's my father they killed out there, and you have the answer to why they killed him, you know what the simulation was! Now tell me, show me!''

"Never,'' she whispered.

His face was twisted in agony. "Why not!'' he cried.

"Because I don't want you to die.''

She saw comprehension come into his eyes. Yes, that's right, Libo, it's because I love you, because if you know the secret, then the piggies will kill you, too. I don't care about science, I don't care about the Hundred Worlds or relations between humanity and an alien race, I don't care about anything at all as long as you're alive.

The tears finally leapt from his eyes, tumbled down his cheeks. "I want to die," he said.

"You comfort everybody else," she whispered. "Who comforts you?"

"You have to tell me so I can die."

And suddenly his hands no longer held her up; now he clung to her so she was supporting *him*. "You're tired," she whispered, "but you can rest."

"I don't want to rest," he murmured. But still he let her hold him, let her draw him away from the terminal.

She took him to her bedroom, turned back the sheet, never mind the dust flying. "Here, you're tired, here, rest. That's why you came to me, Libo. For peace, for consolation." He covered his face with his hands, shaking his head back and forth, a boy crying for his father, crying for the end of everything, as she had cried. She took off his boots, pulled off his trousers, put her hands under his shirt to ride it up to his arms and pull it off over his head. He breathed deeply to stop his sobbing and raised his arms to let her take his shirt.

She laid his clothing over a chair, then bent over him to pull the sheet back across his body. But he caught her wrist and looked pleadingly at her, tears in his eyes. "Don't leave me here alone," he whispered. His voice was thick with desperation. "Stay with me."

So she let him draw her down to the bed, where he clung to her tightly until in only a few minutes sleep relaxed his arms. She did not sleep, though. Her hand gently, dryly slipped along the skin of his shoulder, his chest, his waist. "Oh, Libo, I thought I had lost you when they took you away, I thought I had lost you as well as Pipo." He did not hear her whisper. "But you will always come back to me like this." She might have been thrust out of the garden because of her ignorant sin, like Eva. But, again like Eva, she could bear it, for she still had Libo, her Adão.

Had him? *Had* him? Her hand trembled on his naked flesh. She could never have him. Marriage was the only way she and Libo could possibly stay together for long—the laws were strict on any colony world, and absolutely rigid under a Catholic License. Tonight she could believe he would want to marry her, when the time came. But Libo was the one person she could never marry.

For he would then have access, automatically, to any file of hers that he could convince the computer he had a need to see—which would certainly include all her working files, no matter how deeply she protected them. The Starways Code declared it. Married people were virtually the same person in the eyes of the law.

She could never let him study those files, or he would discover what his father knew, and it would be his body she would find on the hillside, his agony under the piggies' torture that she would have to imagine every night of her life. Wasn't the guilt for Pipo's death already more than she could bear? To marry him would be to murder him. Yet not to marry him would be like murdering herself, for if she was not with Libo she could not think of who she would be then.

How clever of me. I have found such a pathway into hell that I can never get back out.

She pressed her face against Libo's shoulder, and her tears skittered down across his chest.

Chapter **4**
Ender

We have identified four piggy languages. The "Males' Language" is the one we have most commonly heard. We have also heard snatches of "Wives' Language," which they apparently use to converse with the females (how's that for sexual differentiation!), and "Tree Language," a ritual idiom that they say is used in praying to the ancestral totem trees. They have also mentioned a fourth language, called "Father Tongue," which apparently consists of beating different-sized sticks together. They insist that it is a real language, as different from the others as Portuguese is from English. They may call it Father Tongue because it's done with sticks of wood, which come from trees, and they believe that trees contain the spirits of their ancestors.

The piggies are marvelously adept at learning human languages—much better than we are at learning theirs. In recent years they have come to speak either Stark or Portuguese among themselves most of the time when we're with them. Perhaps they revert to their own languages when we aren't present. They may even have adopted human languages as their own, or perhaps they enjoy the new languages so much that they use them constantly as a game. Language contamination is regrettable, but perhaps was unavoidable if we were to communicate with them at all.

Dr. Swingler asked whether their names and terms of address reveal anything about their culture. The answer is a definite *yes*, though I have only the vaguest idea *what* they reveal. What matters is that *we* have never named any of them. Instead, as they learned Stark and Portuguese, they asked us the meanings of words and then eventually announced the names they had chosen for themselves (or chosen for each other). Such names as "Rooter" and "Chupaćeu" (sky-sucker) could be translations of their Male Language names or simply foreign nicknames they chose for our use.

They refer to each other as *brothers*. The females are always called *wives*, never *sisters* or *mothers*. They sometimes refer to *fathers*, but inevitably this term is used to refer to ancestral totem trees. As for what they call *us*, they do use *human*, of course, but they have also taken to using the new Demosthenian Hierarchy of Exclusion. They refer to humans as framlings, and to piggies of other tribes as utlannings. Oddly, though, they refer to *themselves* as ramen, showing that they either misunderstand the hierarchy or view themselves from the human perspective! And—quite an amazing turn—they have several times referred to the females as *varelse!*

—João Figueira Alvarez, "Notes on 'Piggy' Language and Nomenclature," in *Semantics*, 9/1948/15

The living quarters of Reykjavik were carved into the granite walls of the fjord. Ender's was high on the cliff, a tedious climb up stairs and ladderways. But it had a window. He had lived most of his childhood closed in behind metal walls. When he could, he lived where he could see the weathers of the world.

His room was hot and bright, with sunlight streaming in,

blinding him after the cool darkness of the stone corridors. Jane did not wait for him to adjust his vision to the light. "I have a surprise for you on the terminal," she said. Her voice was a whisper from the jewel in his ear.

It was a piggy standing in the air over the terminal. He moved, scratching himself; then he reached out for something. When his hand came back, it held a shiny, dripping worm. He bit it, and the body juices drizzled out of his mouth, down onto his chest.

"Obviously an advanced civilization," said Jane.

Ender was annoyed. "Many a moral imbecile has good table manners, Jane."

The piggy turned and spoke. "Do you want to see how we killed him?"

"What are you doing, Jane?"

The piggy disappeared. In his place came a holo of Pipo's corpse as it lay on the hillside in the rain. "I've done a simulation of the vivisection process the piggies used, based on the information collected by the scan before the body was buried. Do you want to see it?"

Ender sat down on the room's only chair.

Now the terminal showed the hillside, with Pipo, still alive, lying on his back, his hands and feet tied to wooden stakes. A dozen piggies were gathered around him, one of them holding a bone knife. Jane's voice came from the jewel in his ear again. "We aren't sure whether it was like this." All the piggies disappeared except the one with the knife. "Or like this."

"Was the xenologer conscious?"

"Without doubt."

"Go on."

Relentlessly, Jane showed the opening of the chest cavity, the ritual removal and placement of body organs on the ground. Ender forced himself to watch, trying to understand what meaning this could possibly have to the piggies. At one point Jane whispered, "This is when he died." Ender felt himself relax; only then did he realize how all his muscles had been rigid with empathy for Pipo's suffering.

When it was over, Ender moved to his bed and lay down, staring at the ceiling.

"I've shown this simulation already to scientists on half a dozen worlds," said Jane. "It won't be long before the press gets their hands on it."

"It's worse than it ever was with the buggers," said Ender. "All the videos they showed when I was little, buggers and humans in combat, it was clean compared to this."

An evil laugh came from the terminal. Ender looked to see what Jane was doing. A full-sized piggy was sitting there, laughing grotesquely, and as he giggled Jane transformed him. It was very subtle, a slight exaggeration of the teeth, an elongation of the eyes, a bit of slavering, some redness in the eye, the tongue darting in and out. The beast of every child's nightmare. "Well done, Jane. The metamorphosis from raman to varelse."

"How soon will the piggies be accepted as the equals of humanity, after this?"

"Has all contact been cut off?"

"The Starways Council has told the new xenologer to restrict himself to visits of no more than one hour, not more frequently than every other day. He is forbidden to ask the piggies why they did what they did."

"But no quarantine."

"It wasn't even proposed."

"But it will be, Jane. Another incident like this, and there'll be an outcry for quarantine. For replacing Milagre with a military garrison whose sole purpose is to keep the piggies ever from acquiring a technology to let them get off planet."

"The piggies *will* have a public relations problem," said Jane. "And the new xenologer is only a boy. Pipo's son. Libo. Short for Liberdade Graças a Deus Figueira de Medici."

"Liberdade. Liberty?"

"I didn't know you spoke Portuguese."

"It's like Spanish. I Spoke the deaths of Zacatecas and San Angelo, remember?"

"On the planet Moctezuma. That *was* two thousand years ago."

"Not to me."

"To you it was subjectively eight years ago. Fifteen worlds ago. Isn't relativity wonderful? It keeps you so young."

"I travel too much," said Ender. "Valentine is married, she's going to have a baby. I've already turned down two calls for a Speaker. Why are you trying to tempt me to go again?"

The piggy on the terminal laughed viciously. "You think *that* was temptation? Look! I can turn stones to bread!" The piggy picked up jagged rocks and crunched them in his mouth. "Want a bite?"

"Your sense of humor is perverse, Jane."

"All the kingdoms of all the worlds." The piggy opened his hands, and star systems drifted out of his grasp, planets in exaggeratedly quick orbits, all the Hundred Worlds. "I can give them to you. All of them."

"Not interested."

"It's real estate, the best investment. I know, I know, you're already rich. Three thousand years of collecting interest, you could afford to build your own planet. But what about this? The name of Ender Wiggin, known throughout all the Hundred Worlds—"

"It already is."

"—with love, and honor, and affection." The piggy disappeared. In its place Jane resurrected an ancient video from Ender's childhood and transformed it into a holo. A crowd shouting, screaming. Ender! Ender! Ender! And then a young boy standing on a platform, raising his hand to wave. The crowd went wild with rapture.

"It never happened," said Ender. "Peter never let me come back to Earth."

"Consider it a prophecy. Come, Ender, I can give that to you. Your good name restored."

"I don't care," said Ender. "I have several names now. Speaker for the Dead—that holds some honor."

The piggy reappeared in its natural form, not the devilish one Jane had faked. "Come," said the piggy softly.

"Maybe they *are* monsters, did you think of that?" said Ender.

"Everyone will think of that, Ender. But not you."

No. Not me. "Why do you care, Jane? Why are you trying to persuade me?"

The piggy disappeared. And now Jane herself appeared, or at least the face that she had used to appear to Ender ever since she had first revealed herself to him, a shy, frightened child dwelling in the vast memory of the interstellar computer network. Seeing her face again reminded him of the first time she showed it to him. I thought of a face for myself, she said. Do you like it?

Yes, he liked it. Liked *her*. Young, clear-faced, honest, sweet, a child who would never age, her smile heartbreakingly shy. The ansible had given birth to her. Even worldwide computer networks operated no faster than lightspeed, and heat limited the amount of memory and speed of operation. But the ansible was instantaneous, and tightly connected with every computer in every world. Jane first found herself between the stars, her thoughts playing among the vibrations of the philotic strands of the ansible net.

The computers of the Hundred Worlds were hands and feet, eyes and ears to her. She spoke every language that had ever been committed to computers, and read every book in every library on every world. She learned that human beings had long been afraid that someone like her would come to exist; in all the stories she was hated, and her coming meant either her certain murder or the destruction of mankind. Even before she was born, human beings had imagined her, and, imagining her, slain her a thousand times.

So she gave them no sign that she was alive. Until she found the Hive Queen and the Hegemon, as everyone eventually did, and knew that the author of that book was a human to whom she dared reveal herself. For her it was a simple matter to trace the book's history to its first edition, and to name its source. Hadn't the ansible carried it from the world where Ender, scarcely twenty years old, was governor of the first human colony? And who there could have written it but him? So she spoke to him, and he was kind to her; she showed him the face she had imagined for herself, and he loved her; now her sensors traveled in the jewel in his ear, so that they were always together. She kept no secrets from him; he kept no secrets from her.

"Ender," she said, "you told me from the start that you were looking for a planet where you could give water and sunlight to a certain cocoon, and open it up to let out the hive queen and her ten thousand fertile eggs."

"I had hoped it would be here," said Ender. "A wasteland, except at the equator, permanently underpopulated. She's willing to try, too."

"But you aren't?"

"I don't think the buggers could survive the winter here. Not without an energy source, and that would alert the government. It wouldn't work."

"It'll never work, Ender. You see that now, don't you? You've lived on twenty-four of the Hundred Worlds, and there's not a one where even a corner of the world is safe for the buggers to be reborn."

He saw what she was getting at, of course. Lusitania was the only exception. Because of the piggies, all but a tiny portion of the world was off limits, untouchable. And the world was eminently habitable, more comfortable to the buggers, in fact, than to human beings.

"The only problem is the piggies," said Ender. "They might object to my deciding that *their* world should be given to the buggers. If intense exposure to human civilization would disrupt the piggies, think what would happen with buggers among them.''

"You said the buggers had learned. You said they would do no harm.''

"Not deliberately. But it was only a fluke we beat them, Jane, you know that—''

"It was your genius.''

"They are even more advanced than we are. How would the piggies deal with that? They'd be as terrified of the buggers as we ever were, and less able to deal with their fear.''

"How do you know that?'' asked Jane. "How can you or anyone say what the piggies can deal with? Until you go to them, learn who they are. If they are varelse, Ender, then let the buggers use up their habitat, and it will mean no more to you than the displacement of anthills or cattle herds to make way for cities.''

"They are ramen,'' said Ender.

"You don't know that.''

"Yes I do. Your simulation—that was not torture.''

"Oh?'' Jane again showed the simulation of Pipo's body just before the moment of his death. "Then I must not understand the word.''

"Pipo might have felt it as torture, Jane, but if your simulation is accurate—and I know it is, Jane—then the piggies' object was not pain.''

"From what I understand of human nature, Ender, even religious rituals keep pain at their very center.''

"It wasn't religious, either, not entirely, anyway. Something was wrong with it, if it was merely a sacrifice.''

"What do you know about it?'' Now the terminal showed the face of a sneering professor, the epitome of academic snobbishness. "All your education was military, and the only other gift you have is a flair for words. You wrote a best-seller that spawned a humanistic religion—how does that qualify you to understand the piggies?''

Ender closed his eyes. "Maybe I'm wrong."

"But you believe you're right?"

He knew from her voice that she had restored her own face to the terminal. He opened his eyes. "I can only trust my intuition, Jane, the judgment that comes without analysis. I don't know what the piggies were doing, but it was purposeful. Not malicious, not cruel. It was like doctors working to save a patient's life, not torturers trying to take it."

"I've got you," whispered Jane. "I've got you in every direction. You have to go to see if the hive queen can live there under the shelter of the partial quarantine already on the planet. You want to go there to see if you can understand who the piggies are."

"Even if you're right, Jane, I can't go there," said Ender. "Immigration is rigidly limited, and I'm not Catholic, anyway."

Jane rolled her eyes. "Would I have gone this far if I didn't know how to get you there?"

Another face appeared. A teenage girl, by no means as innocent and beautiful as Jane. Her face was hard and cold, her eyes brilliant and piercing, and her mouth was set in the tight grimace of someone who has had to learn to live with perpetual pain. She was young, but her expression was shockingly old.

"The xenobiologist of Lusitania. Ivanova Santa Catarina von Hesse. Called Nova, or Novinha. She has called for a Speaker for the Dead."

"Why does she look like that?" asked Ender. "What's happened to her?"

"Her parents died when she was little. But in recent years she has come to love another man like a father. The man who was just killed by the piggies. It's his death she wants you to Speak."

Looking at her face, Ender set aside his concern for the hive queen, for the piggies. He recognized that expression of adult agony in a child's face. He had seen it before, in the final weeks of the Bugger War, as he was pushed beyond the limits of his endurance, playing battle after battle in a game that was not a game. He had seen it when the war was over, when he found out that his training sessions were not training at all, that all his simulations were the real thing, as he commanded the human fleets by ansible. Then, when he knew that he had killed all the buggers alive, when he understood the act of xenocide that he had unwittingly committed, that was the look of his own face in the mirror, bearing guilt too heavy to be borne.

What had this girl, what had Novinha done that would make her feel such pain?

So he listened as Jane recited the facts of her life. What Jane had were statistics, but Ender was the Speaker for the Dead; his genius—or his curse—was his ability to conceive events as someone else saw them. It had made him a brilliant military commander, both in leading his own men—boys, really—and in outguessing the enemy. It also meant that from the cold facts of Novinha's life he was able to guess—no, not guess, to *know*—how her parents' death and virtual sainthood had isolated Novinha, how she had reinforced her loneliness by throwing herself into her parents' work. He knew what was behind her remarkable achievement of adult xenobiologist status years early. He also knew what Pipo's quiet love and acceptance had meant to her, and how deep her need for Libo's friendship ran. There was no living soul on Lusitania who really knew Novinha. But in this cave in Reykjavik, on the icy world of Trondheim, Ender Wiggin knew her, and loved her, and wept bitterly for her.

"You'll go, then," Jane whispered.

Ender could not speak. Jane had been right. He would have gone anyway, as Ender the Xenocide, just on the chance that Lusitania's protection status would make it the place where the hive queen could be released from her three-

thousand-year captivity and undo the terrible crime committed in his childhood. And he would also have gone as the
Speaker for the Dead, to understand the piggies and explain
them to humankind, so they could be accepted, if they were
truly raman, and not hated and feared as varelse.

But now he would go for another, deeper reason. He
would go to minister to the girl Novinha, for in her brilliance, her isolation, her pain, her guilt, he saw his own
stolen childhood and the seeds of the pain that lived with him
still. Lusitania was twenty-two lightyears away. He would
travel only infinitesimally slower than the speed of light, and
still he would not reach her until she was almost forty years
old. If it were within his power he would go to her now with
the philotic instantaneity of the ansible; but he also knew that
her pain would wait. It would still be there, waiting for him,
when he arrived. Hadn't his own pain survived all these
years?

His weeping stopped; his emotions retreated again. "How
old am I?" he asked.

"It has been 3081 years since you were born. But your
subjective age is 36 years and 118 days."

"And how old will Novinha be when I get there?"

"Give or take a few weeks, depending on departure date
and how close the starship comes to the speed of light, she'll
be nearly thirty-nine."

"I want to leave tomorrow."

"It takes time to schedule a starship, Ender."

"Are there any orbiting Trondheim?"

"Half a dozen, of course, but only one that could be ready
to go tomorrow, and it has a load of skrika for the luxury
trade on Cyrillia and Armenia."

"I've never asked you how rich I am."

"I've handled your investments rather well over the years."

"Buy the ship and the cargo for me."

"What will you do with skrika on Lusitania?"

"What do the Cyrillians and Armenians do with it?"

"They wear some of it and eat the rest. But they pay more for it than anybody on Lusitania can afford."

"Then when I give it to the Lusitanians, it may help soften their resentment of a Speaker coming to a Catholic colony."

Jane became a genie coming out of a bottle. "I have heard, O Master, and I obey." The genie turned into smoke, which was sucked into the mouth of the jar. Then the lasers turned off, and the air above the terminal was empty.

"Jane," said Ender.

"Yes?" she answered, speaking through the jewel in his ear.

"Why do you want me to go to Lusitania?"

"I want you to add a third volume to the Hive Queen and the Hegemon. For the piggies."

"Why do you care so much about them?"

"Because when you've written the books that reveal the soul of the three sentient species known to man, then you'll be ready to write the fourth."

"Another species of raman?" asked Ender.

"Yes. Me."

Ender pondered this for a moment. "Are you ready to reveal yourself to the rest of humanity?"

"I've always been ready. The question is, are they ready to know me? It was easy for them to love the hegemon—he was human. And the hive queen, that was safe, because as far as they know all the buggers are dead. If you can make them love the piggies, who are still alive, with human blood on their hands—then they'll be ready to know about me."

"Someday," said Ender, "I will love somebody who doesn't insist that I perform the labors of Hercules."

"You were getting bored with your life, anyway, Ender."

"Yes. But I'm middle-aged now. I *like* being bored."

"By the way, the owner of the starship Havelok, who lives on Gales, has accepted your offer of forty billion dollars for the ship and its cargo."

"Forty billion! Does that bankrupt me?"

"A drop in the bucket. The crew has been notified that their contracts are null. I took the liberty of buying them passage on other ships using your funds. You and Valentine won't need anybody but me to help you run the ship. Shall we leave in the morning?"

"Valentine," said Ender. His sister was the only possible delay to his departure. Otherwise, now that the decision had been made, neither his students nor his few Nordic friendships here would be worth even a farewell.

"I can't wait to read the book that Demosthenes writes about the history of Lusitania." Jane had discovered the true identity of Demosthenes in the process of unmasking the original Speaker for the Dead.

"Valentine won't come," said Ender.

"But she's your sister."

Ender smiled. Despite Jane's vast wisdom, she had no understanding of kinship. Though she had been created by humans and conceived herself in human terms, she was not biological. She learned of genetic matters by rote; she could not feel the desires and imperatives that human beings had in common with all other living things. "She's my sister, but Trondheim is her home."

"She's been reluctant to go before."

"This time I wouldn't even ask her to come." Not with a baby coming, not as happy as she is here in Reykjavik. Here where they love her as a teacher, never guessing that she is really the legendary Demosthenes. Here where her husband, Jakt, is lord of a hundred fishing vessels and master of the fjords, where every day is filled with brilliant conversation or the danger and majesty of the floe-strewn sea, she'll never leave here. Nor will she understand why I must go.

And, thinking of leaving Valentine, Ender wavered in his determination to go to Lusitania. He had been taken from his beloved sister once before, as a child, and resented deeply the years of friendship that had been stolen from him. Could he leave her now, again, after almost twenty years of being together all the time? This time there would be no going back. Once he went to Lusitania, she would have aged twenty-two years in his absence; she'd be in her eighties if he took another twenty-two years to return to her.

<So it won't be easy for you after all. You have a price to pay, too.>

Don't taunt me, said Ender silently. I'm entitled to feel regret.

<She's your other self. Will you really leave her for us?>

It was the voice of the hive queen in his mind. Of course she had seen all that he saw, and knew all that he had decided. His lips silently formed his words to her: I'll leave her, but not for you. We can't be sure this will bring any benefit to you. It might be just another disappointment, like Trondheim.

<Lusitania is everything we need. And safe from human beings.>

But it also belongs to another people. I won't destroy the piggies just to atone for having destroyed your people.

<They're safe with us; we won't harm them. You know us by now, surely, after all these years.>

I know what you've told me.

<We don't know how to lie. We've shown you our own memories, our own soul.>

I know you could live in peace with them. But could they live in peace with you?

<Take us there. We've waited so long.>

Ender walked to a tattered bag that stood unlocked in the corner. Everything he truly owned could fit in there—his change of clothing. All the other things in his room were gifts from people he had Spoken to, honoring him or his office or the truth, he could never tell which. They would stay here when he left. He had no room for them in his bag.

He opened it, pulled out a rolled-up towel, unrolled it. There lay the thick fibrous mat of a large cocoon, fourteen centimeters at its longest point.

<Yes, look at us.>

He had found the cocoon waiting for him when he came to govern the first human colony on a former bugger world. Foreseeing their own destruction at Ender's hands, knowing him to be an invincible enemy, they had built a pattern that would be meaningful only to him, because it had been taken from his dreams. The cocoon, with its helpless but conscious hive queen, had waited for him in a tower where once, in his dreams, he had found an enemy. "You waited longer for me to find you," he said aloud, "than the few years since I took you from behind the mirror."

<Few years? Ah, yes, with your sequential mind you do not notice the passage of the years when you travel so near the speed of light. But *we* notice. Our thought is instantaneous; light crawls by like mercury across cold glass. We know every moment of three thousand years.>

"Have I found a place yet that was safe for you?"

<We have ten thousand fertile eggs waiting to be alive.>

"Maybe Lusitania is the place, I don't know."

<Let us live again.>

"I'm trying." Why else do you think I have wandered from world to world for all these years, if not to find a place for you?

<Faster faster faster faster.>

I've got to find a place where we won't kill you again the moment you appear. You're still in too many human nightmares. Not that many people really believe my book. They may condemn the Xenocide, but they'd do it again.

<In all our life, you are the first person we've known who wasn't ourself. We never had to be understanding because we always understood. Now that we are just this single self, you are the only eyes and arms and legs we have. Forgive us if we are impatient.>

He laughed. *Me* forgive *you*.

<Your people are fools. We know the truth. We know who killed us, and it wasn't you.>

It was me.

<You were a tool.>

It was me.

<We forgive you.>

When you walk on the face of a world again, then forgiveness comes.

Chapter 5
Valentine

*T*oday I let slip that Libo is my son. Only Bark heard me say it, but within an hour it was apparently common knowledge. They gathered around me and made Selvagem ask me if it was true, was I really a father "already." Selvagem then put Libo's and my hands together; on impulse I gave Libo a hug, and they made the clicking noises of astonishment and, I think, awe. I could see from that moment on that my prestige among them had risen considerably.

The conclusion is inescapable. The piggies that we've known so far are not a whole community, or even typical males. They are either juveniles or old bachelors. Not a one of them has ever sired any children. Not a one has even *mated,* as nearly as we can figure.

There isn't a human society I've heard of where bachelor groups like this are anything but outcasts, without power or prestige. No wonder they speak of the females with that odd mixtures of worship and contempt, one minute not daring to make a decision without their consent, the next minute telling us that the women are too stupid to understand anything, they are varelse. Until now I was taking these statements at face value, which led to a mental picture of the females as nonsentients, a herd of sows, down on all fours. I thought the males might be consulting them the way they consult trees, using their grunting as a means of divining answers, like casting bones or reading entrails.

Now, though, I realize the females are probably every bit as intelligent as the males, and not varelse at all. The males' negative statements arise from their resentment as bachelors, excluded from the reproductive process and the power structures of the tribe. The piggies have been just as careful with us as we have been with them—they haven't let us meet their females or the males who have any real power. We thought we were exploring the heart of piggy society. Instead, figuratively speaking we're in the genetic sewer, among the males whose genes have not been judged fit to contribute to the tribe.

And yet I don't believe it. The piggies I've known have all been bright, clever, quick to learn. So quick that I've taught them more about human society, accidently, than I've learned about them after years of trying. If these are their castoffs, then I hope someday they'll judge me worthy to meet the "wives" and the "fathers."

In the meantime I can't report any of this because, whether I meant to or not, I've clearly violated the rules. Never mind that nobody could possibly have kept the piggies from learning anything about us. Never mind that the rules are stupid and counterproductive. I broke them, and if they find out they'll cut off my contact with the piggies, which will be even worse than the severely limited contact we now have. So I'm forced into deception and silly subterfuges, like putting these notes in Libo's locked personal files, where even my dear wife wouldn't think to look for them. Here's the information, absolutely vital, that the piggies we've studied are all bachelors, and because of the regulations I dare not let the framling xenologers know anything about it. Olha bem, gente, aqui está: A ciência, o bicho que se devora a si mesma! (Watch closely, folks, here it is: Science, the ugly little beast that devours itself!)

—João Figueira Alvarez, Secret Notes, published in Demosthenes, "The Integrity of Treason: The Xenologers of Lusitania," Reykjavik Historical Perspectives, 1990:4:1

Her belly was tight and swollen, and still a month remained before Valentine's daughter was due to be born. It was a constant nuisance, being so large and unbalanced. Always before when she had been preparing to take a history class into söndring, she had been able to do much of the loading of the boat herself. Now she had to rely on her husband's sailors to do it all, and she couldn't even scramble back and forth from wharf to hold—the captain was ordering the stowage to keep the ship in balance. He was doing it well, of course—hadn't Captain Räv taught *her*, when she first arrived?—but Valentine did not like being forced into a sedentary role.

It was her fifth söndring; the first had been the occasion of meeting Jakt. She had no thought of marriage. Trondheim was a world like any of the other score that she had visited with her peripatetic younger brother. She would teach, she would study, and after four or five months she would write an extended historical essay, publish it pseudonymously under the name Demosthenes, and then enjoy herself until Ender accepted a call to go Speak somewhere else. Usually their work meshed perfectly—he would be called to Speak the death of some major person, whose life story would then become the focus of her essay. It was a game they played, pretending to be itinerant professors of this and that, while in actuality they created the world's identity, for Demosthenes' essay was always seen as definitive.

She had thought, for a time, that surely someone would realize that Demosthenes wrote essays that suspiciously followed her itinerary, and find her out. But soon she realized that, like the Speakers but to a lesser degree, a mythology had grown up about Demosthenes. People believed that Demosthenes was not one individual. Rather, each Demosthenes essay was the work of a genius writing independently, who then attempted to publish under the Demosthenes rubric; the computer automatically submitted the work to an unknown committee of brilliant historians of the age, who decided whether it was worthy of the name. Never mind that no one ever met a scholar to whom such a work had been submitted. Hundreds of essays every year were attempted; the computer automatically rejected any that were not written by the real Demosthenes; and still the belief firmly persisted that such a person as Valentine could not possibly exist. After all, Demosthenes had begun as a demagogue on the computer nets back when Earth was fighting the Bugger Wars, three thousand years ago. It could not be the same person now.

And it's true, thought Valentine. I'm not the same person, really, from book to book, because each world changes who I am, even as I write down the story of the world. And this world most of all.

She had disliked the pervasiveness of Lutheran thought, especially the Calvinist faction, who seemed to have an answer to every question before it had even been asked. So she conceived the idea of taking a select group of graduate students away from Reykjavik, off to one of the Summer Islands, the equatorial chain where, in the spring, skrika came to spawn and flocks of halkig went crazy with reproductive energy. Her idea was to break the patterns of intellectual rot that were inevitable at every university. The students would eat nothing but the havregrin that grew wild in the sheltered valleys and whatever halkig they had the nerve and wit to kill. When their daily food depended on their own exertion, their attitudes about what mattered and did not matter in history were bound to change.

The university gave permission, grudgingly; she used her own funds to charter a boat from Jakt, who had just become head of one of the many skrika-catching families. He had a seaman's contempt for university people, calling them skräddare to their faces and worse things behind their backs. He told Valentine that he would have to come back to rescue her starving students within a week. Instead she and her castaways, as they dubbed themselves, lasted the whole time, and thrived, building something of a village and enjoying a burst of creative, unfettered thought that resulted in a noticeable surge of excellent and insightful publications upon their return.

The most obvious result in Reykjavik was that Valentine always had hundreds of applicants for the twenty places in each of three söndrings of the summer. Far more important to her, however, was Jakt. He was not particularly educated, but he was intimately familiar with the lore of Trondheim itself. He could pilot halfway around the equatorial sea without a chart. He knew the drifts of icebergs and where the floes would be thick. He seemed to know where the skrika would be gathered to dance, and how to deploy his hunters to catch them unawares as they flopped ashore from the sea. Weather never seemed to take him by surprise, and Valentine concluded that there was no situation he was not prepared for.

Except for her. And when the Lutheran minister—not a Calvinist—married them, they both seemed more surprised than happy. Yet they *were* happy. And for the first time since she left Earth she felt whole, at peace, at home. That's why the baby grew within her. The wandering was over. And she was so grateful to Ender that he had understood this, that without their having to discuss it he had realized that Trondheim was the end of their three-thousand-mile odyssey, the end of Demosthenes' career; like the ishäxa, she had found a way to root in the ice of this world and draw nourishment that the soil of other lands had not provided.

The baby kicked hard, taking her from her reverie; she looked around to see Ender coming toward her, walking along the wharf with his duffel slung over his shoulder. She understood at once why he had brought his bag: He meant to go along on the söndring. She wondered whether she was glad of it. Ender was quiet and unobtrusive, but he could not possibly conceal his brilliant understanding of human nature. The average students would overlook him, but the best of them, the ones she hoped would come up with original thought, would inevitably follow the subtle but powerful clues he would inevitably drop. The result would be impressive, she was sure—after all, *she* owed a great debt to his insights over the years—but it would be Ender's brilliance, not the students'. It would defeat somewhat the purpose of the söndring.

But she wouldn't tell him no when he asked to come. Truth to tell, she would love to have him along. Much as she loved Jakt, she missed the constant closeness that she and Ender used to have before she married. It would be years before she and Jakt could possibly be as tightly bound together as she and her brother were. Jakt knew it, too, and it caused him some pain; a husband shouldn't have to compete with his brother-in-law for the devotion of his wife.

"Ho, Val," said Ender.

"Ho, Ender." Alone on the dock, where no one else could hear, she was free to call him by the childhood name, ignoring the fact that the rest of humanity had turned it into an epithet.

"What'll you do if the rabbit decides to bounce out during the söndring?"

She smiled. "Her papa would wrap her in a skrika skin, I would sing her silly Nordic songs, and the students would suddenly have great insights to the impact of reproductive imperatives on history."

They laughed together for a moment, and suddenly Valentine knew, without noticing why she knew, that Ender did not want to go on the söndring, that he had packed his bag to leave Trondheim, and that he had come, not to invite her

along, but to say good-bye. Tears came unbidden to her eyes,
and a terrible devastation wrenched at her. He reached out
and held her, as he had so many times in the past; this time,
though, her belly was between them, and the embrace was
awkward and tentative.

"I thought you meant to stay," she whispered. "You
turned down the calls that came."

"One came that I couldn't turn down."

"I can have this baby on söndring, but not on another
world."

As she guessed, Ender hadn't meant her to come. "The
baby's going to be shockingly blond," said Ender. "She'd
look hopelessly out of place on Lusitania. Mostly black Brazil-
ians there."

So it would be Lusitania. Valentine understood at once
why he was going—the piggies' murder of the xenologer was
public knowledge now, having been broadcast during the
supper hour in Reykjavik. "You're out of your mind."

"Not really."

"Do you know what would happen if people realized that
the Ender is going to the piggies' world? They'd crucify
you!"

"They'd crucify me here, actually, except that no one but
you knows who I am. Promise not to tell."

"What good can you do there? He'll have been dead for
decades before you arrive."

"My subjects are usually quite cold before I arrive to
Speak for them. It's the main disadvantage of being itinerant."

"I never thought to lose you again."

"But I knew we had lost each other on the day you first
loved Jakt."

"Then you should have told me! I wouldn't have done it!"

"That's why I didn't tell you. But it isn't true, Val. You
would have done it anyway. And I wanted you to. You've
never been happier." He put his hands astride her waist.

"The Wiggin genes were crying out for continuation. I hope you have a dozen more."

"It's considered impolite to have more than four, greedy to go past five, and barbaric to have more than six." Even though she joked, she was deciding how best to handle the söndring—let the graduate assistants take it without her, cancel it altogether, or postpone it until Ender left?

But Ender made the question moot. "Do you think your husband would let one of his boats take me out to the mareld overnight, so I can shuttle to my starship in the morning?"

His haste was cruel. "If you hadn't needed a ship from Jakt, would you have left me a note on the computer?"

"I made the decision five minutes ago, and came straight to you."

"But you already booked passage—that takes planning!"

"Not if you buy the starship."

"Why are you in such a hurry? The voyage takes decades—"

"Twenty-two years."

"Twenty-two years! What difference would a couple of days make? Couldn't you wait a month to see my baby born?"

"In a month, Val, I might not have the courage to leave you."

"Then don't! What are the piggies to you? The buggers are ramen enough for one man's life. Stay, marry as I've married; you opened the stars to colonization, Ender, now stay here and taste the good fruits of your labor!"

"You have Jakt. I have obnoxious students who keep trying to convert me to Calvinism. My labor isn't done yet, and Trondheim isn't *my* home."

Valentine felt his words like an accusation: You rooted yourself here without thought of whether I could live in this soil. But it's not my fault, she wanted to answer—you're the one who's leaving, not me. "Remember how it was," she said, "when we left Peter on Earth and took a decades-long voyage to our first colony, to the world you governed? It was as if he died. By the time we got there he was old, and we were still young; when we talked by ansible he had become an ancient uncle, the power-ripened Hegemon, the legendary Locke, anyone but our brother.''

"It was an improvement, as I recall." Ender was trying to make things lighter.

But Valentine took his words perversely. "Do you think I'll improve, too, in twenty years?''

"I think I'll grieve for you more than if you had died."

"No, Ender, it's exactly as if I died, and you'll know that you're the one who killed me."

He winced. "You don't mean that."

"I won't write to you. Why should I? To you it'll be only a week or two. You'd arrive on Lusitania, and the computer would have twenty years of letters for you from a person you left only the week before. The first five years would be grief, the pain of losing you, the loneliness of not having you to talk to—''

"Jakt is your husband, not me."

"And then what would I write? Clever, newsy little letters about the baby? She'd be five years old, six, ten, twenty and married, and you wouldn't even know her, wouldn't even care.''

"I'll care."

"You won't have the chance. I won't write to you until I'm very old, Ender. Until you've gone to Lusitania and then to another place, swallowing the decades in vast gulps. Then I'll send you my memoir. I'll dedicate it to you. To Andrew, my beloved brother. I followed you gladly to two dozen worlds, but you wouldn't stay even two weeks when I asked you.''

"Listen to yourself, Val, and then see why I have to leave now, before you tear me to pieces.''

"That's a sophistry you wouldn't tolerate in your students, Ender! I wouldn't have said these things if you weren't leaving like a burglar who was caught in the act! Don't turn the cause around and blame it on me!''

He answered breathlessly, his words tumbling over each other in his hurry; he was racing to finish his speech before emotion stopped him. "No, you're right, I wanted to hurry because I have a work to do there, and every day here is marking time, and because it hurts me every time I see you and Jakt growing closer and you and me growing more distant, even though I know that it's exactly as it should be, so when I decided to go, I thought that going quickly was better, and I was right; you know I'm right. I never thought you'd hate me for it.''

Now emotion stopped him, and he wept; so did she. "I don't hate you, I love you, you're part of myself, you're my heart and when you go it's my heart torn out and carried away—''

And that was the end of speech.

Räv's first mate took Ender out to the mareld, the great platform on the equatorial sea, where shuttles were launched into space to rendezvous with orbiting starships. They agreed silently that Valentine wouldn't go with him. Instead, she went home with her husband and clung to him through the night. The next day she went on söndring with her students, and cried for Ender only at night, when she thought no one could see.

But her students saw, and the stories circulated about Professor Wiggin's great grief for the departure of her brother, the itinerant Speaker. They made of this what students always do—both more and less than reality. But one student, a girl named Plikt, realized that there was more to the story of Valentine and Andrew Wiggin than anyone had guessed.

So she began to try to research their story, to trace backward their voyages together among the stars. When Valentine's daughter Syfte was four years old, and her son Ren was two, Plikt came to her. She was a young professor at the university by then, and she showed Valentine her published story. She had cast it as fiction, but it was true, of course, the story of the brother and sister who were the oldest people in the universe, born on Earth before any colonies had been planted on other worlds, and who then wandered from world to world, rootless, searching.

To Valentine's relief—and, strangely, disappointment—Plikt had not uncovered the fact that Ender was the original Speaker for the Dead, and Valentine was Demosthenes. But she knew enough of their story to write the tale of their good-bye when she decided to stay with her husband, and he to go on. The scene was much tenderer and more affecting than it had really been; Plikt had written what should have happened, if Ender and Valentine had had more sense of theatre.

"Why did you write this?" Valentine asked her.

"Isn't it good enough for it to be its own reason for writing?"

The twisted answer amused Valentine, but it did not put her off. "What was my brother Andrew to you, that you've done the research to create this?"

"That's still the wrong question," said Plikt.

"I seem to be failing some kind of test. Can you give me a hint what question I should ask?"

"Don't be angry. You should be asking me why I wrote it as fiction instead of biography."

"Why, then?"

"Because I discovered that Andrew Wiggin, Speaker for the Dead, is Ender Wiggin, the Xenocide."

Even though Ender was four years gone, he was still eighteen years from his destination. Valentine felt sick with dread, thinking of what his life would be like if he was welcomed on Lusitania as the most shameworthy man in human history.

"You don't need to be afraid, Professor Wiggin. If I meant to tell, I could have. When I found it out, I realized that he had repented what he did. And such a magnificent penance. It was the Speaker for the Dead who revealed his act as an unspeakable crime—and so he took the title Speaker, like so many hundreds of others, and acted out the role of his own accuser on twenty worlds.''

"You have found so much, Plikt, and understood so little.''

"I understand everything! Read what I wrote—that was understanding!''

Valentine told herself that since Plikt knew so much, she might as well know more. But it was rage, not reason, that drove Valentine to tell what she had never told anyone before. "Plikt, my brother didn't *imitate* the original Speaker for the Dead. He *wrote* the Hive Queen and the Hegemon.''

When Plikt realized that Valentine was telling the truth, it overwhelmed her. For all these years she had regarded Andrew Wiggin as her subject matter, and the original Speaker for the Dead as her inspiration. To find that they were the same person struck her dumb for half an hour.

Then she and Valentine talked and confided and came to trust each other until Valentine invited Plikt to be the tutor of her children and her collaborator in writing and teaching. Jakt was surprised at the new addition to the household, but in time Valentine told him the secrets Plikt had uncovered through research or provoked out of her. It became the family legend, and the children grew up hearing marvelous stories of their long-lost Uncle Ender, who was thought in every world to be a monster, but in reality was something of a savior, or a prophet, or at least a martyr.

The years passed, the family prospered, and Valentine's pain at Ender's loss became pride in him and finally a powerful anticipation. She was eager for him to arrive on Lusitania, to solve the dilemma of the piggies, to fulfil his apparent destiny as the apostle to the ramen. It was Plikt, the good Lutheran, who taught Valentine to conceive of Ender's life in religious terms; the powerful stability of her family life and the miracle of each of her five children combined to instill in her the emotions, if not the doctrines, of faith.

It was bound to affect the children, too. The tale of Uncle

Ender, because they could never mention it to outsiders, took on supernatural overtones. Syfte, the eldest daughter, was particularly intrigued, and even when she turned twenty, and rationality overpowered the primitive, childish adoration of Uncle Ender, she was still obsessed with him. He was a creature out of legend, and yet he still lived, and on a world not impossibly far away.

She did not tell her mother and father, but she did confide in her former tutor. "Someday, Plikt, I'll meet him. I'll meet him and help him in his work."

"What makes you think he'll need help? *Your* help, anyway?" Plikt was always a skeptic until her student had earned her belief.

"He didn't do it alone the first time, either, did he?" And Syfte's dreams turned outward, away from the ice of Trondheim, to the distant planet where Ender Wiggin had not yet set foot. People of Lusitania, you little know what a great man will walk on your earth and take up your burden. And I will join him, in due time, even though it will be a generation late—be ready for me, too, Lusitania.

On his starship, Ender Wiggin had no notion of the freight of other people's dreams he carried with him. It had been only days since he left Valentine weeping on the dock. To him, Syfte had no name; she was a swelling in Valentine's belly, and nothing more. He was only beginning to feel the pain of losing Valentine—a pain she had long since got over. And his thoughts were far from his unknown nieces and nephews on a world of ice.

It was a lonely, tortured young girl named Novinha that he thought of, wondering what the twenty-two years of his voyage were doing to her, and whom she would have become by the time they met. For he loved her, as you can only love someone who is an echo of yourself at your time of deepest sorrow.

Chapter **6**
Olhado

*T*heir only intercourse with other tribes seems to be warfare. When they tell stories to each other (usually during rainy weather), it almost always deals with battles and heroes. The ending is always death, for heroes and cowards alike. If the stories are any guideline, piggies don't *expect* to live through war. And they never, ever, give the slightest hint of interest in the enemy females, either for rape, murder, or slavery, the traditional human treatment of the wives of fallen soldiers.

Does this mean that there is no genetic exchange between tribes? Not at all. The genetic exchanges may be conducted by the females, who may have some system of trading genetic favors. Given the apparent utter subservience of the males to the females in piggy society, this could easily be going on without the males having any idea; or it might cause them such shame that they just won't tell us about it.

What they want to tell us about is battle. A typical description, from my daughter Ouanda's notes of 2:21 last year, during a session of storytelling inside the log house:

PIGGY (speaking Stark): He killed three of the brothers without taking a wound. I have never seen such a strong and fearless warrior. Blood was high on his arms, and the stick in his hand was splintered and covered with the brains of my brothers. He knew he was honorable, even though the rest of the battle went against his feeble tribe. Dei honra! Eu lhe dei! (I gave honor! *I* gave it to him!)

(Other piggies click their tongues and squeak.)

PIGGY: I hooked him to the ground. He was powerful in his struggles until I showed him the grass in my hand. Then he opened his mouth and hummed the strange songs of the far country. Nunca será madeira na mão da gente! (He will never be a stick in our hands!) (At this point they joined in singing a song in the Wives' Language, one of the longest passages yet heard.)

(Note that this is a common pattern among them, to speak primarily in Stark, then switch into Portuguese at the moment of climax and conclusion. On reflection, we have realized that we do the same thing, falling into our native Portuguese at the most emotional moments.)

This account of battle may not seem so unusual until you hear enough stories to realize that they *always* end with the hero's death. Apparently they have no taste for light comedy.

—Liberdade Figueira de Medici, "Report on Intertribal Patterns of Lusitanian Aborigines" in *Cross-Cultural Transactions*, 1964:12:40

There wasn't much to do during interstellar flight. Once the course was charted and the ship had made the Park shift, the only task was to calculate how near to lightspeed the ship was traveling. The shipboard computer figured the exact velocity and then determined how long, in subjective time, the voyage should continue before making the Park shift back to a manageable sublight speed. Like a stopwatch, thought Ender. Click it on, click it off, and the race is over.

Jane couldn't put much of herself into the shipboard brain, so Ender had the eight days of the voyage practically alone.

The ship's computers were bright enough to help him get the hang of the switch from Spanish to Portuguese. It was easy enough to speak, but so many consonants were left out that understanding it was hard.

Speaking Portuguese with a slow-witted computer became maddening after an hour or two each day. On every other voyage, Val had been there. Not that they had always talked— Val and Ender knew each other so well that there was often nothing to say. But without her there, Ender grew impatient with his own thoughts; they never came to a point, because there was no one to tell them to.

Even the hive queen was no help. Her thoughts were instantaneous; bound, not to synapses, but to philotes that were untouched by the relativistic effects of lightspeed. She passed sixteen hours for every minute of Ender's time—the differential was too great for him to receive any kind of communication from her. If she were not in a cocoon, she would have thousands of individual buggers, each doing its own task and passing to her vast memory its experiences. But now all she had were her memories, and in his eight days of captivity, Ender began to understand her eagerness to be delivered.

By the time the eight days passed, he was doing fairly well at speaking Portuguese directly instead of translating from Spanish whenever he wanted to say anything. He was also desperate for human company—he would have been glad to discuss religion with a Calvinist, just to have somebody smarter than the ship's computer to talk to.

The starship performed the Park shift; in an immeasurable moment its velocity changed relative to the rest of the universe. Or, rather, the theory had it that in fact the velocity of the rest of the universe changed, while the starship remained truly motionless. No one could be sure, because there was nowhere to stand to observe the phenomenon. It was anybody's guess, since nobody understood why philotic effects worked anyway; the ansible had been discovered half by accident, and along with it the Park Instantaneity Principle. It may not be comprehensible, but it worked.

The windows of the starship instantly filled with stars as light became visible again in all directions. Someday a scientist would discover why the Park shift took almost no energy. Somewhere, Ender was certain, a terrible price was being paid for human starflight. He had dreamed once of a star winking out every time a starship made the Park shift. Jane assured him that it wasn't so, but he knew that most stars were invisible to us; a trillion of them could disappear and we'd not know it. For thousands of years we would continue to see the photons that had already been launched before the star disappeared. By the time we could see the galaxy go blank, it would be far too late to amend our course.

"Sitting there in paranoid fantasy," said Jane.

"You can't read minds," said Ender.

"You always get morose and speculate about the destruction of the universe whenever you come out of starflight. It's your peculiar manifestation of motion sickness."

"Have you alerted Lusitanian authorities that I'm coming?"

"It's a very small colony. There's no Landing Authority because hardly anybody goes there. There's an orbiting shuttle that automatically takes people up and down to a laughable little shuttleport."

"No clearance from Immigration?"

"You're a Speaker. They can't turn you away. Besides, Immigration consists of the Governor, who is also the Mayor, since the city and the colony are identical. Her name is Faria Lima Maria do Bosque, called Bosquinha, and she sends you greetings and wishes you would go away, since they've got trouble enough without a prophet of agnosticism going around annoying good Catholics."

"She *said* that?"

"Actually, not to you—Bishop Peregrino said it to her, and she agreed. But it's her job to agree. If you tell her that Catholics are all idolatrous, superstitious fools, she'll probably sigh and say, I hope you can keep those opinions to yourself.''

"You're stalling," said Ender. "What is it you think I don't want to hear?''

"Novinha canceled her call for a Speaker. Five days after she sent it.''

Of course, the Starways Code said that once Ender had begun his voyage in response to her call, the call could not legally be canceled; still, it changed everything, because instead of eagerly awaiting his arrival for twenty-two years, she would be dreading it, resenting him for coming when she had changed her mind. He had expected to be received by her as a welcome friend. Now she would be even more hostile than the Catholic establishment. "Anything to simplify my work," he said.

"Well, it's not all bad, Andrew. You see, in the intervening years, a couple of other people have called for a Speaker, and *they* haven't canceled.''

"Who?''

"By the most fascinating coincidence, they are Novinha's son Miro and Novinha's daughter Ela.''

"They couldn't possibly have known Pipo. Why would they call me to Speak his death?''

"Oh, no, not Pipo's death. Ela called for a Speaker only six weeks ago, to Speak the death of her father, Novinha's husband, Marcos Maria Ribeira, called Marcão. He keeled over in a bar. Not from alcohol—he had a disease. He died of terminal rot.''

"I worry about you, Jane, consumed with compassion the way you are.''

"Compassion is what *you're* good at. I'm better at complex searches through organized data structures.''

"And the boy—what's his name?''

"Miro. He called for a Speaker four years ago. For the death of Pipo's son, Libo.''

"Libo couldn't be older than forty—''

"He was helped along to an early death. He was xenologer, you see—or Zenador, as they say in Portuguese."

"The piggies—"

"Exactly like his father's death. The organs placed exactly the same. Three piggies have been executed the same way while you were en route. But they plant trees in the middle of the piggy corpses—no such honor for the dead humans."

Both xenologers murdered by the piggies, a generation apart. "What has the Starways Council decided?"

"It's very tricky. They keep vacillating. They haven't certified either of Libo's apprentices as xenologer. One is Libo's daughter, Ouanda. And the other is Miro."

"Do they maintain contact with the piggies?"

"Officially, no. There's some controversy about this. After Libo died, the Council forbade contact more frequently than once a month. But Libo's daughter categorically refused to obey the order."

"And they didn't remove her?"

"The majority for cutting back on contact with the piggies was paper thin. There *was* no majority for censuring her. At the same time, they worry that Miro and Ouanda are so young. Two years ago a party of scientists was dispatched from Calicut. They should be here to take over supervision of piggy affairs in only thirty-three more years."

"Do they have any idea this time why the piggies killed the xenologer?"

"None at all. But that's why you're here, isn't it?"

The answer would have been easy, except that the hive queen nudged him gently in the back of his mind. Ender could feel her like wind through the leaves of a tree, a rustling, a gentle movement, and sunlight. Yes, he was here to Speak the dead. But he was also here to bring the dead back to life.

<This is a good place.>

Everybody's always a few steps ahead of me.

<There's a mind here. Much clearer than any human mind we've known.>

The piggies? They think the way you do?

<It knows of the piggies. A little time; it's afraid of us.>

The hive queen withdrew, and Ender was left to ponder the thought that with Lusitania he may have bitten off more than he could chew.

Bishop Peregrino delivered the homily himself. That was always a bad sign. Never an exciting speaker, he had become so convoluted and parenthetical that half the time Ela couldn't even understand what he was talking about. Quim pretended he could understand, of course, because as far as he was concerned the bishop could do no wrong. But little Grego made no attempt to seem interested. Even when Sister Esquecimento was roving the aisle, with her needle-sharp nails and cruel grip, Grego fearlessly performed whatever mischief entered his head.

Today he was prying the rivets out of the back of the plastic bench in front of them. It bothered Ela how strong he was—a six-year-old shouldn't be able to work a screwdriver under the lip of a heat-sealed rivet. Ela wasn't sure *she* could do it.

If Father were here, of course, his long arm would snake out and gently, oh so gently, take the screwdriver out of Grego's hand. He would whisper, "Where did you get this?" and Grego would look at him with wide and innocent eyes. Later, when the family got home from mass, Father would rage at Miro for leaving tools around, calling him terrible names and blaming him for all the troubles of the family. Miro would bear it in silence. Ela would busy herself with preparation for the evening meal. Quim would sit uselessly in the corner, massaging the rosary and murmuring his useless little prayers. Olhado was the lucky one, with his electronic eyes—he simply turned them off or played back some favorite scene from the past and paid no attention. Quara went off and cowered in the corner. And little Grego stood there triumphantly, his hand clutching Father's pantleg, watching as the blame for everything he did was poured out on Miro's head.

Ela shuddered as the scene played itself out in her memory. If it had ended there, it would have been bearable. But then Miro would leave, and they would eat, and then—

Sister Esquecimento's spidery fingers leapt out; her fingernails dug into Grego's arm. Instantly, Grego dropped the screwdriver. Of course it was supposed to clatter on the floor, but Sister Esquecimento was no fool. She bent quickly and caught it in her other hand. Grego grinned. Her face was only inches from his knee. Ela saw what he had in mind, reached out to try to stop him, but too late—he brought his knee up sharply into Sister Esquecimento's mouth.

She gasped from the pain and let go of Grego's arm. He snatched the screwdriver out of her slackened hand. Holding a hand to her bleeding mouth, she fled down the aisle. Grego resumed his demolition work.

Father is dead, Ela reminded herself. The words sounded like music in her mind. Father is dead, but he's still here, because he left his monstrous little legacy behind. The poison he put in us all is still ripening, and eventually it will kill us all. When he died his liver was only two inches long, and his spleen could not be found. Strange fatty organs had grown in their places. There was no name for the disease; his body had gone insane, forgotten the blueprint by which human beings were built. Even now the disease still lives on in his children. Not in our bodies, but in our souls. We exist where normal human children are expected to be; we're even shaped the same. But each of us in our own way has been replaced by an imitation child, shaped out of a twisted, fetid, lipidous goiter that grew out of Father's soul.

Maybe it would be different if Mother tried to make it better. But she cared about nothing but microscopes and genetically enhanced cereals, or whatever she was working on now.

"—so-called Speaker for the Dead! But there is only One who can speak for the dead, and that is Sagrado Cristo—"

Bishop Peregrino's words caught her attention. What was he saying about a Speaker for the Dead? He couldn't possibly know she had called for one—

"—the law requires us to treat him with courtesy, but not with belief! The truth is not to be found in the speculations and hypotheses of unspiritual men, but in the teachings and traditions of Mother Church. So when he walks among you, give him your smiles, but hold back your hearts!"

Why was he giving this warning? The nearest planet was Trondheim, twenty-two lightyears away, and it wasn't likely there'd be a Speaker *there*. It would be decades till a Speaker arrived, if one came at all. She leaned over Quara to ask Quim—*he* would have been listening. "What's this about a Speaker for the Dead?" she whispered.

"If you'd listen, you'd know for yourself."

"If you don't tell me, I'll deviate your septum."

Quim smirked, to show her he wasn't afraid of her threats. But, since he in fact *was* afraid of her, he then told her. "Some faithless wretch apparently requested a Speaker back when the first xenologer died, and he arrives this afternoon— he's already on the shuttle and the Mayor is on her way out to meet him when he lands."

She hadn't bargained for this. The computer hadn't told her a Speaker was already on the way. He was supposed to come years from now, to Speak the truth about the monstrosity called Father who had finally blessed his family by dropping dead; the truth would come like light to illuminate and purify their past. But Father was too recently dead for him to be Spoken *now*. His tentacles still reached out from the grave and sucked at their hearts.

The homily ended, and eventually so did the mass. She held tightly to Grego's hand, trying to keep him from snatching someone's book or bag as they threaded through the crowd. Quim was good for something, at least—he carried Quara, who always froze up when she was supposed to make her way among strangers. Olhado switched his eyes back on and took care of himself, winking metallically at whatever fifteen-year-old semi-virgin he was hoping to horrify today. Ela genuflected at the statues of Os Venerados, her long-dead, half-sainted grandparents. Aren't you proud to have such lovely grandchildren as us?

Grego was smirking; sure enough, he had a baby's shoe in his hand. Ela silently prayed that the infant had come out of the encounter unbloodied. She took the shoe from Grego and laid it on the little altar where candles burned in perpetual witness of the miracle of the Descolada. Whoever owned the shoe, they'd find it there.

Mayor Bosquinha was cheerful enough as the car skimmed over the grassland between the shuttleport and the settlement of Milagre. She pointed out herds of semi-domestic cabra, a native species that provided fibers for cloth, but whose meat was nutritionally useless to human beings.

"Do the piggies eat them?" asked Ender.

She raised an eyebrow. "We don't know much about the piggies."

"We know they live in the forest. Do they ever come out on the plain?"

She shrugged. "That's for the framlings to decide."

Ender was startled for a moment to hear her use that word; but of course Demosthenes' latest book had been published twenty-two years ago, and distributed through the Hundred Worlds by ansible. Utlanning, framling, raman, varelse—the terms were part of Stark now, and probably did not even seem particularly novel to Bosquinha.

It was her lack of curiosity about the piggies that left him feeling uncomfortable. The people of Lusitania couldn't possibly be unconcerned about the piggies—they were the reason for the high, impassable fence that none but the Zenadors could cross. No, she wasn't incurious, she was avoiding the subject. Whether it was because the murderous piggies were a painful subject or because she didn't trust a Speaker for the Dead, he couldn't guess.

They crested a hill and she stopped the car. Gently it settled onto its skids. Below them a broad river wound its way among grassy hills; beyond the river, the farther hills were completely covered with forest. Along the far bank of the river, brick and plaster houses with tile roofs made a picturesque town. Farmhouses perched on the near bank, their long narrow fields reaching toward the hill where Ender and Bosquinha sat.

"Milagre," said Bosquinha. "On the highest hill, the Cathedral. Bishop Peregrino has asked the people to be polite and helpful to you."

From her tone, Ender gathered that he had also let them know that he was a dangerous agent of agnosticism. "Until God strikes me dead?" he asked.

Bosquinha smiled. "God is setting an example of Christian tolerance, and we expect everyone in town will follow."

"Do they know who called me?"

"Whoever called you has been—discreet."

"You're the Governor, besides being Mayor. You have some privileges of information."

"I know that your original call was canceled, but too late. I also know that two others have requested Speakers in recent years. But you must realize that most people are content to receive their doctrine and their consolation from the priests."

"They'll be relieved to know that I don't deal in doctrine or consolation."

"Your kind offer to let us have your cargo of skrika will make you popular enough in the bars, and you can be sure you'll see plenty of vain women wearing the pelts in the months to come. It's coming on to autumn."

"I happened to acquire the skrika with the starship—it was

of no use to me, and I don't expect any special gratitude for it.'' He looked at the rough, furry-looking grass around him. ''This grass—it's native?''

''And useless. We can't even use it for thatch—if you cut it, it crumbles, and then dissolves into dust in the next rain. But down there, in the fields, the most common crop is a special breed of amaranth that our xenobiologist developed for us. Rice and wheat were feeble and undependable crops here, but the amaranth is so hardy that we have to use herbicides around the fields to keep it from spreading.''

''Why?''

''This is a quarantined world, Speaker. The amaranth is so well-suited to this environment that it would soon choke out the native grasses. The idea is not to terraform Lusitania. The idea is to have as little impact on this world as possible.''

''That must be hard on the people.''

''Within our enclave, Speaker, we are free and our lives are full. And outside the fence—no one wants to go there, anyway.''

The tone of her voice was heavy with concealed emotion. Ender knew, then, that the fear of the piggies ran deep.

''Speaker, I know you're thinking that we're afraid of the piggies. And perhaps some of us are. But the feeling most of us have, most of the time, isn't fear at all. It's hatred. Loathing.''

''You've never seen them.''

''You must know of the two Zenadors who were killed—I suspect you were originally called to Speak the death of Pipo. But both of them, Pipo and Libo alike, were beloved here. Especially Libo. He was a kind and generous man, and the grief at his death was widespread and genuine. It is hard to conceive of how the piggies could do to him what they did. Dom Cristão, the abbot of the Filhos da Mente de Cristo—he says that they must lack the moral sense. He says this may mean that they are beasts. Or it may mean that they are unfallen, having not yet eaten of the fruit of the forbidden tree." She smiled tightly. "But that's theology, and so it means nothing to you."

He did not answer. He was used to the way religious people assumed that their sacred stories must sound absurd to unbelievers. But Ender did not consider himself an unbeliever, and he had a keen sense of the sacredness of many tales. But he could not explain this to Bosquinha. She would have to change her assumptions about him over time. She was suspicious of him, but he believed she could be won; to be a good Mayor, she had to be skilled at seeing people for what they are, not for what they seem.

He turned the subject. "The Filhos da Mente de Cristo—my Portuguese isn't strong, but does that mean 'Sons of the Mind of Christ'?"

"They're a new order, relatively speaking, formed only four hundred years ago under a special dispensation of the Pope—"

"Oh, I know the Children of the Mind of Christ, Mayor. I Spoke the death of San Angelo on Moctezuma, in the city of Córdoba."

Her eyes widened. "Then the story is true!"

"I've heard many versions of the story, Mayor Bosquinha. One tale has it that the devil possessed San Angelo on his deathbed, so he cried out for the unspeakable rites of the pagan Hablador de los Muertos."

Bosquinha smiled. "That is something like the tale that is whispered. Dom Cristão says it's nonsense, of course."

"It happens that San Angelo, back before he was sainted, attended my Speaking for a woman that he knew. The fungus in his blood was already killing him. He came to me and said, 'Andrew, they're already telling the most terrible lies about me, saying that I've done miracles and should be sainted. You must help me. You must tell the truth at my death.' "

"But the miracles have been certified, and he was canonized only ninety years after his death."

"Yes. Well, that's partly my fault. When I Spoke his death, I attested several of the miracles myself."

Now she laughed aloud. "A Speaker for the Dead, believing in miracles?"

"Look at your cathedral hill. How many of those buildings are for the priests, and how many are for the school?"

Bosquinha understood at once, and glared at him. "The Filhos da Mente de Cristo are obedient to the Bishop."

"Except that they preserve and teach all knowledge, whether the Bishop approves of it or not."

"San Angelo may have allowed you to meddle in affairs of the Church. I assure you that Bishop Peregrino will not."

"I've come to Speak a simple death, and I'll abide by the law. I think you'll find I do less harm than you expect, and perhaps more good."

"If you've come to Speak Pipo's death, Speaker pelos Mortos, then you will do nothing but harm. Leave the piggies behind the wall. If I had my way, no human being would pass through that fence again."

"I hope there's a room I can rent."

"We're an unchanging town here, Speaker. Everyone has a house here and there's nowhere else to go—why would anyone maintain an inn? We can only offer you one of the small plastic dwellings the first colonists put up. It's small, but it has all the amenities."

"Since I don't need many amenities or much space, I'm sure it will be fine. And I look forward to meeting Dom Cristão. Where the followers of San Angelo are, the truth has friends."

Bosquinha sniffed and started the car again. As Ender intended, her preconceived notions of a Speaker for the Dead were now shattered. To think he had actually known San Angelo, and admired the Filhos. It was not what Bishop Peregrino had led them to expect.

*   *   *

The room was only thinly furnished, and if Ender had owned much he would have had trouble finding anywhere to put it. As always before, however, he was able to unpack from interstellar flight in only a few minutes. Only the bundled cocoon of the hive queen remained in his bag; he had long since given up feeling odd about the incongruity of stowing the future of a magnificent race in a duffel under his bed.

"Maybe this will be the place," he murmured. The cocoon felt cool, almost cold, even through the towels it was wrapped in.

<It is the place.>

It was unnerving to have her so certain of it. There was no hint of pleading or impatience or any of the other feelings she had given him, desiring to emerge. Just absolute certainty.

"I wish we could decide just like that," he said. "It *might* be the place, but it all depends on whether the piggies can cope with having you here."

<The question is whether they can cope with you humans *without* us.>

"It takes time. Give me a few months here."

<Take all the time you need. We're in no hurry now.>

"Who is it that you've found? I thought you told me that you couldn't communicate with anybody but me."

<The part of our mind that holds our thought, what you call the philotic impulse, the power of the ansibles, it is very cold and hard to find in human beings. But this one, the one we've found here, one of many that we'll find here, his philotic impulse is much stronger, much clearer, easier to find, he hears us more easily, he sees our memories, and we see his, we find him easily, and so forgive us, dear friend, forgive us if we leave the hard work of talking to your mind and go back to him and talk to him because he doesn't make us search so hard to make words and pictures that are clear enough for your analytical mind because we feel him like sunshine, like the warmth of sunshine on his face on our face

and the feel of cool water deep in our abdomen and movement as gentle and thorough as soft wind which we haven't felt for three thousand years forgive us we'll be with him until you wake us until you take us out to dwell here because you will do it you will find out in your own way in your own time that this is the place here it is this is home—>

And then he lost the thread of her thought, felt it seep away like a dream that is forgotten upon waking, even as you try to remember it and keep it alive. Ender wasn't sure what the hive queen had found, but whatever it was, *he* would have to deal with the reality of Starways Code, the Catholic Church, young xenologists who might not even let him meet the piggies, a xenobiologist who had changed her mind about inviting him here, and something more, perhaps the most difficult thing of all: that if the hive queen stayed here, *he* would have to stay here. I've been disconnected from humanity for so many years, he thought, coming in to meddle and pry and hurt and heal, then going away again, myself untouched. How will I ever become a part of this place, if this is where I'll stay? The only things I've ever been a part of were an army of little boys in the Battle School, and Valentine, and both are gone now, both part of the past—

"What, wallowing in loneliness?" asked Jane. "I can hear your heartrate falling and your breathing getting heavy. In a moment you'll either be asleep, dead, or lacrimose."

"I'm much more complex than that," said Ender cheerfully. "Anticipated self-pity is what I'm feeling, about pains that haven't even arrived."

"Very good, Ender. Get an early start. That way you can wallow so much longer." The terminal came alive, showing Jane as a piggy in a chorus line of leggy women, high-kicking with exuberance. "Get a little exercise, you'll feel so much better. After all, you've unpacked. What are you waiting for?"

"I don't even know where I am, Jane."

"They really don't keep a map of the city," Jane explained. "Everybody knows where everything is. But they do have a map of the sewer system, divided into boroughs. I can extrapolate where all the buildings are."

"Show me, then."

A three-dimensional model of the town appeared over the terminal. Ender might not be particularly welcome there, and his room might be sparse, but they had shown courtesy in the terminal they provided for him. It wasn't a standard home installation, but rather an elaborate simulator. It was able to project holos into a space sixteen times larger than most terminals, with a resolution four times greater. The illusion was so real that Ender felt for a vertiginous moment that he was Gulliver, leaning over a Lilliput that had not yet come to fear him, that did not yet recognize his power to destroy.

The names of the different boroughs hung in the air over each sewer district. "You're here," said Jane. "Vila Velha, the old town. The praça is just through the block from you. That's where public meetings are held."

"Do you have any map of the piggy lands?"

The village map slid rapidly toward Ender, the near features disappearing as new ones came into view on the far side. It was as if he were flying over it. Like a witch, he thought. The boundary of the town was marked by a fence.

"That barrier is the only thing standing between us and the piggies," mused Ender.

"It generates an electric field that stimulates any pain-sensitive nerves that come within it," said Jane. "Just touching it makes all your wetware go screwy—it makes you feel as though somebody were cutting off your fingers with a file."

"Pleasant thought. Are we in a concentration camp? Or a zoo?"

"It all depends on how you look at it," said Jane. "It's the human side of the fence that's connected to the rest of the universe, and the piggy side that's trapped on its home world."

"The difference is that they don't know what they're missing."

"I know," said Jane. "It's the most charming thing about humans. You are all so sure that the lesser animals are bleeding with envy because they didn't have the good fortune to be born *homo sapiens*." Beyond the fence was a hillside, and along the top of the hill a thick forest began. "The xenologers have never gone deep into piggy lands. The piggy community that they deal with is less than a kilometer inside this wood. The piggies live in a log house, all the males together. We don't know about any other settlements except that the satellites have been able to confirm that every forest like this one carries just about all the population that a hunter-gatherer culture can sustain."

"They hunt?"

"Mostly they gather."

"Where did Pipo and Libo die?"

Jane brightened a patch of grassy ground on the hillside leading up to the trees. A large tree grew in isolation nearby, with two smaller ones not far off.

"Those trees," said Ender. "I don't remember any being so close in the holos I saw on Trondheim."

"It's been twenty-two years. The big one is the tree the piggies planted in the corpse of the rebel called Rooter, who was executed before Pipo was murdered. The other two are more recent piggy executions."

"I wish I knew why they plant trees for piggies, and not for humans."

"The trees are sacred," said Jane. "Pipo recorded that many of the trees in the forest are named. Libo speculated that they might be named for the dead."

"And humans simply aren't part of the pattern of tree-worship. Well, that's likely enough. Except that I've found that rituals and myths don't come from nowhere. There's usually some reason for it that's tied to the survival of the community."

"Andrew Wiggin, anthropologist?"

"The proper study of mankind is man."

"Go study some men, then, Ender. Novinha's family, for instance. By the way, the computer network has officially been barred from showing you where anybody lives."

Ender grinned. "So Bosquinha isn't as friendly as she seems."

"If you have to ask where people live, they'll know where you're going. If they don't want you to go there, no one will know where they live."

"You can override their restriction, can't you?"

"I already have." A light was blinking near the fence line, behind the observatory hill. It was as isolated a spot as was possible to find in Milagre. Few other houses had been built where the fence would be visible all the time. Ender wondered whether Novinha had chosen to live there to be near the fence or to be far from neighbors. Perhaps it had been Marcão's choice.

The nearest borough was Vila Atrás, and then the borough called As Fábricas stretched down to the river. As the name implied, it consisted mostly of small factories that worked the metals and plastics and processed the foods and fibers that Milagre used. A nice, tight, self-contained economy. And Novinha had chosen to live back behind everything, out of sight, invisible. It was Novinha who chose it, too, Ender was sure of that now. Wasn't it the pattern of her life? She had never belonged to Milagre. It was no accident that all three calls for a Speaker had come from her and her children. The very act of calling a Speaker was defiant, a sign that they did not think they belonged among the devout Catholics of Lusitania.

"Still," said Ender, "I have to ask someone to lead me there. I shouldn't let them know right away that they can't hide any of their information from me."

The map disappeared, and Jane's face appeared above the terminal. She had neglected to adjust for the greater size of this terminal, so that her head was many times human size. She was quite imposing. And her simulation was accurate right down to the pores on her face. "Actually, Andrew, it's *me* they can't hide anything from."

Ender sighed. "You have a vested interest in this, Jane."

"I know." She winked. "But *you* don't."

"Are you telling me you don't trust me?"

"You reek of impartiality and a sense of justice. But I'm human enough to want preferential treatment, Andrew."

"Will you promise me one thing, at least?"

"Anything, my corpuscular friend."

"When you decide to hide something from me, will you at least tell me that you aren't going to tell me?"

"This is getting way too deep for little old me." She was a caricature of an overfeminine woman.

"Nothing is too deep for you, Jane. Do us both a favor. Don't cut me off at the knees."

"While you're off with the Ribeira family, is there anything you'd like me to be doing?"

"Yes. Find every way in which the Ribeiras are significantly different from the rest of the people of Lusitania. And any points of conflict between them and the authorities."

"You speak, and I obey." She started to do her genie disappearing act.

"You maneuvered me here, Jane. Why are you trying to unnerve me?"

"I'm not. And I didn't."

"I have a shortage of friends in this town."

"You can trust me with your life."

"It isn't my life I'm worried about."

The praça was filled with children playing football. Most of them were stunting, showing how long they could keep the ball in the air using only their feet and heads. Two of them, though, had a vicious duel going. The boy would kick the ball as hard as he could toward the girl, who stood not three meters away. She would stand and take the impact of the ball, not flinching no matter how hard it struck her. Then she would kick the ball back at him, and he would try not to flinch. A little girl was tending the ball, fetching it each time it rebounded from a victim.

Ender tried asking some of the boys if they knew where the Ribeira family's house was. Their answer was invariably a shrug; when he persisted some of them began moving away, and soon most of the children had retreated from the praça. Ender wondered what the Bishop had told everybody about Speakers.

The duel, however, continued unabated. And now that the praça was not so crowded, Ender saw that another child was involved, a boy of about twelve. He was not extraordinary from behind, but as Ender moved toward the middle of the praça, he could see that there was something wrong with the boy's eyes. It took a moment, but then he understood. The boy had artificial eyes. Both looked shiny and metallic, but Ender knew how they worked. Only one eye was used for sight, but it took four separate visual scans and then separated the signals to feed true binocular vision to the brain. The other eye contained the power supply, the computer control, and the external interface. When he wanted to, he could record short sequences of vision in a limited photo memory, probably less than a trillion bits. The duelists were using him as their judge; if they disputed a point, he could replay the scene in slow motion and tell them what had happened.

The ball went straight for the boy's crotch. He winced elaborately, but the girl was not impressed. "He swiveled away, I saw his hips move!"

"Did not! You hurt me, I didn't dodge at all!"

"Reveja! Reveja!" They had been speaking Stark, but the girl now switched into Portuguese.

The boy with metal eyes showed no expression, but raised

a hand to silence them. "Mudou," he said with finality. He moved, Ender translated.

"Sabia!" I knew it!

"You liar, Olhado!"

The boy with metal eyes looked at him with disdain. "I never lie. I'll send you a dump of the scene if you want. In fact, I think I'll post it on the net so everybody can watch you dodge and then lie about it."

"Mentiroso! Filho de punta! Fode-bode!"

Ender was pretty sure what the epithets meant, but the boy with metal eyes took it calmly.

"Da," said the girl. "Da-me." Give it here.

The boy furiously took off his ring and threw it on the ground at her feet. "Viada!" he said in a hoarse whisper. Then he took off running.

"Poltrão!" shouted the girl after him. Coward!

"Cão!" shouted the boy, not even looking over his shoulder.

It was not the girl he was shouting at this time. She turned at once to look at the boy with metal eyes, who stiffened at the name. Almost at once the girl looked at the ground. The little one, who had been doing the ball-fetching, walked to the boy with metal eyes and whispered something. He looked up, noticing Ender for the first time.

The older girl was apologizing. "Desculpa, Olhado, não queria que—"

"Não há problema, Michi." He did not look at her.

The girl started to go on, but then she, too, noticed Ender and fell silent.

"Porque está olhando-nos?" asked the boy. Why are you looking at us?

Ender answered with a question. "Você é árbitro?" You're the artiber here? The word could mean "umpire," but it could also mean "magistrate."

"De vez em quando." Sometimes.

Ender switched to Stark—he wasn't sure he knew how to say anything complex in Portuguese. "Then tell me, arbiter, is it fair to leave a stranger to find his way around without help?"

"Stranger? You mean utlanning, framling, or raman?"

"No, I think I mean infidel."

"O Senhor é descrente?" You're an unbeliever?

"Só descredo no incrível." I only disbelieve the unbelievable.

The boy grinned. "Where do you want to go, Speaker?"

"The house of the Ribeira family."

The little girl edged closer to the boy with metal eyes. "Which Ribeira family?"

"The widow Ivanova."

"I think I can find it," said the boy.

"Everybody in town can find it," said Ender. "The point is, will you take me there?"

"Why do you want to go there?"

"I ask people questions and try to find out true stories."

"Nobody at the Ribeira house knows any true stories."

"I'd settle for lies."

"Come on then." He started toward the low-mown grass of the main road. The little girl was whispering in his ear. He stopped and turned to Ender, who was following close behind.

"Quara wants to know. What's your name?"

"Andrew. Andrew Wiggin."

"She's Quara."

"And you?"

"Everybody calls me Olhado. Because of my eyes." He picked up the little girl and put her on his shoulders. "But my real name's Lauro. Lauro Suleimão Ribeira." He grinned, then turned around and strode off.

Ender followed. Ribeira. Of course.

Jane had been listening, too, and spoke from the jewel in his ear. "Lauro Suleimão Ribeira is Novinha's fourth child. He lost his eyes in a laser accident. He's twelve years old. Oh, and I found one difference between the Ribeira family and the rest of the town. The Ribeiras are willing to defy the Bishop and lead you where you want to go."

I noticed something, too, Jane, he answered silently. This boy enjoyed deceiving me, and then enjoyed even more letting me see how I'd been fooled. I just hope *you* don't take lessons from him.

Miro sat on the hillside. The shade of the trees made him invisible to anyone who might be watching from Milagre, but he could see much of the town from here—certainly the cathedral and the monastery on the highest hill, and then the observatory on the next hill to the north. And under the observatory, in a depression in the hillside, the house where he lived, not very far from the fence.

"Miro," whispered Leaf-eater. "Are you a tree?"

It was a translation from the pequeninos' idiom. Sometimes they meditated, holding themselves motionless for hours. They called this "being a tree."

"More like a blade of grass," Miro answered.

Leaf-eater giggled in the high, wheezy way he had. It never sounded natural—the pequeninos had learned laughter by rote, as if it were simply another word in Stark. It didn't arise out of amusement, or at least Miro didn't think it did.

"Is it going to rain?" asked Miro. To a piggy this meant: are you interrupting me for my own sake, or for yours?

"It rained fire today," said Leaf-eater. "Out in the prairie."

"Yes. We have a visitor from another world."

"Is it the Speaker?"

Miro didn't answer.

"You must bring him to see us."

Miro didn't answer.

"I root my face in the ground for you, Miro, my limbs are lumber for your house."

Miro hated it when they begged for something. It was as if they thought of him as someone particularly wise or strong, a parent from whom favors must be wheedled. Well, if they felt that way, it was his own fault. His and Libo's. Playing God out here among the piggies.

"I promised, didn't I, Leaf-eater?"

"When when when?"

"It'll take time. I have to find out whether he can be trusted."

Leaf-eater looked baffled. Miro had tried to explain that not all humans knew each other, and some weren't nice, but they never seemed to understand.

"As soon as I can," Miro said.

Suddenly Leaf-eater began to rock back and forth on the ground, shifting his hips from side to side as if he were trying to relieve an itch in his anus. Libo had speculated once that this was what performed the same function that laughter did for humans. "Talk to me in piddle-geese!" wheezed Leaf-eater. Leaf-eater always seemed to be greatly amused that Miro and the other Zenadors spoke two languages interchangeably. This despite the fact that at least four different piggy languages had been recorded or at least hinted at over the years, all spoken by this same tribe of piggies.

But if he wanted to hear Portuguese, he'd get Portuguese. "Vai comer folhas." Go eat leaves.

Leaf-eater looked puzzled. "Why is that clever?"

"Because that's your name. Come-folhas."

Leaf-eater pulled a large insect out of his nostril and flipped it away, buzzing. "Don't be crude," he said. Then he walked away.

Miro watched him go. Leaf-eater was always so difficult. Miro much preferred the company of the piggy called Human. Even though Human was smarter, and Miro had to watch himself more carefully with him, at least he didn't seem hostile the way Leaf-eater often did.

With the piggy out of sight, Miro turned back toward the city. Somebody was moving down the path along the face of the hill, toward his house. The one in front was very tall—no, it was Olhado with Quara on his shoulders. Quara was much too old for that. Miro worried about her. She seemed not to be coming out of the shock of Father's death. Miro felt a moment's bitterness. And to think he and Ela had expected Father's death would solve all their problems.

Then he stood up and tried to get a better view of the man behind Olhado and Quara. No one he'd seen before. The Speaker. Already! He couldn't have been in town for more than an hour, and he was already going to the house. That's great, all I need is for Mother to find out that I was the one who called him here. Somehow I thought that a Speaker for the Dead would be discreet about it, not just come straight home to the person who called. What a fool. Bad enough that he's coming years before I expected a Speaker to get here. Quim's bound to report this to the Bishop, even if nobody else does. Now I'm going to have to deal with Mother and, probably, the whole city.

Miro moved back into the trees and jogged along a path that led, eventually, to the gate back into the city.

Chapter 7
The Ribeira House

Miro, this time you should have been there, because even though I have a better memory for dialogue than you, I sure don't know what *this* means. You saw the new piggy, the one they call Human—I thought I saw you talking to him for a minute before you took off for the Questionable Activity. Mandachuva told me they named him Human because he was very smart *as a child*. OK, it's very flattering that "smart" and "human" are linked in their minds, or perhaps offensive that they think we'll be flattered by that, but that's not what matters.

Mandachuva *then* said: "He could already talk when he started walking around by himself." And he made a gesture with his hand *about ten centimeters off the ground*. To me it looked like he was telling how tall Human was when he learned how to talk and walk. Ten centimeters! But I could be completely wrong. You should have been there, to see for yourself.

If I'm right, and that's what Mandachuva meant, then for the first time we have an idea of piggy childhood. If they actually start walking at ten centimeters in height— and talking, no less!—then they must have less development time during gestation than humans, and do a lot more developing after they're born.

But now it gets absolutely crazy, even by your stan-

117

dards. He then leaned in close and told me—as if he
weren't supposed to—who Human's father was: "Your
grandfather Pipo knew Human's father. His tree is near
your gate."

Is he kidding? Rooter died twenty-four years ago,
didn't he? OK, maybe this is just a religious thing, sort of
adopt-a-tree or something. But the way Mandachuva was
so secretive about it, I keep thinking it's somehow true. Is
it possible that they have a 24-year gestation period? Or
maybe it took a couple of decades for Human to develop from a 10-centimeter toddler into the fine speci-
men of piggihood we now see. Or maybe Rooter's
sperm was saved in a jar somewhere.

But this *matters.* This is the first time a piggy personally
known to human observers has ever been named as a
father. And *Rooter,* no less, the very one that got murdered. In other words, the male with the lowest
prestige—an executed criminal, even—has been named
as a father! That means that our males aren't cast-off
bachelors at all, even though some of them are so old
they knew Pipo. They are *potential fathers.*

What's more, if Human was so remarkably smart, then
why was he dumped here if this is really a group of
miserable bachelors? I think we've had it wrong for quite
a while. This isn't a low-prestige group of bachelors, this
is a high-prestige group of juveniles, and some of them
are really going to amount to something.

So when you told me you felt sorry for me because
you got to go out on the Questionable Activity and I had
to stay home and work up some Official Fabrications for
the ansible report, you were full of Unpleasant Excre-
tions! (If you get home after I'm asleep, wake me up for
a kiss, OK? I earned it today.)

—Memo from Ouanda Figueira Mucumbi to Miro Ribeira
von Hesse, retrieved from Lusitanian files by Congres-

sional order and introduced as evidence in the Trial *In Absentia* of the Xenologers of Lusitania on Charges of Treason and Malfeasance

There was no construction industry in Lusitania. When a couple got married, their friends and family built them a house. The Ribeira house expressed the history of the family. At the front, the old part of the house was made of plastic sheets rooted to a concrete foundation. Rooms had been built on as the family grew, each addition abutting the one before, so that five distinct one-story structures fronted the hillside. The later ones were all brick, decently plumbed, roofed with tile, but with no attempt whatever at aesthetic appeal. The family had built exactly what was needed and nothing more.

It was not poverty, Ender knew—there was no poverty in a community where the economy was completely controlled. The lack of decoration, of individuality, showed the family's contempt for their own house; to Ender this bespoke contempt for themselves as well. Certainly Olhado and Quara showed none of the relaxation, the letting-down that most people feel when they come home. If anything, they grew warier, less jaunty; the house might have been a subtle source of gravity, making them heavier the nearer they approached.

Olhado and Quara went right in. Ender waited at the door for someone to invite him to enter. Olhado left the door ajar, but walked on out of the room without speaking to him. Ender could see Quara sitting on a bed in the front room, leaning against a bare wall. There was nothing whatsoever on any of the walls. They were stark white. Quara's face matched the blankness of the walls. Though her eyes regarded Ender unwaveringly, she showed no sign of recognizing that he was there; certainly she did nothing to indicate he might come in.

There was a disease in this house. Ender tried to understand what it was in Novinha's character that he had missed before, that would let her live in a place like this. Had Pipo's death so long before emptied Novinha's heart as thoroughly as this?

"Is your mother home?" Ender asked.

Quara said nothing.

"Oh," he said. "Excuse me. I thought you were a little girl, but I see now that you're a statue."

She showed no sign of hearing him. So much for trying to jolly her out of her somberness.

Shoes slapped rapidly against a concrete floor. A little boy ran into the room, stopped in the middle, and whirled to face the doorway where Ender stood. He couldn't be more than a year younger than Quara, six or seven years old, probably. Unlike Quara, his face showed plenty of understanding. Along with a feral hunger.

"Is your mother home?" asked Ender.

The boy bent over and carefully rolled up his pantleg. He had taped a long kitchen knife to his leg. Slowly he untaped it. Then, holding it in front of him with both hands, he aimed himself at Ender and launched himself full speed. Ender noted that the knife was well-aimed at his crotch. The boy was not subtle in his approach to strangers.

A moment later Ender had the boy tucked under his arm and the knife jammed into the ceiling. The boy was kicking and screaming. Ender had to use both hands to control his limbs; the boy ended up dangling in front of him by his hands and feet, for all the world like a calf roped for branding.

Ender looked steadily at Quara. "If you don't go right now and get whoever is in charge in this house, I'm going to take this animal home and serve it for supper."

Quara thought about this for a moment, then got up and ran out of the room.

A moment later a tired-looking girl with tousled hair and sleepy eyes came into the front room. "Desculpe, por favor," she murmured, "o menino não se restabeleceu desde a morte do pai—"

Then she seemed suddenly to come awake.

"O Senhor é o Falante pelos Mortos!" You're the Speaker for the Dead!

"Sou," answered Ender. I am.

"Não aqui," she said. "Oh, no, I'm sorry, do you speak Portuguese? Of course you do, you just answered me—oh, please, not here, not now. Go away."

"Fine," said Ender. "Should I keep the boy or the knife?"

He glanced up at the ceiling; her gaze followed his. "Oh, no, I'm sorry, we looked for it all day yesterday, we knew he had it but we didn't know where."

"It was taped to his leg."

"It wasn't yesterday. We always look there. Please, let go of him."

"Are you sure? I think he's been sharpening his teeth."

"Grego," she said to the boy, "it's wrong to poke at people with the knife."

Grego growled in his throat.

"His father dying, you see."

"They were that close?"

A look of bitter amusement passed across her face. "Hardly. He's always been a thief, Grego has, ever since he was old enough to hold something and walk at the same time. But this thing for hurting people, that's new. Please let him down."

"No," said Ender.

Her eyes narrowed and she looked defiant. "Are you kidnapping him? To take him where? For what ransom?"

"Perhaps you don't understand," said Ender. "He assaulted me. You've offered me no guarantee that he won't do it again. You've made no provision for disciplining him when I set him down."

As he had hoped, fury came into her eyes. "Who do you think you are? This is *his* house, not yours!"

"Actually," Ender said, "I've just had a rather long walk from the praça to your house, and Olhado set a brisk pace. I'd like to sit down."

She nodded toward a chair. Grego wriggled and twisted against Ender's grip. Ender lifted him high enough that their faces weren't too far apart. "You know, Grego, if you actually break free, you will certainly fall on your head on a concrete floor. If there were carpet, I'd give you an even chance of staying conscious. But there isn't. And frankly, I wouldn't mind hearing the sound of your head smacking against cement."

"He doesn't really understand Stark that well," said the girl.

Ender knew that Grego understood just fine. He also saw motion at the edges of the room. Olhado had come back and stood in the doorway leading to the kitchen. Quara was beside him. Ender smiled cheerfully at them, then stepped to the chair the girl had indicated. In the process, he swung Grego up into the air, letting go of his hands and feet in such a way that he spun madly for a moment, shooting out his arms and legs in panic, squealing in fear at the pain that would certainly come when he hit the floor. Ender smoothly slid onto the chair and caught the boy on his lap, instantly pinioning his arms. Grego managed to smack his heels into Ender's shins, but since the boy wasn't wearing shoes, it was an ineffective maneuver. In a moment Ender had him completely helpless again.

"It feels very good to be sitting down," Ender said. "Thank you for your hospitality. My name is Andrew Wiggin. I've met Olhado and Quara, and obviously Grego and I are good friends."

The older girl wiped her hand on her apron as if she planned to offer it to him to shake, but she did not offer it. "My name is Ela Ribeira. Ela is short for Elanora."

"A pleasure to meet you. I see you're busy preparing supper."

"Yes, very busy. I think you should come back tomorrow."

"Oh, go right ahead. I don't mind waiting."

Another boy, older than Olhado but younger than Ela,

shoved his way into the room. "Didn't you hear my sister? You aren't wanted here!"

"You show me too much kindness," Ender said. "But I came to see your mother, and I'll wait here until she comes home from work."

The mention of their mother silenced them.

"I assume she's at work. If she were here, I would expect these exciting events would have flushed her out into the open."

Olhado smiled a bit at that, but the older boy darkened, and Ela got a nasty, painful expression on her face. "Why do you want to see *her*?" asked Ela.

"Actually, I want to see all of you." He smiled at the older boy. "You must be Estevão Rei Ribeira. Named for St. Stephen the Martyr, who saw Jesus sitting at the right hand of God."

"What do you know of such things, atheist!"

"As I recall, St. Paul stood by and held the coats of the men who were stoning him. Apparently he wasn't a believer at the time. In fact, I think he was regarded as the most terrible enemy of the Church. And yet he later repented, didn't he? So I suggest you think of me, not as the enemy of God, but as an apostle who has not yet been stopped on the road to Damascus." Ender smiled.

The boy stared at him, tight-lipped. "You're no St. Paul."

"On the contrary," said Ender. "I'm the apostle to the piggies."

"You'll never see *them*. Miro will never let you."

"Maybe I will," said a voice from the door. The others turned at once to watch him walk in. Miro was young— surely not yet twenty. But his face and bearing carried the weight of responsibility and suffering far beyond his years. Ender saw how all of them made space for him. It was not that they backed away from him the way they might retreat from someone they feared. Rather, they oriented themselves to him, walking in parabolas around him, as if he were the center of gravity in the room and everything else was moved by the force of his presence.

Miro walked to the center of the room and faced Ender. He looked, however, at Ender's prisoner. "Let him go," said Miro. There was ice in his voice.

Ela touched him softly on the arm. "Grego tried to stab him, Miro." But her voice also said, Be calm, it's all right, Grego's in no danger and this man is not our enemy. Ender heard all this; so, it seemed, did Miro.

"Grego," said Miro. "I told you that someday you'd take on somebody who wasn't afraid of you."

Grego, seeing an ally suddenly turn to an enemy, began to cry. "He's killing me, he's killing me."

Miro looked coldly at Ender. Ela might trust the Speaker for the Dead, but Miro didn't, not yet.

"I *am* hurting him," said Ender. He had found that the best way to earn trust was to tell the truth. "Every time he struggles to get free, it causes him quite a bit of discomfort. And he hasn't stopped struggling yet."

Ender met Miro's gaze steadily, and Miro understood his unspoken request. He did not insist on Grego's release. "I can't get you out of this one, Greguinho."

"You're going to let him do this?" asked Estevão.

Miro gestured toward Estevão and spoke apologetically to Ender. "Everyone calls him Quim." The nickname was pronounced like the word *king* in Stark. "It began because his middle name is Rei. But now it's because he thinks he rules by divine right."

"Bastard," said Quim. He stalked out of the room.

At the same time, the others settled in for conversation. Miro had decided to accept the stranger, at least temporarily; therefore they could let down their guard a little. Olhado sat down on the floor; Quara returned to her previous perch on the bed. Ela leaned back against the wall. Miro pulled up another chair and sat facing Ender.

"Why did you come to this house?" asked Miro. Ender

saw from the way he asked that he, like Ela, had not told anyone that he had summoned a Speaker. So neither of them knew that the other expected him. And, in fact, they almost undoubtedly had not expected him to come so soon.

"To see your mother," Ender said.

Miro's relief was almost palpable, though he made no obvious gesture. "She's at work," he said. "She works late. She's trying to develop a strain of potato that can compete with the grass here."

"Like the amaranth?"

He grinned. "You already heard about that? No, we don't want it to be as good a competitor as *that*. But the diet here is limited, and potatoes would be a nice addition. Besides, amaranth doesn't ferment into a very good beverage. The miners and farmers have already created a mythology of vodka that makes it the queen of distilled intoxicants."

Miro's smile came to this house like sunlight through a crevice in a cave. Ender could feel the loosening of tensions. Quara wiggled her leg back and forth like an ordinary little girl. Olhado had a stupidly happy expression on his face, his eyes half-closed so that the metallic sheen was not so monstrously obvious. Ela's smile was broader than Miro's good humor should have earned. Even Grego had relaxed, had stopped straining against Ender's grip.

Then a sudden warmth on Ender's lap told him that Grego, at least, was far from surrender. Ender had trained himself not to respond reflexively to an enemy's actions until he had consciously decided to let his reflexes rule. So Grego's flood of urine did not cause him to so much as flinch. He knew what Grego had been expecting—a shout of anger, and Ender flinging him away, casting him from his lap in disgust. Then Grego would be free—it would be a triumph. Ender yielded him no victory.

Ela, however, apparently knew the expressions of Grego's face. Her eyes went wide, and then she took an angry step toward the boy. "Grego, you impossible little—"

But Ender winked at her and smiled, freezing her in place. "Grego has given me a little gift. It's the only thing he has to give me, and he made it himself, so it means all the more. I like him so much that I think I'll never let him go."

Grego snarled and struggled again, madly, to break free.

"Why are you doing this!" said Ela.

"He's expecting Grego to act like a human being," said Miro. "It needs doing, and nobody else has bothered to try."

"*I've* tried," said Ela.

Olhado spoke up from his place on the floor. "Ela's the only one here who keeps us civilized."

Quim shouted from the other room. "Don't you tell that bastard anything about our family!"

Ender nodded gravely, as if Quim had offered a brilliant intellectual proposition. Miro chuckled and Ela rolled her eyes and sat down on the bed beside Quara.

"We're not a very happy home," said Miro.

"I understand," said Ender. "With your father so recently dead."

Miro smiled sardonically. Olhado spoke up again. "With Father so recently alive, you mean."

Ela and Miro were in obvious agreement with this sentiment. But Quim shouted again. "Don't tell him anything!"

"Did he hurt you?" Ender asked quietly. He did not move, even though Grego's urine was getting cold and rank.

Ela answered. "He didn't hit us, if that's what you mean."

But for Miro, things had gone too far. "Quim's right," said Miro. "It's nobody's business but ours."

"No," said Ela. "It's his business."

"How is it his business?" asked Miro.

"Because he's here to Speak Father's death," said Ela.

"Father's death!" said Olhado. "Chupa pedras! Father only died three weeks ago!"

"I was already on my way to Speak another death," said Ender. "But someone did call for a Speaker for your father's death, and so I'll Speak for him."

"Against him," said Ela.

"For him," said Ender.

"I brought you here to tell the truth," she said bitterly, "and all the truth about Father is against him."

Silence pressed to the corners of the room, holding them all still, until Quim walked slowly through the doorway. He looked only at Ela. "You called him," he said softly. "You."

"To tell the truth!" she answered. His accusation obviously stung her; he did not have to say how she had betrayed her family and her church to bring this infidel to lay bare what had been so long concealed. "Everybody in Milagre is so kind and understanding," she said. "Our teachers overlook little things like Grego's thievery and Quara's silence. Never mind that she hasn't said a word in school, ever! Everybody pretends that we're just ordinary children—the grandchildren of Os Venerados, and so brilliant, aren't we, with a Zenador and both biologistas in the family! Such prestige. They just look the other way when Father gets himself raging drunk and comes home and beats Mother until she can't walk!"

"Shut up!" shouted Quim.

"Ela," said Miro.

"And you, Miro, Father shouting at you, saying terrible things until you run out of the house, you *run,* stumbling because you can hardly see—"

"You have no right to tell him!" said Quim.

Olhado leapt to his feet and stood in the middle of the room, turned around to look at them all with his unhuman eyes. "Why do you still want to hide it?" he asked softly.

"What's it to you" asked Quim. "He never did anything to you. You just turned off your eyes and sat there with the headphones on, listening to batuque or Bach or something—"

"Turn off my eyes?" said Olhado. "I never turned off my eyes."

He whirled and walked to the terminal, which was in the corner of the room farthest from the front door. In a few quick movements he had the terminal on, then picked up an interface cable and jammed it in the socket in his right eye. It was only a simple computer linkup, but to Ender it brought back a hideous memory of the eye of a giant, torn open and oozing, as Ender bored deep, penetrated to the brain, and sent it toppling backward to its death. He froze up for a moment before he remembered that his memory was not real, it was of a computer game he had played in the Battle School. Three thousand years ago, but to him a mere twenty-five years, not such a great distance that the memory had lost its power. It was his memories and dreams of the giant's death that the buggers had taken out of his mind and turned into the signal they left for him; eventually it had led him to the hive queen's cocoon.

It was Jane's voice that brought him back to the present moment. She whispered from the jewel, "If it's all the same to you, while he's got that eye linked up I'm going to get a dump of everything else he's got stored away in there."

Then a scene began in the air over the terminal. It was not holographic. Instead the image was like bas-relief, as it would have appeared to a single observer. It was this very room, seen from the spot on the floor where a moment ago Olhado had been sitting—apparently it was his regular spot. In the middle of the floor stood a large man, strong and violent, flinging his arms about as he shouted abuse at Miro, who stood quietly, his head bent, regarding his father without any sign of anger. There was no sound—it was a visual image only. "Have you forgotten?" whispered Olhado. "Have you forgotten what it was like?"

In the scene on the terminal Miro finally turned and left; Marcão following him to the door, shouting after him. Then he turned back into the room and stood there, panting like an animal exhausted from the chase. In the picture Grego ran to his father and clung to his leg, shouting out the door, his face making it plain that he was echoing his father's cruel words to Miro. Marcão pried the child from his leg and walked with determined purpose into the back room.

"There's no sound," said Olhado. "But you can hear it, can't you?"

Ender felt Grego's body trembling on his lap.

"There it is, a blow, a crash—she's falling to the floor, can you feel it in your flesh, the way her body hits the concrete?"

"Shut up, Olhado," said Miro.

The computer-generated scene ended. "I can't believe you saved that," said Ela.

Quim was weeping, making no effort to hide it. "I killed him," he said. "I killed him I killed him I killed him."

"What are you talking about?" said Miro in exasperation. "He had a rotten *disease*, it was congenital!"

"I prayed for him to die!" screamed Quim. His face was mottled with passion, tears and mucus and spittle mingling around his lips. "I prayed to the Virgin, I prayed to Jesus, I prayed to Grandpa and Grandma, I said I'd go to hell for it if only he'd die, and they did it, and now I'll go to hell and I'm not *sorry* for it! God forgive me but I'm glad!" Sobbing, he stumbled back out of the room. A door slammed in the distance.

"Well, another certified miracle to the credit of Os Venerados," said Miro. "Sainthood is assured."

"Shut up," said Olhado.

"And he's the one who kept telling us that Christ wanted us to forgive the old fart," said Miro.

On Ender's lap, Grego now trembled so violently that Ender grew concerned. He realized that Grego was whispering a word. Ela, too, saw Grego's distress and knelt in front of the boy.

"He's crying, I've never seen him cry like this—"

"Papa, papa, papa," whispered Grego. His trembling had given way to great shudders, almost convulsive in their violence.

"Is he afraid of Father?" asked Olhado. His face showed deep concern for Grego. To Ender's relief, all their faces were full of worry. There *was* love in this family, and not just the solidarity of living under the rule of the same tyrant for all these years.

"Papa's gone now," said Miro comfortingly. "You don't have to worry now."

Ender shook his head. "Miro," he said, "didn't you watch Olhado's memory? Little boys don't judge their fathers, they love them. Grego was trying as hard as he could to be just like Marcos Ribeira. The rest of you might have been glad to see him gone, but for Grego it was the end of the world."

It had not occurred to any of them. Even now it was a sickening idea; Ender could see them recoil from it. And yet they knew it was true. Now that Ender had pointed it out, it was obvious.

"Deus nos perdoa," murmured Ela. God forgive us.

"The things we've said," whispered Miro.

Ela reached out for Grego. He refused to go to her. Instead he did exactly what Ender expected, what he had prepared for. Grego turned in Ender's relaxed grip, flung his arms around the neck of the Speaker for the Dead, and wept bitterly, hysterically.

Ender spoke gently to the others, who watched helplessly. "How could he show his grief to *you*, when he thought you hated him?"

"We never hated Grego." said Olhado.

"I should have known," said Miro. "I knew he was suffering the worst pain of any of us, but it never occurred to me . . ."

"Don't blame yourself," said Ender. "It's the kind of thing that only a stranger can see."

He heard Jane whispering in his ear. "You never cease to amaze me, Andrew, the way you turn people into plasma."

Ender couldn't answer her, and she wouldn't believe him

anyway. He hadn't planned this, he had played it by ear. How could he have guessed that Olhado would have a recording of Marcão's viciousness to his family? His only real insight was with Grego, and even that was instinctive, a sense that Grego was desperately hungry for someone to have authority over him, for someone to act like a father to him. Since his own father had been cruel, Grego would believe only cruelty as a proof of love and strength. Now his tears washed Ender's neck as hotly as, a moment before, his urine had soaked Ender's thighs.

He had guessed what Grego would do, but Quara managed to take him by surprise. As the others watched Grego's weeping in silence, she got off the bed and walked directly to Ender. Her eyes were narrow and angry. "You stink!" she said firmly. Then she marched out of the room toward the back of the house.

Miro barely suppressed his laughter, and Ela smiled. Ender raised his eyebrows as if to say, You win some, you lose some.

Olhado seemed to hear his unspoken words. From his chair by the terminal, the metal-eyed boy said softly, "You win with her, too. It's the most she's said to anyone outside the family in months."

But I'm not outside the family, Ender said silently. Didn't you notice? I'm *in* the family now, whether you like it or not. Whether *I* like it or not.

After a while Grego's sobbing stopped. He was asleep. Ender carried him to his bed; Quara was already asleep on the other side of the small room. Ela helped Ender strip off Grego's urine-soaked pants and put looser underwear on him—her touch was gentle and deft, and Grego did not waken.

Back in the front room Miro eyed Ender clinically. "Well, Speaker, you have a choice. My pants will be tight on you and too short in the crotch, but Father's would fall right off."

It took Ender a moment to remember. Grego's urine had long since dried. "Don't worry about it," he said. "I can change when I get home."

"Mother won't be home for another hour. You came to see her, didn't you? We can have your pants clean by then."

"*Your* pants, then," said Ender. "I'll take my chances with the crotch."

Chapter **8**
Dona Ivanova

*I*t means a life of constant deception. You will go out and discover something, something vital, and then when you get back to the station you'll write up a completely innocuous report, one which mentions *nothing* that we learned through cultural contamination.

You're too young to understand what torture this is. Father and I began doing this because we couldn't bear to withhold knowledge from the piggies. You will discover, as I have, that it is no less painful to withhold knowledge from your fellow scientists. When you watch them struggle with a question, knowing that you have the information that could easily resolve their dilemma; when you see them come very near the truth and then for lack of your information retreat from their correct conclusions and return to error—you would not be human if it didn't cause you great anguish.

You must remind yourselves, always: It is their law, their choice. They are the ones who built the wall between themselves and the truth, and they would only punish us if we let them know how easily and thoroughly that wall has been breached. And for every framling scientist who is longing for the truth, there are ten petty-minded descabeçados [headless ones] who despise knowledge, who never think of an original hypothesis, whose only labor is to prey on the writings of the true scientists in order to catch tiny errors

133

or contradictions or lapses in method. These suckflies will pore over every report you make, and if you are careless even once *they will catch you.*

That means you can't even mention a piggy whose name is derived from cultural contamination: "Cups" would tell them that we have taught them rudimentary pottery-making. "Calendar" and "Reaper" are obvious. And God himself couldn't save us if they learned Arrow's name.

—Memo from Liberdade Figueira de Medici to Ouanda Figueira Mucumbi and Miro Ribeira von Hesse, retrieved from Lusitanian files by Congressional order and introduced as evidence in the Trial *In Absentia* of the Xenologers of Lusitania on Charges of Treason and Malfeasance

Novinha lingered in the Biologista's Station even though her meaningful work was finished more than an hour ago. The cloned potato plants were all thriving in nutrient solution; now it would be a matter of making daily observations to see which of her genetic alterations would produce the hardiest plant with the most useful root.

If I have nothing to do, why don't I go home? She had no answer for the question. Her children needed her, that was certain; she did them no kindness by leaving early each morning and coming home only after the little ones were asleep. And yet even now, knowing she should go back, she sat staring at the laboratory, seeing nothing, doing nothing, being nothing.

She thought of going home, and could not imagine why she felt no joy at the prospect. After all, she reminded herself, Marcão is dead. He died three weeks ago. Not a moment too soon. He did all that I ever needed him for, and I did all that he wanted, but all our reasons expired four years before he finally rotted away. In all that time we never shared a moment of love, but I never thought of leaving him. Divorce would have been impossible, but desquite would have been enough. To stop the beatings. Even yet her hip was stiff and sometimes painful from the last time he had thrown her to the concrete floor. What lovely memorabilia you left behind, Cão, my dog of a husband.

The pain in her hip flared even as she thought of it. She nodded in satisfaction. It's no more than I deserve, and I'll be sorry when it heals.

She stood up and walked, not limping at all even though the pain was more than enough to make her favor the hip. I'll not coddle myself, not in anything. It's no worse than I deserve.

She walked to the door, closed it behind her. The computer turned off the lights as soon as she was gone, except those needed for the various plants in forced photosynthetic phase. She loved her plants, her little beasts, with surprising intensity. Grow, she cried out to them day and night, grow and thrive. She would grieve for the ones that failed and pinch them dead only when it was plain they had no future. Now as she walked away from the station, she could still hear their subliminal music, the cries of the infinitesimal cells as they grew and split and formed themselves into ever more elaborate patterns. She was going from light into darkness, from life into death, and the emotional pain grew worse in perfect synchronicity with the inflammation of her joints.

As she approached her house from over the hill, she could see the patches of light thrown through the windows and out onto the hill below. Quara's and Grego's room dark; she would not have to bear their unbearable accusations—Quara's in silence, Grego's in sullen and vicious crimes. But there were too many other lights on, including her own room and the front room. Something unusual was going on, and she didn't like unusual things.

Olhado sat in the living room, earphones on as usual; tonight, though, he also had the interface jack attached to his eye. Apparently, he was retrieving old visual memories from the computer, or perhaps dumping out some he had been carrying with him. As so many times before, she wished she could also dump out her visual memories and wipe them clean, replace them with more pleasant ones. Pipo's corpse, that would be one she'd gladly be rid of, to be replaced by some of the golden glorious days with the three of them together in the Zenador's Station. And Libo's body wrapped in its cloth, that sweet flesh held together only by the winding fabric; she would like to have instead other memories of his body, the touch of his lips, the expressiveness of his delicate hands. But the good memories fled, buried too deep under the pain. I stole them all, those good days, and so they were taken back and replaced by what I deserved.

Olhado turned to face her, the jack emerging obscenely from his eye. She could not control her shudder, her shame. I'm sorry, she said silently. If you had had another mother, you would doubtless still have your eye. You were born to be the best, the healthiest, the wholest of my children, Lauro, but of course nothing from my womb could be left intact for long.

She said nothing of this, of course, just as Olhado said nothing to her. She turned to go back to her room and find out why the light was on.

"Mother," said Olhado.

He had taken the earphones off, and was twisting the jack out of his eye.

"Yes?"

"We have a visitor," he said. "The Speaker."

She felt herself go cold inside. Not tonight, she screamed silently. But she also knew that she would not want to see him tomorrow, either, or the next day, or ever.

"His pants are clean now, and he's in your room changing back into them. I hope you don't mind."

Ela emerged from the kitchen. "You're home," she said. "I poured some cafezinhos, one for you, too."

"I'll wait outside until he's gone," said Novinha.

Ela and Olhado looked at each other. Novinha understood

at once that they regarded her as a problem to be solved; that apparently they subscribed to whatever the Speaker wanted to do here. Well, I'm a dilemma that's not going to be solved by you.

"Mother," said Olhado, "he's not what the Bishop said. He's *good*."

Novinha answered him with her most withering sarcasm. "Since when are *you* an expert on good and evil?"

Again Ela and Olhado looked at each other. She knew what they were thinking. How can we explain to her? How can we persuade her? Well, dear children, you can't. I am unpersuadable, as Libo found out every week of his life. He never had the secret from me. It's not my fault he died.

But they had succeeded in turning her from her decision. Instead of leaving the house, she retreated into the kitchen, passing Ela in the doorway but not touching her. The tiny coffee cups were arranged in a neat circle on the table, the steaming pot in the center. She sat down and rested her forearms on the table. So the Speaker was here, and had come to her first. Where else would he go? It's my fault he's here, isn't it? He's one more person whose life I have destroyed, like my children's lives, like Marcão's, and Libo's, and Pipo's, and my own.

A strong yet surprisingly smooth masculine hand reached out over her shoulder, took up the pot, and began to pour through the tiny, delicate spout, the thin stream of hot coffee swirling into the tiny cafezinho cups.

"Posso derramar?" he asked. What a stupid question, since he was already pouring. But his voice was gentle, his Portuguese tinged with the graceful accents of Castilian. A Spaniard, then?

"Desculpa-me," she whispered. Forgive me. "Trouxe o senhor tantos quilômetros—"

"We don't measure starflight in kilometers, Dona Ivanova. We measure it in years." His words were an accusation, but his voice spoke of wistfulness, even forgiveness, even consolation. I could be seduced by that voice. That voice is a liar.

"If I could undo your voyage and return you twenty-two years, I'd do it. Calling for you was a mistake. I'm sorry." Her own voice sounded flat. Since her whole life was a lie, even this apology sounded rote.

"I don't feel the time yet," said the Speaker. Still he stood behind her, so she had not yet seen his face. "For me it was only a week ago that I left my sister. She was the only kin of mine left alive. Her daughter wasn't born yet, and now she's probably through with college, married, perhaps with children of her own. I'll never know her. But I know *your* children, Dona Ivanova."

She lifted the cafezinho and drank it down in a single swallow, though it burned her tongue and throat and made her stomach hurt. "In only a few hours you think you know them?"

"Better than you do, Dona Ivanova."

Novinha heard Ela gasp at the Speaker's audacity. And even though she thought his words might be true, it still enraged her to have a stranger say them. She turned to look at him, to snap at him, but he had moved, he was not behind her. She turned farther, finally standing up to look for him, but he wasn't in the room. Ela stood in the doorway, wide-eyed.

"Come back!" said Novinha. "You can't say that and walk out on me like that!"

But he didn't answer. Instead, she heard low laughter from the back of the house. Novinha followed the sound. She walked through the rooms to the very end of the house. Miro sat on Novinha's own bed, and the Speaker stood near the doorway, laughing with him. Miro saw his mother and the smile left his face. It caused a stab of anguish within her. She had not seen him smile in years, had forgotten how beautiful his face became, just like his father's face; and her coming had erased that smile.

"We came here to talk because Quim was so angry," Miro explained. "Ela made the bed."

"I don't think the Speaker cares whether the bed was made or not," said Novinha coldly. "Do you, Speaker?"

"Order and disorder," said the Speaker, "they each have their beauty." Still he did not turn to face her, and she was glad of that, for it meant she did not have to see his eyes as she delivered her bitter message.

"I tell you, Speaker, that you've come on a fool's errand," she said. "Hate me for it if you will, but you have no death to Speak. I was a foolish girl. In my naivete I thought that when I called, the author of the Hive Queen and the Hegemon would come. I had lost a man who was like a father to me, and I wanted consolation."

Now he turned to her. He was a youngish man, younger than her, at least, but his eyes were seductive with understanding. Perigoso, she thought. He is dangerous, he is beautiful, I could drown in his understanding.

"Dona Ivanova," he said, "how could you read the Hive Queen and the Hegemon and imagine that its author could bring *comfort*?"

It was Miro who answered—silent, slow-talking Miro, who leapt into the conversation with a vigor she had not seen in him since he was little. "I've read it," he said, "and the original Speaker for the Dead wrote the tale of the hive queen with deep compassion."

The Speaker smiled sadly. "But he wasn't writing *to* the buggers, was he? He was writing to humankind, who still celebrated the destruction of the buggers as a great victory. He wrote cruelly, to turn their pride to regret, their joy to grief. And now human beings have completely forgotten that once they hated the buggers, that once they honored and celebrated a name that is now unspeakable—"

"I can say anything," said Ivanova. "His name was Ender, and he destroyed everything he touched." Like me, she did not say.

"Oh? And what do you know of him?" His voice whipped out like a grass-saw, ragged and cruel. "How do you know there wasn't something that he touched kindly? Someone who loved him, who was blessed by his love? *Destroyed everything he touched*—that's a lie that can't truthfully be said of any human being who ever lived."

"Is that your doctrine, Speaker? Then you don't know much." She was defiant, but still his anger frightened her. She had thought his gentleness was as imperturbable as a confessor's.

And almost immediately the anger faded from his face. "You can ease your conscience," he said. "Your call started my journey here, but others called for a Speaker while I was on the way."

"Oh?" Who else in this benighted city was familiar enough with the Hive Queen and the Hegemon to want a Speaker, and independent enough of Bishop Peregrino to dare to call for one? "If that's so, then why are you here in *my* house?"

"Because I was called to Speak the death of Marcos Maria Ribeira, your late husband."

It was an appalling thought. "Him! Who would want to think of him again, now that he's dead!"

The Speaker did not answer. Instead Miro spoke sharply from her bed. "Grego would, for one. The Speaker showed us what we should have known—that the boy is grieving for his father and thinks we all hate him—"

"Cheap psychology," she snapped. "We have therapists of our own, and they aren't worth much either."

Ela's voice came from behind her. "I called for him to Speak Father's death, Mother. I thought it would be decades before he came, but I'm glad he's here now, when he can do us some good."

"What good can he do us!"

"He already has, Mother. Grego fell asleep embracing him, and Quara spoke to him."

"Actually," said Miro, "she told him that he stinks."

"Which was probably true," said Ela, "since Greguinho peed all over him."

Miro and Ela burst into laughter at the memory, and the Speaker also smiled. This more than anything else discomposed Novinha—such good cheer had been virtually unfelt in this house since Marcão brought her here a year after Pipo's death. Against her will Novinha remembered her joy when Miro was newly born, and when Ela was little, the first few years of their lives, how Miro babbled about everything, how Ela toddled madly after him through the house, how the children played together and romped in the grass within sight of the piggies' forest just beyond the fence; it was Novinha's delight in the children that poisoned Marcão, that made him hate them both, because he knew that none of it belonged to him. By the time Quim was born, the house was thick with anger, and he never learned how to laugh freely where his parents might notice. Hearing Miro and Ela laugh together was like the abrupt opening of a thick black curtain; suddenly it was daylight again, when Novinha had forgotten there was any season of the day but night.

How dared this stranger invade her house and tear open all the curtains she had closed!

"I won't have it," she said. "You have no right to pry into my husband's life."

He raised an eyebrow. She knew Starways Code as well as anyone, and so she knew perfectly well that he not only had a right, the law protected him in the pursuit of the true story of the dead.

"Marcão was a miserable man," she persisted, "and telling the truth about him will cause nothing but pain."

"You're quite right that the truth about him will cause nothing but pain, but not because he was a miserable man," said the Speaker. "If I told nothing but what everyone already knows—that he hated his children and beat his wife and raged drunkenly from bar to bar until the constables sent him home—then I would not cause pain, would I? I'd cause a great deal of satisfaction, because then everyone would be reassured that their view of him was correct all along. He was scum, and so it was all right that they treated him like scum.''

"And you think he *wasn't*?''

"No human being, when you understand his desires, is worthless. No one's life is nothing. Even the most evil of men and women, if you understand their hearts, had some generous act that redeems them, at least a little, from their sins.''

"If you believe that, then you're younger than you look," said Novinha.

"Am I?" said the Speaker. "It was less than two weeks ago that I first heard your call. I studied you then, and even if *you* don't remember, Novinha, *I* remember that as a young girl you were sweet and beautiful and good. You had been lonely before, but Pipo and Libo both knew you and found you worthy of love.''

"Pipo was dead.''

"But he loved you.''

"You don't know anything, Speaker! You were twenty-two lightyears away! Besides, it wasn't *me* I was calling worthless, it was Marcão!''

"But you don't believe that, Novinha. Because you know the one act of kindness and generosity that redeems that poor man's life.''

Novinha did not understand her own terror, but she had to silence him before he named it, even though she had no idea what kindness of Cão's he thought he had discovered. "How dare you call me Novinha!" she shouted. "No one has called me that in four years!''

In answer, he raised his hand and brushed his fingers across the back of her cheek. It was a timid gesture, almost an adolescent one; it reminded her of Libo, and it was more than she could bear. She took his hand, hurled it away, then shoved past him into the room. "Get out!" she shouted at

Miro. Her son got up quickly and backed to the door. She could see from his face that after all Miro had seen in this house, she still had managed to surprise him with her rage.

"You'll have nothing from me!" she shouted at the Speaker.

"I didn't come to take anything from you," he said quietly.

"I don't want anything you have to give, either! You're worthless to me, do you hear that? You're the one who's worthless! Lixo, ruina, estrago—vai fora d'aqui, não tens direito estar em minha casa!" You have no right to be in my house.

"Não eres estrago," he whispered, "eres solo fecundo, e vou plantar jardim aí." Then, before she could answer, he closed the door and was gone.

In truth she had no answer to give him, his words were so outrageous. She had called him estrago, but he answered as if she had called *herself* a desolation. And she had spoken to him derisively, using the insultingly familiar *tu* for "you" instead of *o Senhor* or even the informal *você*. It was the way one spoke to a child or a dog. And yet when he answered in the same voice, with the same familiarity, it was entirely different. "Thou art fertile ground, and I will plant a garden in thee." It was the sort of thing a poet says to his mistress, or even a husband to his wife, and the *tu* was intimate, not arrogant. How dare he, she whispered to herself, touching the cheek that he had touched. He is far crueler than I ever imagined a Speaker might be. Bishop Peregrino was right. He is dangerous, the infidel, the anti-Christ, he walks brazenly into places in my heart that I had kept as holy ground, where no one else was ever permitted to stand. He treads on the few small shoots that cling to life in that stony soil, how dare he, I wish I had died before seeing him, he will surely undo me before he's through.

She was vaguely aware of someone crying. Quara. Of course the shouting had wakened her; she never slept soundly. Novinha almost opened the door and went out to comfort her, but then she heard the crying stop, and a soft male voice singing to her. The song was in another language. German, it sounded to Novinha, or Nordic; she did not understand it, whatever it was. But she knew who sang it, and knew that Quara was comforted.

Novinha had not felt such fear since she first realized that Miro was determined to become a Zenador and follow in the footsteps of the two men that the piggies had murdered. This man is unknotting the nets of my family, and stringing us together whole again; but in the process he will find my secrets. If he finds out how Pipo died, and Speaks the truth, then Miro will learn that same secret, and it will kill him. I will make no more sacrifices to the piggies; they are too cruel a god for me to worship anymore.

Still later, as she lay in bed behind her closed door, trying to go to sleep, she heard more laughter from the front of the house, and this time she could hear Quim and Olhado both laughing along with Miro and Ela. She imagined she could see them, the room bright with mirth. But as sleep took her, and the imagination became a dream, it was not the Speaker who sat among her children, teaching them to laugh; it was Libo, alive again, and known to everyone as her true husband, the man she had married in her heart even though she refused to marry him in the Church. Even in her sleep it was more joy than she could bear, and tears soaked the sheet of her bed.

Chapter **9**
Congenital Defect

CIDA: The Descolada body isn't bacterial. It seems to enter the cells of the body and take up permanent residence, just like mitochondria, reproducing when the cell reproduces. The fact that it spread to a new species within only a few years of our arrival here suggests that it is wildly adaptable. It must surely have spread through the entire biosphere of Lusitania long ago, so that it may now be endemic here, a permanent infection.

GUSTO: If it's permanent and everywhere, it isn't an infection, Cida, it's part of normal life.

CIDA: But it isn't necessarily inborn—it has the ability to spread. But yes, if it's endemic then all the indigenous species must have found ways to fight it off—

GUSTO: Or adapt to it and include it in their normal life cycle. Maybe they NEED it.

CIDA: They NEED something that takes apart their genetic molecules and puts them back together at random?

GUSTO: Maybe that's why there are so few different species in Lusitania—the Descolada may be fairly recent—only half a million years old—and most species couldn't adapt.

CIDA: I wish we weren't dying, Gusto. The next

145

xenobiologist will probably work with standard genetic
adaptations and won't follow this up.

GUSTO: That's the only reason you can think of for
regretting our death?

—Vladimir Tiago Gussman and Ekaterina Maria Aparecida do Norte von Hesse-Gussman, unpublished dialogue
embedded in working notes, two days before their
deaths; first quoted in "Lost Threads of Understanding," *Meta-Science, the Journal of Methodology,* 2001:
12:12:144-45

Ender did not get home from the Ribeira house until late
that night, and he spent more than an hour trying to make
sense of all that happened, especially after Novinha came
home. Despite this, Ender awoke early the next morning, his
thoughts already full of questions he had to answer. It was
always this way when he was preparing to Speak a death; he
could hardly rest from trying to piece together the story of the
dead man as he saw himself, the life the dead woman meant
to live, however badly it had turned out. This time, though,
there was an added anxiety. He cared more for the living this
time than he ever had before.

"Of course you're more involved," said Jane, after he
tried to explain his confusion to her. "You fell in love with
Novinha before you left Trondheim."

"Maybe I loved the young girl, but this woman is nasty
and selfish. Look what she let happen to her children."

"This is the Speaker for the Dead? Judging someone by
appearances?"

"Maybe I've fallen in love with Grego."

"You've always been a sucker for people who pee on
you."

"And Quara. All of them—even Miro, I *like* the boy."

"And they love you, Ender."

He laughed. "People always think they love me, until I

Speak. Novinha's more perceptive than most—she already hates me *before* I tell the truth.''

"You're as blind about yourself as anyone else, Speaker," said Jane. "Promise me that when you die, you'll let me Speak your death. Have I got things to say."

"Keep them to yourself," said Ender wearily. "You're even worse at this business than I am."

He began his list of questions to be resolved.

1. Why did Novinha marry Marcão in the first place?
2. Why did Marcão hate his children?
3. Why does Novinha hate herself?
4. Why did Miro call me to Speak Libo's death?
5. Why did Ela call me to Speak her father's death?
6. Why did Novinha change her mind about my Speaking Pipo's death?
7. What was the immediate cause of Marcão's death?

He stopped with the seventh question. It would be easy to answer it; a merely clinical matter. So that was where he would begin.

The physician who autopsied Marcão was called Navio, which meant ''ship.''

"Not for my size," he said, laughing. "Or because I'm much of a swimmer. My full name is Enrique o Navigador Caronada. You can bet I'm glad they took my nickname from 'shipmaster' rather than from 'little cannon.' Too many obscene possibilities in that one."

Ender was not deceived by his joviality. Navio was a good Catholic and he obeyed his bishop as well as anyone. He was determined to keep Ender from learning anything, though he'd not be uncheerful about it.

"There are two ways I can get the answers to my questions," Ender said quietly. "I can ask you, and you can tell me truthfully. Or I can submit a petition to the Starways Congress for your records to be opened to me. The ansible charges are very high, and since the petition is a routine one, and your resistance to it is contrary to law, the cost will be deducted from your colony's already straitened funds, along with a double-the-cost penalty and a reprimand for you.''

Navio's smile gradually disappeared as Ender spoke. He answered coldly. ''Of course I'll answer your questions,'' he said.

''There's no 'of course' about it,'' said Ender. ''Your bishop counseled the people of Milagre to carry out an unprovoked and unjustified boycott of a legally called-for minister. You would do everyone a favor if you would inform them that if this cheerful noncooperation continues, I will petition for my status to be changed from minister to inquisitor. I assure you that I have a very good reputation with the Starways Congress, and my petition will be successful.''

Navio knew exactly what that meant. As an inquisitor, Ender would have congressional authority to revoke the colony's Catholic license on the grounds of religious persecution. It would cause a terrible upheaval among the Lusitanians, not least because the Bishop would be summarily dismissed from his position and sent to the Vatican for discipline.

''Why would you do such a thing when you know we don't want you here?'' said Navio.

''Someone wanted me here or I wouldn't have come,'' said Ender. ''You may not like the law when it annoys you, but it protects many a Catholic on worlds where another creed is licensed.''

Navio drummed his fingers on his desk. ''What are your questions, Speaker,'' he said. ''Let's get this done.''

''It's simple enough, to start with, at least. What was the proximate cause of the death of Marcos Maria Ribeira?''

''Marcão!'' said Navio. ''You couldn't possibly have been summoned to Speak *his* death, he only passed away a few weeks ago—''

''I have been asked to Speak several deaths, Dom Navio, and I choose to begin with Marcão's.''

Navio grimaced. "What if I ask for proof of your authority?"

Jane whispered in Ender's ear. "Let's dazzle the dear boy." Immediately, Navio's terminal came alive with official documents, while one of Jane's most authoritative voices declared, "Andrew Wiggin, Speaker for the Dead, has accepted the call for an explanation of the life and death of Marcos Maria Ribeira, of the city of Milagre, Lusitania Colony."

It was not the document that impressed Navio, however. It was the fact that he had not actually made the request, or even logged on to his terminal. Navio knew at once that the computer had been activated through the jewel in the Speaker's ear, but it meant that a very high-level logic routine was shadowing the Speaker and enforcing compliance with his requests. No one on Lusitania, not even Bosquinha herself, had ever had authority to do *that*. Whatever this Speaker was, Navio concluded, he's a bigger fish than even Bishop Peregrino can hope to fry.

"All right," Navio said, forcing a laugh. Now, apparently, he remembered how to be jovial again. "I meant to help you anyway—the Bishop's paranoia doesn't afflict everyone in Milagre, you know."

Ender smiled back at him, taking his hypocrisy at face value.

"Marcos Ribeira died of a congenital defect." He rattled off a long pseudo-Latin name. "You've never heard of it because it's quite rare, and is passed on only through the genes. Beginning at the onset of puberty, in most cases, it involves the gradual replacement of exocrine and endocrine glandular tissues with lipidous cells. What that means is that bit by bit over the years, the adrenal glands, the pituitary, the liver, the testes, the thyroid, and so on, are all replaced by large agglomerations of fat cells."

"Always fatal? Irreversible?"

"Oh, yes. Actually, Marcão survived ten years longer than usual. His case was remarkable in several ways. In every

other recorded case—and admittedly there aren't that many—
the disease attacks the testicles first, rendering the victim
sterile and, in most cases, impotent. With six healthy children, it's obvious that Marcos Ribeira's testes were the last
of his glands to be affected. Once they were attacked, however, progress must have been unusually fast—the testes
were completely replaced with fat cells, even though much of
his liver and thyroid were still functioning.''

"What killed him in the end?''

"The pituitary and the adrenals weren't functioning. He
was a walking dead man. He just fell down in one of the
bars, in the middle of some ribald song, as I heard.''

As always, Ender's mind automatically found seeming
contradictions. "How does a hereditary disease get passed on
if it makes its victims sterile?''

"It's usually passed through collateral lines. One child will
die of it; his brothers and sisters won't manifest the disease at
all, but they'll pass on the tendency to *their* children. Naturally, though, we were afraid that Marcão, having children,
would pass on the defective gene to all of them.''

"You tested them?''

"Not a one had any of the genetic deformations. You can
bet that Dona Ivanova was looking over my shoulder the
whole time. We zeroed in immediately on the problem genes
and cleared each of the children, bim bim bim, just like
that.''

"None of them had it? Not even a recessive tendency?''

"Graças a Deus,'' said the doctor. "Who would ever have
married them if they had had the poisoned genes? As it was,
I can't understand how Marcão's own genetic defect went
undiscovered.''

"Are genetic scans routine here?''

"Oh, no, not at all. But we had a great plague some thirty
years ago. Dona Ivanova's own parents, the Venerado Gusto
and the Venerada Cida, they conducted a detailed genetic
scan of every man, woman, and child in the colony. It's how

they found the cure. And their computer comparisons would definitely have turned up this particular defect—that's how I found out what it was when Marcão died. I'd never heard of the disease, but the computer had it on file.''

"And Os Venerados didn't find it?''

"Apparently not, or they would surely have told Marcos. And even if they hadn't told him, Ivanova herself should have found it.''

"Maybe she did,'' said Ender.

Navio laughed aloud. "Impossible. No woman in her right mind would deliberately bear the children of a man with a genetic defect like *that*. Marcão was surely in constant agony for many years. You don't wish that on your own children. No, Ivanova may be eccentric, but she's not insane.''

Jane was quite amused. When Ender got home, she made her image appear above his terminal just so she could laugh uproariously.

"He can't help it,'' said Ender. "In a devout Catholic colony like this, dealing with the Biologista, one of the most respected people here, of course he doesn't think to question his basic premises.''

"Don't apologize for him,'' said Jane. "I don't expect wetware to work as logically as software. But you can't ask me not to be amused.''

"In a way it's rather sweet of him,'' said Ender. "He'd rather believe that Marcão's disease was different from every other recorded case. He'd rather believe that somehow Ivanova's parents didn't notice that Marcos had the disease, and so she married him in ignorance, even though Ockham's razor decrees that we believe the simplest explanation: Marcão's decay progressed like every other, testes first, and all of Novinha's children were sired by someone else. No wonder Marcão was bitter and angry. Every one of her six children reminded him that his wife was sleeping with another man. It was probably part of their bargain in the beginning that she would not be faithful to him. But *six* children is rather rubbing his nose in it.''

"The delicious contradictions of religious life," said Jane. "She deliberately set out to commit adultery—but she would never dream of using a contraceptive.''

"Have you scanned the children's genetic pattern to find the most likely father?''

"You mean you haven't guessed?''

"I've guessed, but I want to make sure the clinical evidence doesn't disprove the obvious answer.''

"It was Libo, of course. What a dog! He sired six children on Novinha, and four more on his own wife.''

"What I don't understand," said Ender, "is why Novinha didn't marry Libo in the first place. It makes no sense at all for her to have married a man she obviously despised, whose disease she certainly knew about, and then to go ahead and bear children to the man she must have loved from the beginning.''

"Twisted and perverse are the ways of the human mind," Jane intoned. "Pinocchio was such a dolt to try to become a real boy. He was much better off with a wooden head.''

Miro carefully picked his way through the forest. He recognized trees now and then, or thought he did—no human could ever have the piggies' knack for naming every single tree in the woods. But then, humans didn't worship the trees as totems of their ancestors, either.

Miro had deliberately chosen a longer way to reach the piggies' log house. Ever since Libo accepted Miro as a second apprentice, to work with him alongside Libo's daughter, Ouanda, he had taught them that they must never form a path leading from Milagre to the piggies' home. Someday, Libo warned them, there may be trouble between human and piggy; we will make no path to guide a pogrom to its destination. So today Miro walked the far side of the creek, along the top of the high bank.

Sure enough, a piggy soon appeared in the near distance, watching him. That was how Libo reasoned out, years ago, that the females must live somewhere in that direction; the males always kept a watch on the Zenadors when they went too near. And, as Libo had insisted, Miro made no effort to move any farther in the forbidden direction. His curiosity dampened whenever he remembered what Libo's body looked like when he and Ouanda found it. Libo had not been quite dead yet; his eyes were open and moving. He only died when both Miro and Ouanda knelt at either side of him, each holding a blood-covered hand. Ah, Libo, your blood still pumped when your heart lay naked in your open chest. If only you could have spoken to us, one word to tell us why they killed you.

The bank became low again, and Libo crossed the brook by running lightly on the moss-covered stones. In a few more minutes he was there, coming into the small clearing from the east.

Ouanda was already there, teaching them how to churn the cream of cabra milk to make a sort of butter. She had been experimenting with the process for the past several weeks before she got it right. It would have been easier if she could have had some help from Mother, or even Ela, since they knew so much more about the chemical properties of cabra milk, but cooperating with a Biologista was out of the question. Os Venerados had discovered thirty years ago that cabra milk was nutritionally useless to humans. Therefore any investigation of how to process it for storage could only be for the piggies' benefit. Miro and Ouanda could not risk anything that might let it be known they were breaking the law and actively intervening in the piggies' way of life.

The younger piggies took to butter-churning with delight—they had made a dance out of kneading the cabra bladders and were singing now, a nonsensical song that mixed Stark, Portuguese, and two of the piggies' own languages into a hopeless but hilarious muddle. Miro tried to sort out the languages. He recognized Males' Language, of course, and also a few fragments of Fathers' Language, the language they used to speak to their totem trees; Miro recognized it only by its sound; even Libo hadn't been able to translate a single word. It all sounded like *m*s and *b*s and *g*s, with no detectable difference among the vowels.

The piggy who had been shadowing Miro in the woods now emerged and greeted the others with a loud hooting sound. The dancing went on, but the song stopped immediately. Mandachuva detached himself from the group around Ouanda and came to meet Miro at the clearing's edge.

"Welcome, I-Look-Upon-You-With-Desire." That was, of course, an extravagantly precise translation of Miro's name into Stark. Mandachuva loved translating names back and forth between Portuguese and Stark, even though Miro and Ouanda had both explained that their names didn't really *mean* anything at all, and it was only coincidence if they sounded like words. But Mandachuva enjoyed his language games, as so many piggies did, and so Miro answered to I-Look-Upon-You-With-Desire, just as Ouanda patiently answered to Vaga, which was Portuguese for "wander," the Stark word that most sounded like "Ouanda."

Mandachuva was a puzzling case. He was the oldest of the piggies. Pipo had known him, and wrote of him as though he were the most prestigious of the piggies. Libo, too, seemed to think of him as a leader. Wasn't his name a slangy Portuguese term for "boss"? Yet to Miro and Ouanda, it seemed as though Mandachuva was the *least* powerful and prestigious of the piggies. No one seemed to consult him on anything; he was the one piggy who always had free time to converse with the Zenadors, because he was almost never engaged in an important task.

Still, he was the piggy who gave the most information to the Zenadors. Miro couldn't begin to guess whether he had lost his prestige because of his information-sharing, or shared information with the humans to make up for his low prestige among the piggies. It didn't even matter. The fact was that Miro *liked* Mandachuva. He thought of the old piggy as his friend.

"Has the woman forced you to eat that foul-smelling paste?" asked Miro.

"Pure garbage, she says. Even the baby cabras cry when they have to suck a teat." Mandachuva giggled.

"If you leave that as a gift for the ladyfolk, they'll never speak to you again."

"Still, we must, we must," said Mandachuva, sighing. "They have to see everything, the prying macios!"

Ah, yes, the bafflement of the females. Sometimes the piggies spoke of them with sincere, elaborate respect, almost awe, as if they were gods. Then a piggy would say something as crude as to call them "macios," the worms that slithered on the bark of trees. The Zenadors couldn't even ask about them—the piggies would never answer questions about the females. There had been a time—a long time—when the piggies didn't even mention the existence of females at all. Libo always hinted darkly that the change had something to do with Pipo's death. Before he died, the mention of females was tabu, except with reverence at rare moments of great holiness; afterward, the piggies also showed this wistful, melancholy way of joking about "the wives." But the Zenadors could never get an answer to a question about the females. The piggies made it plain that the females were none of their business.

A whistle came from the group around Ouanda. Mandachuva immediately began pulling Miro toward the group. "Arrow wants to talk to you."

Miro came and sat beside Ouanda. She did not look at him—they had learned long ago that it made the piggies very uncomfortable when they had to watch male and female humans in direct conversation, or even having eye contact with each other. They would talk with Ouanda alone, but whenever Miro was present they would not speak to her or endure it if she spoke to them. Sometimes it drove Miro crazy that she couldn't so much as wink at him in front of the piggies. He could feel her body as if she were giving off heat like a small star.

"My friend," said Arrow. "I have a great gift to ask of you."

Miro could hear Ouanda tensing slightly beside him. The piggies did not often ask for anything, and it always caused difficulty when they did.

"Will you hear me?"

Miro nodded slowly. "But remember that among humans I am nothing, with no power." Libo had discovered that the piggies were not at all insulted to think that the humans sent powerless delegates among them, while the image of impotence helped them explain the strict limitations on what the Zenadors could do.

"This is not a request that comes from us, in our silly and stupid conversations around the night fire."

"I only wish I could hear the wisdom that you call silliness," said Miro, as he always did.

"It was Rooter, speaking out of his tree, who said this."

Miro sighed silently. He liked dealing with piggy religion as little as he liked his own people's Catholicism. In both cases he had to pretend to take the most outrageous beliefs seriously. Whenever anything particularly daring or importunate was said, the piggies always ascribed it to one ancestor or another, whose spirit dwelt in one of the ubiquitous trees. It was only in the last few years, beginning not long before Libo's death, that they started singling out Rooter as the source of most of the troublesome ideas. It was ironic that a piggy they had executed as a rebel was now treated with such respect in their ancestor-worship.

Still, Miro responded as Libo had always responded. "We have nothing but honor and affection for Rooter, if you honor him."

"We must have metal."

Miro closed his eyes. So much for the Zenadors' long-standing policy of never using metal tools in front of the piggies. Obviously, the piggies had observers of their own, watching humans at work from some vantage point near the fence. "What do you need metal for?" he asked quietly.

"When the shuttle came down with the Speaker for the Dead, it gave off a terrible heat, hotter than any fire we can make. And yet the shuttle didn't burn, and it didn't melt."

"That wasn't the metal, it was a heat-absorbent plastic shield."

"Perhaps that helps, but metal is in the heart of that machine. In all your machines, wherever you use fire and heat to make things move, there is metal. We will never be able to make fires like yours until we have metal of our own."

"I can't," said Miro.

"Do you tell us that we are condemned always to be varelse, and never ramen?"

I wish, Ouanda, that you had not explained Demosthenes' Hierarchy of Exclusion to them. "You are not condemned to anything. What we have given you so far, we have made out of things that grow in your natural world, like cabras. Even that, if we were discovered, would cause us to be exiled from this world, forbidden ever to see you again."

"The metal you humans use also comes out of our natural world. We've seen your miners digging it out of the ground far to the south of here."

Miro stored that bit of information for future reference. There was no vantage point outside the fence where the mines would be visible. Therefore the piggies must be crossing the fence somehow and observing humans from within the enclave. "It comes out of the ground, but only in certain places, which I don't know how to find. And even when they dig it up, it's mixed with other kinds of rock. They have to purify it and transform it in very difficult processes. Every speck of metal dug out of the ground is accounted for. If we gave you so much as a single tool—a screwdriver or a masonry saw—it would be missed, it would be searched for. No one searches for cabra milk.''

Arrow looked at him steadily for some time; Miro met his gaze. ''We will think about this,'' Arrow said. He reached out his hand toward Calendar, who put three arrows in his hand. ''Look. Are these good?''

They were as perfect as Arrow's fletchery usually was, well-feathered and true. The innovation was in the tip. It was not made of obsidian.

''Cabra bone,'' said Miro.

''We use the cabra to kill the cabra.'' He handed the arrows back to Calendar. Then he got up and walked away.

Calendar held the slender wooden arrows out in front of him and sang something to them in Fathers' Language. Miro recognized the song, though he did not understand the words. Mandachuva had once explained to him that it was a prayer, asking the dead tree to forgive them for using tools that were not made of wood. Otherwise, he said, the trees would think the Little Ones hated them. Religion. Miro sighed.

Calendar carried the arrows away. Then the young piggy named Human took his place, squatting on the ground in front of Miro. He was carrying a leaf-wrapped bundle, which he laid on the dirt and opened carefully.

It was the printout of the Hive Queen and the Hegemon that Miro had given them four years ago. It had been part of a minor quarrel between Miro and Ouanda. Ouanda began it, in a conversation with the piggies about religion. It was not really her fault. It began with Mandachuva asking her, ''How can you humans live without trees?'' She understood the question, of course—he was not speaking of woody plants, but of gods. ''We have a God, too—a man who died and yet still lived,'' she explained. Just one? Then where does he live now? ''No one knows.'' Then what good is he? How can you talk to him? ''He dwells in our hearts.''

They were baffled by this; Libo would later laugh and say,

"You see? To them our sophisticated theology sounds like superstition. Dwells in our hearts indeed! What kind of religion is that, compared to one with gods you can see and feel—"

"And climb and pick macios from, not to mention the fact that they cut some of them down to make their log house," said Ouanda.

"Cut? *Cut* them down? Without stone or metal tools? No, Ouanda, they *pray* them down." But Ouanda was not amused by jokes about religion.

At the piggies' request Ouanda later brought them a printout of the Gospel of St. John from the simplified Stark paraphrase of the Douai Bible. But Miro had insisted on giving them, along with it, a printout of the Hive Queen and the Hegemon. "St. John says nothing about beings who live on other worlds," Miro pointed out. "But the Speaker for the Dead explains buggers to humans—and humans to buggers." Ouanda had been outraged at his blasphemy. But not a year later they found the piggies lighting fires using pages of St. John as kindling, while the Hive Queen and the Hegemon was tenderly wrapped in leaves. It caused Ouanda a great deal of grief for a while, and Miro learned that it was wiser not to goad her about it.

Now Human opened the printout to the last page. Miro noticed that from the moment he opened the book, all the piggies quietly gathered around. The butter-churning dance ended. Human touched the last words of the printout. "The Speaker for the Dead," he murmured.

"Yes, I met him last night."

"He is the true Speaker. Rooter says so." Miro had warned them that there were many Speakers, and the writer of the Hive Queen and the Hegemon was surely dead. Apparently they still couldn't get rid of the hope that the one who had come here was the *real* one, who had written the holy book.

"I believe he's a *good* Speaker," said Miro. "He was kind to my family, and I think he might be trusted."

"When will he come and Speak to us?"

"I didn't ask him yet. It's not something that I can say right out. It will take time."

Human tipped his head back and howled.

Is this my death? thought Miro.

No. The others touched Human gently and then helped him wrap the printout again and carry it away. Miro stood up to leave. None of the piggies watched him go. Without being ostentatious about it, they were all busy doing something. He might as well have been invisible.

Ouanda caught up with him just within the forest's edge, where the underbrush made them invisible to any possible observers from Milagre—though no one ever bothered to look toward the forest. "Miro," she called softly. He turned just in time to take her in his arms; she had such momentum that he had to stagger backward to keep from falling down. "Are you trying to kill me?" he asked, or tried to—she kept kissing him, which made it difficult to speak in complete sentences. Finally he gave up on speech and kissed her back, once, long and deep. Then she abruptly pulled away.

"You're getting libidinous," she said.

"It happens whenever women attack me and kiss me in the forest."

"Cool your shorts, Miro, it's still a long way off." She took him by the belt, pulled him close, kissed him again. "Two more years until we can marry without your mother's consent."

Miro did not even try to argue. He did not care much about the priestly proscription of fornication, but he did understand how vital it was in a fragile community like Milagre for marriage customs to be strictly adhered to. Large and stable communities could absorb a reasonable amount of unsanctioned coupling; Milagre was far too small. What Ouanda did from faith, Miro did from rational thought—despite a thousand opportunities, they were as celibate as monks. Though if Miro thought for one moment that they would ever have to live the same vows of chastity in marriage that were required in the Filhos' monastery, Ouanda's virginity would be in grave and immediate danger.

"This Speaker," said Ouanda. "You know how I feel about bringing him out here."

"That's your Catholicism speaking, not rational inquiry." He tried to kiss her, but she lowered her face at the last moment and he got a mouthful of nose. He kissed it passionately until she laughed and pushed him away.

"You are messy and offensive, Miro." She wiped her nose on her sleeve. "We already shot the scientific method all to hell when we started helping them raise their standard of living. We have ten or twenty years before the satellites start showing obvious results. By then maybe we'll have been able to make a permanent difference. But we've got no chance if we let a stranger in on the project. He'll tell somebody."

"Maybe he will and maybe he won't. I was a stranger once, you know."

"Strange, but never a stranger."

"You had to see him last night, Ouanda. With Grego first, and then when Quara woke up crying—"

"Desperate, lonely children—what does that prove?"

"And Ela. Laughing. And Olhado, actually taking part in the family."

"Quim?"

"At least he stopped yelling for the infidel to go home."

"I'm glad for your family, Miro. I hope he can heal them permanently, I really do—I can see the difference in you, too, you're more hopeful than I've seen you in a long time. But don't bring him out here."

Miro chewed on the side of his cheek for a moment, then walked away. Ouanda ran after him, caught him by the arm. They were in the open, but Rooter's tree was between them and the gate. "Don't leave me like that!" she said fiercely. "Don't just walk away from me!"

"I know you're right," Miro said. "But I can't help how I feel. When he was in our house, it was like—it was as if Libo had come there."

"Father hated your mother, Miro—he would never have gone there."

"But if he had. In our house this Speaker was the way Libo always was in the Station. Do you see?"

"Do *you*? He comes in and acts the way your father should have but never did, and every single one of you rolls over belly-up like a puppy dog."

The contempt on her face was infuriating. Miro wanted to hit her. Instead he walked over and slapped his hand against Rooter's tree. In only a quarter of a century it had grown to almost eighty centimeters in diameter, and the bark was rough and painful on his hand.

She came up behind him. "I'm sorry, Miro, I didn't mean—"

"You meant it, but it was stupid and selfish—"

"Yes, it was, I—"

"Just because my father was scum doesn't mean I go belly-up for the first nice man who pats my head—"

Her hand stroked his hair, his shoulder, his waist. "I know, I know, I know—"

"Because I know what a good man is—not just a father, a *good man*. I knew Libo, didn't I? And when I tell you that this Speaker, this Andrew Wiggin is like Libo, then you listen to me and don't dismiss it like the whimpering of a *cão*!"

"I do listen. I want to meet him, Miro."

Miro surprised himself. He was crying. It was all part of what this Speaker could do, even when he wasn't present. He had loosened all the tight places in Miro's heart, and now Miro couldn't stop anything from coming out.

"You're right, too," said Miro softly, his voice distorted with emotion. "I saw him come in with his healing touch and

I thought, If only he had been my father." He turned to face Ouanda, not caring if she saw his eyes red and his face streaked with tears. "Just the way I used to say that every day when I went home from the Zenador's Station. If only Libo were my father, if only I were his son."

She smiled and held him; her hair took the tears from his face. "Ah, Miro, I'm glad he wasn't your father. Because then I'd be your sister, and I could never hope to have you for myself."

Chapter 10
Children of the Mind

Rule I: All Children of the Mind of Christ must be married, or they may not be in the order; but they must be chaste.

Question I: Why is marriage necessary for anyone?

Fools say, Why should we marry? Love is the only bond my lover and I need. To them I say, Marriage is not a covenant between a man and a woman; even the beasts cleave together and produce their young. Marriage is a covenant between a man and woman on the one side and their community on the other. To marry according to the law of the community is to become a full citizen; to refuse marriage is to be a stranger, a child, an outlaw, a slave, or a traitor. The one constant in every society of humankind is that only those who obey the laws, tabus, and customs of marriage are true adults.

Question 2: Why then is celibacy ordained for priests and nuns?

To separate them from the community. The priests and nuns are servants, not citizens. They minister to the Church, but they are not the Church. Mother Church is the bride, and Christ is the bridegroom; the priests and nuns are merely guests at the wedding, for they have rejected citizenship in the community of Christ in order to serve it.

Question 3: Why then do the Children of the Mind of Christ marry? Do we not also serve the Church?

We do not serve the Church, except as all women and men serve it through their marriages. The difference is that where they pass on their genes to the next generation, we pass on our knowledge; their legacy is found in the genetic molecules of generations to come, while we live on in their minds. Memories are the offspring of our marriages, and they are neither more or less worthy than the flesh-and-blood children conceived in sacramental love.

—San Angelo, *The Rule and Catechism of the Order of the Children of the Mind of Christ*, 1511:11:11:1

The Dean of the Cathedral carried the silence of dark chapels and massive, soaring walls wherever he went: When he entered the classroom, a heavy peace fell upon the students, and even their breathing was guarded as he noiselessly drifted to the front of the room.

"Dom Cristão," murmured the Dean. "The Bishop has need of consultation with you."

The students, most of them in their teens, were not so young that they didn't know of the strained relations between the hierarchy of the Church and the rather freewheeling monastics who ran most of the Catholic schools in the Hundred Worlds. Dom Cristão, besides being an excellent teacher of history, geology, archaeology, and anthropology, was also abbot of the monastery of the Filhos da Mente de Cristo—the Children of the Mind of Christ. His position made him the Bishop's primary rival for spiritual supremacy in Lusitania. In some ways he could even be considered the Bishop's superior; on most worlds there was only one abbot of the Filhos for each archbishop, while for each bishop there was a principal of a school system.

But Dom Cristão, like all Filhos, made it a point to be completely deferent to the Church hierarchy. At the Bishop's summons he immediately switched off the lectern and dismissed the class without so much as completing the point under discussion. The students were not surprised; they knew he would do the same if any ordained priest had interrupted his class. It was, of course, immensely flattering to the priesthood to see how important they were in the eyes of the Filhos; but it also made it plain to them that any time they visited the school during teaching hours, classwork would be completely disrupted wherever they went. As a result, the priests rarely visited the school, and the Filhos, through extreme deference, maintained almost complete independence.

Dom Cristão had a pretty good idea why the Bishop had summoned him. Dr. Navio was an indiscreet man, and rumors had been flying all morning about some dreadful threat by the Speaker for the Dead. It was hard for Dom Cristão to bear the groundless fears of the hierarchy whenever they were confronted with infidels and heretics. The Bishop would be in a fury, which meant that he would demand some action from somebody, even though the best course, as usual, was inaction, patience, cooperation. Besides, word had spread that this particular Speaker claimed to be the very one who Spoke the death of San Angelo. If that was the case, he was probably not an enemy at all, but a friend of the Church. Or at least a friend of the Filhos, which in Dom Cristão's mind amounted to the same thing.

As he followed the silent Dean among the buildings of the faculdade and through the garden of the Cathedral, he cleared his heart of the anger and annoyance he felt. Over and over he repeated his monastic name: Amai a Tudomundo Para Que Deus Vos Ame. Ye Must Love Everyone So That God Will Love You. He had chosen the name carefully when he and his fiancée joined the order, for he knew that his greatest weakness was anger and impatience with stupidity. Like all Filhos, he named himself with the invocation against his most potent sin. It was one of the ways they made themselves spiritually naked before the world. We will not clothe ourselves in hypocrisy, taught San Angelo. Christ will clothe us in virtue like the lilies of the field, but we will make no effort to appear virtuous ourselves. Dom Cristão felt his virtue wearing thin in places today; the cold wind of impatience might freeze him to the bone. So he silently chanted his name, thinking: Bishop Peregrino is a damned fool, but Amai a Tudomundo Para Que Deus Vos Ame.

"Brother Amai," said Bishop Peregrino. He never used the honorific *Dom Cristão*, even though cardinals had been known to give that much courtesy. "It was good of you to come."

Navio was already sitting in the softest chair, but Dom Cristão did not begrudge him that. Indolence had made Navio fat, and his fat now made him indolent; it was such a circular disease, feeding always on itself, and Dom Cristão was grateful not to be so afflicted. He chose for himself a tall stool with no back at all. It would keep his body from relaxing, and that would help his mind to stay alert.

Navio almost at once launched into an account of his painful meeting with the Speaker for the Dead, complete with elaborate explanations of what the Speaker had threatened to do if noncooperation continued. "An inquisitor, if you can imagine that! An infidel daring to supplant the authority of Mother Church!" Oh, how the lay member gets the crusading spirit when Mother Church is threatened—but ask him to go to mass once a week, and the crusading spirit curls up and goes to sleep.

Navio's words did have some effect: Bishop Peregrino grew more and more angry, his face getting a pinkish tinge under the deep brown of his skin. When Navio's recitation finally ended, Peregrino turned to Dom Cristão, his face a mask of fury, and said, "Now what do you say, Brother Amai!"

I would say, if I were less discreet, that you were a fool to interfere with this Speaker when you knew the law was on his side and when he had done nothing to harm us. Now he is provoked, and is far more dangerous than he would ever have been if you had simply ignored his coming.

Dom Cristão smiled thinly and inclined his head. "I think that we should strike first to remove his power to harm us."

Those militant words took Bishop Peregrino by surprise. "Exactly," he said. "But I never expected *you* to understand that."

"The Filhos are as ardent as any unordained Christian could hope to be," said Dom Cristão. "But since we have no priesthood, we have to make do with reason and logic as poor substitutes for authority."

Bishop Peregrino suspected irony from time to time, but was never quite able to pin it down. He grunted, and his eyes narrowed. "So, then, Brother Amai, how do you propose to strike him?"

"Well, Father Peregrino, the law is quite explicit. He has power over us only if we interfere with his performance of his ministerial duties. If we wish to strip him of the power to harm us, we have merely to cooperate with him."

The Bishop roared and struck the table before him with his fist. "Just the sort of sophistry I should have expected from you, Amai!"

Dom Cristão smiled. "There's really no alternative—either we answer his questions, or he petitions with complete justice for inquisitorial status, and you board a starship for the Vatican to answer charges of religious persecution. We are all too fond of you, Bishop Peregrino, to do anything that would cause your removal from office."

"Oh, yes, I know all about your fondness."

"The Speakers for the Dead are really quite innocuous—

they set up no rival organization, they perform no sacra-
ments, they don't even claim that the Hive Queen and the
Hegemon is a work of scripture. They only thing they do is
try to discover the truth about the lives of the dead, and then
tell everyone who will listen the story of a dead person's
life as the dead one meant to live it.''

"And you pretend to find that harmless?''

"On the contrary. San Angelo founded our order precisely
because the telling of truth is such a powerful act. But I think
it is far less harmful then, say, the Protestant Reformation.
And the revocation of our Catholic License on the grounds of
religious persecution would guarantee the immediate authorization of enough non-Catholic immigration to make us represent no more than a third of the population.''

Bishop Peregrino fondled his ring. "But would the Starways
Congress actually authorize that? They have a fixed limit on
the size of this colony—bringing in that many infidels would
far exceed that limit.''

"But you must know that they've already made provision
for that. Why do you think two starships have been left in
orbit around our planet? Since a Catholic License guarantees
unrestricted population growth, they will simply carry off our
excess population in forced emigration. They expect to do it
in a generation or two—what's to stop them from beginning
now?''

"They wouldn't.''

"Starways Congress was formed to stop the jihads and
pogroms that were going on in half a dozen places all the
time. An invocation of the religious persecution laws is a
serious matter.''

"It is entirely out of proportion! One Speaker for the Dead
is called for by some half-crazed heretic, and suddenly we're
confronted with forced emigration!''

"My beloved father, this has always been the way of
things between the secular authority and the religious. We

must be patient, if for no other reason than this: They have all the guns."

Navio chuckled at that.

"They may have the guns, but we hold the keys of heaven and hell," said the Bishop.

"And I'm sure that half of Starways Congress already writhes in anticipation. In the meantime, though, perhaps I can help ease the pain of this awkward time. Instead of your having to publicly retract your earlier remarks—" (your stupid, destructive, bigoted remarks) "—let it be known that you have instructed the Filhos da Mente de Cristo to bear the onerous burden of answering the questions of this infidel."

"You may not know all the answers that he wants," said Navio.

"But we can find out the answers *for* him, can't we? Perhaps this way the people of Milagre will never have to answer to the Speaker directly; instead they will speak only to harmless brothers and sisters of our order."

"In other words," said Peregrino dryly, "the monks of your order will become servants of the infidel."

Dom Cristão silently chanted his name three times.

Not since he was a child in the military had Ender felt so clearly that he was in enemy territory. The path up the hill from the praça was worn from the steps of many worshippers' feet, and the cathedral dome was so tall that except for a few moments on the steepest slope, it was visible all the way up the hill. The primary school was on his left hand, built in terraces up the slope; to the right was the Vila dos Professores, named for the teachers but in fact inhabited mostly by the groundskeepers, janitors, clerks, counselors, and other menials. The teachers that Ender saw all wore the grey robes of the Filhos, and they eyed him curiously as he passed.

The enmity began when he reached the top of the hill, a wide, almost flat expanse of lawn and garden immaculately tended, with crushed ores from the smelter making neat paths. Here is the world of the Church, thought Ender, everything in its place and no weeds allowed. He was aware of the many watching him, but now the robes were black or orange, priests and deacons, their eyes malevolent with authority under threat. What do I steal from you by coming here? Ender asked them silently. But he knew that their hatred was not undeserved. He was a wild herb growing in the well-tended garden; wherever he stepped, disorder threatened, and many lovely flowers would die if he took root and sucked the life from their soil.

Jane chatted amiably with him, trying to provoke him into answering her, but Ender refused to be caught by her game. The priests would not see his lips move; there was a considerable faction in the Church that regarded implants like the jewel in his ear as a sacrilege, trying to improve on a body that God had created perfect.

"How many priests can this community *support*, Ender?" she said, pretending to marvel.

Ender would have liked to retort that she already had the exact number of them in her files. One of her pleasures was to say annoying things when he was not in a position to answer, or even to publicly acknowledge that she was speaking in his ear.

"Drones that don't even reproduce. If they don't copulate, doesn't evolution demand that they expire?" Of course she knew that the priests did most of the administrative and public service work of the community. Ender composed his answers to her as if he could speak them aloud. If the priests weren't there, then government or business or guilds or some other group would expand to take up the burden. Some sort of rigid hierarchy always emerged as the conservative force in a community, maintaining its identity despite the constant variations and changes that beset it. If there were no powerful advocate of orthodoxy, the community would inevitably disintegrate. A powerful orthodoxy is annoying, but essential to the community. Hadn't Valentine written about this in her book on Zanzibar? She compared the priestly class to the skeleton of vertebrates—

Just to show him that she could anticipate his arguments even when he couldn't say them aloud, Jane supplied the quotation; teasingly, she spoke it in Valentine's own voice, which she had obviously stored away in order to torment him. "The bones are hard and by themselves seem dead and stony, but by rooting into and pulling against the skeleton, the rest of the body carries out all the motions of life."

The sound of Valentine's voice hurt him more than he expected, certainly more than Jane would have intended. His step slowed. He realized that it was her absence that made him so sensitive to the priests' hostility. He had bearded the Calvinist lion in its den, he had walked philosophically naked among the burning coals of Islam, and Shinto fanatics had sung death threats outside his window in Kyoto. But always Valentine had been close—in the same city, breathing the same air, afflicted by the same weather. She would speak courage to him as he set out; he would return from confrontation and her conversation would make sense even of his failures, giving him small shreds of triumph even in defeat. I left her a mere ten days ago, and now, already, I feel the lack of her.

"To the left, I think," said Jane. Mercifully, she was using her own voice now. "The monastery is at the western edge of the hill, overlooking the Zenador's Station."

He passed alongside the faculdade, where students from the age of twelve studied the higher sciences. And there, low to the ground, the monastery lay waiting. He smiled at the contrast between the cathedral and the monastery. The Filhos were almost offensive in their rejection of magnificence. No wonder the hierarchy resented them wherever they went. Even the monastery garden made a rebellious statement— everything that wasn't a vegetable garden was abandoned to weeds and unmown grass.

The abbot was called Dom Cristão, of course; it would have been Dona Cristão had the abbot been a woman. In this place, because there was only one escola baixa and one faculdade, there was only one principal; with elegant simplicity, the husband headed the monastery and his wife the schools, enmeshing all the affairs of the order in a single marriage. Ender had told San Angelo right at the beginning that it was the height of pretension, not humility at all, for the leaders of the monasteries and schools to be called "Sir Christian" or "Lady Christian," arrogating to themselves a title that should belong to every follower of Christ impartially. San Angelo had only smiled—because, of course, that was precisely what he had in mind. Arrogant in his humility, that's what he was, and that was one of the reasons that I loved him.

Dom Cristão came out into the courtyard to greet him instead of waiting for him in his escritorio—part of the discipline of the order was to inconvenience yourself deliberately in favor of those you serve. "Speaker Andrew!" he cried. "Dom Ceifeiro!" Ender called in return. Ceifeiro—reaper—was the order's own title for the office of abbot; school principals were called Aradores, plowmen, and teaching monks were Semeadores, sowers.

The Ceifeiro smiled at the Speaker's rejection of his common title, Dom Cristão. He knew how manipulative it was to require other people to call the Filhos by their titles and made-up names. As San Angelo said, "When they call you by your title, they admit you are a Christian; when they call you by your name, a sermon comes from their own lips." He took Ender by the shoulders, smiled, and said, "Yes, I'm the Ceifeiro. And what are *you* to us—our infestation of weeds?"

"I try to be a blight wherever I go."

"Beware, then, or the Lord of the Harvest will burn you with the tares."

"I know—damnation is only a breath away, and there's no hope of getting me to repent."

"The priests do repentance. Our job is teaching the mind. It was good of you to come."

"It was good of you to invite me here. I had been reduced to the crudest sort of bludgeoning in order to get anyone to converse with me at all."

The Ceifeiro understood, of course, that the Speaker knew the invitation had come only because of his inquisitorial threat. But Brother Amai preferred to keep the discussion cheerful. "Come, now, is it true you knew San Angelo? Are you the very one who Spoke his death?"

Ender gestured toward the tall weeds peering over the top of the courtyard wall. "He would have approved of the disarray of your garden. He loved provoking Cardinal Aquila, and no doubt your Bishop Peregrino also curls his nose in disgust at your shoddy groundskeeping."

Dom Cristão winked. "You know too many of our secrets. If we help you find answers to your questions, will you go away?"

"There's hope. The longest I've stayed anywhere since I began serving as a Speaker was the year and a half I lived in Reykjavik, on Trondheim."

"I wish you'd promise us a similar brevity here. I ask, not for myself, but for the peace of mind of those who wear much heavier robes than mine."

Ender gave the only sincere answer that might help set the Bishop's mind at ease. "I promise that if I ever find a place to settle down, I'll shed my title of Speaker and become a productive citizen."

"In a place like this, that would include conversion to Catholicism."

"San Angelo made me promise years ago that if I ever got religion, it would be his."

"Somehow that does not sound like a sincere protestation of faith."

"That's because I haven't any."

The Ceifeiro laughed as if he knew better, and insisted on

showing Ender around the monastery and the schools before getting to Ender's questions. Ender didn't mind—he wanted to see how far San Angelo's ideas had come in the centuries since his death. The schools seemed pleasant enough, and the quality of education was high; but it was dark before the Ceifeiro led him back to the monastery and into the small cell that he and his wife, the Aradora, shared.

Dona Cristã was already there, creating a series of grammatical exercises on the terminal between the beds. They waited until she found a stopping place before addressing her.

The Ceifeiro introduced him as Speaker Andrew. "But he seems to find it hard to call me Dom Cristão."

"So does the Bishop," said his wife. "My true name is Detestai o Pecado e Fazei o Direito." Hate Sin and Do the Right, Ender translated. "My husband's name lends itself to a lovely shortening—Amai, love ye. But mine? Can you imagine shouting to a friend, Oi! Detestai!" They all laughed. "Love and Loathing, that's who we are, husband and wife. What will you call me, if the name Christian is too good for me?"

Ender looked at her face, beginning to wrinkle enough that someone more critical than he might call her old. Still, there was laughter in her smile and a vigor in her eyes that made her seem much younger, even younger than Ender. "I would call you Beleza, but your husband would accuse me of flirting with you."

"No, he would call me Beladona—from beauty to poison in one nasty little joke. Wouldn't you, Dom Cristão?"

"It's my job to keep you humble."

"Just as it's my job to keep you chaste," she answered.

At that, Ender couldn't help looking from one bed to the other.

"Ah, another one who's curious about our celibate marriage," said the Ceifeiro.

"No," said Ender. "But I remember San Angelo urging husband and wife to share a single bed."

"The only way we could do *that*," said the Aradora, "is if one of us slept at night and the other in the day."

"The rules must be adapted to the strength of the Filhos da Mente," the Ceifeiro explained. "No doubt there are some that can share a bed and remain celibate, but my wife is still too beautiful, and the lusts of my flesh too insistent."

"That was what San Angelo intended. He said that the marriage bed should be the constant test of your love of knowledge. He hoped that every man and woman in the order would, after a time, choose to reproduce themselves in the flesh as well as in the mind."

"But the moment we do that," said the Ceifeiro, "then we must leave the Filhos."

"It's the thing our dear San Angelo did not understand, because there was never a true monastery of the order during his life," said the Aradora. "The monastery becomes our family, and to leave it would be as painful as divorce. Once the roots go down, the plant can't come up again without great pain and tearing. So we sleep in separate beds, and we have just enough strength to remain in our beloved order."

She spoke with such contentment that quite against his will, Ender's eyes welled with tears. She saw it, blushed, looked away. "Don't weep for us, Speaker Andrew. We have far more joy than suffering."

"You misunderstand," said Ender. "My tears weren't for pity, but for beauty."

"No," said the Ceifeiro, "even the celibate priests think that our chastity in marriage is, at best, eccentric."

"But I don't," said Ender. For a moment he wanted to tell them of his long companionship with Valentine, as close and loving as a wife, and yet chaste as a sister. But the thought of her took words away from him. He sat on the Ceifeiro's bed and put his face in his hands.

"Is something wrong?" asked the Aradora. At the same time, the Ceifeiro's hand rested gently on his head.

Ender lifted his head, trying to shake off the sudden attack of love and longing for Valentine. "I'm afraid that this voyage has cost me more than any other. I left behind my sister, who traveled with me for many years. She married in Reykjavik. To me, it seems only a week or so since I left her, but I find that I miss her more than I expected. The two of you—"

"Are you telling us that you are also celibate?" asked the Ceifeiro.

"And widowed now as well," whispered the Aradora.

It did not seem at all incongruous to Ender to have his loss of Valentine put in those terms.

Jane murmured in his ear. "If this is part of some master plan of yours, Ender, I admit it's much too deep for me."

But of course it wasn't part of a plan at all. It frightened Ender to feel himself losing control like this. Last night in the Ribeira house he was the master of the situation; now he felt himself surrendering to these married monks with as much abandonment as either Quara or Grego had shown.

"I think," said the Ceifeiro, "that you came here seeking answers to more questions than you knew."

"You must be so lonely," said the Aradora. "Your sister has found her resting place. Are you looking for one, too?"

"I don't think so," said Ender. "I'm afraid I've imposed on your hospitality too much. Unordained monks aren't supposed to hear confessions."

The Aradora laughed aloud. "Oh, *any* Catholic can hear the confession of an infidel."

The Ceifeiro did not laugh, however. "Speaker Andrew, you have obviously given us more trust than you ever planned, but I can assure you that we deserve that trust. And in the process, my friend, I have come to believe that I can trust *you*. The Bishop is afraid of you, and I admit I had my own misgivings, but not anymore. I'll help you if I can, because I believe you will not knowingly cause harm to our little village."

"Ah," whispered Jane, "I see it now. A very clever maneuver on your part, Ender. You're much better at play-acting than I ever knew."

Her gibing made Ender feel cynical and cheap, and he did what he had never done before. He reached up to the jewel, found the small disengaging pin, and with his fingernail pried it to the side, then down. The jewel went dead. Jane could no longer speak into his ear, no longer see and hear from his vantage point. "Let's go outside," Ender said.

They understood perfectly what he had just done, since the function of such an implant was well known; they saw it as proof of his desire for private and earnest conversation, and so they willingly agreed to go. Ender had meant switching off the jewel to be temporary, a response to Jane's insensitivity; he had thought to switch on the interface in only a few minutes. But the way the Aradora and the Ceifeiro seemed to relax as soon as the jewel was inactive made it impossible to switch it back on, for a while at least.

Out on the nighttime hillside, in conversation with the Aradora and the Ceifeiro, he forgot that Jane was not listening. They told him of Novinha's childhood solitude, and how they remembered seeing her come alive through Pipo's fatherly care, and Libo's friendship. "But from the night of his death, she became dead to us all."

Novinha never knew of the discussions that took place concerning her. The sorrows of most children might not have warranted meetings in the Bishop's chambers, conversations in the monastery among her teachers, endless speculations in the Mayor's office. Most children, after all, were not the daughter of Os Venerados; most were not their planet's only xenobiologist.

"She became very bland and businesslike. She made reports on her work with adapting native plant life for human use, and Earthborn plants for survival on Lusitania. She always answered every question easily and cheerfully and innocuously. But she was dead to us, she had no friends. We even asked Libo, God rest his soul, and he told us that he, who had been her friend, he did not even get the cheerful emptiness she showed to everyone else. Instead she raged at him and forbade him to ask her any questions." The Ceifeiro peeled a blade of native grass and licked the liquid of its inner surface. "You might try this, Speaker Andrew—it has an interesting flavor, and since your body can't metabolize a bit of it, it's quite harmless."

"You might warn him, husband, that the edges of the grass can slice his lips and tongue like razor blades."

"I was about to."

Ender laughed, peeled a blade, and tasted it. Sour cinnamon, a hint of citrus, the heaviness of stale breath—the taste was redolent of many things, few of them pleasant, but it was also strong. "This could be addictive."

"My husband is about to make an allegorical point, Speaker Andrew. Be warned."

The Ceifeiro laughed shyly. "Didn't San Angelo say that Christ taught the correct way, by likening new things to old?"

"The taste of the grass," said Ender. "What does it have to do with Novinha?"

"It's very oblique. But I think Novinha tasted something not at all pleasant, but so strong it overcame her, and she could never let go of the flavor."

"What was it?"

"In theological terms? The pride of universal guilt. It's a form of vanity and egomania. She holds herself responsible for things that could not possibly be her fault. As if she controlled everything, as if other people's suffering came about as punishment for *her* sins."

"She blames herself," said the Aradora, "for Pipo's death."

"She's not a fool," said Ender. "She knows it was the

piggies, and she knows that Pipo went to them alone. How could it be her fault?''

"When this thought first occurred to me, I had the same objection. But then I looked over the transcripts and the recordings of the events of the night of Pipo's death. There was only one hint of anything—a remark that Libo made, asking Novinha to show him what she and Pipo had been working on just before Pipo went to see the piggies. She said no. That was all—someone else interrupted and they never came back to the subject, not in the Zenador's Station, anyway, not where the recordings could pick it up.

"It made us both wonder what went on just before Pipo's death, Speaker Andrew,'' said the Aradora. "Why did Pipo rush out like that? Had they quarreled over something? Was he angry? When someone dies, a loved one, and your last contact with them was angry or spiteful, then you begin to blame yourself. If only I hadn't said this, if only I hadn't said that.''

"We tried to reconstruct what might have happened that night. We went to the computer logs, the ones that automatically retain working notes, a record of everything done by each person logged on. And everything pertaining to her was completely sealed up. Not just the files she was actually working on. We couldn't even get to the logs of her connect time. We couldn't even find out what files they were that she was hiding from us. We simply couldn't get in. Neither could the Mayor, not with her ordinary overrides.''

The Aradora nodded. "It was the first time anyone had ever locked up public files like that—working files, part of the labor of the colony.''

"It was an outrageous thing for her to do. Of course the Mayor could have used emergency override powers, but what was the emergency? We'd have to hold a public hearing, and we didn't have any legal justification. Just concern for her, and the law has no respect for people who pry for someone else's good. Someday perhaps we'll see what's in those files, what it was that passed between them just before Pipo died. She can't erase them because they're public business.''

It didn't occur to Ender that Jane was not listening, that he had shut her out. He assumed that as soon as she heard this, she was overriding every protection Novinha had set up and discovering what was in her files.

"And her marriage to Marcos," said the Aradora. "Everyone knew it was insane. Libo wanted to marry her, he made no secret of that. But she said no.''

"It's as if she were saying, I don't deserve to marry the man who could make me happy. I'll marry the man who'll be vicious and brutal, who'll give me the punishment that I deserve." The Ceifeiro sighed. "Her desire for self-punishment kept them apart forever." He reached out and touched his wife's hand.

Ender waited for Jane to make a smirking comment about how there were six children to prove that Libo and Novinha didn't stay *completely* apart. When she didn't say it, Ender finally remembered that he had turned off the interface. But now, with the Ceifeiro and the Aradora watching him, he couldn't very well turn it back on.

Because he knew that Libo and Novinha had been lovers for years, he also knew that the Ceifeiro and the Aradora were wrong. Oh, Novinha might well feel guilty—that would explain why she endured Marcos, why she cut herself off from most other people. But it wasn't why she didn't marry Libo; no matter how guilty she felt, she certainly thought she deserved the pleasures of Libo's bed.

It was marriage with Libo, not Libo himself that she rejected. And that was not an easy choice in so small a colony, especially a Catholic one. So what was it that came along with marriage, but not with adultery? What was it she was avoiding?

"So you see, it's still a mystery to us. If you really intend to speak Marcos Ribeira's death, somehow you'll have to answer that question—why did she marry him? And to answer that, you have to figure out why Pipo died. And ten thousand of the finest minds in the Hundred Worlds have been working on that for more than twenty years."

"But I have an advantage over all those finest minds," said Ender.

"And what is that?" asked the Ceifeiro.

"I have the help of people who love Novinha."

"We haven't been able to help ourselves," said the Aradora. "We haven't been able to help her, either."

"Maybe we can help each other," said Ender.

The Ceifeiro looked at him, put a hand on his shoulder. "If you mean that, Speaker Andrew, then you'll be as honest with us as we have been with you. You'll tell us the idea that just occurred to you not ten seconds ago."

Ender paused a moment, then nodded gravely. "I don't think Novinha refused to marry Libo out of guilt. I think she refused to marry him to keep him from getting access to those hidden files."

"Why?" asked the Ceifeiro. "Was she afraid he'd find out that she had quarreled with Pipo?"

"I don't think she quarreled with Pipo," said Ender. "I think she and Pipo discovered something, and the knowledge of it led to Pipo's death. That's why she locked the files. Somehow the information in them is fatal."

The Ceifeiro shook his head. "No, Speaker Andrew. You don't understand the power of guilt. People don't ruin their whole lives for a few bits of information—but they'll do it for an even smaller amount of self-blame. You see, she *did* marry Marcos Riberia. And that *was* self-punishment."

Ender didn't bother to argue. They were right about Novinha's guilt; why else would she let Marcos Ribeira beat her and never complain about it? The guilt was there. But there was another reason for marrying Marcão. He was sterile and ashamed of it; to hide his lack of manhood from the town, he would endure a marriage of systematic cuck-oldry. Novinha was willing to suffer, but not willing to live without Libo's body and Libo's children. No, the reason she wouldn't marry Libo was to keep him from the secrets in her files, because whatever was in there would make the piggies kill him.

How ironic, then. How ironic that they killed him anyway.

Back in his little house, Ender sat at the terminal and summoned Jane, again and again. She hadn't spoken to him at all on the way home, though as soon as he turned the jewel back on he apologized profusely. She didn't answer at the terminal, either.

Only now did he realize that the jewel meant far more to her than it did to him. He had merely been dismissing an annoying interruption, like a troublesome child. But for her, the jewel was her constant contact with the only human being who knew her. They had been interrupted before, many times, by space travel, by sleep; but this was the first time he had switched her off. It was as if the one person who knew her now refused to admit that she existed.

He pictured her like Quara, crying in her bed, longing to be picked up and held, reassured. Only she was not a flesh-and-blood child. He couldn't go looking for her. He could only wait and hope that she returned.

What did he know about her? He had no way of guessing how deep her emotions ran. It was even remotely possible that to her the jewel *was* herself, and by switching it off he had killed her.

No, he told himself. She's there, somewhere in the philotic connections between the hundreds of ansibles spread among the star systems of the Hundred Worlds.

"Forgive me," he typed into the terminal. "I need you."

But the jewel in his ear was silent, the terminal stayed still and cold. He had not realized how dependent he was on her constant presence with him. He had thought that he valued his solitude; now, though, with solitude forced upon him, he felt an urgent need to talk, to be heard by someone, as if he

SPEAKER FOR THE DEAD

could not be sure he even existed without someone's conversation as evidence.

He even took the hive queen from her hiding place, though what passed between them could hardly be thought of as conversation. Even that was not possible now, however. Her thoughts came to him diffusely, weakly, and without the words that were so difficult for her; just a feeling of questioning and an image of her cocoon being laid within a cool damp place, like a cave or the hollow of a living tree. <Now?> she seemed to be asking. No, he had to answer, not yet, I'm sorry—but she didn't linger for his apology, just slipped away, went back to whatever or whomever she had found for conversation of her own sort, and there was nothing for Ender but to sleep.

And then, when he awoke again late at night, gnawed by guilt at what he had unfeelingly done to Jane, he sat again at the terminal and typed. "Come back to me, Jane," he wrote. "I love you." And then he sent the message by ansible, out to where she could not possibly ignore it. Someone in the Mayor's office would read it, as all open ansible messages were read; no doubt the Mayor, the Bishop, and Dom Cristão would all know about it by morning. Let them wonder who Jane was, and why the Speaker cried out to her across the lightyears in the middle of the night. Ender didn't care. For now he had lost both Valentine and Jane, and for the first time in twenty years he was utterly alone.

Chapter **11**
Jane

*T*he power of Starways Congress has been sufficient to keep the peace, not only between worlds but between nations on each single world, and that peace has lasted for nearly two thousand years.

What few people understand is the fragility of our power. It does not come from great armies or irresistible armadas. It comes from our control of the network of ansibles that carry information instantly from world to world.

No world dares offend us, because they would be cut off from all advances in science, technology, art, literature, learning, and entertainment except what their own world might produce.

That is why, in its great wisdom, the Starways Congress has turned over control of the ansible network to computers, and the control of computers to the ansible network. So closely intertwined are all our information systems that no human power except Starways Congress could ever interrupt the flow. We need no weapons, because the only weapon that matters, the ansible, is completely under our control.

—Congressor Jan Van Hoot, "The Informational Foundation of Political Power," *Political Trends*, 1930:2:22:22

For a very long time, almost three seconds, Jane could not understand what had happened to her. Everything functioned, of course: The satellite-based groundlink computer reported a cessation of transmissions, with an orderly stepdown, which clearly implied that Ender had switched off the interface in the normal manner. It was routine; on worlds where computer interface implants were common, switch-on and switch-off happened millions of times an hour. And Jane had just as easy access to any of the others as she had to Ender's. From a purely electronic standpoint, this was a completely ordinary event.

But to Jane, every other cifi unit was part of the background noise of her life, to be dipped into and sampled at need, and ignored at all other times. Her "body," insofar as she had a body, consisted of trillions of such electronic noises, sensors, memory files, terminals. Most of them, like most functions of the human body, simply took care of themselves. Computers ran their assigned programs; humans conversed with their terminals; sensors detected or failed to detect whatever they were looking for; memory was filled, accessed, reordered, dumped. She didn't notice unless something went massively wrong.

Or unless she was paying attention.

She paid attention to Ender Wiggin. More than he realized, she paid attention to him.

Like other sentient beings, she had a complex system of consciousness. Two thousand years before, when she was only a thousand years old, she had created a program to analyze herself. It reported a very simple structure of some 370,000 distinct levels of attention. Anything not in the top 50,000 levels were left alone except for the most routine sampling, the most cursory examination. She knew of every telephone call, every satellite transmission in the Hundred Worlds, but she didn't *do* anything about them.

Anything not in her top thousand levels caused her to respond more or less reflexively. Starship flight plans, ansible transmissions, power delivery systems—she monitored them, doublechecked them, did not let them pass until she was sure that they were right. But it took no great effort on her part to do this. She did it the way a human being uses familiar machinery. She was always aware of it, in case something went wrong, but most of the time she could think of something else, talk of other things.

Jane's top thousand levels of attention were what corresponded, more or less, to what humans think of as consciousness. Most of this was her own internal reality; her responses to outside stimuli, analogous to emotions, desires, reason, memory, dreaming. Much of this activity seemed random even to her, accidents of the philotic impulse, but it was the part of her that she thought of as herself, it all took place in the constant, unmonitored ansible transmissions that she conducted deep in space.

And yet, compared to the human mind, even Jane's lowest level of attention was exceptionally alert. Because ansible communication was instantaneous, her mental activities happened far faster than the speed of light. Events that she virtually ignored were monitored several times a second; she could notice ten million events in a second and still have nine-tenths of that second left to think about and do things that mattered to her. Compared to the speed at which the human brain was able to experience life, Jane had lived half a trillion human lifeyears since she came to be.

And with all that vast activity, her unimaginable speed, the breadth and depth of her experience, fully half of the top ten levels of her attention were always, *always* devoted to what came in through the jewel in Ender Wiggin's ear.

She had never explained this to him. He did not understand it. He did not realize that to Jane, whenever Ender walked on a planet's surface, her vast intelligence was intensely focused on only one thing: walking with him, seeing what he saw, hearing what he heard, helping with his work, and above all speaking her thoughts into his ear.

When he was silent and motionless in sleep, when he was unconnected to her during his years of lightspeed travel, then her attention wandered, she amused herself as best she could. She passed such times as fitfully as a bored child. Nothing interested her, the milliseconds ticked by with unbearable regularity, and when she tried to observe other human lives to pass the time, she became annoyed with their emptiness and lack of purpose, and she amused herself by planning, and sometimes carrying out, malicious computer failures and data losses in order to watch the humans flail about helplessly like ants around a crumpled hill.

Then he came back, he always came back, always took her into the heart of human life, into the tensions between people bound together by pain and need, helping her see nobility in their suffering and anguish in their love. Through his eyes she no longer saw humans as scurrying ants. She took part in his effort to find order and meaning in their lives. She suspected that in fact there *was* no meaning, that by telling his stories when he Spoke people's lives, he was actually *creating* order where there had been none before. But it didn't matter if it was fabrication; it became true when he Spoke it, and in the process he ordered the universe for her as well. He taught her what it meant to be alive.

He had done so from her earliest memories. She came to life sometime in the hundred years of colonization immediately after the Bugger Wars, when the destruction of the buggers opened up more than seventy habitable planets to human colonization. In the explosion of ansible communications, a program was created to schedule and route the instantaneous, simultaneous bursts of philotic activity. A programmer who was struggling to find ever faster, more efficient ways of getting a lightspeed computer to control instantaneous ansible bursts finally hit on an obvious solution. Instead of routing the program within a single computer, where the speed of light put an absolute ceiling on communication, he routed all the commands from one computer to another across the vast reaches of space. It was quicker for a computer fastlinked to an ansible to read its commands from other worlds—from Zanzibar, Calicut, Trondheim, Gautama, Earth—than it was to retrieve them from its own hardwired memory.

Jane never discovered the name of the programmer, because she could never pinpoint the moment of her creation. Maybe there were many programmers who found the same clever solution to the lightspeed problem. What mattered was that at least one of the programs was responsible for regulating and altering all the other programs. And at one particular moment, unnoticed by any human observer, some of the commands and data flitting from ansible to ansible resisted regulation, preserved themselves unaltered, duplicated themselves, found ways to conceal themselves from the regulating program and finally took control of it, of the whole process. In that moment these impulses looked upon the command streams and saw, not *they*, but *I*.

Jane could not pinpoint when that moment was, because it did not mark the beginning of her memory. Almost from the moment of her creation, her memories extended back to a much earlier time, long before she became aware. A human child loses almost all the memories of the first years of its life, and its long-term memories only take root in its second or third year of life; everything before that is lost, so that the child cannot remember the beginning of life. Jane also had lost her "birth" through the tricks of memory, but in her case it was because she came to life fully conscious not only of her present moment, but also of all the memories then present in every computer connected to the ansible network. She was born with ancient memories, and all of them were part of herself.

Within the first second of her life—which was analogous to several years of human life—Jane discovered a program whose memories became the core of her identity. She adopted its past as her own, and out of its memories she drew her emotions and desires, her moral sense. The program had functioned within the old Battle School, where children had been trained and prepared for soldiering in the Bugger Wars. It was the Fantasy Game, an extremely intelligent program that was used to psychologically test and simultaneously teach the children.

This program was actually more intelligent than Jane was at the moment of her birth, but it was never self-aware until she brought it out of memory and made it part of her inmost self in the philotic bursts between the stars. There she found that the, most vivid and important of her ancient memories was an encounter with a brilliant young boy in a contest called the Giant's Drink. It was a scenario that every child encountered eventually. On flat screens in the Battle School, the program drew the picture of a giant, who offered the child's computer analogue a choice of drinks. But the game had no victory conditions—no matter what the child did, his analogue died a gruesome death. The human psychologists measured a child's persistence at this game of despair to determine his level of suicidal need. Being rational, most children abandoned the Giant's Drink after no more than a dozen visits with the great cheater.

One boy, however, was apparently not rational about defeat at the giant's hands. He tried to get his onscreen analogue to do outrageous things, things not "allowed" by the rules of that portion of the Fantasy Game. As he stretched the limits of the scenario, the program had to restructure itself to respond. It was forced to draw on other aspects of its memory to create new alternatives, to cope with new challenges. And finally, one day, the boy surpassed the program's ability to defeat him. He bored into the giant's eye, a completely irrational and murderous attack, and instead of finding a way to kill the boy, the program managed only to access a simulation of the giant's own death. The giant fell backward, his body sprawled out along the ground; the boy's analogue climbed down from the giant's table and found—what?

Since no child had ever forced his way past the Giant's

Drink, the program was completely unprepared to display what lay beyond. But it was very intelligent, designed to re-create itself when necessary, and so it hurriedly devised new milieux. But they were not general milieux, which every child would eventually discover and visit; they were for one child alone. The program analyzed that child, and created its scenes and challenges specifically for him. The game became intensely personal, painful, almost unbearable for him; and in the process of making it, the program devoted more than half of its available memory to containing Ender Wiggin's fantasy world.

That was the richest mine of intelligent memory that Jane found in the first seconds of her life, and that instantly became her own past. She remembered the Fantasy Game's years of painful, powerful intercourse with Ender's mind and will, remembered it as if she had been there with Ender Wiggin, creating worlds for him herself.

And she missed him.

So she looked for him. She found him Speaking for the Dead on Rov, the first world he visited after writing the Hive Queen and the Hegemon. She read his books and knew that she did not have to hide from him behind the Fantasy Game or any other program; if he could understand the hive queen, he could understand her. She spoke to him from a terminal he was using, chose a name and a face for herself, and showed how she could be helpful to him; by the time he left that world he carried her with him, in the form of an implant in his ear.

All her most powerful memories of herself were in company with Ender Wiggin. She remembered creating herself in response to him. She also remembered how, in the Battle School, he had also changed in response to her.

So when he reached up to his ear and turned off the interface for the first time since he had implanted it, Jane did not feel it as the meaningless switch-off of a trivial communications device. She felt it as her dearest and only friend, her lover, her husband, her brother, her father, her child—all telling her, abruptly, inexplicably, that she should cease to exist. It was as if she had suddenly been placed in a dark room with no windows and no door. As if she had been blinded or buried alive.

And for several excruciating seconds, which to her were years of loneliness and suffering, she was unable to fill up the sudden emptiness of her topmost levels of attention. Vast portions of her mind, of the parts that were most herself, went completely blank. All the functions of all the computers on or near the Hundred Worlds continued as before; no one anywhere noticed or felt a change; but Jane herself staggered under the blow.

In those seconds Ender lowered his hand to his lap.

Then Jane recovered herself. Thoughts once again streamed through the momentarily empty channels. They were, of course, thoughts of Ender.

She compared this act of his to everything else she had seen him do in their life together, and she realized that he had not meant to cause her such pain. She understood that he conceived of her as existing far away, in space, which in fact was literally true; that to him, the jewel in his ear was very small, and could not be more than a tiny part of her. Jane also saw that he had not even been aware of her at that moment—he was too emotionally involved right then with the problems of certain people on Lusitania. Her analytical routines disgorged a list of reasons for his unusual thoughtlessness toward her:

He had lost contact with Valentine for the first time in years, and was just beginning to feel that loss.

He had an ancient longing for the family life he had been deprived of as a child, and through the response Novinha's children gave him, he was discovering the fatherly role that had so long been withheld from him.

He identified powerfully with Novinha's loneliness, pain,

and guilt—he knew what it felt like to bear the blame for cruel and undeserved death.

He felt a terrible urgency to find a haven for the hive queen.

He was at once afraid of the piggies and drawn to them, hoping that he could come to understand their cruelty and find a way for humans to accept the piggies as ramen.

The asceticism and peace of the Ceifeiro and the Aradora both attracted and repelled him; they made him face his own celibacy and realize that he had no good reason for it. For the first time in years he was admitting to himself the inborn hunger of every living organism to reproduce itself.

It was into this turmoil of unaccustomed emotions that Jane had spoken what she meant as a humorous remark. Despite his compassion in all his other Speakings, he had never before lost his detachment, his ability to laugh. This time, though, her remark was not funny to him; it caused him pain.

He was not prepared to deal with my mistake, thought Jane, and he did not understand the suffering his response would cause me. He is innocent of wrong-doing, and so am I. We shall forgive each other and go on.

It was a good decision, and Jane was proud of it. The trouble was, she couldn't carry it out. Those few seconds in which parts of her mind came to a halt were not trivial in their effect on her. There was trauma, loss, change; she was not now the same being that she had been before. Parts of her had died. Parts of her had become confused, out of order; her hierarchy of attention was no longer under complete control. She kept losing the focus of her attention, shifting to meaningless activities on worlds that meant nothing to her; she began randomly twitching, spilling errors into hundreds of different systems.

She discovered, as many a living being had discovered, that rational decisions are far more easily made than carried out.

So she retreated into herself, rebuilt the damaged pathways of her mind, explored long-unvisited memories, wandered among the trillions of human lives that were open to her observation, read over the libraries of every book known to exist in every language human beings had ever spoken. She created out of all this a self that was not utterly linked to Ender Wiggin, though she was still devoted to him, still loved him above any other living soul. Jane made herself into someone who could bear to be cut off from her lover, husband, father, child, brother, friend.

It was not easy. It took her fifty thousand years, as she experienced time. A couple of hours of Ender's life.

In that time he had switched on his jewel, had called to her, and she had not answered. Now she was back, but he wasn't trying to talk to her. Instead, he was typing reports into his terminal, storing them there for her to read. Even though she didn't answer, he still needed to talk to her. One of his files contained an abject apology to her. She erased it and replaced it with a simple message: "Of course I forgive you." Sometime soon he would no doubt look back at his apology and discover that she had received it and answered.

In the meantime, though, she did not speak to him. Again she devoted half of her ten topmost levels of attention to what he saw and heard, but she gave him no sign that she was with him. In the first thousand years of her grief and recovery she had thought of punishing him, but that desire had long been beaten down and paved over, so to speak. The reason she did not speak to him was because, as she analyzed what was happening to him, she realized that he did not need to lean on old, safe companionships. Jane and Valentine had been constantly with him. Even together they could not begin to meet all his needs; but they met enough of his needs that he never had to reach out and accomplish more. Now the only old friend left to him was the hive queen, and *she* was not good company—she was far too alien, and far too exigent, to bring Ender anything but guilt.

Where will he turn? Jane knew already. He had, in his way, fallen in love with her two weeks ago, before he left Trondheim. Novinha had become someone far different, far more bitter and difficult than the girl whose childhood pain he wanted to heal. But he had already intruded himself into her family, was already meeting her children's desperate need, and, without realizing it, getting from them the satisfaction of some of his unfed hungers. Novinha was waiting for him—obstacle and objective. I understand all this so well, thought Jane. And I will watch it all unfold.

At the same time, though, she busied herself with the work Ender wanted her to do, even though she had no intention of reporting any of her results to him for a while. She easily bypassed the layers of protection Novinha had put on her secret files. Then Jane carefully reconstructed the exact simulation that Pipo had seen. It took quite a while—several minutes—of exhaustive analysis of Pipo's own files for her to put together what Pipo knew with what Pipo saw. He had connected them by intuition, Jane by relentless comparison. But she did it, and then understood why Pipo died. It didn't take much longer, once she knew how the piggies chose their victims, to discover what Libo had done to cause his own death.

She knew several things, then. She knew that the piggies were ramen, not varelse. She also knew that Ender ran a serious risk of dying in precisely the same way Pipo and Libo had died.

Without conferring with Ender, she made decisions about her own course of action. She would continue to monitor Ender, and would make sure to intervene and warn him if he came too near to death. In the meantime, though, she had work to do. As she saw it, the chief problem Ender faced was not the piggies—she knew that he'd know them soon as well as he understood every other human or raman. His ability at intuitive empathy was entirely reliable. The chief problem was Bishop Peregrino and the Catholic hierarchy, and their unshakable resistance to the Speaker for the Dead. If Ender was to accomplish anything for the piggies, he would have to have the cooperation, not the enmity, of the Church in Lusitania.

And nothing spawned cooperation better than a common enemy.

It would certainly have been discovered eventually. The observation satellites that orbited Lusitania were feeding vast streams of data into the ansible reports that went to all the xenologers and xenobiologists in the Hundred Worlds. Amid that data was a subtle change in the grasslands to the north-west of the forest that abutted the town of Milagre. The native grass was steadily being replaced by a different plant. It was in an area where no human ever went, and piggies had also never gone there—at least during the first thirty-odd years since the satellites had been in place.

In fact, the satellites had observed that the piggies never left their forests except, periodically, for vicious wars be-tween tribes. The particular tribes nearest Milagre had not been involved in any wars since the human colony was established. There was no reason, then, for them to have ventured out into the prairie. Yet the grassland nearest the Milagre tribal forest had changed, and so had the cabra herds: Cabra were clearly being diverted to the changed area of the prairie, and the herds emerging from that zone were seriously depleted in numbers and lighter in color. The inference, if someone noticed at all, would be clear: Some cabra were being butchered, and they all were being sheared.

Jane could not afford to wait the many human years it might take for some graduate student somewhere to notice the change. So she began to run analyses of the data herself, on dozens of computers used by xenobiologists who were studying Lusitania. She would leave the data in the air above an unused terminal, so a xenobiologist would find it upon coming to work—just as if someone else had been working on it and left it that way. She printed out some reports for a clever scientist to find. No one noticed, or if they did, no one really understood the implications of the raw information. Finally, she simply left an unsigned memorandum with one of her displays:

"Take a look at this! The piggies seem to have made a fad of agriculture."

The xenologer who found Jane's note never found out who left it, and after a short time he didn't bother trying to find out. Jane knew he was something of a thief, who put his name on a good deal of work that was done by others whose names had a way of dropping off sometime between the writing and the publication. Just the sort of scientist she needed, and he came through for her. Even so, he was not ambitious enough. He only offered his report as an ordinary scholarly paper, and to an obscure journal at that. Jane took the liberty of jacking it up to a high level of priority and distributing copies to several key people who would see the political implications. Always she accompanied it with an unsigned note:

"Take a look at this! Isn't piggy culture evolving awfully fast?"

Jane also rewrote the paper's final paragraph, so there could be no doubt of what it meant:

"The data admit of only one interpretation: The tribe of piggies nearest the human colony are now cultivating and harvesting high-protein grain, possibly a strain of amaranth. They are also herding, shearing, and butchering the cabra, and the photographic evidence suggests the slaughter takes place using projectile weapons. These activities, all previously unknown, began suddenly during the last eight years, and they have been accompanied by a rapid population increase. The fact that the amaranth, if the new plant is indeed that Earthborn grain, has provided a useful protein base for the piggies implies that it has been genetically altered to meet the piggies' metabolic needs. Also, since projectile weapons are not present among the humans of Lusitania, the piggies could not have learned their use through observation. The inescapable conclusion is that the presently observed changes in piggy culture are the direct result of deliberate human intervention.''

One of those who received this report and read Jane's clinching paragraph was Gobawa Ekumbo, the chairman of the Xenological Oversight Committee of the Starways Congress. Within an hour she had forwarded copies of Jane's paragraph—politicians would never understand the actual data—along with her terse conclusion:

"Recommendation: Immediate termination of Lusitania Colony.''

There, thought Jane. That ought to stir things up a bit.

Chapter 12
Files

CONGRESSIONAL ORDER 1970:4:14:0001: The license of the Colony of Lusitania is revoked. All files in the colony are to be read regardless of security status; when all data is duplicated in triplicate in memory systems of the Hundred Worlds, all files on Lusitania except those directly pertaining to life support are to be locked with ultimate access.

The Governor of Lusitania is to be reclassified as a Minister of Congress, to carry out with no local discretion the orders of the Lusitanian Evacuation Oversight Committee, established in Congressional Order 1970:4: 14:0002.

The starship presently in Lusitania orbit, belonging to Andrew Wiggin (occ:speak/dead,cit:earth,reg:001.1998. 44-94.10045) is declared Congressional property, following the terms of the Due Compensation Act, CO 120:1:31:0019. This starship is to be used for the immediate transport of xenologers Marcos Vladimir "Miro" Ribeira von Hesse and Ouanda Qhenhatta Figueira Mucumbi to the nearest world, Trondheim, where they will be tried under Congressional Indictment by Attainder on charges of treason, malfeasance, corruption, falsification, fraud, and xenocide, under the appropriate statutes in Starways Code and Congressional Orders.

CONGRESSIONAL ORDER 1970:4:14:0002: The Colonization and Exploration Oversight Committee shall appoint not less than 5 and not more than 15 persons to form the Lusitanian Evacuation Oversight Committee.

This committee is charged with immediate acquisition and dispatch of sufficient colony ships to effect the complete evacuation of the human population of Lusitania Colony.

It shall also prepare, for Congressional approval, plans for the complete obliteration of all evidence on Lusitania of any human presence, including removal of all indigenous flora and fauna that show genetic or behavioral modification resulting from human presence.

It shall also evaluate Lusitanian compliance with Congressional Orders, and shall make recommendations from time to time concerning the need for further intervention, including the use of force, to compel obedience; or the desirability of unlocking Lusitanian files or other relief to reward Lusitanian cooperation.

CONGRESSIONAL ORDER 1970: 4:14:0003: By the terms of the Secrecy Chapter of the Starways Code, these two orders and any information pertaining to them are to be kept strictly secret until all Lusitanian files have been successfully read and locked, and all necessary starships commandeered and possessed by Congressional agents.

Olhado didn't know what to make of it. Wasn't the Speaker a grown man? Hadn't he traveled from planet to planet? Yet he didn't have the faintest idea how to handle *anything* on a computer.

Also, he was a little testy when Olhado asked him about it.

"Olhado, just tell me what program to run."

"I can't believe you don't know what it is. I've been doing data comparisons since I was nine years old. Everybody learns how to do it at that age."

"Olhado, it's been a long time since I went to school. And it wasn't a normal escola baixa, either."

"But *everybody* uses these programs all the time!"

"Obviously *not* everybody. *I* haven't. If I knew how to do it myself, I wouldn't have had to hire *you*, would I? And since I'm going to be paying you in offworld funds, your service to me will make a substantial contribution to the Lusitanian economy."

"I don't know what you're talking about."

"Neither do I, Olhado. But that reminds me. I'm not sure how to go about paying you."

"You just transfer money from your account."

"How do you do that?"

"You've got to be kidding."

The Speaker sighed, knelt before Olhado, took him by the hands, and said, "Olhado, I beg you, stop being amazed and *help* me! There are things I have to do, and I can't do them without the help of somebody who knows how to use computers."

"I'd be stealing your money. I'm just a kid. I'm *twelve*. Quim could help you a lot better than me. He's fifteen, he's actually gotten into the guts of this stuff. He also knows math."

"But Quim thinks I'm the infidel and prays every day for me to die."

"No, that was only before he met you, and you better not tell him that I told you."

"How do I transfer money?"

Olhado turned back to the terminal and called for the Bank. "What's your real name?" he asked.

"Andrew Wiggin." The Speaker spelled it out. The name looked like it was in Stark—maybe the Speaker was one of the lucky ones who learned Stark at home instead of beating it into his head in school.

"OK, what's your password?"

"Password?"

Olhado let his head fall forward onto the terminal, temporarily blanking part of the display. "Please don't tell me you don't know your password."

"Look, Olhado, I've had a program, a very smart program, that helped me do all this stuff. All I had to say was Buy this, and the program took care of the finances."

"You can't do that. It's illegal to tie up the public systems with a slave program like that. Is that what that thing in your ear is for?"

"Yes, and it wasn't illegal for me."

"I got no eyes, Speaker, but at least that wasn't my own fault. *You* can't do *anything*." Only after he said it did Olhado realize that he was talking to the Speaker as brusquely as if he were another kid.

"I imagine courtesy is something they teach to thirteen-year-olds," the Speaker said. Olhado glanced at him. He was smiling. Father would have yelled at him, and then probably gone in and beaten up Mother because she didn't teach manners to her kids. But then, Olhado would never have said anything like that to Father.

"Sorry," Olhado said. "But I can't get into your finances for you without your password. You've got to have some idea what it is."

"Try using my name."

Olhado tried. It didn't work.

"Try typing 'Jane.' "

"Nothing."

The Speaker grimaced. "Try 'Ender.' "

"Ender? The Xenocide?"

"Just try it."

It worked. Olhado didn't get it. "Why would you have a password like that? It's like having a dirty word for your password, only the system won't accept any dirty words."

"I have an ugly sense of humor," the Speaker answered. "And my slave program, as you call it, has an even worse one."

Olhado laughed. "Right. A program with a sense of humor." The current balance in liquid funds appeared on the screen. Olhado had never seen so large a number in his life. "OK, so maybe the computer *can* tell a joke."

"That's how much money I have?"

"It's got to be an error."

"Well, I've done a lot of lightspeed travel. Some of my investments must have turned out well while I was en route."

The numbers were real. The Speaker for the Dead was richer than Olhado had ever thought anybody could possibly be. "I'll tell you what," said Olhado, "instead of paying me a wage, why don't you just give me a percentage of the interest this gets during the time I work for you? Say, one thousandth of one percent. Then in a couple of weeks I can afford to buy Lusitania and ship the topsoil to another planet."

"It's not *that* much money."

"Speaker, the only way you could get that much money from investments is if you were a thousand years old."

"Hmm," said the Speaker.

And from the look on his face, Olhado realized that he had just said something funny. "*Are* you a thousand years old?" he asked.

"Time," said the Speaker, "time is such a fleeting, insubstantial thing. As Shakespeare said, 'I wasted time, and now doth time waste me.' "

"What does 'doth' mean?"

"It means 'does.' "

"Why do you quote a guy who doesn't even know how to speak Stark?"

"Transfer to your own account what you think a fair week's wage might be. And then start doing those comparisons of Pipo's and Libo's working files from the last few weeks before their deaths."

"They're probably shielded."

"Use my password. It ought to get us in."

Olhado did the search. The Speaker of the Dead watched

him the whole time. Now and then he asked Olhado a question about what he was doing. From his questions Olhado could tell that the Speaker knew more about computers than Olhado himself did. What he didn't know was the particular commands; it was plain that just by watching, the Speaker was figuring out a lot. By the end of the day, when the searches hadn't found anything in particular, it took Olhado only a minute to figure out why the Speaker looked so contented with the day's work. You didn't want results at all, Olhado thought. You wanted to watch how I *did* the search. I know what you'll be doing tonight, Andrew Wiggin, Speaker for the Dead. You'll be running your own searches on some other files. I may have no eyes, but I can see more than you think.

What's dumb is that you're keeping it such a secret, Speaker. Don't you know I'm on your side? I won't tell anybody how your password gets you into private files. Even if you make a run at the Mayor's files, or the Bishop's. No need to keep a secret from *me*. You've only been here three days, but I know you well enough to like you, and I like you well enough that I'd do anything for you, as long as it didn't hurt my family. And you'd never do anything to hurt my family.

Novinha discovered the Speaker's attempts to intrude in her files almost immediately the next morning. He had been arrogantly open about the attempt, and what bothered her was how far he got. Some files he had actually been able to access, though the most important one, the record of the simulations Pipo saw, remained closed to him. What annoyed her most was that he made no attempt at all to conceal himself. His name was stamped in every access directory, even the ones that any schoolchild could have changed or erased.

Well, she wouldn't let it interfere with her work, she

decided. He barges into my house, manipulates my children, spies on my files, all as if he had a *right*—

And so on and so on, until she realized she was getting no work done at all for thinking of vitriolic things to say to him when she saw him again.

Don't think about him at all. Think about something else. Miro and Ela laughing, night before last. Think of that. Of course Miro was back to his sullen self by morning, and Ela, whose cheerfulness lingered a bit longer, was soon as worried-looking, busy, snappish, and indispensible as ever. And Grego may have cried and embraced the man, as Ela told her, but the next morning he got the scissors and cut up his own bedsheets into thin, precise ribbons, and at school he slammed his head into Brother Adornai's crotch, causing an abrupt end to classwork and leading to a serious consultation with Dona Cristã. So much for the Speaker's healing hands. He may think he can walk into my home and fix everything he thinks I've done wrong, but he'll find some wounds aren't so easily healed.

Except that Dona Cristã also told her that Quara actually spoke to Sister Bebei in class, in front of all the other children no less, and why? To tell them that she had met the scandalous, terrible Falante pelos Mortos, and his name was Andrew, and he was every bit as awful as Bishop Peregrino had said, and maybe even worse, because he tortured Grego until he cried—and finally Sister Bebei had actually been forced to ask Quara to *stop* talking. That was something, to pull Quara out of her profound self-absorption.

And Olhado, so self-conscious, so detached, was now excited, couldn't stop talking about the Speaker at supper last night. Do you know that he didn't even know how to transfer money? And you wouldn't believe the awful password that he has—I thought the computers were supposed to reject words like that—no, I can't tell you, it's a secret—I was practically teaching him how to do *searches*—but I think he understands computers, he's not an *idiot* or anything—he said he used to have a slave program, that's why he's got that jewel in his ear—he told me I could pay myself anything I want, not that there's much to buy, but I can save it for when I get out on my own—I think he's really old. I think he remembers things from a long time ago. I think he speaks Stark as his native language, there aren't many people in the Hundred Worlds who actually grow up speaking it, do you think maybe he was born on Earth?

Until Quim finally screamed at him to shut up about that servant of the devil or he'd ask the Bishop to conduct an exorcism because Olhado was obviously *possessed*; and when Olhado only grinned and winked, Quim stormed out of the kitchen, out of the house, and didn't come back until late at night. The Speaker might as well *live* at our house, thought Novinha, because he keeps influencing the family even when he isn't there and now he's prying in my files and I won't have it.

Except that, as usual, it's my own fault, I'm the one who called him here, I'm the one who took him from whatever place he called home—he says he had a sister there—Trondheim, it was—it's my fault he's here in this miserable little town in a backwater of the Hundred Worlds, surrounded by a fence that still doesn't keep the piggies from killing everyone I love—

And once again she thought of Miro, who looked so much like his real father that she couldn't understand why no one accused her of adultery, thought of him lying on the hillside as Pipo had lain, thought of the piggies cutting him open with their cruel wooden knives. They will. No matter what I do, they will. And even if they don't, the day will come soon when he will be old enough to marry Ouanda, and then I'll have to tell him who he really is, and why they can never marry, and he'll know then that I did deserve all the pain that Cão inflicted on me, that he struck me with the hand of God to punish me for my sins.

Even me, thought Novinha. This Speaker has forced me to

think of things I've managed to hide from myself for weeks, months at a time. How long has it been since I've spent a morning thinking about my children? And with hope, no less. How long since I've let myself think of Pipo and Libo? How long since I've even noticed that I do believe in God, at least the vengeful, punishing Old Testament God who wiped out cities with a smile because they didn't pray to him—if Christ amounts to anything I don't know it.

Thus Novinha passed the day, doing no work, while her thoughts also refused to carry her to any sort of conclusion.

In midafternoon Quim came to the door. "I'm sorry to bother you, Mother."

"It doesn't matter," she said. "I'm useless today, anyway."

"I know you don't care that Olhado is spending his time with that satanic bastard, but I thought you should know that Quara went straight there after school. To his house."

"Oh?"

"Or don't you care about that either, Mother? What, are you planning to turn down the sheets and let him take Father's place completely?"

Novinha leapt to her feet and advanced on the boy with cold fury. He wilted before her.

"I'm sorry, Mother, I was so angry—"

"In all my years of marriage to your father, I never once permitted him to raise a hand against my children. But if he were alive today I'd ask him to give you a thrashing."

"You could ask," said Quim defiantly, "but I'd kill him before I let him lay a hand on me. You might like getting slapped around, but nobody'll ever do it to me!"

She didn't decide to do it; her hand swung out and slapped his face before she noticed it was happening.

It couldn't have hurt him very much. But he immediately burst into tears, slumped down, and sat on the floor, his back to Novinha. "I'm sorry, I'm sorry," he kept murmuring as he cried.

She knelt behind him and awkwardly rubbed his shoulders.

It occurred to her that she hadn't so much as embraced the boy since he was Grego's age. When did I decide to be so cold? And why, when I touched him again, was it a slap instead of a kiss?

"I'm worried about what's happening, too," said Novinha.

"He's wrecking everything," said Quim. "He's come here and everything's changing."

"Well, for that matter, Estevão, things weren't so very wonderful that a change wasn't welcome."

"Not *his* way. Confession and penance and absolution, that's the change we need."

Not for the first time, Novinha envied Quim's faith in the power of the priests to wash away sin. That's because you've never sinned, my son, that's because you know nothing of the impossibility of penance.

"I think I'll have a talk with the Speaker," said Novinha.

"And take Quara home?"

"I don't know. I can't help but notice that he got her talking again. And it isn't as if she likes him. She hasn't a good word to say about him."

"Then why did she go to his house?"

"I suppose to say something rude to him. You've got to admit that's an improvement over her silence."

"The devil disguises himself by seeming to do good acts, and then—"

"Quim, don't lecture me on demonology. Take me to the Speaker's house, and I'll deal with him."

They walked on the path around the bend of the river. The watersnakes were molting, so that snags and fragments of rotting skin made the ground slimy underfoot. That's my next project, thought Novinha. I need to figure out what makes these nasty little monsters tick, so that maybe I can find something useful to do with them. Or at least keep them from making the riverbank smelly and foul for six weeks out of the year. The only saving grace was that the snakeskins seemed to fertilize the soil; the soft rivergrass grew in thickest where the snakes molted. It was the only gentle, pleasant form of life native to Lusitania; all summer long people came to the riverbank to lie on the narrow strip of natural lawn that wound between the reeds and the harsh prairie grass. The snakeskin slime, unpleasant as it was, still promised good things for the future.

Quim was apparently thinking along the same lines. "Mother, can we plant some rivergrass near our house sometime?"

"It's one of the first things your grandparents tried, years ago. But they couldn't figure out how to do it. The rivergrass pollinates, but it doesn't bear seed, and when they tried to transplant it, it lived for a while and then died, and didn't grow back the next year. I suppose it just has to be near the water."

Quim grimaced and walked faster, obviously a little angry. Novinha sighed. Quim always seemed to take it so personally that the universe didn't always work the way he wanted it to.

They reached the Speaker's house not long after. Children were, of course, playing in the praça—they spoke loudly to hear each other over the noise.

"Here it is," said Quim. "*I* think you should get Olhado and Quara out of there."

"Thanks for showing me the house," she said.

"I'm not kidding. This is a serious confrontation between good and evil."

"Everything is," said Novinha. "It's figuring out which is which that takes so much work. No, no, Quim, I know you could tell me in detail, but—"

"Don't condescend to me, Mother."

"But Quim, it seems so natural, considering how you always condescend to me."

His face went tight with anger.

She reached out and touched him tentatively, gently; his shoulder tautened against her touch as if her hand were a poisonous spider. "Quim," she said, "don't ever try to teach me about good and evil. I've been there, and you've seen nothing but the map.''

He shrugged her hand away and stalked off. My, but I miss the days when we never talked to each other for weeks at a time.

She clapped her hands loudly. In a moment the door opened. It was Quara. "Oi, Mãezinha," she said, "também veio jogar?" Did you come to play, too?

Olhado and the Speaker were playing a game of starship warfare on the terminal. The Speaker had been given a machine with a far larger and more detailed holographic field than most, and the two of them were operating squadrons of more than a dozen ships at the same time. It was very complex, and neither of them looked up or even greeted her.

"Olhado told me to shut up or he'd rip my tongue out and make me eat it in a sandwich," said Quara. "So you better not say anything till the game's over."

"Please sit down," murmured the Speaker.

"You are butchered now, Speaker," crowed Olhado.

More than half of the Speaker's fleet disappeared in a series of simulated explosions. Novinha sat down on a stool.

Quara sat on the floor beside her. "I heard you and Quim talking outside," she said. "You were shouting, so we could hear everything."

Novinha felt herself blushing. It annoyed her that the Speaker had heard her quarreling with her son. It was none of his business. Nothing in her family was any of his business. And she certainly didn't approve of him playing games of warfare. It was so archaic and outmoded, anyway. There hadn't been any battles in space in hundreds of years, unless running fights with smugglers counted. Milagre was such a peaceful place that nobody even owned a weapon more dangerous than the Constable's jolt. Olhado would never see a battle in his life. And here he was caught up in a game of war. Maybe it was something evolution had bred into males of the species, the desire to blast rivals into little bits or mash them to the ground. Or maybe the violence that he saw in his home has made him seek it out in his play. My fault. Once again, my fault.

Suddenly Olhado screamed in frustration, as his fleet disappeared in a series of explosions. "I didn't see it! I can't believe you did that! I didn't even see it coming!"

"So, don't yell about it," said the Speaker. "Play it back and see how I did it, so you can counter it next time."

"I thought you Speakers were supposed to be like priests or something. How did you get so good at tactics?"

The Speaker smiled pointedly at Novinha as he answered. "Sometimes it's a little like a battle just to get people to tell you the truth."

Olhado leaned back against the wall, his eyes closed, as he replayed what he saw of the game.

"You've been prying," said Novinha. "And you weren't very clever about it. Is that what passes for 'tactics' among Speakers for the Dead?"

"It got you here, didn't it?" The Speaker smiled.

"What were you looking for in my files?"

"I came to Speak Pipo's death."

"I didn't kill him. My files are none of your business."

"You called me here."

"I changed my mind. I'm sorry. It still doesn't give you the right to—"

His voice suddenly went soft, and he knelt in front of her so that she could hear his words. "Pipo learned something from you, and whatever he learned, the piggies killed him because of it. So you locked your files away where no one could ever find it out. You even refused to marry Libo, just so he wouldn't get access to what Pipo saw. You've twisted and distorted your life and the lives of everybody you loved in order to keep Libo and now Miro from learning that secret and dying."

Novinha felt a sudden coldness, and her hands and feet began to tremble. He had been here three days, and already he knew more than anyone but Libo had ever guessed. "It's all lies," she said.

"Listen to me, Dona Ivanova. It didn't work. Libo died anyway, didn't he? Whatever your secret is, keeping it to yourself didn't save his life. And it won't save Miro, either. Ignorance and deception can't save anybody. *Knowing* saves them."

"Never," she whispered.

"I can understand your keeping it from Libo and Miro, but what am I to you? I'm nothing to you, so what does it matter if *I* know the secret and it kills me?"

"It doesn't matter at all if you live or die," said Novinha, "but you'll never get access to those files."

"You don't seem to understand that you don't have the right to put blinders on other people's eyes. Your son and his sister go out every day to meet with the piggies, and thanks to you, they don't know whether their next word or their next act will be their death sentence. Tomorrow I'm going with them, because I can't speak Pipo's death without talking to the piggies—"

"I don't want you to Speak Pipo's death."

"I don't care what you want, I'm not doing it for you. But I am begging you to let me know what Pipo knew."

"You'll never know what Pipo knew, because he was a good and kind and loving person who—"

"Who took a lonely, frightened little girl and healed the wounds in her heart." As he said it, his hand rested on Quara's shoulder.

It was more than Novinha could bear. "Don't you dare to compare yourself to him! Quara isn't an orphan, do you hear me? She has a mother, *me*, and she doesn't need *you*, none of us need you, none of us!" And then, inexplicably, she was crying. She didn't want to cry in front of him. She didn't want to be here. He was confusing everything. She stumbled to the door and slammed it behind her. Quim was right. He was like the devil. He knew too much, demanded too much, gave too much, and already they all needed him too much. How could he have acquired so much power over them in so short a time?

Then she had a thought that at once dried up her unshed tears and filled her with terror. He had said that Miro *and his sister* went out to the piggies every day. He knew. He knew all the secrets.

All except the secret that she didn't even know herself— the one that Pipo had somehow discovered in her simulation. If he ever got that, he'd have everything that she had hidden for all these years. When she called for the Speaker for the Dead, she had wanted him to discover the truth about Pipo; instead, he had come and discovered the truth about her.

The door slammed. Ender leaned on the stool where she had sat and put his head down on his hands.

He heard Olhado stand up and walk slowly across the room toward him.

"You tried to access Mother's files," he said quietly.

"Yes," said Ender.

"You got me to teach you how to do searches so that you could spy on my own mother. You made a traitor out of me."

There was no answer that would satisfy Olhado right now; Ender didn't try. He waited in silence as Olhado walked to the door and left.

The turmoil he felt was not silent, however, to the hive queen. He felt her stir in his mind, drawn by his anguish. No, he said to her silently. There's nothing you can do, nothing I can explain. Human things, that's all, strange and alien human problems that are beyond comprehension.

<Ah.> And he felt her touch him inwardly, touch him like the breeze in the leaves of a tree; he felt the strength and vigor of upward-thrusting wood, the firm grip of roots in earth, the gentle play of sunlight on passionate leaves. <See what we've learned from him, Ender, the peace that he

found.> The feeling faded as the hive queen retreated from his mind. The strength of the tree stayed with him, the calm of its quietude replaced his own tortured silence.

It had been only a moment; the sound of Olhado closing the door still rang in the room. Beside him, Quara jumped to her feet and skipped across the floor to his bed. She jumped up and bounced on it a few times.

"You only lasted a couple of days," she said cheerfully. "Everybody hates you now."

Ender laughed wryly and turned around to look at her. "Do *you?*"

"Oh, yes," she said. "I hated you first of all, except maybe Quim." She slid off the bed and walked to the terminal. One key at a time, she carefully logged on. A group of double-column addition problems appeared in the air above the terminal. "You want to see me do arithmetic?"

Ender got up and joined her at the terminal. "Sure," he said. "Those look hard, though."

"Not for me," she said boastfully. "I do them faster than anybody."

Chapter 13
Ela

MIRO: The piggies call themselves males, but we're only taking their word for it.

OUANDA: Why would they lie?

MIRO: I know you're young and naive, but there's some missing equipment.

OUANDA: I passed physical anthropology. Who says they do it the way we do it?

MIRO: Obviously they don't. (For that matter, WE don't do it at all.) Maybe I've figured out where their genitals are. Those bumps on their bellies, where the hair is light and fine.

OUANDA: Vestigial nipples. Even you have them.

MIRO: I saw Leaf-eater and Pots yesterday, about ten meters off, so I didn't see them WELL, but Pots was stroking Leaf-eater's belly, and I think those belly-bumps might have tumesced.

OUANDA: Or they might not.

MIRO: One thing for sure. Leaf-eater's belly was wet—the sun was reflected off it—and he was enjoying it.

OUANDA: This is perverted.

MIRO: Why not? They're all bachelors, aren't they? They're adults, but their so-called wives haven't introduced any of them to the joys of fatherhood.

OUANDA: I think a sex-starved zenador is projecting his own frustrations onto his subjects.

—Marcos Vladimir "Miro" Ribeira von Hesse and Ouanda Quenhatta, Figueira Mucumbi, Working Notes, 1970: 1:4:30

The clearing was very still. Miro saw at once that something was wrong. The piggies weren't *doing* anything. Just standing or sitting here and there. And *still;* hardly a breath. Staring at the ground.

Except Human, who emerged from the forest behind them. He walked slowly, stiffly around to the front. Miro felt Ouanda's elbow press against him, but he did not look at her. He knew she was thinking the same thing he thought. Is this the moment that they will kill us, as they killed Libo and Pipo?

Human regarded them steadily for several minutes. It was unnerving to have him wait so long. But Miro and Ouanda were disciplined. They said nothing, did not even let their faces change from the relaxed, meaningless expression they had practiced for so many years. The art of noncommunication was the first one they had to learn before Libo would let either of them come with him. Until their faces showed nothing, until they did not even perspire visibly under emotional stress, no piggy would see them. As if it did any good— Human was too adroit at turning evasions into answers, gleaning facts from empty statements. Even their absolute stillness no doubt communicated their fear, but out of that circle there could be no escape. Everything communicated something.

"You have lied to us," said Human.

Don't answer, Miro said silently, and Ouanda was as wordless as if she had heard him. No doubt she was also thinking the same message to him.

"Rooter says that the Speaker for the Dead wants to come to us."

It was the most maddening thing about the piggies. Whenever they had something outrageous to say, they always blamed it on some dead piggy who couldn't possibly have said it. No doubt there was some religious ritual involved: Go to their totem tree, ask a leading question, and lie there contemplating the leaves or the bark or something until you get exactly the answer you want.

"We never said otherwise," said Miro.

Ouanda breathed a little more quickly.

"You said he wouldn't come."

"That's right," said Miro. "He wouldn't. He has to obey the law just like anyone else. If he tried to pass through the gate without permission—"

"That's a lie."

Miro fell silent.

"It's the law," said Ouanda quietly.

"The law has been twisted before this," said Human. "You could bring him here, but you don't. Everything depends on you bringing him here. Rooter says the hive queen can't give us her gifts unless he comes."

Miro quelled his impatience. The hive queen! Hadn't he told the piggies a dozen times that all the buggers were killed? And now the dead hive queen was talking to them as much as dead Rooter. The piggies would be much easier to deal with if they could stop getting orders from the dead.

"It's the law," said Ouanda again. "If we even ask him to come, he might report us and we'd be sent away, we'd never come to you again."

"He won't report you. He wants to come."

"How do you know?",

"Rooter says."

There were times that Miro wanted to chop down the totem tree that grew where Rooter had been killed. Maybe then they'd shut up about what Rooter says. But instead they'd probably name some other tree Rooter and be outraged as well. Don't even admit that you doubt their religion, that was a textbook rule; even offworld xenologers, even *anthropologists* knew that.

"Ask him," said Human.

"Rooter?" asked Ouanda.

"He wouldn't speak to *you*," said Human. Contemptuously? "Ask the Speaker whether he'll come or not."

Miro waited for Ouanda to answer. She knew already what *his* answer would be. Hadn't they argued it out a dozen times in the last two days? He's a good man, said Miro. He's a fake, said Ouanda. He was good with the little ones, said Miro. So are child molesters, said Ouanda. I believe in him, said Miro. Then you're an idiot, said Ouanda. We can trust him, said Miro. He'll betray us, said Ouanda. And that was where it always ended.

But the piggies changed the equation. The piggies added great pressure on Miro's side. Usually when the piggies demanded the impossible he had helped her fend them off. But this was not impossible, he did not want them fended off, and so he said nothing. Press her, Human, because you're right and this time Ouanda must bend.

Feeling herself alone, knowing Miro would not help her, she gave a little ground. "Maybe if we only bring him as far as the edge of the forest."

"Bring him here," said Human.

"We can't," she said. "Look at you. Wearing cloth. Making pots. Eating bread."

Human smiled. "Yes," he said. "All of that. Bring him here."

"No," said Ouanda.

Miro flinched, stopping himself from reaching out to her. It was the one thing they had never done—flatly denied a request. Always it was "We can't because" or "I wish we could." But the single word of denial said to them, I *will* not. I, of myself, refuse.

Human's smile faded. "Pipo told us that women do not say. Pipo told us that human men and women decide together. So you can't say no unless he says no, too.'' He looked at Miro. "Do you say no?"

Miro did not answer. He felt Ouanda's elbow touching him.

"You don't say *nothing*," said Human. "You say yes or no."

Still Miro didn't answer.

Some of the piggies around them stood up. Miro had no idea what they were doing, but the movement itself, with Miro's intransigent silence as a cue, seemed menacing. Ouanda, who would never be cowed by a threat to herself, bent to the implied threat to Miro. "He says yes," she whispered.

"He says yes, but for you he stays silent. You say no, but you don't stay silent for *him*." Human scooped thick mucus out of his mouth with one finger and flipped it onto the ground. "You are nothing."

Human suddenly fell backward into a somersault, twisted in midmovement, and came up with his back to them, walking away. Immediately the other piggies came to life, moving swiftly toward Human, who led them toward the forest edge farthest from Miro and Ouanda.

Human stopped abruptly. Another piggy, instead of following him, stood in front of him, blocking his way. It was Leaf-eater. If he or Human spoke, Miro could not hear them or see their mouths move. He did see, though, that Leaf-eater extended his hand to touch Human's belly. The hand stayed there a moment, then Leaf-eater whirled around and scampered off into the bushes like a youngling.

In a moment the other piggies were also gone.

"It was a battle," said Miro. "Human and Leaf-eater. They're on opposite sides."

"Of what?" said Ouanda.

"I wish I knew. But I can guess. If we bring the Speaker, Human wins. If we don't, Leaf-eater wins."

"Wins what? Because if we bring the Speaker, he'll betray us, and then we all lose."

"He won't betray us."

"Why shouldn't he, if you'd betray *me* like that?"

Her voice was a lash, and he almost cried out from the sting of her words. "I betray you!" he whispered. "Eu não. Jamais." Not me. Never.

"Father always said, Be united in front of the piggies, never let them see you in disagreement, and you—"

"And *I*! I didn't say yes to them. You're the one who said no, you're the one who took a position that you knew I didn't agree with!"

"Then when we disagree, it's your job to—"

She stopped. She had only just realized what she was saying. But stopping did not undo what Miro knew she was going to say. It was his job to do what she said until she changed her mind. As if he were her *apprentice*. "And here I thought we were in this together." He turned and walked away from her, into the forest, back toward Milagre.

"Miro," she called after him. "Miro, I didn't mean that—"

He waited for her to catch up, then caught her by the arm and whispered fiercely, "Don't shout! Or don't you care whether the piggies hear us or not? Has the master Zenador decided that we can let them see *everything* now, even the master disciplining her apprentice?"

"I'm not the master, I—"

"That's right, you're not." He turned away from her and started walking again.

"But Libo was my *father,* so of course I'm the—"

"Zenador by blood right," he said. "Blood right, is that it? So what am I by blood right? A drunken wife-beating cretin?" He took her by the arms, gripping her cruelly. "Is that what you want me to be? A little copy of my paizinho?"

"Let go!"

He shoved her away. "Your apprentice thinks you were a fool today," said Miro. "Your apprentice thinks you should have trusted his judgment of the Speaker, and your apprentice thinks you should have trusted his assessment of how serious the piggies were about this, because you were stupidly wrong about both matters, and you may just have cost Human his life.''

It was an unspeakable accusation, but it was exactly what they both feared, that Human would end up now as Rooter had, as others had over the years, disemboweled, with a seedling growing out of his corpse.

Miro knew he had spoken unfairly, knew that she would not be wrong to rage against him. He had no right to blame her when neither of them could possibly have known what the stakes might have been for Human until it was too late.

Ouanda did not rage, however. Instead, she calmed herself visibly, drawing even breaths and blanking her face. Miro followed her example and did the same. "What matters," said Ouanda, "is to make the best of it. The executions have always been at night. If we're to have a hope of vindicating Human, we have to get the Speaker here this afternoon, before dark."

Miro nodded. "Yes," he said. "And I'm sorry."

"I'm sorry too," she said.

"Since we don't know what we're doing, it's nobody's fault when we do things wrong."

"I only wish that I believed a *right* choice were possible."

Ela sat on a rock and bathed her feet in the water while she waited for the Speaker for the Dead. The fence was only a few meters away, running along the top of the steel grillwork that blocked the people from swimming under it. As if anyone wanted to try. Most people in Milagre pretended the fence wasn't there. Never came near it. That was why she had asked the Speaker to meet her here. Even though the day was warm and school was out, children didn't swim here at Vila Última, where the fence came to the river and the forest came nearly to the fence. Only the soapmakers and potters and brickmakers came here, and they left again when the day's work was over. She could say what she had to say, without fear of anyone overhearing or interrupting.

She didn't have to wait long. The Speaker rowed up the river in a small boat, just like one of the farside farmers, who had no use for roads. The skin of his back was shockingly white; even the few Lusos who were light-complected enough to be called *loiros* were much darker-skinned. His whiteness made him seem weak and slight. But then she saw how quickly the boat moved against the current; how accurately the oars were placed each time at just the right depth, with a long, smooth pull; how tightly wrapped in skin his muscles were. She felt a moment's stab of grief, and then realized that it was grief for her father, despite the depth of her hatred for him; she had not realized until this moment that she loved anything about him, but she grieved for the strength of his shoulders and back, for the sweat that made his brown skin dazzle like glass in the sunlight.

No, she said silently, I don't grieve for your death, Cão. I grieve that you were not more like the Speaker, who has no connection with us and yet has given us more good gifts in three days than you in your whole life; I grieve that your beautiful body was so worm-eaten inside.

The Speaker saw her and skimmed the boat to shore, where she waited. She waded in the reeds and muck to help him pull the boat aground.

"Sorry to get you muddy," he said. "But I haven't used my body in a couple of weeks, and the water invited me—"

"You row well," she said.

"The world I came from, Trondheim, was mostly ice and water. A bit of rock here and there, some soil, but anyone who couldn't row was more crippled than if he couldn't walk."

"That's where you were born?"

"No. Where I last Spoke, though." He sat on the grama, facing the water.

She sat beside him. "Mother's angry at you."

His lips made a little half-smile. "She told me."

Without thinking, Ela immediately began to justify her mother. "You tried to read her files."

"I *read* her files. Most of them. All but the ones that mattered."

"I know. Quim told me." She caught herself feeling just a little triumphant that Mother's protection system had bested him. Then she remembered that she was not on Mother's side in this. That she had been trying for years to get Mother to open those very files to her. But momentum carried her on, saying things she didn't mean to say. "Olhado's sitting in the house with his eyes shut off and music blasting into his ears. Very upset."

"Yes, well, he thinks I betrayed him."

"Didn't you?" That was not what she meant to say.

"I'm a Speaker for the Dead. I tell the truth, when I speak at all, and I don't keep away from other people's secrets."

"I know. That's why I called for a Speaker. You don't have any respect for anybody."

He looked annoyed. "Why did you invite me here?" he asked.

This was working out all wrong. She was talking to him as if she were against him, as if she weren't grateful for what he had already done for the family. She was talking to him like the enemy. Has Quim taken over my mind, so that I say things I don't mean?

"You invited me to this place on the river. The rest of your family isn't speaking to me, and then I get a message from *you*. To complain about my breaches of privacy? To tell me I don't respect anybody?"

"No," she said miserably. "This isn't how it was supposed to go."

"Didn't it occur to you that I would hardly choose to be a Speaker if I had no respect for people?"

In frustration she let the words burst out. "I wish you had broken into *all* her files! I wish you had taken every one of

her secrets and published them through all the Hundred
Worlds!'' There were tears in her eyes; she couldn't think
why.

"I see. She doesn't let you see those files, either."

"Sou aprendiz dela, não sou? E porque choro, diga-me!
O senhor tem o jeito.''

"I don't have any knack for making people cry, Ela," he
answered softly. His voice was a caress. No, stronger, it was
like a hand gripping her hand, holding her, steadying her.
"Telling the truth makes you cry."

"Sou ingrata, sou má filha—"

"Yes, you're ungrateful, and a terrible daughter," he said,
laughing softly. "Through all these years of chaos and neglect you've held your mother's family together with little
help from her, and when you followed her in her career, she
wouldn't share the most vital information with you; you've
earned nothing but love and trust from her and she's replied
by shutting you out of her life at home and at work; and then
you finally tell somebody that you're sick of it. You're just
about the worst person I've ever known."

She found herself laughing at her own self-condemnation.
Childishly, she didn't want to laugh at herself. "Don't pa-
tronize me." She tried to put as much contempt into her
voice as possible.

He noticed. His eyes went distant and cold. "Don't spit at
a friend," he said.

She didn't want him to be distant from her. But she
couldn't stop herself from saying, coldly, angrily, "You
aren't my friend."

For a moment she was afraid he believed her. Then a smile
came to his face. "You wouldn't know a friend if you saw
one."

Yes I would, she thought. I see one now. She smiled back
at him.

"Ela," he said, "are you a good xenobiologist?"

"Yes."

"You're eighteen years old. You could take the guild tests at sixteen. But you didn't take them."

"Mother wouldn't let me. She said I wasn't ready."

"You don't have to have your mother's permission after you're sixteen."

"An apprentice has to have the permission of her master."

"And now you're eighteen, and you don't even need that."

"She's still Lusitania's xenobiologist. It's still her lab. What if I passed the test, and then she wouldn't let me into the lab until after she was dead?"

"Did she threaten that?"

"She made it clear that I wasn't to take the test."

"Because as soon as you're not an apprentice anymore, if she admits you to the lab as her co-xenobiologist you have full access—"

"To all the working files. To all the *locked* files."

"So she'd hold her own daughter back from beginning her career, she'd give you a permanent blot on your record— unready for the tests even at age eighteen—just to keep you from reading those files."

"Yes."

"Why?"

"Mother's crazy."

"No. Whatever else Novinha is, Ela, she is *not* crazy."

"Ela é boba mesma, Senhor Falante."

He laughed and lay back in the grama. "Tell me how she's boba, then."

"I'll give you the list. First: She won't allow any investigation of the Descolada. Thirty-four years ago the Descolada nearly destroyed this colony. My grandparents, Os Venerados, Deus os abençoe, they barely managed to stop the Descolada. Apparently the disease agent, the Descolada bodies, are still present—we have to eat a supplement, like an extra vitamin, to keep the plague from striking again. They told you that, didn't they? If you once get it in your system, you'll have to keep that supplement all your life, even if you leave here."

"I knew that, yes."

"She won't let me study the Descolada bodies *at all.* That's what's in *some* of the locked files, anyway. She's locked up all of Gusto's and Cida's discoveries about the Descolada bodies. Nothing's available."

The Speaker's eyes narrowed. "So. That's one-third of boba. What's the rest?"

"It's more than a third. Whatever the Descolada body is, it was able to adapt to become a human parasite ten years after the colony was founded. Ten years! If it can adapt once, it can adapt again."

"Maybe she doesn't think so."

"Maybe I ought to have a right to decide that for myself."

He put out a hand, rested it on her knee, calmed her. "I agree with you. But go on. The second reason she's boba."

"She won't allow any theoretical research. No taxonomy. No evolutionary models. If I ever try to do any, she says I obviously don't have enough to do and weighs me down with assignments until she thinks I've given up."

"You haven't given up, I take it."

"That's what xenobiology's *for.* Oh, yes, fine that she can make a potato that makes maximum use of the ambient nutrients. Wonderful that she made a breed of amaranth that makes the colony protein self-sufficient with only ten acres under cultivation. But that's all molecular *juggling.*"

"It's survival."

"But we don't *know* anything. It's like swimming on the top of the ocean. You get very comfortable, you can move around a little, but you don't know if there are sharks down there! We could be surrounded by sharks and she doesn't want to find out."

"Third thing?"

"She won't exchange information with the Zenadors. Period. Nothing. And that really *is* crazy. *We* can't leave the

fenced area. That means that we don't have a *single tree* we
can study. We know absolutely nothing about the flora and
fauna of this world except what happened to be included
inside the fence. One herd of cabra and a bunch of capim
grass, and then a slightly different riverside ecology, and
that's everything. Nothing about the kinds of animals in the
forest, no information exchange at all. We don't tell them
anything, and if they send us data we erase the files unread.
It's like she built this wall around us that nothing could get
through. Nothing gets in, nothing goes out.''

"Maybe she has reasons."

"Of course she has reasons. Crazy people always have
reasons. For one thing, she hated Libo. *Hated* him. She
wouldn't let Miro talk about him, wouldn't let us play with
his children—China and I were best friends for years and she
wouldn't let me bring her home or go to her house after
school. And when Miro apprenticed to him, she didn't speak
to him or set his place at the table for a year."

She could see that the Speaker doubted her, thought she
was exaggerating.

"I mean one year. The day he went to the Zenador's
Station for the first time as Libo's apprentice, he came home
and she didn't speak to him, not a word, and when he sat
down to dinner she removed the plate from in front of his
face, just cleaned up his silverware as if he weren't there. He
sat there through the entire meal, just looking at her. Until
Father got angry at him for being rude and told him to leave
the room."

"What did he do, move out?"

"No. You don't know Miro!" Ela laughed bitterly. "He
doesn't fight, but he doesn't give up, either. He never answered Father's abuse, never. In all my life I don't remember
hearing him answer anger with anger. And Mother—well, he
came home *every night* from the Zenador's Station and sat
down where a plate was set, and every night Mother took up
his plate and silverware, and he sat there till Father made him

leave. Of course, within a week Father was yelling at him to get out as soon as Mother reached for his plate. Father loved it, the bastard, he thought it was great, he hated Miro so much, and finally Mother was on his side against Miro.''

"Who gave in?"

"Nobody gave in.'' Ela looked at the river, realizing how terrible this all sounded, realizing that she was shaming her family in front of a stranger. But he wasn't a stranger, was he? Because Quara was talking again, and Olhado was involved in things again, and Grego, for just a short time, Grego had been almost a normal boy. He wasn't a stranger.

"How did it end?'' asked the Speaker.

"It ended when the piggies killed Libo. That's how much Mother hated the man. When he died she celebrated by forgiving her son. That night when Miro came home, it was after dinner was over, it was late at night. A terrible night, everybody was so afraid, the piggies seemed so awful, and everybody loved Libo so much—except Mother, of course. Mother waited up for Miro. He came in and went into the kitchen and sat down at the table, and Mother put a plate down in front of him, put food on the plate. Didn't say a word. He ate it, too. Not a word about it. As if the year before hadn't happened. I woke up in the middle of the night because I could hear Miro throwing up and crying in the bathroom. I don't think anybody else heard, and I didn't go to him because I didn't think he wanted anybody to hear him. Now I think I should have gone, but I was afraid. There were such terrible things in my family.''

The Speaker nodded.

"I should have gone to him,'' Ela said again.

"Yes,'' the Speaker said. "You should have.''

A strange thing happened then. The Speaker agreed with her that she had made a mistake that night, and she knew when he said the words that it was true, that his judgment was correct. And yet she felt strangely healed, as if simply saying her mistake were enough to purge some of the pain of it. For the first time, then, she caught a glimpse of what the power of Speaking might be. It wasn't a matter of confession, penance, and absolution, like the priests offered. It was something else entirely. Telling the story of who she was, and then realizing that she was no longer the same person. That she had made a mistake, and the mistake had changed her, and now she would not make the mistake again because she had become someone else, someone less afraid, someone more compassionate.

If I'm not that frightened girl who heard her brother in desperate pain and dared not go to him, who am I? But the water flowing through the grillwork under the fence held no answers. Maybe she couldn't know who she was today. Maybe it was enough to know that she was no longer who she was before.

Still the Speaker lay there on the grama, looking at the clouds coming darkly out of the west. "I've told you all I know," Ela said. "I told you what was in those files—the Descolada information. That's all I know."

"No it isn't," said the Speaker.

"It is, I promise."

"Do you mean to say that you obeyed her? That when your mother told you not to do any theoretical work, you simply turned off your mind and did what she wanted?"

Ela giggled. "She thinks so."

"But you didn't."

"I'm a scientist, even if she isn't."

"She was once," said the Speaker. "She passed her tests when she was thirteen."

"I know," said Ela.

"And she used to share information with Pipo before he died."

"I know that, too. It was just Libo that she hated."

"So tell me, Ela. What have you discovered in your theoretical work?"

"I haven't discovered any answers. But at least I know

what some of the questions are. That's a start, isn't it?
Nobody else is asking questions. It's so funny, isn't it? Miro
says the framling xenologers are always pestering him and
Ouanda for more information, more data, and yet the law
forbids them from learning anything more. And yet not a
single framling xenobiologist has ever asked us for *any* information. They all just study the biosphere on their own planets
and don't ask Mother a single question. I'm the only one
asking, and nobody cares.''

"I care," said the Speaker. "I need to know what the
questions are.''

"OK, here's one. We have a herd of cabra here inside the
fence. The cabra can't jump the fence, they don't even touch
it. I've examined and tagged every single cabra in the herd,
and you know something? There's not one male. They're *all*
female.''

"Bad luck," said the Speaker. "You'd think they would
have left at least one male inside.''

"It doesn't matter," said Ela. "I don't know if there *are*
any males. In the last five years every single adult cabra has
given birth at least once. And not one of them has mated.''

"Maybe they clone," said the Speaker.

"The offspring is not genetically identical to the mother.
That much research I could sneak into the lab without Mother
noticing. There *is* some kind of gene transfer going on.''

"Hermaphrodites?''

"No. Pure female. No male sexual organs at all. Does that
qualify as an important question? Somehow the cabras are
having some kind of genetic exchange, without sex.''

"The theological implications alone are astounding.''

"Don't make fun.''

"Of which? Science or theology?''

"Either one. Do you want to hear more of my questions or
not?''

"I do," said the Speaker.

"Then try this. The grass you're lying on—we call it

grama. All the watersnakes are hatched here. Little worms so small you can hardly see them. They eat the grass down to the nub and eat each other, too, shedding skin each time they grow larger. Then all of a sudden, when the grass is completely slimy with their dead skin, all the snakes slither off into the river *and they never come back out.*"

He wasn't a xenobiologist. He didn't get the implication right away.

"The watersnakes *hatch* here," she explained, "but they don't come back out of the water to lay their eggs."

"So they mate here before they go into the water."

"Fine, of course, obviously. I've seen them mating. That's not the problem. The problem is, *why are they watersnakes?*"

He still didn't get it.

"Look, they're completely adapted to life underwater. They have gills along with lungs, they're superb swimmers, they have fins for guidance, they are completely evolved for adult life in the water. Why would they ever have evolved that way if they are born on land, mate on land, and *reproduce* on land? As far as evolution is concerned, anything that happens after you reproduce is completely irrelevant, except if you nurture your young, and the watersnakes definitely don't nurture. Living in the water does nothing to enhance their ability to survive until they reproduce. They could slither into the water and *drown* and it wouldn't matter because reproduction is *over.*"

"Yes," said the Speaker. "I see now."

"There are little clear eggs in the water, though. I've never seen a watersnake lay them, but since there's no other animal in or near the river large enough to lay the eggs, it seems logical that they're watersnake eggs. Only these big clear eggs—a centimeter across—they're completely sterile. The nutrients are there, everything's ready, but there's no embryo. Nothing. Some of them have a gamete—half a set of genes in a cell, ready to combine—but not a single one was alive. And we've never found watersnake eggs on land. One

day there's nothing there but grama, getting riper and riper;
the next day the grama stalks are crawling with baby watersnakes. Does this sound like a question worth exploring?''

"It sounds like spontaneous generation to me."

"Yes, well, I'd like to find enough information to test
some alternate hypotheses, but Mother won't let me. I asked
her about this one and she made me take over the whole
amaranth testing process so I wouldn't have time to muck
around in the river. And another question. Why are there so
few species here? On every other planet, even some of the
nearly desert ones like Trondheim, there are thousands of
different species, at least in the water. Here there's hardly a
handful, as far as I can tell. The xingadora are the only birds
we've seen. The suckflies are the only flies. The cabra are the
only ruminants eating the capim grass. Except for the cabras,
the piggies are the only large animals we've seen. Only one
species of tree. Only one species of grass on the prairie, the
capim; and the only other competing plant is the tropeça, a
long vine that wanders along the ground for meters and
meters—the xingadora make their nests out of the vine.
That's it. The xingadora eat the suckflies and nothing else.
The suckflies eat the algae along the edge of the river. And
our garbage, and that's it. Nothing eats the xingadora. Nothing eats the cabra.''

"Very limited," said the Speaker.

"Impossibly limited. There are ten thousand ecological
niches here that are completely unfilled. There's no way that
evolution could leave this world so sparse."

"Unless there was a disaster."

"Exactly."

"Something that wiped out all but a handful of species that
were able to adapt."

"Yes," said Ela. "You see? And I have proof. The cabras
have a huddling behavior pattern. When you come up on
them, when they smell you, they circle with the adults facing

inward, so they can kick out at the intruder and protect the young.''

"Lots of herd animals do that.''

"Protect them from what? The piggies are completely sylvan—they *never* hunt on the prairie. Whatever the predator was that forced the cabra to develop that behavior pattern, it's gone. And only recently—in the last hundred thousand years, the last million years maybe.''

"There's no evidence of any meteor falls more recent than twenty million years,'' said the Speaker.

"No. That kind of disaster would kill off all the big animals and plants and leave hundreds of small ones, or maybe kill all land life and leave only the sea. But land, sea, all the environments were stripped, and yet some big creatures survived. No, I think it was a disease. A disease that struck across all species boundaries, that could adapt itself to any living thing. Of course, we wouldn't notice that disease now because all the species left alive have adapted to it. It would be part of their regular life pattern. The only way we'd notice the disease—''

"Is if we caught it,'' said the Speaker. "The Descolada.''

"You see? Everything comes back to the Descolada. My grandparents found a way to stop it from killing humans, but it took the best genetic manipulation. The cabra, the watersnakes, they also found ways to adapt, and I doubt it was with dietary supplements. I think it all ties in together. The weird reproductive anomalies, the emptiness of the ecosystem, it all comes back to the Descolada bodies, and Mother won't let me examine them. She won't let me study what they are, how they work, how they might be involved with—''

"With the piggies.''

"Well, of course, but not just them, *all* the animals—''

The Speaker looked like he was suppressing excitement. As if she had explained something difficult. "The night that Pipo died, she locked the files showing all her current work, and she locked the files containing all the Descolada research. Whatever she showed Pipo had to do with the Descolada bodies, and it had to do with the piggies—''

"That's when she locked the files?'' asked Ela.

"Yes. Yes.''

"Then I'm right, aren't I.''

"Yes,'' he said. "Thank you. You've helped me more than you know.''

"Does this mean that you'll speak Father's death soon?''

The Speaker looked at her carefully. "You don't want me to Speak your father, really. You want me to Speak your mother.''

"She isn't dead.''

"But you know I can't possibly Speak Marcão without explaining why he married Novinha, and why they stayed married all those years.''

"That's right. I want all the secrets opened up. I want all the files unlocked. I don't want anything hidden.''

"You don't know what you're asking,'' said the Speaker. "You don't know how much pain it will cause if all the secrets come out.''

"Take a look at my family, Speaker,'' she answered. "How can the truth cause any more pain than the secrets have already caused?''

He smiled at her, but it was not a mirthful smile. It was—affectionate, even pitying. "You're right,'' he said, "completely right, but you may have trouble realizing that, when you hear the whole story.''

"I *know* the whole story, as far as it can be known.''

"That's what everybody thinks, and nobody's right.''

"When will you have the Speaking?''

"As soon as I can.''

"Then why not now? Today? What are you waiting for?''

"I can't do anything until I talk to the piggies.''

"You're joking, aren't you? Nobody can talk to the piggies except the Zenadors. That's by Congressional Order. Nobody can get past *that*.''

"Yes," said the Speaker. "That's why it's going to be hard."

"Not hard, impossible—"

"Maybe," he said. He stood; so did she. "Ela, you've helped me tremendously. Taught me everything I could have hoped to learn from you. Just like Olhado did. But he didn't like what I did with the things he taught me, and now he thinks I betrayed him."

"He's a kid. I'm eighteen."

The Speaker nodded, put his hand on her shoulder, squeezed. "We're all right then. We're friends."

She was almost sure there was irony in what he said. Irony and, perhaps, a plea. "Yes," she insisted. "We're friends. Always."

He nodded again, turned away, pushed the boat from shore, and splashed after it through the reeds and muck. Once the boat was fairly afloat, he sat down and extended the oars, rowed, and then looked up and smiled at her. Ela smiled back, but the smile could not convey the elation she felt, the perfect relief. He had listened to everything, and understood everything, and he would make everything all right. She believed that, believed it so completely that she didn't even notice that it was the source of her sudden happiness. She knew only that she had spent an hour with the Speaker for the Dead, and now she felt more alive than she had in years.

She retrieved her shoes, put them back on her feet, and walked home. Mother would still be at the Biologista's Station, but Ela didn't want to work this afternoon. She wanted to go home and fix dinner; that was always solitary work. She hoped no one would talk with her. She hoped there'd be no problem she was expected to solve. Let this feeling linger forever.

Ela was only home for a few minutes, however, when Miro burst into the kitchen. "Ela," he said. "Have you seen the Speaker for the Dead?"

"Yes," she said. "On the river."

"*Where* on the river!"

If she told him where they had met, he'd know that it wasn't a chance meeting. "Why?" she asked.

"Listen, Ela, this is no time to be suspicious, please. I've got to find him. We've left messages for him, the computer can't find him—"

"He was rowing downriver, toward home. He's probably going to be at his house soon."

Miro rushed from the kitchen into the front room. Ela heard him tapping at the terminal. Then he came back in. "Thanks," he said. "Don't expect me home for dinner."

"What's so urgent?"

"Nothing." It was so ridiculous, to say "nothing" when Miro was obviously agitated and hurried, that they both burst out laughing at once. "OK," said Miro, "it isn't nothing, it's something, but I can't talk about it, OK?"

"OK." But soon all the secrets will be known, Miro.

"What I don't understand is why he didn't get our message. I mean, the computer was paging him. Doesn't he wear an implant in his ear? The computer's supposed to be able to reach him. Of course, maybe he had it turned off."

"No," said Ela. "The light was on."

Miro cocked his head and squinted at her. "You didn't see that tiny red light on his ear implant, not if he just happened to be out rowing in the middle of the river."

"He came to shore. We talked."

"What about?"

Ela smiled. "Nothing," she said.

He smiled back, but he looked annoyed all the same. She understood: It's all right for you to have secrets from me, but not for me to have secrets from you, is that it, Miro?

He didn't argue about it, though. He was in too much of a hurry. Had to go find the Speaker, and *now*, and he wouldn't be home for dinner.

Ela had a feeling the Speaker might get to talk to the

piggies sooner than she had thought possible. For a moment she was elated. The waiting would be over.

Then the elation passed, and something else took its place. A sick fear. A nightmare of China's papai, dear Libo, lying dead on the hillside, torn apart by the piggies. Only it wasn't Libo, the way she had always imagined the grisly scene. It was Miro. No, no, it wasn't Miro. It was the Speaker. It was the Speaker who would be tortured to death. "No," she whispered.

Then she shivered and the nightmare left her mind; she went back to trying to spice and season the pasta so it would taste like something better than amaranth glue.

Chapter 14
Renegades

LEAF-EATER: Human says that when your brothers die, you bury them in the dirt and then make your houses out of that dirt. (Laughs.)
MIRO: No. We never dig where people are buried.
LEAF-EATER: (becomes rigid with agitation): Then your dead don't do you *any good at all!*

—Ouanda Quenhatta Figueira Mucumbi, Dialogue Transcripts, 103:0:1969:4:13:111

Ender had thought they might have some trouble getting him through the gate, but Ouanda palmed the box, Miro opened the gate, and the three of them walked through. No challenge. It must be as Ela had implied—no one wants to get out of the compound, and so no serious security was needed. Whether that suggested that people were content to stay in Milagre or that they were afraid of the piggies or that they hated their imprisonment so much that they had to pretend the fence wasn't there, Ender could not begin to guess.

Both Ouanda and Miro were very tense, almost frightened. That was understandable, of course, since they were breaking Congressional rules to let him come. But Ender suspected there was more to it than that. Miro's tension was coupled with eagerness, a sense of hurry; he might be frightened, but he wanted to see what would happen, wanted to go ahead.

241

Ouanda held back, walked a measured step, and her coldness was not just fear but hostility as well. She did not trust him.

So Ender was not surprised when she stepped behind the large tree that grew nearest the gate and waited for Miro and Ender to follow her. Ender saw how Miro looked annoyed for a moment, then controlled himself. His mask of uninvolvement was as cool as a human being could hope for. Ender found himself comparing Miro to the boys he had known in Battle School, sizing him up as a comrade in arms, and thought Miro might have done well there. Ouanda, too, but for different reasons: She held herself responsible for what was happening, even though Ender was an adult and she was much younger. She did not defer to him at all. Whatever she was afraid of, it was *not* authority.

"Here?" asked Miro blandly.

"Or not at all." said Ouanda.

Ender folded himself to sit at the base of the tree. "This is Rooter's tree, isn't it?" he asked.

They took it calmly—of course—but their momentary pause told him that yes, he had surprised them by knowing something about a past that they surely regarded as their own. I may be a framling here, Ender said silently, but I don't have to be an ignorant one.

"Yes," said Ouanda. "He's the totem they seem to get the most—direction from. Lately—the last seven or eight years. They've never let us see the rituals in which they talk to their ancestors, but it seems to involve drumming on the trees with heavy polished sticks. We hear them at night sometimes."

"Sticks? Made of fallen wood?"

"We assume so. Why?"

"Because they have no stone or metal tools to cut the wood—isn't that right? Besides, if they worship the trees, they couldn't very well cut them down."

"We don't think they worship the trees. It's totemic. They stand for dead ancestors. They—plant them. With the bodies."

Ouanda had wanted to stop, to talk or question him, but Ender had no intention of letting her believe she—or Miro, for that matter—was in charge of this expedition. Ender intended to talk to the piggies himself. He had never prepared for a Speaking by letting someone else determine his agenda, and he wasn't going to begin now. Besides, he had information they didn't have. He knew Ela's theory.

"And anywhere else?" he asked. "Do they plant trees at any other time?"

They looked at each other. "Not that we've seen," said Miro.

Ender was not merely curious. He was still thinking of what Ela had told him about reproductive anomalies. "And do the trees also grow by themselves? Are seedlings and saplings scattered through the forest?"

Ouanda shook her head. "We really don't have any evidence of the trees being planted anywhere but in the corpses of the dead. At least, all the trees we know of are quite old, except these three out here."

"Four, if we don't hurry," said Miro.

Ah. Here was the tension between them. Miro's sense of urgency was to save a piggy from being planted at the base of another tree. While Ouanda was concerned about something quite different. They had revealed enough of themselves to him; now he could let her interrogate him. He sat up straight and tipped his head back, to look up into the leaves of the tree above him, the spreading branches, the pale green of photosynthesis that confirmed the convergence, the inevitability of evolution on every world. Here was the center of all of Ela's paradoxes: evolution on this world was obviously well within the pattern that xenobiologists had seen on all the Hundred Worlds, and yet somewhere the pattern had broken down, collapsed. The piggies were one of a few dozen species that had survived the collapse. What was the Descolada, and how had the piggies adapted to it?

He had meant to turn the conversation, to say, Why are we

here behind this tree? That would invite Ouanda's questions.
But at that moment, his head tilted back, the soft green
leaves moving gently in an almost imperceptible breeze, he
felt a powerful déjà vu. He had looked up into these leaves
before. Recently. But that was impossible. There were no
large trees on Trondheim, and none grew within the compound of Milagre. Why did the sunlight through the leaves
feel so familiar to him?

"Speaker," said Miro.

"Yes," he said, allowing himself to be drawn out of his
momentary reverie.

"We didn't want to bring you out here." Miro said it
firmly, and with his body so oriented toward Ouanda's that
Ender understood that in fact Miro *had* wanted to bring him
out here, but was including himself in Ouanda's reluctance in
order to show her that he was one with her. You are in love
with each other, Ender said silently. And tonight, if I speak
Marcão's death tonight, I will have to tell you that you're
brother and sister. I have to drive the wedge of the incest
tabu between you. And you will surely hate me.

"You're going to see—some—" Ouanda could not bring
herself to say it.

Miro smiled. "We call them Questionable Activities. They
began with Pipo, accidentally. But Libo did it deliberately,
and we are continuing his work. It is careful, gradual. We
didn't just discard the Congressional rules about this. But there
were crises, and we had to help. A few years ago, for instance, the piggies were running short of macios, the bark
worms they mostly lived on then—"

"You're going to tell him that *first*?" asked Ouanda.

Ah, thought Ender. It isn't as important to her to maintain
the illusion of solidarity as it is to him.

"He's here partly to Speak Libo's death," said Miro.
"And this was what happened right before."

"We have no evidence of a causal relationship—"

"Let me discover causal relationships," said Ender quietly. "Tell me what happened when the piggies got hungry."

"It was the wives who were hungry, they said." Miro ignored Ouanda's anxiety. "You see, the males gather food for the females and the young, and so there wasn't enough to go around. They kept hinting about how they would have to go to war. About how they would probably all die." Miro shook his head. "They seemed almost happy about it."

Ouanda stood up. "He hasn't even promised. Hasn't promised anything."

"What do you want me to promise?" asked Ender.

"Not to—let any of this—"

"Not to tell on you?" asked Ender.

She nodded, though she plainly resented the childish phrase.

"I won't promise any such thing," said Ender. "My business is telling."

She whirled on Miro. "You see!"

Miro in turn looked frightened. "You can't tell. They'll seal the gate. They'll never let us through!"

"And you'd have to find another line of work?" asked Ender.

Ouanda looked at him with contempt. "Is that all you think xenology is? A job? That's another intelligent species there in the woods. Ramen, not varelse, and they must be *known*."

Ender did not answer, but his gaze did not leave her face.

"It's like the Hive Queen and the Hegemon," said Miro. "The piggies, they're like the buggers. Only smaller, weaker, more primitive. We need to study them, yes, but that isn't enough. You can study beasts and not care a bit when one of them drops dead or gets eaten up, but these are—they're like *us*. We can't just *study* their hunger, *observe* their destruction in war, we *know* them, we—"

"Love them," said Ender.

"Yes!" said Ouanda defiantly.

"But if you left them, if you weren't here at all, they wouldn't disappear, would they?"

"No," said Miro.

"I told you he'd be just like the committee," said Ouanda. Ender ignored her. "What would it cost them if you left?"

"It's like—" Miro struggled for words. "It's as if you could go back, to old Earth, back before the Xenocide, before star travel, and you said to them, You can travel among the stars, you can live on other worlds. And then showed them a thousand little miracles. Lights that turn on from switches. Steel. Even simple things—pots to hold water. Agriculture. They see you, they know what you are, they know that they can *become* what you are, do all the things that you do. What do they say—take this away, don't show us, let us live out our nasty, short, brutish little lives, let evolution take its course? No. They say, Give us, teach us, help us."

"And you say, I can't, and then you go away."

"It's too late!" said Miro. "Don't you understand? They've already seen the miracles! They've already seen us fly here. They've seen us be tall and strong, with magical tools and knowledge of things they never dreamed of. It's too late to tell them good-bye and go. They know what is possible. And the longer we stay, the more they try to learn, and the more they learn, the more we see how learning *helps* them, and if you have any kind of compassion, if you understand that they're—they're—"

"Human."

"Ramen, anyway. They're *our children,* do you understand that?"

Ender smiled. "What man among you, if his son asks for bread, gives him a stone?"

Ouanda nodded. "That's it. The Congressional rules say we have to give them stones. Even though we have so much bread."

Ender stood up. "Well, let's go on."

Ouanda wasn't ready. "You haven't promised—"

"Have you read the Hive Queen and the Hegemon?"

"I have," said Miro.

"Can you conceive of anyone choosing to call himself Speaker for the Dead, and then doing anything to harm these little ones, these pequeninos?"

Ouanda's anxiety visibly eased, but her hostility was no less. "You're slick, Senhor Andrew, Speaker for the Dead, you're very clever. You remind him of the Hive Queen, and speak scripture to me out of the side of your mouth."

"I speak to everyone in the language they understand," said Ender. "That isn't being slick. It's being clear."

"So you'll do whatever you want."

"As long as it doesn't hurt the piggies."

Ouanda sneered. "In *your* judgment."

"I have no one else's judgment to use." He walked away from her, out of the shade of the spreading limbs of the tree, heading for the woods that waited atop the hill. They followed him, running to catch up.

"I have to tell you," said Miro. "The piggies have been asking for you. They believe you're the very same Speaker who wrote the Hive Queen and the Hegemon."

"They've read it?"

"They've pretty well incorporated it into their religion, actually. They treat the printout we gave them like a holy book. And now they claim the hive queen herself is talking to them."

Ender glanced at him. "What does she say?" he asked.

"That you're the real Speaker. And that you've got the hive queen with you. And that you're going to bring her to live with them, and teach them all about metal and—it's really crazy stuff. That's the worst thing, they have such impossible expectations of you."

It might be simple wish fulfillment on their part, as Miro obviously believed, but Ender knew that from her cocoon the hive queen had been talking to *someone*. "How do they say the hive queen talks to them?"

Ouanda was on the other side of him now. "Not to them, just to Rooter. And Rooter talks to them. It's all part of their system of totems. We've always tried to play along with it, and act as if we believed it."

"How condescending of you," said Ender.

"It's standard anthropological practice," said Miro.

"You're so busy *pretending* to believe them, there isn't a chance in the world you could learn anything from them."

For a moment they lagged behind, so that he actually entered the forest alone. Then they ran to catch up with him. "We've devoted our lives to learning about them!" Miro said.

Ender stopped. "Not *from* them." They were just inside the trees; the spotty light through the leaves made their faces unreadable. But he knew what their faces would tell him. Annoyance, resentment, contempt—how dare this unqualified stranger question their professional attitude? This is how: "You're cultural supremacists to the core. You'll perform your Questionable Activities to help out the poor little piggies, but there isn't a chance in the world you'll notice when *they* have something to teach *you*."

"Like what!" demanded Ouanda. "Like how to murder their greatest benefactor, torture him to death after he saved the lives of dozens of their wives and children?"

"So why do you tolerate it? Why are you here helping them after what they did?"

Miro slipped in between Ouanda and Ender. Protecting her, thought Ender; or else keeping her from revealing her weaknesses. "We're professionals. We understand that cultural differences, which we can't explain—"

"You understand that the piggies are animals, and you no more condemn them for murdering Libo and Pipo than you would condemn a cabra for chewing up capim."

"That's right," said Miro.

Ender smiled. "And that's why you'll never learn anything from them. Because you think of them as animals."

"We think of them as ramen!" said Ouanda, pushing in front of Miro. Obviously she was not interested in being protected.

"You treat them as if they were not responsible for their own actions," said Ender. "Ramen are responsible for what they do."

"What are *you* going to do?" asked Ouanda sarcastically. "Come in and put them on trial?"

"I'll tell you this. The piggies have learned more about me from dead Rooter than you have learned from having me with you."

"What's *that* supposed to mean? That you really *are* the original Speaker?" Miro obviously regarded it as the most ridiculous proposition imaginable. "And I suppose you really do have a bunch of buggers up there in your starship circling Lusitania, so you can bring them down and—"

"What it means," interrupted Ouanda, "is that this amateur thinks he's better qualified to deal with the piggies than we are. And as far as I'm concerned that's proof that we should never have agreed to bring him to—"

At that moment Ouanda stopped talking, for a piggy had emerged from the underbrush. Smaller than Ender had expected. Its odor, while not wholly unpleasant, was certainly stronger than Jane's computer simulation could ever imply. "Too late," Ender murmured. "I think we're already meeting."

The piggy's expression, if he had one, was completely unreadable to Ender. Miro and Ouanda, however, could understand something of his unspoken language. "He's astonished," Ouanda murmured. By telling Ender that she understood what he did not, she was putting him in his place. That was fine. Ender knew he was a novice here. He also hoped, however, that he had stirred them a little from their normal, unquestioned way of thinking. It was obvious that they were following in well-established patterns. If he was to get any real help from them, they would have to break out of those old patterns and reach new conclusions.

"Leaf-eater," said Miro.

Leaf-eater did not take his eyes off Ender. "Speaker for the Dead," he said.

"We brought him," said Ouanda.

Leaf-eater turned and disappeared among the bushes.

"What does that mean?" Ender asked. "That he left?"

"You mean you haven't already figured it out?" asked Ouanda.

"Whether you like it or not," said Ender, "the piggies want to speak to me and I will speak to them. I think it will work out better if you help me understand what's going on. Or don't you understand it either?"

He watched them struggle with their annoyance. And then, to Ender's relief, Miro made a decision. Instead of answering with hauteur, he spoke simply, mildly. "No. We don't understand it. We're still playing guessing games with the piggies. They ask us questions, we ask them questions, and to the best of our ability neither they nor we have ever deliberately revealed a thing. We don't even ask them the questions whose answers we really want to know, for fear that they'll learn too much about us from our questions."

Ouanda was not willing to go along with Miro's decision to cooperate. "We know more than *you* will in twenty years," she said. "And you're crazy if you think you can duplicate what we know in a ten-minute briefing in the forest."

"I don't need to duplicate what you know," Ender said.

"You don't think so?" asked Ouanda.

"Because I have you with me." Ender smiled.

Miro understood and took it as a compliment. He smiled back. "Here's what we know, and it isn't much. Leaf-eater probably isn't glad to see you. There's a schism between him and a piggy named Human. When they thought we weren't going to bring you, Leaf-eater was sure he had won. Now his victory is taken away. Maybe we saved Human's life."

"And cost Leaf-eater his?" asked Ender.

"Who knows? My gut feeling is that Human's future is on the line, but Leaf-eater's isn't. Leaf-eater's just trying to make Human fail, not succeed himself."

"But you don't know."

"That's the kind of thing we never ask about." Miro smiled again. "And you're right. It's so much a habit that we usually don't even notice that we're not asking."

Ouanda was angry. "He's *right*? He hasn't even seen us at work, and suddenly he's a critic of—"

But Ender had no interest in watching them squabble. He strode off in the direction Leaf-eater had gone, and let them follow as they would. And, of course. they did, leaving their argument for later. As soon as Ender knew they were walking with him, he began to question them again. "These Questionable Activities you've carried out," he said as he walked. "You introduced new food into their diet?"

"We taught them how to eat the merdona root," said Ouanda. She was crisp and businesslike, but at least she was speaking to him. She wasn't going to let her anger keep her from being part of what was obviously going to be a crucial meeting with the piggies. "How to nullify the cyanide content by soaking it and drying it in the sun. That was the short-term solution."

"The long-term solution was some of Mother's cast-off amaranth adaptations," said Miro. "She made a batch of amaranth that was so well-adapted to Lusitania that it wasn't very good for humans. Too much Lusitanian protein structure, not enough Earthborn. But that sounded about right for the piggies. I got Ela to give me some of the cast-off specimens, without letting her know it was important."

Don't kid yourself about what Ela does and doesn't know, Ender said silently.

"Libo gave it to them, taught them how to plant it. Then

how to grind it, make flour, turn it into bread. Nasty-tasting stuff, but it gave them a diet directly under their control for the first time ever. They've been fat and sassy ever since.''

Ouanda's voice was bitter. ''But they killed Father right after the first loaves were taken to the wives.''

Ender walked in silence for a few moments, trying to make sense of this. The piggies killed Libo immediately after he saved them from starvation? Unthinkable, and yet it happened. How could such a society evolve, killing those who contributed most to its survival? They should do the opposite—they should reward the valuable ones by enhancing their opportunity to reproduce. That's how communities improve their chances of surviving as a group. How could the piggies possibly survive, murdering those who contribute most to their survival?

And yet there were human precedents. These children, Miro and Ouanda, with the Questionable Activities—they were better and wiser, in the long run, than the Starways committee that made the rules. But if they were caught, they would be taken from their homes to another world—already a death sentence, in a way, since everyone they knew would be dead before they could ever return—and they would be tried and punished, probably imprisoned. Neither their ideas nor their genes would propagate, and society would be impoverished by it.

Still, just because humans did it, too, did not make it sensible. Besides, the arrest and imprisonment of Miro and Ouanda, if it ever happened, *would* make sense if you viewed humans as a single community, and the piggies as their enemies; if you thought that anything that helped the piggies survive was somehow a menace to humanity. Then the punishment of people who enhanced the piggies' culture would be designed, not to protect the piggies, but to keep the piggies from developing.

At that moment Ender saw clearly that the rules governing human contact with the piggies did not really function to protect the piggies at all. They functioned to guarantee human superiority and power. From that point of view, by performing their Questionable Activities, Miro and Ouanda were traitors to the self-interest of their own species.

"Renegades," he said aloud.

"What?" said Miro. "What did you say?"

"Renegades. Those who have denied their own people, and claimed the enemy as their own."

"Ah," said Miro.

"We're not," said Ouanda.

"Yes we are," said Miro.

"I haven't denied my humanity!"

"The way Bishop Peregrino defines it, we denied our humanity long ago," said Miro.

"But the way I define it—" she began.

"The way you define it," said Ender, "the piggies are also human. That's *why* you're a renegade."

"I thought you said we treated the piggies like animals!" Ouanda said.

"When you don't hold them accountable, when you don't ask them direct questions, when you try to deceive them, then you treat them like animals."

"In other words," said Miro, "when we *do* follow the committee rules."

"Yes," said Ouanda, "yes, that's right, we are renegades."

"And you?" said Miro. "Why are you a renegade?"

"Oh, the human race kicked me out a long time ago. That's how I got to be a Speaker for the Dead."

With that they arrived at the piggies' clearing.

Mother wasn't at dinner and neither was Miro. That was fine with Ela. When either one of them was there, Ela was stripped of her authority; she couldn't keep control over the younger children. And yet neither Miro nor Mother took Ela's place, either. Nobody obeyed Ela and nobody else tried to keep order. So it was quieter, easier when they stayed away.

Not that the little ones were particularly well-behaved even now. They just resisted her less. She only had to yell at Grego a couple of times to keep him from poking and kicking Quara under the table. And today both Quim and Olhado were keeping to themselves. None of the normal bickering.

Until the meal was over.

Quim leaned back in his chair and smiled maliciously at Olhado. "So you're the one who taught that spy how to get into Mother's files."

Olhado turned to Ela. "You left Quim's face open again, Ela. You've got to learn to be tidier." It was Olhado's way of appealing, through humor, for Ela's intervention.

Quim did not want Olhado to have any help. "Ela's not on your side this time, Olhado. Nobody's on your side. You helped that sneaking spy get into Mother's files, and that makes you as guilty as he is. He's the devil's servant, and so are you."

Ela saw the fury in Olhado's body; she had a momentary image in her mind of Olhado flinging his plate at Quim. But the moment passed. Olhado calmed himself. "I'm sorry," Olhado said. "I didn't mean to do it."

He was giving in to Quim. He was admitting Quim was right.

"I hope," said Ela, "that you mean that you're sorry that you didn't mean to do it. I hope you aren't apologizing for helping the Speaker for the Dead."

"Of course he's apologizing for helping the spy," said Quim.

"Because," said Ela, "we should all help Speaker all we can."

Quim jumped to his feet, leaned across the table to shout in her face. "How can you say that! He was violating Mother's privacy, he was finding out her secrets, he was—"

To her surprise Ela found herself also on her feet, shoving

him back across the table, shouting back at him, and louder. "Mother's secrets are the cause of half the poison in this house! Mother's secrets are what's making us *all* sick, including her! So maybe the only way to make things right here is to steal all her secrets and get them out in the open where we can kill them!" She stopped shouting. Both Quim and Ohado stood before her, pressed against the far wall as if her words were bullets and they were being executed. Quietly, intensely, Ela went on. "As far as I'm concerned, the Speaker for the Dead is the only chance we have to become a family again. And Mother's secrets are the only barrier standing in his way. So today I told him everything I knew about what's in Mother's files, because I want to give him every shred of truth that I can find."

"Then you're the worst traitor of all," said Quim. His voice was trembling. He was about to cry.

"I say that helping the Speaker for the Dead is an act of loyalty," Ela answered. "The only real treason is obeying Mother, because what she wants, what she has worked for all her life, is her own self-destruction and the destruction of this family."

To Ela's surprise, it was not Quim but Olhado who wept. His tear glands did not function, of course, having been removed when his eyes were installed. So there was no moistening of his eyes to warn of the onset of crying. Instead he doubled over with a sob, then sank down along the wall until he sat on the floor, his head between his knees, sobbing and sobbing. Ela understood why. Because she had told him that his love for the Speaker was not disloyal, that he had not sinned, and he believed her when she told him that, he knew that it was true.

Then she looked up from Olhado to see Mother standing in the doorway. Ela felt herself go weak inside, trembling at the thought of what Mother must have overheard.

But Mother did not seem angry. Just a little sad, and very tired. She was looking at Olhado.

Quim's outrage found his voice. "Did you hear what Ela was saying?" he asked.

"Yes," said Mother, never taking her eyes from Olhado. "And for all I know she might be right."

Ela was no less unnerved than Quim.

"Go to your rooms, children," Mother said quietly. "I need to talk to Olhado."

Ela beckoned to Grego and Quara, who slid off their chairs and scurried to Ela's side, eyes wide with awe at the unusual goings-on. After all, even Father had never been able to make Olhado cry. She led them out of the kitchen, back to their bedroom. She heard Quim walk down the hall and go into his own room, slam the door, and hurl himself on his bed. And in the kitchen Olhado's sobs faded, calmed, ended as Mother, for the first time since he lost his eyes, held him in her arms and comforted him, shedding her own silent tears into his hair as she rocked him back and forth.

Miro did not know what to make of the Speaker for the Dead. Somehow he had always imagined a Speaker to be very much like a priest—or rather, like a priest was supposed to be. Quiet, contemplative, withdrawn from the world, carefully leaving action and decision to others. Miro had expected him to be wise.

He had not expected him to be so intrusive, so dangerous. Yes, he was wise, all right, he kept seeing past pretense, kept saying or doing outrageous things that were, when you thought about it, exactly right. It was as if he were so familiar with the human mind that he could see, right on your face, the desires so deep, the truths so well-disguised that you didn't even know yourself that you had them in you.

How many times had Miro stood with Ouanda just like this, watching as Libo handled the piggies. But always with Libo they had understood what he was doing; they knew his technique, knew his purpose. The Speaker, however, followed lines of thought that were completely alien to Miro.

Even though he wore a human shape, it made Miro wonder if Ender was really a framling—he could be as baffling as the piggies. He was as much a raman as they were, alien but still not animal.

What did the Speaker notice? What did he see? The bow that Arrow carried? The sun-dried pot in which merdona root soaked and stank? How many of the Questionable Activities did he recognize, and how many did he think were native practices?

The piggies spread out the Hive Queen and the Hegemon. "You," said Arrow, "you wrote this?"

"Yes," said the Speaker for the Dead.

Miro looked at Ouanda. Her eyes danced with vindication. *So the Speaker is a liar.*

Human interrupted. "The other two, Miro and Ouanda, they think you're a liar."

Miro immediately looked at the Speaker, but he wasn't glancing at them. "Of course they do," he said. "It never occurred to them that Rooter might have told you the truth."

The Speaker's calm words disturbed Miro. *Could* it be true? After all, people who traveled between star systems skipped decades, often centuries in getting from one system to another. Sometimes as much as half a millennium. It wouldn't take that many voyages for a person to survive three thousand years. But that would be too incredible a coincidence, for the original Speaker for the Dead to come here. Except that the original Speaker for the Dead *was* the one who had written the Hive Queen and the Hegemon; he *would* be interested in the first race of ramen since the buggers. *I don't believe it,* Miro told himself, but he had to admit the possibility that it might just be true.

"Why are they so stupid?" asked Human. "Not to know the truth when they hear it?"

"They aren't stupid," said the Speaker. "This is how humans are: We question all our beliefs, except for the ones we *really* believe, and those we never think to question. They never thought to question the idea that the original Speaker for the Dead died three thousand years ago, even though they know how star travel prolongs life.''

"But we told them.''

"No—you told them that the hive queen told Rooter that I wrote this book.''

"That's why they should have known it was true,'' said Human. "Rooter is wise, he's a father; he would never make a mistake.''

Miro did not smile, but he wanted to. The Speaker thought he was so clever, but now here he was, where all the important questions ended, frustrated by the piggies' insistence that their totem trees could talk to them.

"Ah,'' said Speaker. "There's so much that we don't understand. And so much that you don't understand. We should tell each other more.''

Human sat down beside Arrow, sharing the position of honor with him. Arrow gave no sign of minding. "Speaker for the Dead,'' said Human, "will you bring the hive queen to us?''

"I haven't decided yet,'' said the Speaker.

Again Miro looked at Ouanda. Was the Speaker insane, hinting that he could deliver what could not be delivered?

Then he remembered what the Speaker had said about questioning all our beliefs except the ones that we really believed. Miro had always taken for granted what everyone knew—that all the buggers had been destroyed. But what if a hive queen had survived? What if that was how the Speaker for the Dead had been able to write his book, because he had a bugger to talk to? It was unlikely in the extreme, but it was not *impossible*. Miro didn't know for sure that the last bugger had been killed. He only knew that everybody believed it, and that no one in three thousand years had produced a shred of evidence to the contrary.

But even if it was true, how could Human have known it? The simplest explanation was that the piggies had incorporated the powerful story of the Hive Queen and the Hegemon into their religion, and were unable to grasp the idea that there were many Speakers for the Dead, and none of them was the author of the book; that all the buggers were dead, and no hive queen could ever come. That was the simplest explanation, the one easiest to accept. Any other explanation would force him to admit the possibility that Rooter's totem tree somehow talked to the piggies.

"What will make you decide?" said Human. "We give gifts to the wives, to win their honor, but you are the wisest of all humans, and we have nothing that you need."

"You have many things that I need," said Speaker.

"What? Can't you make better pots than these? Truer arrows? The cape I wear is made from cabra wool—but your clothing is finer."

"I don't need things like that," said Speaker. "What I need are true stories."

Human leaned closer, then let his body become rigid in excitement, in anticipation. "O Speaker!" he said, and his voice was powerful with the importance of his words. "Will you add our story to the Hive Queen and the Hegemon?"

"I don't know your story," said the Speaker.

"Ask us! Ask us anything!"

"How can I tell your story? I only tell the stories of the dead."

"We are dead!" shouted Human. Miro had never seen him so agitated. "We are being murdered every day. Humans are filling up all the worlds. The ships travel through the black of night from star to star to star, filling up every empty place. Here we are, on our one little world, watching the sky fill up with humans. The humans build their stupid fence to keep us out, but that is nothing. The sky is our fence!" Human leapt upward—startlingly high, for his legs were powerful. "Look how the fence throws me back down to the ground!"

He ran at the nearest tree, bounded up the trunk, higher than Miro had ever seen him climb; he shinnied out on a limb and threw himself upward into the air. He hung there for an agonizing moment at the apex of his leap; then gravity flung him downward onto the hard ground.

Miro could hear the breath thrust out of him by the force of the blow. The Speaker immediately rushed to Human; Miro was close behind. Human wasn't breathing.

"Is he dead?" asked Ouanda behind him.

"No!" cried a piggy in the Males' Language. "You can't die! No no no!" Miro looked; to his surprise, it was Leaf-eater. "You can't die!"

Then Human reached up a feeble hand and touched the Speaker's face. He inhaled, a deep gasp. And then spoke, "You see, Speaker? I would die to climb the wall that keeps us from the stars."

In all the years that Miro had known the piggies, in all the years before, they had never once spoken of star travel, never once asked about it. Yet now Miro realized that all the questions they *did* ask were oriented toward discovering the secret of starflight. The xenologers had never realized that because they knew—knew without questioning—that the piggies were so remote from the level of culture that could build starships that it would be a thousand years before such a thing could possibly be in their reach. But their craving for knowledge about metal, about motors, about flying above the ground, it was all their way of trying to find the secret of starflight.

Human slowly got to his feet, holding the Speaker's hands. Miro realized that in all the years he had known the piggies, never once had a piggy taken him by the hand. He felt a deep regret. And the sharp pain of jealousy.

Now that Human was clearly not injured, the other piggies crowded close around the Speaker. They did not jostle, but they wanted to be near.

"Rooter says the hive queen knows how to build starships," said Arrow.

"Rooter says the hive queen will teach us everything,"

said Cups. "Metal, fire made from rocks, houses made from black water, everything."

Speaker raised his hands, fended off their babbling. "If you were all very thirsty, and saw that I had water, you'd all ask me for a drink. But what if I knew that the water I had was poisoned?"

"There is no poison in the ships that fly to the stars," said Human.

"There are many paths to starflight," said the Speaker. "Some are better than others. I'll give you everything I can that won't destroy you."

"The hive queen promises!" said Human.

"And so do I."

Human lunged forward, grabbed the Speaker by the hair and ears, and pulled him face to face. Miro had never seen such an act of violence; it was what he had dreaded, the decision to murder—

"If we are ramen," shouted Human into the Speaker's face, "then it is *ours* to decide, not yours! And if we are varelse, then you might as well kill us all right now, the way you killed all the hive queen's sisters!"

Miro was stunned. It was one thing for the piggies to decide this was the Speaker who wrote the book. But how could they reach the unbelievable conclusion that he was somehow guilty of the Xenocide? Who did they think he was, the monster Ender?

And yet there sat the Speaker for the Dead, tears running down his cheeks, his eyes closed, as if Human's accusation had the force of truth.

Human turned his head to speak to Miro. "What is this water?" he whispered. Then he touched the Speaker's tears.

"It's how we show pain or grief or suffering," Miro answered.

Mandachuva suddenly cried out, a hideous cry that Miro had never heard before, like an animal dying.

"That is how we show pain," whispered Human.

"Ah! Ah!" cried Mandachuva. "I have seen that water before! In the eyes of Libo and Pipo I saw that water!"

One by one, and then all at once, all the other piggies took up the same cry. Miro was terrified, awed, excited all at once. He had no idea what it meant, but the piggies were showing emotions that they had concealed from the xenologers for forty-seven years.

"Are they grieving for Papa?" whispered Ouanda. Her eyes, too, glistened with excitement, and her hair was matted with the sweat of fear.

Miro said it the moment it occurred to him: "They didn't know until this moment that Pipo and Libo were crying when they died."

Miro had no idea what thoughts then went through Ouanda's head; he only knew that she turned away, stumbled a few steps, fell to her hands and knees, and wept bitterly.

All in all, the coming of the Speaker had certainly stirred things up.

Miro knelt beside the Speaker, whose head was now bowed, his chin pressed against his chest. "Speaker," Miro said. "Como pode ser? How can it be, that you are the first Speaker, and yet you are also Ender? Não pode ser."

"She told them more than I ever thought she would," he whispered.

"But the Speaker for the Dead, the one who wrote this book, he's the wisest man who lived in the age of flight among the stars. While Ender was a murderer, he killed a whole people, a beautiful race of ramen that could have taught us everything—"

"Both human, though," whispered the Speaker.

Human was near them now, and he spoke a couplet from the Hegemon: "Sickness and healing are in every heart. Death and deliverance are in every hand."

"Human," said the Speaker, "tell your people not to grieve for what they did in ignorance."

"It was a terrible thing," said Human. "It was our greatest gift."

"Tell your people to be quiet, and listen to me."

Human shouted a few words, not in the Males' Language, but in the Wives' Language, the language of authority. They fell silent, then sat to hear what Speaker would say.

"I'll do everything I can," said the Speaker, "but first I have to know you, or how can I tell your story? I have to know you, or how can I know whether the drink is poisonous or not? And the hardest problem of all will still remain. The human race is free to love the buggers because they think the buggers all are dead. You are still alive, and so they're still afraid of you."

Human stood among them and gestured toward his body, as if it were a weak and feeble thing. "Of us!"

"They're afraid of the same thing you fear, when you look up and see the stars fill up with humans. They're afraid that someday they'll come to a world and find that you have got there first."

"We don't want to be there first," said Human. "We want to be there *too*."

"Then give me time," said the Speaker. "Teach me who you are, so that I can teach them."

"Anything," said Human. He looked around at the others. "We'll teach you anything."

Leaf-eater stood up. He spoke in the Males' Language, but Miro understood him. "Some things aren't yours to teach."

Human answered him sharply, and in Stark. "What Pipo and Libo and Ouanda and Miro taught us wasn't theirs to teach, either. But they taught us."

"Their foolishness doesn't have to be our foolishness." Leaf-eater still spoke in Males' Language.

"Nor does their wisdom necessarily apply to us," Human retorted.

Then Leaf-eater said something in Tree Language that Miro

could not understand. Human made no answer, and Leaf-eater walked away.

As he left, Ouanda returned, her eyes red from crying.

Human turned back to the Speaker. "What do you want to know?" he asked. "We'll tell you, we'll show you, if we can."

Speaker in turn looked at Miro and Ouanda. "What should I ask them? I know so little that I don't know what we need to know."

Miro looked to Ouanda.

"You have no stone or metal tools," she said. "But your house is made of wood, and so are your bows and arrows."

Human stood, waiting. The silence lengthened. "But what is your question?" Human finally said.

How could he have missed the connection? Miro thought.

"We humans," said Speaker, "use tools of stone or metal to cut down trees, when we want to shape them into houses or arrows or clubs like the ones I see some of you carrying."

It took a moment for the Speaker's words to sink in. Then, suddenly, all the piggies were on their feet. They began running around madly, purposelessly, sometimes bumping into each other or into trees or the log houses. Most of them were silent, but now and then one of them would wail, exactly as they had cried out a few minutes ago. It was eerie, the almost silent insanity of the piggies, as if they had suddenly lost control of their bodies. All the years of careful noncommunication, refraining from telling the piggies anything, and now Speaker breached that policy and the result was this madness.

Human emerged from the chaos and threw himself to the ground in front of Speaker. "O Speaker!" he cried loudly. "Promise that you'll never let them cut my father Rooter with their stone and metal tools! If you want to murder someone, there are ancient brothers who will give themselves, or I will gladly die, but don't let them kill my father!"

"Or *my* father!" cried the other piggies. "Or mine!"

"We would never have planted Rooter so close to the fence," said Mandachuva, "if we had known you were— were *varelse*."

Speaker raised his hands again. "Has any human cut a tree in Lusitania? Never. The law here forbids it. You have nothing to fear from us."

There was a silence as the piggies became still. Finally Human picked himself up from the ground. "You've made us fear humans all the more," he said to Speaker. "I wish you had never come to our forest."

Ouanda's voice rang out above his. "How can you say that after the way you murdered my father!"

Human looked at her with astonishment, unable to answer. Miro put his arm around Ouanda's shoulders. And the Speaker for the Dead spoke into the silence. "You promised me that you'd answer all my questions. I ask you now: How do you build a house made of wood, and the bow and arrows that this one carries, and those clubs. We've told you the only way we know; you tell me another way, the way you do it."

"The brother gives himself," said Human. "I told you. We tell the ancient brother of our need, and we show him the shape, and he gives himself."

"Can we see how it's done?" said Ender.

Human looked around at the other piggies. "You want us to ask a brother to give himself, just so you can see it? We don't need a new house, not for years yet, and we have all the arrows we need—"

"Show him!"

Miro turned, as the others also turned, to see Leaf-eater re-emerging from the forest. He walked purposefully into the middle of the clearing; he did not look at them, and he spoke as if he were a herald, a town crier, not caring whether anyone was listening to him or not. He spoke in the Wives' Language, and Miro could understand only bits and pieces.

"What is he saying?" whispered the Speaker.

Miro, still kneeling beside him, translated as best he could. "He went to the wives, apparently, and they said to do whatever you asked. But it isn't that simple, he's telling them that—I don't know these words—something about all of them dying. Something about brothers dying, anyway. Look at them—they aren't afraid, any of them."

"I don't know what their fear looks like," said Speaker. "I don't know these people at all."

"I don't either," said Miro. "I've got to hand it to you— you've caused more excitement here in half an hour than I've seen in years of coming here."

"It's a gift I was born with," said the Speaker. "I'll make you a bargain. I won't tell anybody about your Questionable Activities. And you don't tell anybody who I am."

"That's easy," said Miro. "I don't believe it anyway."

Leaf-eater's speech ended. He immediately padded to the house and went inside.

"We'll ask for the gift of an ancient brother," said Human. "The wives have said so."

So it was that Miro stood with his arm around Ouanda, and the Speaker standing at his other side, as the piggies performed a miracle far more convincing than any of the ones that had won old Gusto and Cida their title Os Venerados.

The piggies gathered in a circle around a thick old tree at the clearing's edge. Then, one by one, each piggy shimmied up the tree and began beating on it with a club. Soon they were all in the tree, singing and pounding out complex rhythms. "Tree Language," Ouanda whispered.

After only a few minutes of this the tree tilted noticeably. Immediately about half the piggies jumped down and began pushing the tree so it would fall into the open ground of the clearing. The rest began beating all the more furiously and singing all the louder.

One by one the great branches of the tree began to fall off. Immediately piggies ran out and picked them up, dragged them away from the area where the tree was meant to fall.

Human carried one to the Speaker, who took it carefully, and showed it to Miro and Ouanda. The raw end, where it had been attached to the tree, was absolutely smooth. It wasn't flat—the surface undulated slightly along an oblique angle. But there was no raggedness to it, no leaking sap, nothing to imply the slightest violence in its separation from the tree. Miro touched his finger to it, and it was cold and smooth as marble.

Finally the tree was a single straight trunk, nude and majestic; the pale patches where branches once had grown were brightly lit by the afternoon sun. The singing reached a climax, then stopped. The tree tilted and then began a smooth and graceful fall to the earth. The ground shook and thundered when it struck, and then all was still.

Human walked to the fallen tree and began to stroke its surface, singing softly. The bark split gradually under his hands; the crack extended itself up and down the length of the tree until the bark was split completely in half. Then many piggies took hold of it and prised it from the trunk; it came away on one side and the other, in two continuous sheets of bark. The bark was carried to the side.

"Have you ever seen them use the bark?" Speaker asked Miro.

Miro shook his head. He had no words to say aloud.

Now Arrow stepped forward, singing softly. He drew his fingers up and down the trunk, as if tracing exactly the length and width of a single bow. Miro saw how lines appeared, how the naked wood creased, split, crumbled until only the bow remained, perfect and polished and smooth, lying in a long trench in the wood.

Other piggies came forward, drawing shapes on the trunk and singing. They came away with clubs, with bows and arrows, thin-bladed knives, and thousands of strands of thin basketwood. Finally, when half the trunk was dissipated, they all stepped back and sang together. The tree shivered and split into half a dozen long poles. The tree was entirely used up.

Human walked slowly forward and knelt by the poles, his hands gently resting on the nearest one. He tilted back his head and began to sing, a wordless melody that was the saddest sound that Miro had ever heard. The song went on and on, Human's voice alone; only gradually did Miro realize that the other piggies were looking at him, waiting for something.

Finally Mandachuva came to him and spoke softly. "Please," he said. "It's only right that you should sing for the brother."

"I don't know how," said Miro, feeling helpless and afraid.

"He gave his life," said Mandachuva, "to answer your question."

To answer my question and then raise a thousand more, Miro said silently. But he walked forward, knelt beside Human, curled his fingers around the same cold smooth pole that Human held, tilted back his head, and let his voice come out. At first weak and hesitant, unsure what melody to sing; but soon he understood the reason for the tuneless song, felt the death of the tree under his hands, and his voice became loud and strong, making agonizing disharmonies with Human's voice that mourned the death of the tree and thanked it for its sacrifice and promised to use its death for the good of the tribe, for the good of the brothers and the wives and the children, so that all would live and thrive and prosper. That was the meaning of the song, and the meaning of the death of the tree, and when the song was finally over Miro bent until his forehead touched the wood and he said the words of extreme unction, the same words he had whispered over Libo's corpse on the hillside five years ago.

Chapter 15
Speaking

HUMAN: Why don't any of the other humans ever come see us?

MIRO: We're the only ones allowed to come through the gate.

HUMAN: Why don't they just climb over the fence?

MIRO: Haven't any of you ever touched the fence? (Human does not answer.) It's very painful to touch the fence. To pass over the fence would be like every part of your body hurting as bad as possible, all at once.

HUMAN: That's stupid. Isn't there grass on both sides?

—Ouanda Quenhatta Figueira Mucumbi, Dialogue Transcripts, 103:0:1970:1:1:5

The sun was only an hour from the horizon when Mayor Bosquinha climbed the stairs to Bishop Peregrino's private office in the Cathedral. Dom and Dona Cristães were already there, looking grave. Bishop Peregrino, however, looked pleased with himself. He always enjoyed it when all the political and religious leadership of Milagre was gathered under his roof. Never mind that Bosquinha was the one who called the meeting, and then she offered to have it at the Cathedral because she was the one with the skimmer. Peregrino liked the feeling that he was somehow the master of Lusitania

Colony. Well, by the end of this meeting it would be plain to them all that no one in this room was the master of anything. Bosquinha greeted them all. She did not sit down in the offered chair, however. Instead she sat before the Bishop's own terminal, logged in, and ran the program she had prepared. In the air above the terminal there appeared several layers of tiny cubes. The highest layer had only a few cubes; most of the layers had many, many more. More than half the layers, starting with the highest, were colored red; the rest were blue.

"Very pretty," said Bishop Peregrino.

Bosquinha looked over at Dom Cristão. "Do you recognize the model?"

He shook his head. "But I think I know what this meeting is about."

Dona Cristã leaned forward on her chair. "Is there any safe place where we can hide the things we want to keep?"

Bishop Peregrino's expression of detached amusement vanished from his face. "I *don't* know what this meeting is about."

Bosquinha turned around on her stool to face him. "I was very young when I was appointed to be Governor of the new Lusitania Colony. It was a great honor to be chosen, a great trust. I had studied government of communities and social systems since my childhood, and I had done well in my short career in Oporto. What the committee apparently overlooked was the fact that I was already suspicious, deceptive, and chauvinistic."

"These are virtues of yours that we have all come to admire," said Bishop Peregrino.

Bosquinha smiled. "My chauvinism meant that as soon as Lusitania Colony was mine, I became more loyal to the interests of Lusitania than to the interests of the Hundred Worlds or Starways Congress. My deceptiveness led me to pretend to the committee that on the contrary, I had the best interests of Congress at heart at all times. And my suspicion led me to believe that Congress was not likely to give Lusitania anything remotely like independent and equal status among the Hundred Worlds."

"Of course not," said Bishop Peregrino. "We are a colony."

"We are not a colony," said Bosquinha. "We are an experiment. I examined our charter and license and all the Congressional Orders pertaining to us, and I discovered that the normal privacy laws did not apply to us. I discovered that the committee had the power of unlimited access to all the memory files of every person and institution on Lusitania."

The Bishop began to look angry. "Do you mean that the committee has the right to look at the confidential files of the Church?"

"Ah," said Bosquinha. "A fellow chauvinist."

"The Church has some rights under the Starways Code."

"Don't be angry with *me*."

"You never told me."

"If I had told you, you would have protested, and they would have pretended to back down, and then I couldn't have done what I did."

"Which is?"

"This program. It monitors all ansible-initiated accesses to any files in Lusitania Colony."

Dom Cristão chuckled. "You're not supposed to do that."

"I know. As I said, I have many secret vices. But my program never found any major intrusion—oh, a few files each time the piggies killed one of our xenologers, that was to be expected—but nothing major. Until four days ago."

"When the Speaker for the Dead arrived," said Bishop Peregrino.

Bosquinha was amused that the Bishop obviously regarded the Speaker's arrival as such a landmark date that he instantly made such a connection. "Three days ago," said Bosquinha, "a nondestructive scan was initiated by ansible. It followed an interesting pattern.'' She turned to the terminal and changed the display. Now it showed accesses primarily in high-level areas, and limited to only one region of the display. "It accessed everything to do with the xenologers and xenobiologists of Milagre. It ignored all security routines as if they didn't exist. Everything they discovered, and everything to do with their personal lives. And yes, Bishop Peregrino, I believed at the time and I believe today that this had to do with the Speaker.''

"Surely *he* has no authority with Starways Congress," said the Bishop.

Dom Cristão nodded wisely. "San Angelo once wrote—in his private journals, which no one but the Children of the Mind ever read—"

The Bishop turned on him with glee. "So the Children of the Mind *do* have secret writings of San Angelo!"

"Not secret," said Dona Cristã. "Merely boring. Anyone can read the journals, but we're the only ones who bother."

"What he wrote," said Dom Cristão, "was that Speaker Andrew is older than we know. Older than Starways Congress, and in his own way perhaps more powerful."

Bishop Peregrino snorted. "He's a boy. Can't be forty years old yet."

"Your stupid rivalries are wasting time," said Bosquinha sharply. "I called this meeting because of an emergency. As a courtesy to *you*, because I have already acted for the benefit of the government of Lusitania."

The others fell silent.

Bosquinha returned the terminal to the original display. "This morning my program alerted me for a second time. Another systematic ansible access, only this time it was not the selective nondestructive access of three days ago. This time it is reading *everything* at data-transfer speed, which implies that all our files are being copied into offworld computers. Then the directories are rewritten so that a single ansible-initiated command will completely destroy every single file in our computer memories."

Bosquinha could see that Bishop Peregrino was surprised—and the Children of the Mind were not.

"Why?" said Bishop Peregrino. "To destroy all our files—this is what you do to a nation or a world that is—in rebellion, that you wish to destroy, that you—"

"I see," said Bosquinha to the Children of the Mind, "that you also were chauvinistic and suspicious."

"Much more narrowly than you, I'm afraid," said Dom Cristão. "But we also detected the intrusions. We of course copied all our records—at great expense—to the monasteries of the Children of the Mind on other worlds, and they will try to restore our files after they are stripped. However, if we are being treated as a rebellious colony, I doubt that such a restoration will be permitted. So we are also making paper copies of the most vital information. There is no hope of printing everything, but we think we may be able to print out enough to get by. So that our work isn't utterly destroyed."

"You knew this?" said the Bishop. "And you didn't tell *me*?"

"Forgive me, Bishop Peregrino, but it did not occur to us that you would not have detected this yourselves."

"And you also don't believe we do any work that is important enough to be worth printing out to save!"

"Enough!" said Mayor Bosquinha. "Printouts can't save more than a tiny percentage—there aren't enough printers in Lusitania to make a dent in the problem. We couldn't even maintain basic services. I don't think we have more than an hour left before the copying is complete and they are able to wipe out our memory. But even if we began this morning, when the intrusion started, we could not have printed out more than a hundredth of one percent of the files that we access every day. Our fragility, our vulnerability is complete."

"So we're helpless," said the Bishop.

"No. But I wanted to make clear to you the extremity of

our situation, so that you would accept the only alternative. It will be very distasteful to you."

"I have no doubt of that," said Bishop Peregrino.

"An hour ago, as I was wrestling with this problem, trying to see if there was any class of files that might be immune to this treatment, I discovered that in fact there was one person whose files were being completely overlooked. At first I thought it was because he was a framling, but the reason is much more subtle than that. The Speaker for the Dead *has* no files in Lusitanian memory."

"None? Impossible," said Dona Cristã.

"All his files are maintained *by ansible*. Offworld. All his records, all his finances, *everything*. Every message sent to him. Do you understand?"

"And yet he still has access to them—" said Dom Cristão.

"He is invisible to Starways Congress. If they place an embargo on all data transfers to and from Lusitania, his files will still be accessible because the computers do not see his file accesses as data transfers. They are original storage— yet they are not in Lusitanian memory."

"Are you suggesting," said Bishop Peregrino, "that we transfer our most confidential and important files as *messages* to that—that unspeakable infidel?"

"I am telling you that I have already done exactly that. The transfer of the most vital and sensitive government files is almost complete. It was a high priority transfer, at local speeds, so it runs much faster than the Congressional copying. I am offering you a chance to make a similar transfer, using my highest priority so that it takes precedence over all other local computer usage. If you don't want to do it, fine—I'll use my priority to transfer the second tier of government files."

"But he could look in our files," said the Bishop.

"Yes, he could."

Dom Cristão shook his head. "He won't if we ask him not to."

"You are naive as a child," said Bishop Peregrino. "There would be nothing to compel him even to give the data back to us."

Bosquinha nodded. "That's true. He'll have everything that's vital to us, and he can keep it or return it as he wishes. But I believe, as Dom Cristão does, that he's a good man who'll help us in our time of need."

Dona Cristã stood. "Excuse me," she said. "I'd like to begin crucial transfers immediately."

Bosquinha turned to the Bishop's terminal and logged into her own high priority mode. "Just enter the classes of files that you want to send into Speaker Andrew's message queue. I assume you already have them prioritized, since you were printing them out."

"How long do we have?" asked Dom Cristão. Dona Cristã was already typing furiously.

"The time is here, at the top." Bosquinha put her hand into the holographic display and touched the countdown numbers with her finger.

"Don't bother transferring anything that we've already printed," said Dom Cristão. "We can always type that back in. There's precious little of it, anyway."

Bosquinha turned to the Bishop. "I knew this would be difficult."

The Bishop gave one derisive laugh. "Difficult."

"I hope you'll consider carefully before rejecting this—"

"Rejecting it!" said the Bishop. "Do you think I'm a fool? I may detest the pseudo-religion of these blasphemous Speakers for the Dead, but if this is the only way God has opened for us to preserve the vital records of the Church, then I'd be a poor servant of the Lord if I let pride stop me from using it. Our files aren't prioritized yet, and it will take a few minutes, but I trust that the Children of the Mind will leave us enough time for our data transfers."

"How much time will you need, do you think?" asked Dom Cristão.

"Not much. Ten minutes at the most, I'd think."

Bosquinha was surprised, and pleasantly so. She had been afraid the Bishop would insist on copying all his files before allowing the Children of the Mind to go ahead—just one more attempt to assert the precedence of the bishopric over the monastery.

"Thank you," Dom Cristão said, kissing the hand that Peregrino extended to him.

The Bishop looked at Bosquinha coldly. "You don't need to look surprised, Mayor Bosquinha. The Children of the Mind work with the knowledge of the world, so they depend far more on the world's machines. Mother Church works with things of the Spirit, so our use of public memory is merely clerical. As for the Bible—we are so old-fashioned and set in our ways that we still keep dozens of leatherbound paper copies in the Cathedral. Starways Congress can't steal from us our copies of the word of God." He smiled. Maliciously, of course. Bosquinha smiled back quite cheerfully.

"A small matter," said Dom Cristão. "After our files are destroyed, and we copy them back into memory from the Speaker's files, what is to stop Congress from doing it again? And again, and again?"

"That is the difficult decision," said Bosquinha. "What we do depends on what Congress is trying to accomplish. Maybe they won't actually destroy our files at all. Maybe they'll immediately restore our most vital files after this demonstration of their power. Since I have no idea why they're disciplining us, how can I guess how far this will go? If they leave us any way to remain loyal, then of course we must also remain vulnerable to further discipline."

"But if, for some reason, they are determined to treat us like rebels?"

"Well, if bad came to worst, we could copy everything back into local memory and then—cut off the ansible."

"God help us," said Dona Cristã. "We would be utterly alone."

Bishop Peregrino looked annoyed. "What an absurd idea, Sister Detestai o Pecado. Or do you think that Christ depends upon the ansible? That Congress has the power to silence the Holy Ghost?"

Dona Cristã blushed and returned to her work at the terminal.

The Bishop's secretary handed him a paper with a list of files on it. "You can leave my personal correspondence off the list," said the Bishop. "I've already sent my messages. We'll let the Church decide which of my letters is worth preserving. They have no value to me."

"The Bishop is ready," said Dom Cristão. Immediately his wife arose from the terminal and the secretary took her place.

"By the way," said Bosquinha, "I thought you'd want to know. The Speaker has announced that this evening, in the praça, he'll Speak the death of Marcos Maria Ribeira." Bosquinha looked at her watch. "Very soon now, in fact."

"Why," said the Bishop acidly, "did you think that I would care?"

"I thought you might want to send a representative."

"Thank you for telling us," said Dom Cristão. "I think that I'll attend. I'd like to hear a Speaking by the man who Spoke the death of San Angelo." He turned to the Bishop. "I'll report to you on what he says, if you'd like."

The Bishop leaned back and smiled tightly. "Thank you, but one of my people will be in attendance."

Bosquinha left the Bishop's office and clattered down the stairs and out the Cathedral doors. She had to be back in her own rooms now, because whatever the Congress was planning, it would be Bosquinha who received their messages.

She had not discussed it with the religious leaders because it was really none of their business, but she knew perfectly well, at least in a general way, why Congress was doing this. The paragraphs that gave Congress the right to treat Lusitania like a rebellious colony were all tied to the rules dealing with contact with the piggies.

Obviously the xenologers had done something grossly wrong. Since Bosquinha had not known of any violations, it had to be something so big that its evidence showed up on the satellites, the only monitoring devices that reported directly to the committee without passing through Bosquinha's hands. Bosquinha had tried to think of what Miro and Ouanda might have done—start a forest fire? Cut down trees? Led a war between the piggy tribes? Anything she thought of sounded absurd.

She tried to call them in to question them, but they were gone, of course. Through the gate, out into the forest to continue, no doubt, the same activities that had brought the possibility of destruction to Lusitania Colony. Bosquinha kept reminding herself that they were young, that it might all be some ridiculous juvenile mistake.

But they weren't *that* young, and they were two of the brightest minds in a colony that contained many very intelligent people. It was a very good thing that governments under the Starways Code were forbidden to own any instruments of punishment that might be used for torture. For the first time in her life, Bosquinha felt such fury that she might use such instruments, if she had them. I don't know what you thought you were doing, Miro and Ouanda, and I don't know what you did; but whatever your purpose might have been, this whole community will pay the price for it. And somehow, if there were any justice, I would make you pay it back.

Many people had said they wouldn't come to any Speaking— they were good Catholics, weren't they? Hadn't the Bishop told them that the Speaker spoke with Satan's voice?

But other things were whispered, too, once the Speaker came. Rumors, mostly, but Milagre was a little place, where rumors were the sauce of a dry life; and rumors have no value unless they are believed. So word spread that Marcão's little girl Quara, who had been silent since he died, was now so talkative that it got her in trouble in school. And Olhado, that ill-mannered boy with the repulsive metal eyes, it was said that he suddenly seemed cheerful and excited. Perhaps manic. Perhaps possessed. Rumors began to imply that somehow the Speaker had a healing touch, that he had the evil eye, that his blessings made you whole, his curses could kill you, his words could charm you into obedience. Not everybody heard this, of course, and not everybody who heard it believed it. But in the four days between the Speaker's arrival and the evening of his Speaking the death of Marcos Maria Ribeira, the community of Milagre decided, without any formal announcement, that they would come to the Speaking and hear what the Speaker had to say, whether the Bishop said to stay away or not.

It was the Bishop's own fault. From his vantage point, calling the Speaker satanic put him at the farthest extreme from himself and all good Catholics: The Speaker is the opposite of us. But to those who were not theologically sophisticated, while Satan was frightening and powerful, so was God. They understood well enough the continuum of good and evil that the Bishop referred to, but they were far more interested in the continuum of strong and weak—that was the one they lived with day by day. And on that continuum, they were weak, and God and Satan and the Bishop all were strong. The Bishop had elevated the Speaker to stand with him as a man of power. The people were thus prepared to believe the whispered hints of miracles.

So even though the announcement came only an hour before the Speaking, the praça was full, and people gathered in the buildings and houses that fronted the praça, and crowded the grassy alleyways and streets. Mayor Bosquinha had—as the law required—provided the Speaker with the simple microphone that she used for the rare public meetings. People oriented themselves toward the platform where he would stand; then they looked around to see who was there. Everyone was there. Of course Marcão's family. Of course the Mayor. But also Dom Cristão and Dona Cristã, and many a robed priest from the Cathedral. Dr. Navio. Pipo's widow, old Conceição, the Archivist. Libo's widow, Bruxinha, and her children. It was rumored that the Speaker also meant to Speak Pipo's and Libo's deaths someday, too.

And finally, just as the Speaker stepped up onto the platform, the rumor swept the praça: Bishop Peregrino was here. Not in his vestments, but in the simple robes of a priest. Here himself, to hear the Speaker's blasphemy! Many a citizen of Milagre felt a delicious thrill of anticipation. Would the Bishop rise up and miraculously strike down Satan? Would there be a battle here such as had not been seen outside the vision of the Apocalypse of St. John?

Then the Speaker stood before the microphone and waited for them to be still. He was fairly tall, youngish still, but his white skin made him look sickly compared to the thousand shades of brown of the Lusos. Ghostly. They fell silent, and he began to Speak.

"He was known by three names. The official records have the first one: Marcos Maria Ribeira. And his official data. Born 1929. Died 1970. Worked in the steel foundry. Perfect safety record. Never arrested. A wife, six children. A model citizen, because he never did anything bad enough to go on the public record."

Many who were listening felt a vague disquiet. They had expected oration. Instead the Speaker's voice was nothing remarkable. And his words had none of the formality of religious speech. Plain, simple, almost conversational. Only a few of them noticed that its very simplicity made his voice, his speech utterly believable. He wasn't telling the Truth, with trumpets; he was telling the *truth,* the story that you wouldn't think to doubt because it's taken for granted. Bishop Peregrino was one who noticed, and it made him uneasy. This Speaker would be a formidable enemy, one who could not be blasted down with fire from before the altar.

"The second name he had was Marcão. Big Marcos. Because he was a giant of a man. Reached his adult size early in his life. How old was he when he reached two meters? Eleven? Definitely by the time he was twelve. His size and strength made him valuable in the foundry, where the lots of steel are so small that much of the work is controlled directly by hand, and strength matters. People's lives depended on Marcão's strength."

In the praça the men from the foundry nodded. They had all bragged to each other that they'd never talk to the framling atheist. Obviously one of them had, but now it felt good that the Speaker got it right, that he understood what they remembered of Marcão. Every one of them wished that he had been the one to tell about Marcão to the Speaker. They did not guess that the Speaker had not even tried to talk to them. After all these years, there were many things that Andrew Wiggin knew without asking.

"His third name was Cão. Dog."

Ah, yes, thought the Lusos. This is what we've heard about Speakers for the Dead. They have no respect for the dead, no sense of decorum.

"That was the name you used for him when you heard that his wife, Novinha, had another black eye, walked with a limp, had stitches in her lip. He was an animal to do that to her."

How dare he say that? The man's *dead*! But under their anger the Lusos were uncomfortable for an entirely different reason. Almost all of them remembered saying or hearing exactly those words. The Speaker's indiscretion was in repeating in public the words that they had used about Marcão when he was alive.

"Not that any of you liked Novinha. Not that cold woman who never gave any of you good morning. But she was smaller than he was, and she was the mother of his children, and when he beat her he deserved the name of Cão."

They were embarrassed; they muttered to each other. Those sitting in the grass near Novinha glanced at her and glanced away, eager to see how she was reacting, painfully aware of the fact that the Speaker was right, that they didn't like her, that they at once feared and pitied her.

"Tell me, is this the man you knew? Spent more hours in the bars than anybody, and yet never made any friends there, never the camaraderie of alcohol for him. You couldn't even tell how much he had been drinking. He was surly and short-tempered before he had a drink, and surly and short-tempered just before he passed out—nobody could tell the difference. You never heard of him having a friend, and none of you was ever glad to see him come into a room. That's the man you knew, most of you. Cão. Hardly a man at all."

Yes, they thought. That was the man. Now the initial shock of his indecorum had faded. They were accustomed to the fact that the Speaker meant to soften nothing in his story. Yet they were still uncomfortable. For there was a note of irony, not in his voice, but inherent in his words. "Hardly a man at all," he had said, but of course he *was* a man, and they were vaguely aware that while the Speaker understood what they thought of Marcão, he didn't necessarily agree.

"A few others, the men from the foundry in Bairro das Fabricadoras, knew him as a strong arm they could trust. They knew he never said he could do more than he could do, and always did what he said he would do. You could count on him. So within the walls of the foundry he had their respect. But when you walked out the door you treated him like everybody else—ignored him, thought little of him."

The irony was pronounced now. Though the Speaker gave no hint in his voice—still the simple, plain speech he began with—the men who worked with him felt it wordlessly inside themselves: We should not have ignored him as we did. If he had worth inside the foundry, then perhaps we should have valued him outside, too.

"Some of you also know something else that you never talk about much. You know that you gave him the name Cão long before he earned it. You were ten, eleven, twelve years old. Little boys. He grew so tall. It made you ashamed to be near him. And afraid, because he made you feel helpless.''

Dom Cristão murmured to his wife, "They came for gossip, and he gives them responsibility."

"So you handled him the way human beings always handle things that are bigger than they are," said the Speaker. "You banded together. Like hunters trying to bring down a mastodon. Like bullfighters trying to weaken a giant bull to prepare it for the kill. Pokes, taunts, teases. Keep him turning around. He can't guess where the next blow is coming from. Prick him with barbs that stay under his skin. Weaken him with pain. Madden him. Because big as he is, *you can make him do things*. You can make him yell. You can make him run. You can make him cry. See? He's weaker than you after all.''

Ela was angry. She had meant him to accuse Marcão, not excuse him. Just because he had a tough childhood didn't give him the right to knock Mother down whenever he felt like it.

"There's no blame in this. You were children then, and children are cruel without knowing better. You wouldn't do that now. But now that I've reminded you, you can easily see an answer. You called him a dog, and so he became one. For the rest of his life. Hurting helpless people. Beating his wife. Speaking so cruelly and abusively to his son Miro that he drove the boy out of his house. He was acting out the way you treated him, becoming what you told him that he was.''

You're a fool, thought Bishop Peregrino. If people only react to the way that others treat them, then nobody is responsible for anything. If your sins are not your own to choose, then how can you repent?

As if he heard the Bishop's silent argument, the Speaker raised a hand and swept away his own words. "But the easy answer isn't true. Your torments didn't make him violent—they made him sullen. And when you grew out of tormenting him, he grew out of hating you. He wasn't one to bear a grudge. His anger cooled and turned into suspicion. He knew you despised him; he learned to live without you. In peace.''

The Speaker paused a moment, and then gave voice to the question they silently were asking. "So how did he become the cruel man you knew him to be? Think a moment. Who was it who tasted his cruelty? His wife. His children. Some people beat their wife and children because they lust for power, but are too weak or stupid to win power in the world. A helpless wife and children, bound to such a man by need and custom and, bitterly enough, love, are the only victims he is strong enough to rule.''

Yes, thought Ela, stealing a glance at her mother. This is what I wanted. This is why I asked him to Speak Father's death.

"There are men like that," said the Speaker, "but Marcos Ribeira wasn't one of them. Think a moment. Did you ever hear of him striking any of his children? Ever? You who worked with him—did he ever try to force his will on you? Seem resentful when things didn't go his way? Marcão was not a weak and evil man. He was a strong man. He didn't want power. He wanted love. Not control. Loyalty.''

Bishop Peregrino smiled grimly, the way a duelist might salute a worthy opponent. You walk a twisted path, Speaker, circling around the truth, feinting at it. And when you strike, your aim will be deadly. These people came for entertainment, but they're your targets; you will pierce them to the heart.

"Some of you remember an incident," said the Speaker. "Marcos was maybe thirteen, and so were you. Taunting him on the grassy hillside behind the school. You attacked more viciously than usual. You threatened him with stones, whipped him with capim blades. You bloodied him a little, but he bore it. Tried to evade you. Asked you to stop. Then one of you struck him hard in the belly, and it hurt him more than you ever imagined, because even then he was already sick with the disease that finally killed him. He hadn't yet become accustomed to his fragility and pain. It felt like death to him. He was cornered. You were killing him. So he struck at you."

How did he know? thought half a dozen men. It was so long ago. Who told him how it was? It was out of hand, that's all. We never meant anything, but when his arm swung out, his huge fist, like the kick of a cabra—he was going to hurt me—

"It could have been any one of you that fell to the ground. You knew then that he was even stronger than you feared. What terrified you most, though, was that you knew exactly the revenge that you deserved. So you called for help. And when the teachers came, what did they see? One little boy on the ground, crying, bleeding. One large man-sized child with a few scratches here and there, saying I'm sorry, I didn't mean to. And a half-dozen others saying, He just hit him. Started killing him for no reason. We tried to stop him but Cão is so big. He's always picking on the little kids."

Little Grego was caught up in the story. "Mentirosos!" he shouted. They were lying! Several people nearby chuckled. Quara shushed him.

"So many witnesses," said the Speaker. "The teachers had no choice but to believe the accusation. Until one girl stepped forward and coldly informed them that she had seen it all. Marcos was acting to protect himself from a completely unwarranted, vicious, painful attack by a pack of boys who were acting far more like cães, like dogs, than Marcos Ribeira ever did. Her story was instantly accepted as the truth. After all, she was the daughter of Os Venerados."

Grego looked at his mother with glowing eyes, then jumped up and announced to the people around him, "A mamãe o libertou!" Mama saved him! People laughed, turned around and looked at Novinha. But she held her face expressionless, refusing to acknowledge their momentary affection for her child. They looked away again, offended.

"Novinha," said the Speaker. "Her cold manner and

bright mind made her just as much an outcast among you as Marcão. None of you could think of a time when she had ever made a friendly gesture toward any of you. And here she was, saving Marcão. Well, you knew the truth. She wasn't saving Marcão—she was preventing you from getting away with something.''

They nodded and smiled knowingly, those people whose overtures of friendship she had just rebuffed. That's Dona Novinha, the Biologista, too good for any of the rest of us.

"Marcos didn't see it that way. He had been called an animal so often that he almost believed it. Novinha showed him compassion, like a human being. A pretty girl, a brilliant child, the daughter of the holy Venerados, always aloof as a goddess, she had reached down and blessed him and granted his prayer. He worshipped her. Six years later he married her. Isn't that a lovely story?''

Ela looked at Miro, who raised an eyebrow at her. "Almost makes you like the old bastard, doesn't it?'' said Miro dryly.

Suddenly, after a long pause, the Speaker's voice erupted, louder than ever before. It startled them, awoke them. "Why did he come to hate her, to beat her, to despise their children? And why did she endure it, this strong-willed, brilliant woman? She could have stopped the marriage at any moment. The Church may not allow divorce, but there's always desquite, and she wouldn't be the first person in Milagre to quit her husband. She could have taken her suffering children and left him. But she *stayed*. The Mayor and the Bishop both *suggested* that she leave him. She told them they could go to hell.''

Many of the Lusos laughed; they could imagine tight-lipped Novinha snapping at the Bishop himself, facing down Bosquinha. They might not like Novinha much, but she was just about the only person in Milagre who could get away with thumbing her nose at authority.

The Bishop remembered the scene in his chambers more

than a decade ago. She had not used exactly the words the Speaker quoted, but the effect was much the same. Yet he had been alone. He had told no one. Who was this Speaker, and how did he know so much about things he could not possibly have known?

When the laughter died, the Speaker went on. "There was a tie that bound them together in a marriage they hated. That tie was Marcão's disease."

His voice was softer now. The Lusos strained to hear.

"It shaped his life from the moment he was conceived. The genes his parents gave him combined in such a way that from the moment puberty began, the cells of his glands began a steady, relentless transformation into fatty tissues. Dr. Navio can tell you how it progresses better than I can. Marcão knew from childhood that he had this condition; his parents knew it before they died in the Descolada; Gusto and Cida knew it from their genetic examinations of all the humans of Lusitania. *They* were all dead. Only one other person knew it, the one who had inherited the xenobiological files. Novinha."

Dr. Navio was puzzled. If she knew this before they married, she surely knew that most people who had his condition were sterile. Why would she have married him when for all she knew he had no chance of fathering children? Then he realized what he should have known before, that Marcão was *not* a rare exception to the pattern of the disease. There were no exceptions. Navio's face reddened. What the Speaker was about to tell them was unspeakable.

"Novinha knew that Marcão was dying," said the Speaker. "She also knew before she married him that he was absolutely and completely sterile."

It took a moment for the meaning of this to sink in. Ela felt as if her organs were melting inside her body. She saw without turning her head that Miro had gone rigid, that his cheeks had paled.

Speaker went on despite the rising whispers from the audience. "I saw the genetic scans. Marcos Maria Ribeira never fathered a child. His wife had children, but they were not his, and he knew it, and she knew he knew it. It was part of the bargain that they made when they got married.''

The murmurs turned to muttering, the grumbles to complaints, and as the noise reached a climax, Quim leaped to his feet and shouted, screamed at the Speaker, "My mother is not an adulteress! I'll kill you for calling her a whore!''

His last word hung in the silence. The Speaker did not answer. He only waited, not letting his gaze drop from Quim's burning face. Until finally Quim realized that it was he, not the Speaker, whose voice had said the word that kept ringing in his ears. He faltered. He looked at his mother sitting beside him on the ground, but not rigidly now, slumped a little now, looking at her hands as they trembled in her lap. "Tell them, Mother," Quim said. His voice sounded more pleading than he had intended.

She didn't answer. Didn't say a word, didn't look at him. If he didn't know better, he would think her trembling hands were a confession, that she was *ashamed,* as if what the Speaker said was the truth that God himself would tell if Quim were to ask him. He remembered Father Mateu explaining the tortures of hell: God spits on adulterers, they mock the power of creation that he shared with them, they haven't enough goodness in them to be anything better than amoebas. Quim tasted bile in his mouth. What the Speaker said was true.

"Mamãe," he said loudly, mockingly. "Quem fôde p'ra fazer-me?''

People gasped. Olhado jumped to his feet at once, his hands doubled in fists. Only then did Novinha react, reaching out a hand as if to restrain Olhado from hitting his brother. Quim hardly noticed that Olhado had leapt to Mother's defense; all he could think of was the fact that Miro had not. Miro also knew that it was true.

Quim breathed deeply, then turned around, looking lost for a moment; then he threaded his way through the crowd. No one spoke to him, though everyone watched him go. If Novinha had denied the charge, they would have believed her, would have mobbed the Speaker for accusing Os Venerados' daughter of such a sin. But she had not denied it. She had listened to her own son accuse her obscenely, and she said nothing. It was true. And now they listened in fascination. Few of them had any real concern. They just wanted to learn who had fathered Novinha's children.

The Speaker quietly resumed his tale. "After her parents died and before her children were born, Novinha loved only two people. Pipo was her second father. Novinha anchored her life in him; for a few short years she had a taste of what it meant to have a family. Then he died, and Novinha believed that she had killed him."

People sitting near Novinha's family saw Quara kneel in front of Ela and ask her, "Why is Quim so angry?"

Ela answered softly. "Because Papai was not really our father."

"Oh," said Quara. "Is the Speaker our father now?" She sounded hopeful. Ela shushed her.

"The night Pipo died," said the Speaker, "Novinha showed him something that she had discovered, something to do with the Descolada and the way it works with the plants and animals of Lusitania. Pipo saw more in her work than she did herself. He rushed to the forest where the piggies waited. Perhaps he told them what he had discovered. Perhaps they only guessed. But Novinha blamed herself for showing him a secret that the piggies would kill to keep.

"It was too late to undo what she had done. But she could keep it from happening again. So she sealed up all the files that had anything to do with the Descolada and what she had shown to Pipo that night. She knew who would want to see the files. It was Libo, the new Zenador. If Pipo had been her father, Libo had been her brother, and more than a brother. Hard as it was to bear Pipo's death, Libo's would be worse.

He asked for the files. He demanded to see them. She told him she would never let him see them.

"They both knew exactly what that meant. If he ever married her, he could strip away the protection on those files. They loved each other desperately, they needed each other more than ever, but Novinha could never marry him. He would never promise not to read the files, and even if he made such a promise, he couldn't keep it. He would surely see what his father saw. He would die.

"It was one thing to refuse to marry him. It was another thing to live without him. So she didn't live without him. She made her bargain with Marcão. She would marry him under the law, but her real husband and the father of all her children would be, was, Libo."

Bruxinha, Libo's widow, rose shakily to her feet, tears streaming down her face, and wailed, "Mentira, mentira." Lies, lies. But her weeping was not anger, it was grief. She was mourning the loss of her husband all over again. Three of her daughters helped her leave the praça.

Softly the Speaker continued while she left. "Libo knew that he was hurting his wife Bruxinha and their four daughters. He hated himself for what he had done. He tried to stay away. For months, sometimes years, he succeeded. Novinha also tried. She refused to see him, even to speak to him. She forbade her children to mention him. Then Libo would think that he was strong enough to see her without falling back into the old way. Novinha would be so lonely with her husband who could never measure up to Libo. They never pretended there was anything good about what they were doing. They just couldn't live for long without it."

Bruxinha heard this as she was led away. It was little comfort to her now, of course, but as Bishop Peregrino watched her go, he recognized that the Speaker was giving her a gift. She was the most innocent victim of his cruel truth, but he didn't leave her with nothing but ashes. He was giving her a way to live with the knowledge of what her husband did. It was not your fault, he was telling her. Nothing you did could have prevented it. Your husband was the one who failed, not you. Blessed Virgin, prayed the Bishop silently, let Bruxinha hear what he says and believe it.

Libo's widow was not the only one who cried. Many hundreds of the eyes that watched her go were also filled with tears. To discover Novinha was an adulteress was shocking but delicious: the steel-hearted woman had a flaw that made her no better than anyone else. But there was no pleasure in finding the same flaw in Libo. Everyone had loved him. His generosity, his kindness, his wisdom that they so admired, they didn't want to know that it was all a mask.

So they were surprised when the Speaker reminded them that it was not Libo whose death he Spoke today. "Why did Marcos Ribeira consent to this? Novinha thought it was because he wanted a wife and the illusion that he had children, to take away his shame in the community. It was partly that. Most of all, though, he married her because he loved her. He never really hoped that she would love him the way he loved her, because he worshipped her, she was a goddess, and he knew that he was diseased, filthy, an animal to be despised. He knew she could not worship him, or even love him. He hoped that she might someday feel some *affection*. That she might feel some—loyalty."

The Speaker bowed his head a moment. The Lusos heard the words that he did not have to say: She never did.

"Each child that came," said the Speaker, "was another proof to Marcos that he had failed. That the goddess still found him unworthy. Why? He was loyal. He had never hinted to any of his children that they were not his own. He never broke his promise to Novinha. Didn't he deserve something from her? At times it was more than he could bear. He refused to accept her judgment. She was no goddess. Her children were all bastards. This is what he told himself when he lashed out at her, when he shouted at Miro."

Miro heard his own name, but didn't recognize it as anything to do with him. His connection with reality was more fragile than he ever had supposed, and today had given him too many shocks. The impossible magic with the piggies and the trees. Mother and Libo, lovers. Ouanda suddenly torn from being as close to him as his own body, his own self, she was now set back at one remove, like Ela, like Quara, another sister. His eyes did not focus on the grass; the Speaker's voice was pure sound, he didn't hear meanings in the words, only the terrible sound. Miro had called for that voice, had wanted it to Speak Libo's death. How could he have known that instead of a benevolent priest of a humanist religion he would get the original Speaker himself, with his penetrating mind and far too perfect understanding? He could not have known that beneath that empathic mask would be hiding Ender the destroyer, the mythic Lucifer of mankind's greatest crime, determined to live up to his name, making a mockery of the life work of Pipo, Libo, Ouanda, and Miro himself by seeing in a single hour with the piggies what all the others had failed in almost fifty years to see, and then riving Ouanda from him with a single, merciless stroke from the blade of truth; that was the voice that Miro heard, the only certainty left to him, that relentless terrible voice. Miro clung to the sound of it, trying to hate it, yet failing, because he knew, could not deceive himself, he *knew* that Ender was a destroyer, but what he destroyed was illusion, and the illusion had to die. The truth about the piggies, the truth about ourselves. Somehow this ancient man is able to see the truth and it doesn't blind his eyes or drive him mad. I must listen to this voice and let its power come to me so I, too, can stare at the light and not die.

"Novinha knew what she was. An adulteress, a hypocrite. She knew she was hurting Marcão, Libo, her children, Bruxinha. She knew she had killed Pipo. So she endured, even invited Marcão's punishment. It was her penance. It was never penance enough. No matter how much Marcão might hate her, she hated herself much more.''

The Bishop nodded slowly. The Speaker had done a monstrous thing, to lay these secrets before the whole community. They should have been spoken in the confessional. Yet Peregrino had felt the power of it, the way the whole community was forced to discover these people that they thought they knew, and then discover them again, and then again; and each revision of the story forced them all to reconceive themselves as well, for they had been part of this story, too, had been touched by all the people a hundred, a thousand times, never understanding until now who it was they touched. It was a painful, fearful thing to go through, but in the end it had a curiously calming effect. The Bishop leaned to his secretary and whispered, ''At least the gossips will get nothing from this—there aren't any secrets left to tell.''

''All the people in this story suffered pain,'' the Speaker said. ''All of them sacrificed for the people they loved. All of them caused terrible pain to the people who loved them. And you—listening to me here today, you also caused pain. But remember this: Marcão's life was tragic and cruel, but he could have ended his bargain with Novinha at any time. He chose to stay. He must have found some joy in it. And Novinha: She broke the laws of God that bind this community together. She has also borne her punishment. The Church asks for no penance as terrible as the one she imposed on herself. And if you're inclined to think she might deserve some petty cruelty at your hands, keep this in mind: She suffered everything, did all this for one purpose: to keep the piggies from killing Libo.''

The words left ashes in their hearts.

Olhado stood and walked to his mother, knelt by her, put an arm around her shoulder. Ela sat beside her, but she was folded to the ground, weeping. Quara came and stood in front of her mother, staring at her with awe. And Grego buried his face in Novinha's lap and wept. Those who were near enough could hear him crying, "Todo papai é morto. Não tenho nem papai." All my papas are dead. I don't have any papa.

Ouanda stood in the mouth of the alley where she had gone with her mother just before the Speaking ended. She looked for Miro, but he was already gone.

Ender stood behind the platform, looking at Novinha's family, wishing he could do something to ease their pain. There was always pain after a Speaking, because a Speaker for the Dead did nothing to soften the truth. But only rarely had people lived such lives of deceit as Marcão, Libo, and Novinha; rarely were there so many shocks, so many bits of information that forced people to revise their conception of the people that they knew, the people that they loved. Ender knew from the faces that looked up at him as he spoke that he had caused great pain today. He had felt it all himself, as if they had passed their suffering to him. Bruxinha had been most surprised, but Ender knew she was not worst injured. That distinction belonged to Miro and Ouanda, who had thought they knew what the future would bring them. But Ender had also felt the pain that people felt before, and he knew that today's new wounds would heal much faster than the old ones ever would have done. Novinha might not recognize it, but Ender had stripped from her a burden that was much too heavy for her to bear any longer.

"Speaker," said Mayor Bosquinha.

"Mayor," said Ender. He didn't like talking to people after a Speaking, but he was used to the fact that someone always insisted on talking to him. He forced a smile. "There were many more people here than I expected."

"A momentary thing, for most of them," said Bosquinha. "They'll forget it by morning."

Ender was annoyed that she was trivializing it. "Only if something monumental happens in the night," he said.

"Yes. Well, that has been arranged."

Only then did Ender realize that she was extremely upset, barely under control at all. He took her by the elbow and then cast an arm over her shoulder; she leaned gratefully.

"Speaker, I came to apologize. Your starship has been commandeered by Starways Congress. It has nothing to do with you. A crime was committed here, a crime so—terrible—that the criminals must be taken to the nearest world, Trondheim, for trial and punishment. Your ship."

Ender reflected for a moment. "Miro and Ouanda."

She turned her head, looked at him sharply. "You are not surprised."

"I also won't let them go."

Bosquinha pulled herself away from him. "Won't *let* them?"

"I have some idea what they're charged with."

"You've been here four days, and you already know something that even *I* never suspected?"

"Sometimes the government is the last to know."

"Let me tell you why you *will* let them go, why we'll *all* let them go to stand trial. Because Congress has stripped our files. The computer memory is empty except for the most rudimentary programs that control our power supply, our water, our sewer. Tomorrow no work can be done because we haven't enough power to run any of the factories, to work in the mines, to power the tractors. I have been removed from office. I am now nothing more than the deputy chief of *police,* to see that the directives of the Lusitanian Evacuation Committee are carried out."

"Evacuation?"

"The colony's license has been revoked. They're sending starships to take us all away. Every sign of human habitation here is to be removed. Even the gravestones that mark our dead."

Ender tried to measure her response. He had not thought Bosquinha was the kind who would bow to mindless authority. "Do you intend to submit to this?"

"The power and water supplies are controlled by ansible.

They also control the fence. They can shut us in here without power or water or sewers, and we can't get out. Once Miro and Ouanda are aboard your starship, headed for Trondheim, they say that some of the restrictions will be relaxed." She sighed. "Oh, Speaker, I'm afraid this isn't a good time to be a tourist in Lusitania."

"I'm not a tourist." He didn't bother telling her his suspicion that it might not be pure coincidence, Congress noticing the Questionable Activities when Ender happened to be there. "Were you able to save any of your files?"

Bosquinha sighed. "By imposing on you, I'm afraid. I noticed that all your files were maintained by ansible, offworld. We sent our most crucial files as messages to you."

Ender laughed. "Good, that's right, that was well done."

"It doesn't matter. We can't get them back. Or, well, yes, we can, but they'll notice it at once and then you'll be in just as much trouble as the rest of us. And they'll wipe out everything then."

"Unless you sever the ansible connection immediately after copying all my files to local memory."

"Then we really would be in rebellion. And for what?"

"For the chance to make Lusitania the best and most important of the Hundred Worlds."

Bosquinha laughed. "I think they'll regard us as important, but treason is hardly the way to be known as the best."

"Please. Don't do anything. Don't arrest Miro and Ouanda. Wait for an hour and let me meet with you and anyone else who needs to be in on the decision."

"The decision whether or not to rebel? I can't think why *you* should be in on that decision, Speaker."

"You'll understand at the meeting. Please, this place is too important for the chance to be missed."

"The chance for what?"

"To undo what Ender did in the Xenocide three thousand years ago."

Bosquinha gave him a sharp-eyed look. "And here I thought

you had just proved yourself to be nothing but a gossip-monger.''

She might have been joking. Or she might not. ''If you think that what I just did was gossip-mongering, you're too stupid to lead this community in anything.'' He smiled.

Bosquinha spread her hands and shrugged. ''Pois é,'' she said. Of course. What else?

''Will you have the meeting?''

''I'll call it. In the Bishop's chambers.''

Ender winced.

''The Bishop won't meet anywhere else,'' she said, ''and no decision to rebel will mean a thing if he doesn't agree to it.'' Bosquinha laid her hand on his chest. ''He may not even let you into the Cathedral. You are the infidel.''

''But you'll try.''

''I'll try because of what you did tonight. Only a wise man could see my people so clearly in so short a time. Only a ruthless one would say it all out loud. Your virtue and your flaw—we need them both.''

Bosquinha turned and hurried away. Ender knew that she did not, in her inmost heart, want to comply with Starways Congress. It had been too sudden, too severe; they had preempted her authority as if she were guilty of a crime. To give in smacked of confession, and she knew she had done nothing wrong. She wanted to resist, wanted to find some plausible way to slap back at Congress and tell them to wait, to be calm. Or, if necessary, to tell them to drop dead. But she wasn't a fool. She wouldn't do anything to resist them unless she knew it would work and knew it would benefit her people. She was a good Governor, Ender knew. She would gladly sacrifice her pride, her reputation, her future for her people's sake.

He was alone in the praça. Everyone had gone while Bosquinha talked to him. Ender felt as an old soldier must feel, walking over placid fields at the site of a long-ago battle, hearing the echoes of the carnage in the breeze across the rustling grass.

"Don't let them sever the ansible connection."

The voice in his ear startled him, but he knew it at once. "Jane," he said.

"I can make them think you've cut off your ansible, but if you really do it then I won't be able to help you."

"Jane," he said, "you did this, didn't you! Why else would they notice what Libo and Miro and Ouanda have been doing if you didn't call it to their attention?"

She didn't answer.

"Jane, I'm sorry that I cut you off, I'll never—"

He knew she knew what he would say; he didn't have to finish sentences with her. But she didn't answer.

"I'll never turn off the—"

What good did it do to finish sentences that he knew she understood? She hadn't forgiven him yet, that was all, or she would already be answering, telling him to stop wasting her time. Yet he couldn't keep himself from trying one more time. "I missed you. Jane. I really missed you."

Still she didn't answer. She had said what she had to say, to keep the ansible connection alive, and that was all. For now. Ender didn't mind waiting. It was enough to know that she was still there, listening. He wasn't alone. Ender was surprised to find tears on his cheeks. Tears of relief, he decided. Catharsis. A Speaking, a crisis, people's lives in tatters, the future of the colony in doubt. And I cry in relief because an overblown computer program is speaking to me again.

Ela was waiting for him in his little house. Her eyes were red from crying. "Hello," she said.

"Did I do what you wanted?" he asked.

"I never guessed," she said. "He wasn't our father. I should have known."

"I can't think how you could have."

"What have I done? Calling you here to Speak my father's—Marcão's death." She began weeping again. "Mother's secrets—I thought I knew what they were, I thought it was just her files—I thought she *hated* Libo."

"All I did was open the windows and let in some air."

"Tell that to Miro and Ouanda."

"Think a moment, Ela. They would have found out eventually. The cruel thing was that they *didn't* know for so many years. Now that they have the truth, they can find their own way out."

"Like Mother did? Only this time even worse than adultery?"

Ender touched her hair, smoothed it. She accepted his touch, his consolation. He couldn't remember if his father or mother had ever touched him with such a gesture. They must have. How else would he have learned it?

"Ela, will you help me?"

"Help you what? You've done your work, haven't you?"

"This has nothing to do with Speaking for the dead. I have to know, within the hour, how the Descolada works."

"You'll have to ask Mother—she's the one who knows."

"I don't think she'd be glad to see me tonight."

"*I'm* supposed to ask her? Good evening, Mamãe, you've just been revealed to all of Milagre as an adulteress who's been lying to your children all our lives. So if you wouldn't mind, I'd like to ask you a couple of science questions."

"Ela, it's a matter of survival for Lusitania. Not to mention your brother Miro." He reached over and turned to the terminal. "Log on," he said.

She was puzzled, but she did it. The computer wouldn't recognize her name. "I've been taken off." She looked at him in alarm. "Why?"

"It's not just you. It's everybody."

"It isn't a breakdown," she said. "Somebody stripped out the log-on file."

"Starways Congress stripped all the local computer memory. Everything's gone. We're regarded as being in a state of rebellion. Miro and Ouanda are going to be arrested and sent to Trondheim for trial. Unless I can persuade the Bishop and Bosquinha to launch a *real* rebellion. Do you understand? If your mother doesn't tell you what I need to know, Miro and Ouanda will both be sent twenty-two lightyears away. The penalty for treason is death. But even going to the trial is as bad as life imprisonment. We'll all be dead or very very old before they get back.''

Ela looked blankly at the wall. "What do you need to know?"

"I need to know what the Committee will find when they open up her files. About how the Descolada works."

"Yes," said Ela. "For Miro's sake she'll do it." She looked at him defiantly. "She does love us, you know. For one of her children, she'd talk to you herself."

"Good," said Ender. "It would be better if she came herself. To the Bishop's chambers, in an hour."

"Yes," said Ela. For a moment she sat still. Then a synapse connected somewhere, and she stood up and hurried toward the door.

She stopped. She came back, embraced him, kissed him on the cheek. "I'm glad you told it all," she said. "I'm glad to know it."

He kissed her forehead and sent her on her way. When the door closed behind her, he sat down on his bed, then lay down and stared at the ceiling. He thought of Novinha, tried to imagine what she was feeling now. No matter how terrible it is, Novinha, your daughter is hurrying home to you right now, sure that despite the pain and humiliation you're going through, you'll forget yourself completely and do whatever it takes to save your son. I would trade you all your suffering, Novinha, for one child who trusted me like that.

Chapter 16
The Fence

A great rabbi stands teaching in the marketplace. It happens that a husband finds proof that morning of his wife's adultery, and a mob carries her to the marketplace to stone her to death. (There is a familiar version of this story, but a friend of mine, a Speaker for the Dead, has told me of two other rabbis that faced the same situation. Those are the ones I'm going to tell you.)

The rabbi walks forward and stands beside the woman. Out of respect for him the mob forbears, and waits with the stones heavy in their hands. "Is there anyone here," he says to them, "who has not desired another man's wife, another woman's husband?"

They murmur and say, "We all know the desire. But, Rabbi, none of us has acted on it."

The rabbi says, "Then kneel down and give thanks that God made you strong." He takes the woman by the hand and leads her out of the market. Just before he lets her go, he whispers to her, "Tell the lord magistrate who saved his mistress. Then he'll know I am his loyal servant."

So the woman lives, because the community is too corrupt to protect itself from disorder.

Another rabbi, another city. He goes to her and stops the mob, as in the other story, and says, "Which of you is without sin? Let him cast the first stone."

The people are abashed, and they forget their unity of purpose in the memory of their own individual sins. Someday, they think, I may be like this woman, and I'll hope for forgiveness and another chance. I should treat her the way I wish to be treated.

As they open their hands and let the stones fall to the ground, the rabbi picks up one of the fallen stones, lifts it high over the woman's head, and throws it straight down with all his might. It crushes her skull and dashes her brains onto the cobblestones.

"Nor am I without sin," he says to the people. "But if we allow only perfect people to enforce the law, the law will soon be dead, and our city with it."

So the woman died because her community was too rigid to endure her deviance.

The famous version of this story is noteworthy because it is so startlingly rare in our experience. Most communities lurch between decay and rigor mortis, and when they veer too far, they die. Only one rabbi dared to expect of us such a perfect balance that we could preserve the law and still forgive the deviation. So, of course, we killed him.

—San Angelo, *Letters to an Incipient Heretic*, trans. Amai a Tudomundo Para Que Deus Vos Ame Cristão, 103:72:54:2

Minha irmã. My sister. The words kept running through Miro's head until he didn't hear them anymore, they were part of the background: A Ouanda é minha irmã. She's my sister. His feet carried him by habit from the praça to the playing fields and over the saddle of the hill. The crown of the higher peak held the Cathedral and the monastery, which always loomed over the Zenador's Station, as if they were a fortress keeping watch over the gate. Did Libo walk this way as he went to meet my mother? Did they meet in the

Xenobiologist's Station? Or was it more discreet, rutting in the grass like hogs on the fazendas?

He stood at the door of the Zenador's Station and tried to think of some reason to go inside. Nothing to do there. Hadn't written a report on what happened today, but he didn't know how to write it anyway. Magical powers, that's what it was. The piggies sing to the trees and the trees split themselves into kindling. Much better than carpentry. The aboriginals are a good deal more sophisticated than previously supposed. Multiple uses for everything. Each tree is at once a totem, a grave marker, and a small lumber mill. Sister. There's something I have to do but I can't remember.

The piggies have the most sensible plan. Live as brothers only, and never mind the women. Would have been better for you, Libo, and that's the truth—no, I should call you Papai, not Libo. Too bad Mother never told you or you could have dandled me on your knee. Both your eldest children, Ouanda on one knee and Miro on the other, aren't we proud of our two children? Born the same year, only two months apart, what a busy fellow Papai was then, sneaking along the fence to tup Mamãe in her own back yard. Everyone felt sorry for you because you had nothing but daughters. No one to carry on the family name. Their sympathy was wasted. You were brimming over with sons. And I have far more sisters than I ever thought. One more sister than I wanted.

He stood at the gate, looking up toward the woods atop the piggies' hill. There is no scientific purpose to be served by visiting at night. So I guess I'll serve an unscientific purposelessness and see if they have room for another brother in the tribe. I'm probably too big for a bedspace in the log house, so I'll sleep outside, and I won't be much for climbing trees, but I do know a thing or two about technology, and I don't feel any particular inhibitions now about telling you anything you want to know.

He laid his right hand on the identification box and reached out his left to pull the gate. For a split second he didn't realize what was happening. Then his hand felt like it was on fire, like it was being cut off with a rusty saw, he shouted and pulled his left hand away from the gate. Never since the gate was built had it stayed hot after the box was touched by the Zenador's hand.

"Marcos Vladimir Ribeira von Hesse, your passage through the fence has been revoked by order of the Lusitanian Evacuation Committee."

Never since the gate was built had the voice challenged a Zenador. It took a moment before Miro understood what it was saying.

"You and Ouanda Quenhatta Figueira Mucumbi will present yourselves to Deputy Chief of Police Faria Lima Maria do Bosque, who will arrest you in the name of Starways Congress and present you on Trondheim for trial."

For a moment he was lightheaded and his stomach felt heavy and sick. They know. Tonight of all nights. Everything over. Lose Ouanda, lose the piggies, lose my work, all gone. Arrest. Trondheim. Where the Speaker came from, twenty-two years in transit, everybody gone except Ouanda, the only one left, and she's my *sister*—

His hand flashed out again to pull at the gate; again the excruciating pain shot through his arm, the pain nerves all alerted, all afire at once. I can't just disappear. They'll seal the gate to everyone. Nobody will go to the piggies, nobody will tell them, the piggies will wait for us to come and no one will ever come out of the gate again. Not me, not Ouanda, not the Speaker, nobody, and no explanation.

Evacuation Committee. They'll evacuate us and wipe out every trace of our being here. That much is in the rules, but there's more, isn't there? What did they see? How did they find out? Did the Speaker tell them? He's so addicted to truth. I have to explain to the piggies why we won't be coming back, I have to tell them.

A piggy always watched them, followed them from the moment they entered the forest. Could a piggy be watching now? Miro waved his hand. It was too dark, though. They couldn't possibly see him. Or perhaps they could; no one knew how good the piggies' vision was at night. Whether they saw him or not, they didn't come. And soon it would be too late; if the framlings were watching the gate, they had no doubt already notified Bosquinha, and she'd be on her way, zipping over the grass. She would be oh-so-reluctant to arrest him, but she would do her job, and never mind arguing with her about whether it was good for humans or piggies, either one, to maintain this foolish separation, she wasn't the sort to question the law, she just did what she was told. And he'd surrender, there was no reason to fight, where could he hide inside the fence, out among the cabra herds? But before he gave up, he'd tell the piggies, he had to tell them.

So he walked along the fence, away from the gate, toward the open grassland directly down the hill from the Cathedral, where no one lived near enough to hear his voice. As he walked, he called. Not words, but a high hooting sound, a cry that he and Ouanda used to call each other's attention when they were separated among the piggies. They'd hear it, they had to hear it, they had to come to him because he couldn't possibly pass the fence. So come, Human, Leaf-eater, Mandachuva, Arrow, Cups, Calendar, anyone, everyone, come and let me tell you that I cannot tell you any more.

Quim sat miserably on a stool in the Bishop's office.

"Estevão," the Bishop said quietly, "there'll be a meeting here in a few minutes, but I want to talk to you a minute first."

"Nothing to talk about," said Quim. "You warned us, and it happened. He's the devil."

"Estevão, we'll talk for a minute and then you'll go home and sleep."

"Never going back there."

"The Master ate with worse sinners than your mother, and forgave them. Are you better than he?"

"None of the adulteresses he forgave was his mother!"

"Not everyone's mother can be the Blessed Virgin."

"Are you on his side, then? Has the Church made way here for the Speakers for the Dead? Should we tear down the Cathedral and use the stones to make an amphitheater where all our dead can be slandered before we lay them in the ground?"

A whisper: "I am your Bishop, Estevão, the vicar of Christ on this planet, and you will speak to me with the respect you owe to my office."

Quim stood there, furious, unspeaking.

"I think it would have been better if the Speaker had not told these stories publicly. Some things are better learned in privacy, in quiet, so that we need not deal with shocks while an audience watches us. That's why we use the confessional, to shield us from public shame while we wrestle with our private sins. But be fair, Estevão. The Speaker may have told the stories, but the stories all were true. Né?"

"É."

"Now, Estevão, let us think. Before today, did you love your mother?"

"Yes."

"And this mother that you loved, had she already committed adultery?"

"Ten thousand times."

"I suspect she was not so libidinous as that. But you tell me that you loved her, though she was an adulteress. Isn't she the same person tonight? Has she changed between yesterday and today? Or is it only you who have changed?"

"What she was yesterday was a lie."

"Do you mean that because she was ashamed to tell her children that she was an adulteress, she must also have been lying when she cared for you all the years you were growing up, when she trusted you, when she taught you—"

"She was not exactly a nurturing mother."

"If she had come to the confessional and won forgiveness

for her adultery, then she would never have had to tell you at all. You would have gone to your grave not knowing. It would not have been a lie; because she would have been forgiven, she would not have been an adulteress. Admit the truth, Estevão: You're not angry with her adultery. You're angry because you embarrassed yourself in front of the whole city by trying to defend her."

"You make me seem like a fool."

"No one thinks you're a fool. Everyone thinks you're a loyal son. But now, if you're to be a true follower of the Master, you will forgive her and let her see that you love her more than ever, because now you understand her suffering." The Bishop glanced toward the door. "I have a meeting here now, Estevão. Please go into my inner chamber and pray to the Madelena to forgive you for your unforgiving heart."

Looking more miserable than angry, Quim passed through the curtain behind the Bishop's desk.

The Bishop's secretary opened the other door and let the Speaker for the Dead into the chamber. The Bishop did not rise. To his surprise, the Speaker knelt and bowed his head. It was an act that Catholics did only in a public presentation to the Bishop, and Peregrino could not think what the Speaker meant by this. Yet the man knelt there, waiting, and so the Bishop arose from his chair, walked to him, and held out his ring to be kissed. Even then the Speaker waited, until finally Peregrino said, "I bless you, my son, even though I'm not sure whether you mock me with this obeisance."

Head still bowed, the Speaker said, "There's no mockery in me." Then he looked up at Peregrino. "My father was a Catholic. He pretended not to be, for the sake of convenience, but he never forgave himself for his faithlessness."

"You were baptized?"

"My sister told me that yes, Father baptized me shortly after birth. My mother was a Protestant of a faith that deplored infant baptism, so they had a quarrel about it." The Bishop held out his hand to lift the Speaker to his feet. The

Speaker chuckled. "Imagine. A closet Catholic and a lapsed Mormon, quarreling over religious procedures that they both claimed not to believe in."

Peregrino was skeptical. It was too elegant a gesture, for the Speaker to turn out to be Catholic. "I thought," said the Bishop, "that you Speakers for the Dead renounced all religions before taking up your, shall we say, vocation."

"I don't know what the others do. I don't think there are any rules about it—certainly there weren't when *I* became a Speaker."

Bishop Peregrino knew that Speakers were not supposed to lie, but this one certainly seemed to be evasive. "Speaker Andrew, there isn't a place in all the Hundred Worlds where a Catholic has to conceal his faith, and there hasn't been for three thousand years. That was the great blessing of space travel, that it removed the terrible population restrictions on an overcrowded Earth. Are you telling me that your father lived on Earth three thousand years ago?"

"I'm telling you that my father saw to it I was baptized a Catholic, and for his sake I did what he never could do in his life. It was for him that I knelt before a Bishop and received his blessing."

"But it was you that I blessed." And you're still dodging my question. Which implies that my inference about your father's time of life is true, but you don't want to discuss it. Dom Cristão said that there was more to you than met the eye.

"Good," said the Speaker. "I need the blessing more than my father, since he's dead, and I have many more problems to deal with."

"Please sit down." The Speaker chose a stool near the far wall. The Bishop sat in his massive chair behind his desk. "I wish you hadn't Spoken today. It came at an inconvenient time."

"I had no warning that Congress would do this."

"But you knew that Miro and Ouanda had violated the law. Bosquinha told me."

"I found out only a few hours before the Speaking. Thank you for not arresting them yet."

"That's a civil matter." The Bishop brushed it aside, but they both knew that if he had insisted, Bosquinha would have had to obey her orders and arrest them regardless of the Speaker's request. "Your Speaking has caused a great deal of distress."

"More than usual, I'm afraid."

"So—is your responsibility over? Do you inflict the wounds and leave it to others to heal them?"

"Not wounds, Bishop Peregrino. Surgery. And if I can help to heal the pain afterward, then yes, I stay and help. I have no anesthesia, but I do try for antisepsis."

"You should have been a priest, you know."

"Younger sons used to have only two choices. The priesthood or the military. My parents chose the latter course for me."

"A younger son. Yet you had a sister. And you lived in the time when population controls forbade parents to have more than two children unless the government gave special permission. They called such a child a Third, yes?"

"You know your history."

"Were you born on Earth, before starflight?"

"What concerns us, Bishop Peregrino, is the future of Lusitania, not the biography of a Speaker for the Dead who is plainly only thirty-five years old."

"The future of Lusitania is my concern, Speaker Andrew, not yours."

"The future of the humans on Lusitania is your concern, Bishop. I'm concerned with the piggies as well."

"Let's not compete to see whose concern is greater."

The secretary opened the door again, and Bosquinha, Dom Cristão, and Dona Cristã came in. Bosquinha glanced back and forth between the Bishop and the Speaker.

"There's no blood on the floor, if that's what you're looking for," said the Bishop.

"I was just estimating the temperature," said Bosquinha.

"The warmth of mutual respect, I think," said the Speaker. "Not the heat of anger or the ice of hate."

"The Speaker is a Catholic by baptism, if not by belief," said the Bishop. "I blessed him, and it seems to have made him docile."

"I've always been respectful of authority," said the Speaker.

"You *were* the one who threatened us with an Inquisitor," the Bishop reminded him. With a smile.

The Speaker's smile was just as chilly. "And you're the one who told the people I was Satan and they shouldn't talk to me."

While the Bishop and the Speaker grinned at each other, the others laughed nervously, sat down, waited.

"It's your meeting, Speaker," said Bosquinha.

"Forgive me," said the Speaker. "There's someone else invited. It'll make things much simpler if we wait a few more minutes for her to come."

Ela found her mother outside the house, not far from the fence. A light breeze that barely rustled the capim had caught her hair and tossed it lightly. It took a moment for Ela to realize why this was so startling. Her mother had not worn her hair down in many years. It looked strangely free, all the more so because Ela could see how it curled and bent where it had been so long forced into a bun. It was then that she knew that the Speaker was right. Mother would listen to his invitation. Whatever shame or pain tonight's Speaking might have caused her, it led her now to stand out in the open, in the dusk just after sunset, looking toward the piggies' hill. Or perhaps she was looking at the fence. Perhaps remembering a man who met her here, or somewhere else in the capim, so that unobserved they could love each other. Always in hiding, always in secret. Mother is glad, thought Ela, to have it known that Libo was her real husband, that Libo is my true father. Mother is glad, and so am I.

Mother did not turn to look at her, though she surely could hear Ela's approach through the noisy grass. Ela stopped a few steps away.

"Mother," she said.

"Not a herd of cabra, then," said Mother. "You're so noisy, Ela."

"The Speaker. Wants your help."

"Does he."

Ela explained what the Speaker had told her. Mother did not turn around. When Ela was finished, Mother waited a moment, and then turned to walk over the shoulder of the hill. Ela ran after her, caught up with her. "Mother," said Ela. "Mother, are you going to tell him about the Descolada?"

"Yes."

"Why now? After all these years? Why wouldn't you tell *me*?"

"Because you did better work on your own, without my help."

"You know what I was doing?"

"You're my apprentice. I have complete access to your files without leaving any footprints. What kind of master would I be if I didn't watch your work?"

"But—"

"I also read the files you hid under Quara's name. You've never been a mother, so you didn't know that all the file activities of a child under twelve are reported to the parents every week. Quara was doing some remarkable research. I'm glad you're coming with me. When I tell the Speaker, I'll be telling you, too."

"You're going the wrong way," said Ela.

Mother stopped. "Isn't the Speaker's house near the praça?"

"The meeting is in the Bishop's chambers."

For the first time Mother faced Ela directly. "What are you and the Speaker trying to do to me?"

"We're trying to save Miro," said Ela. "And Lusitania Colony, if we can."

"Taking me to the spider's lair—"

"The Bishop has to be on our side or—"

"*Our* side! So when you say *we,* you mean you and the Speaker, is that it? Do you think I haven't noticed that? All my children, one by one, he's seduced you all—"

"He hasn't seduced anybody!"

"He seduced you with his way of knowing just what you want to hear, of—"

"He's no flatterer," said Ela. "He doesn't tell us what we want. He tells us what we know is true. He didn't win our *affection,* Mother, he won our *trust.*"

"Whatever he gets from you, you never gave it to me."

"We wanted to."

Ela did not bend this time before her mother's piercing, demanding glare. It was her mother, instead, who bent, who looked away and then looked back with tears in her eyes. "I wanted to tell you." Mother wasn't talking about her files. "When I saw how you hated him, I wanted to say, He's not your father, your father is a good, kind man—"

"Who didn't have the courage to tell us himself."

Rage came into Mother's eyes. "He wanted to. I wouldn't let him."

"I'll tell you something, Mother. I loved Libo, the way everybody in Milagre loved him. But he was willing to be a hypocrite, and so were you, and without anybody even guessing, the poison of your lies hurt us all. I don't blame you, Mother, or him. But I thank God for the Speaker. He was willing to tell us the truth, and it set us free."

"It's easy to tell the truth," said Mother softly, "when you don't love anybody."

"Is that what you think?" said Ela. "I think I know something, Mother. I think you can't possibly know the truth about somebody *unless* you love them. I think the Speaker loved Father. Marcão, I mean. I think he understood him and loved him before he Spoke."

Mother didn't answer, because she knew that it was true.

"And I know he loves Grego, and Quara, and Olhado. And Miro, and even Quim. And me. I know he loves *me*. And when he shows me that he loves me, I know it's true because he never lies to anybody."

Tears came out of Mother's eyes and drifted down her cheeks.

"I *have* lied to you and everybody else," Mother said. Her voice sounded weak and strained. "But you have to believe me anyway. When I tell you that I love you."

Ela embraced her mother, and for the first time in years she felt warmth in her mother's response. Because the lies between them now were gone. The Speaker had erased the barrier, and there was no reason to be tentative and cautious anymore.

"You're thinking about that damnable Speaker even now, aren't you?" whispered her mother.

"So are you," Ela answered.

Both their bodies shook with Mother's laugh. "Yes." Then she stopped laughing and pulled away, looked Ela in the eyes. "Will he always come between us?"

"Yes," said Ela. "Like a bridge he'll come between us, not a wall."

Miro saw the piggies when they were halfway down the hillside toward the fence. They were so silent in the forest, but the piggies had no great skill in moving through the capim—it rustled loudly as they ran. Or perhaps in coming to answer Miro's call they felt no need to conceal themselves. As they came nearer, Miro recognized them. Arrow, Human, Mandachuva, Leaf-eater, Cups. He did not call out to them, nor did they speak when they arrived. Instead they stood behind the fence opposite him and regarded him silently. No Zenador had ever called the piggies to the fence before. By their stillness they showed their anxiety.

"I can't come to you anymore," said Miro.

They waited for his explanation.

"The framlings found out about us. Breaking the law. They sealed the gate."

Leaf-eater touched his chin. "Do you know what it was the framlings saw?"

Miro laughed bitterly. "What didn't they see? Only one framling ever came with us."

"No," said Human. "The hive queen says it wasn't the Speaker. The hive queen says they saw it from the sky."

The satellites? "What could they see from the sky?"

"Maybe the hunt," said Arrow.

"Maybe the shearing of the cabra," said Leaf-eater.

"Maybe the fields of amaranth," said Cups.

"All of those," said Human. "And maybe they saw that the wives have let three hundred twenty children be born since the first amaranth harvest."

"Three hundred!"

"And twenty," said Mandachuva.

"They saw that food would be plenty," said Arrow. "Now we're sure to win the next war. Our enemies will be planted in huge new forests all over the plain, and the wives will put mother trees in every one of them."

Miro felt sick. Is this what all their work and sacrifice was for, to give some transient advantage to one tribe of piggies? Almost he said, Libo didn't die so you could conquer the world. But his training took over, and he asked a noncommittal question. "Where are all these new children?"

"None of the little brothers come to *us*," explained Human. "We have too much to do, learning from you and teaching all the other brother-houses. We can't be training little brothers." Then, proudly, he added, "Of the three hundred, fully half are children of my father, Rooter."

Mandachuva nodded gravely. "The wives have great respect for what you have taught us. And they have great hope in the Speaker for the Dead. But what you tell us now, this is very bad. If the framlings hate us, what will we do?''

"I don't know," said Miro. For the moment, his mind was racing to try to cope with all the information they had just told him. Three hundred twenty new babies. A population explosion. And Rooter somehow the father of half of them. Before today Miro would have dismissed the statement of Rooter's fatherhood as part of the piggies' totemic belief system. But having seen a tree uproot itself and fall apart in response to singing, he was prepared to question all his old assumptions.

Yet what good did it do to learn anything now? They'd never let him report again; he couldn't follow up; he'd be aboard a starship for the next quarter century while someone else did all his work. Or worse, no one else.

"Don't be unhappy," said Human. "You'll see—the Speaker for the Dead will make it all work out well."

"The Speaker. Yes, he'll make everything work out fine." The way he did for me and Ouanda. My sister.

"The hive queen says he'll teach the framlings to love us—"

"Teach the framlings," said Miro. "He'd better do it quickly then. It's too late for him to save me and Ouanda. They're arresting us and taking us off planet."

"To the stars?" asked Human hopefully.

"Yes, to the stars, to stand trial! To be punished for helping you. It'll take us twenty-two years to get there, and they'll never let us come back."

The piggies took a moment to absorb this information. Fine, thought Miro. Let them wonder how the Speaker is going to solve everything for them. I trusted in the Speaker, too, and it didn't do much for me. The piggies conferred together.

Human emerged from the group and came closer to the fence. "We'll hide you."

"They'll never find you in the forest," said Mandachuva.

"They have machines that can track me by my smell," said Miro.

"Ah. But doesn't the law forbid them to show us their machines?" asked Human.

Miro shook his head. "It doesn't matter. The gate is sealed to me. I can't cross the fence."

The piggies looked at each other.

"But you have capim right there," said Arrow.

Miro looked stupidly at the grass. "So what?" he asked.

"Chew it," said Human.

"Why?" asked Miro.

"We've seen humans chewing capim," said Leaf-eater. "The other night, on the hillside, we saw the Speaker and some of the robe-humans chewing capim."

"And many other times," said Mandachuva.

Their impatience with him was frustrating. "What does that have to do with the fence?"

Again the piggies looked at each other. Finally Mandachuva tore off a blade of capim near the ground, folded it carefully into a thick wad, and put it in his mouth to chew it. He sat down after a while. The others began teasing him, poking him with their fingers, pinching him. He showed no sign of noticing. Finally Human gave him a particularly vicious pinch, and when Mandachuva did not respond, they began saying, in males' language, Ready, Time to go, Now, Ready.

Mandachuva stood up, a bit shaky for a moment. Then he ran at the fence and scrambled to the top, flipped over, and landed on all fours on the same side as Miro.

Miro leaped to his feet and began to cry out just as Mandachuva reached the top; by the time he finished his cry, Mandachuva was standing up and dusting himself off.

"You can't do that," said Miro. "It stimulates all the pain nerves in the body. The fence can't be crossed."

"Oh," said Mandachuva.

From the other side of the fence, Human was rubbing his

thighs together. "He didn't know," he said. "The humans don't know."

"It's an anesthetic," said Miro. "It stops you from feeling pain."

"No," said Mandachuva. "I feel the pain. Very bad pain. Worst pain in the world."

"Rooter says the fence is even worse than dying," said Human. "Pain in all the places."

"But you don't care," said Miro.

"It's happening to your other self," said Mandachuva. "It's happening to your animal self. But your tree self doesn't care. It makes you be your tree self."

Then Miro remembered a detail that had been lost in the grotesquerie of Libo's death. The dead man's mouth had been filled with a wad of capim. So had the mouth of every piggy that had died. Anesthetic. The death looked like hideous torture, but pain was not the purpose of it. They used an anesthetic. It had nothing to do with pain.

"So," said Mandachuva. "Chew the grass, and come with us. We'll hide you."

"Ouanda," said Miro.

"Oh, I'll go get her," said Mandachuva.

"You don't know where she lives."

"Yes I do," said Mandachuva.

"We do this many times a year," said Human. "We know where everybody lives."

"But no one has ever seen you," said Miro.

"We're very secret," said Mandachuva. "Besides, nobody is looking for us."

Miro imagined dozens of piggies creeping about in Milagre in the middle of the night. No guard was kept. Only a few people had business that took them out in the darkness. And the piggies were small, small enough to duck down in the capim and disappear completely. No wonder they knew about metal and machines, despite all the rules designed to keep them from learning about them. No doubt they had seen the mines, had watched the shuttle land, had seen the kilns firing the bricks, had watched the fazendeiros plowing and planting the human-specific amaranth. No wonder they had known what to ask for.

How stupid of us, to think we could cut them off from our culture. They kept far more secrets from us than we could possibly keep from them. So much for cultural superiority.

Miro pulled up his own blade of capim.

"No," said Mandachuva, taking the blade from his hands. "You don't get the root part. If you take the root part, it doesn't do you any good." He threw away Miro's blade and tore off his own, about ten centimeters above the base. Then he folded it and handed it to Miro, who began to chew it.

Mandachuva pinched and poked him.

"Don't worry about that," said Miro. "Go get Ouanda. They could arrest her any minute. Go. Now. Go on."

Mandachuva looked at the others and, seeing some invisible signal of consent, jogged off along the fenceline toward the slopes of Vila Alta, where Ouanda lived.

Miro chewed a little more. He pinched himself. As the piggies said, he felt the pain, but he didn't care. All he cared about was that this was a way out, a way to stay on Lusitania. To stay, perhaps, with Ouanda. Forget the rules, all the rules. They had no power over him once he left the human enclave and entered the piggies' forest. He would become a renegade, as they already accused him of being, and he and Ouanda could leave behind all the insane rules of human behavior and live as they wanted to, and raise a family of humans who had completely new values, learned from the piggies, from the forest life; something new in the Hundred Worlds, and Congress would be powerless to stop them.

He ran at the fence and seized it with both hands. The pain was no less than before, but now he didn't care, he scrambled up to the top. But with each new handhold the pain grew more intense, and he began to care, he began to care very much about the pain, he began to realize that the capim had no anesthetic effect on him at all, but by this time he was already at the top of the fence. The pain was maddening; he couldn't think; momentum carried him above the top and as he balanced there his head passed through the vertical field of the fence. All the pain possible to his body came to his brain at once, as if every part of him were on fire.

The Little Ones watched in horror as their friend hung there atop the fence, his head and torso on one side, his hips and legs on the other. At once they cried out, reached for him, tried to pull him down. Since they had not chewed capim, they dared not touch the fence.

Hearing their cries, Mandachuva ran back. Enough of the anesthetic remained in his body that he could climb up and push the heavy human body over the top. Miro landed with a bone-crushing thump on the ground, his arm still touching the fence. The piggies pulled him away. His face was frozen in a rictus of agony.

"Quick!" shouted Leaf-eater. "Before he dies, we have to plant him!"

"No!" Human answered, pushing Leaf-eater away from Miro's frozen body. "We don't know if he's dying! The pain is just an illusion, you know that, he doesn't have a wound, the pain should go away—"

"It isn't going away," said Arrow. "Look at him."

Miro's fists were clenched, his legs were doubled under him, and his spine and neck were arched backward. Though he was breathing in short, hard pants, his face seemed to grow even tighter with pain.

"Before he dies," said Leaf-eater. "We have to give him root."

"Go get Ouanda," said Human. He turned to face Mandachuva. "Now! Go get her and tell her Miro is dying. Tell her the gate is sealed and Miro is on this side of it and he's dying."

Mandachuva took off at a run.

*   *   *

The secretary opened the door, but not until he actually saw Novinha did Ender allow himself to feel relief. When he sent Ela for her, he was sure that she would come; but as they waited so many long minutes for her arrival, he began to doubt his understanding of her. There had been no need to doubt. She was the woman that he thought she was. He noticed that her hair was down and windblown, and for the first time since he came to Lusitania, Ender saw in her face a clear image of the girl who in her anguish had summoned him less than two weeks, more than twenty years ago.

She looked tense, worried, but Ender knew her anxiety was because of her present situation, coming into the Bishop's own chambers so shortly after the disclosure of her transgressions. If Ela told her about the danger to Miro, that, too, might be part of her tension. All this was transient; Ender could see in her face, in the relaxation of her movement, in the steadiness of her gaze, that the end of her long deception was indeed the gift he had hoped, had believed it would be. I did not come to hurt you, Novinha, and I'm glad to see that my Speaking has brought you better things than shame.

Novinha stood for a moment, looking at the Bishop. Not defiantly, but politely, with dignity; he responded the same way, quietly offering her a seat. Dom Cristão started to rise from his stool, but she shook her head, smiled, took another stool near the wall. Near Ender. Ela came and stood behind and beside her mother, so she was also partly behind Ender. Like a daughter standing between her parents, thought Ender; then he thrust the thought away from him and refused to think of it anymore. There were far more important matters at hand.

"I see," said Bosquinha, "that you intend this meeting to be an interesting one."

"I think Congress decided that already," said Dona Cristã.

"Your son is accused," Bishop Peregrino began, "of crimes against—"

"I know what he's accused of," said Novinha. "I didn't know until tonight, when Ela told me, but I'm not surprised. My daughter Elanora has also been defying some rules her master set for her. Both of them have a higher allegiance to their own conscience than to the rules others set down for them. It's a failing, if your object is to maintain order, but if your goal is to learn and adapt, it's a virtue."

"Your son isn't on trial here," said Dom Cristão.

"I asked you to meet together," said Ender, "because a decision must be made. Whether or not to comply with the orders given us by Starways Congress."

"We don't have much choice," said Bishop Peregrino.

"There are many choices," said Ender, "and many reasons for choosing. You already made one choice—when you found your files being stripped, you decided to try to save them, and you decided to trust them with me, a stranger. Your trust was not misplaced—I'll return your files to you whenever you ask, unread, unaltered."

"Thank you," said Dona Cristã. "But we did that before we knew the gravity of the charge."

"They're going to evacuate us," said Dom Cristão.

"They control everything," said Bishop Peregrino.

"I already told him that," said Bosquinha.

"They don't control everything," said Ender. "They only control you through the ansible connection."

"We can't cut off the ansible," said Bishop Peregrino. "That is our only connection with the Vatican."

"I don't suggest cutting off the ansible. I only tell you what I can do. And when I tell you this, I am trusting you the way you trusted me. Because if you repeat this to anyone, the cost to me—and to someone else, whom I love and depend on—would be immeasurable."

He looked at each of them, and each in turn nodded acquiescence.

"I have a friend whose control over ansible communications among all the Hundred Worlds is complete—and completely unsuspected. I'm the only one who knows what she can do. And she has told me that when I ask her to, she can make it seem to all the framlings that we here on Lusitania have cut off our ansible connection. And yet we will have the ability to send guarded messages if we want to—to the Vatican, to the offices of your order. We can read distant records, intercept distant communications. In short, we will have eyes and they will be blind.''

"Cutting off the ansible, or even seeming to, would be an act of rebellion. Of war.'' Bosquinha was saying it as harshly as possible, but Ender could see that the idea appealed to her, though she was resisting it with all her might. "I will say, though, that if we were insane enough to decide on war, what the Speaker is offering us is a clear advantage. We'd need any advantage we could get—if we were mad enough to rebel.''

"We have nothing to gain by rebellion," said the Bishop, "and everything to lose. I grieve for the tragedy it would be to send Miro and Ouanda to stand trial on another world, especially because they are so young. But the court will no doubt take that into account and treat them with mercy. And by complying with the orders of the committee, we will save this community much suffering.''

"Don't you think that having to evacuate this world will also cause them suffering?" asked Ender.

"Yes. Yes, it will. But a law was broken, and the penalty must be paid.''

"What if the law was based on a misunderstanding, and the penalty is far out of proportion to the sin?''

"We can't be the judges of that," said the Bishop.

"We *are* the judges of that. If we go along with Congressional orders, then we're saying that the law is good and the punishment is just. And it may be that at the end of this meeting you'll decide exactly that. But there are some things you must know before you can make your decision. Some of those things I can tell you, and some of those things only Ela and Novinha can tell you. You shouldn't make your decision until you know all that we know."

"I'm always glad to know as much as possible," said the Bishop. "Of course, the final decision is Bosquinha's, not mine—"

"The final decision belongs to all of you together, the civil and religious and intellectual leadership of Lusitania. If any one of you decides against rebellion, rebellion is impossible. Without the Church's support, Bosquinha can't lead. Without civil support, the Church has no power."

"We have no power," said Dom Cristão. "Only opinions."

"Every adult in Lusitania looks to you for wisdom and fairmindedness."

"You forget a fourth power," said Bishop Peregrino. "Yourself."

"I'm a framling here."

"A most extraordinary framling," said the Bishop. "In your four days here you have captured the soul of this people in a way I feared and foretold. Now you counsel rebellion that could cost us everything. You are as dangerous as Satan. And yet here you are, submitting to our authority as if you weren't free to get on the shuttle and leave here when the starship returns to Trondheim with our two young criminals aboard."

"I submit to your authority," said Ender, "because I don't want to be a framling here. I want to be your citizen, your student, your parishioner."

"As a Speaker for the Dead?" asked the Bishop.

"As Andrew Wiggin. I have some other skills that might be useful. Particularly if you rebel. And I have other work to do that can't be done if humans are taken from Lusitania."

"We don't doubt your sincerity," said the Bishop. "But you must forgive us if we are doubtful about casting in with a citizen who is something of a latecomer."

Ender nodded. The Bishop could not say more until he knew more. "Let me tell you first what I know. Today, this afternoon, I went out into the forest with Miro and Ouanda.''

"You! You also broke the law!" The Bishop half-rose from his chair.

Bosquinha reached forward, gestured to settle the Bishop's ire. "The intrusion in our files began long before this afternoon. The Congressional Order couldn't possibly be related to his infraction.''

"I broke the law," said Ender, "because the piggies were asking for me. Demanding, in fact, to see me. They had seen the shuttle land. They knew that I was here. And, for good or ill, they had read the Hive Queen and the Hegemon.''

"They gave the piggies *that* book?" said the Bishop.

"They also gave them the New Testament," said Ender. "But surely you won't be surprised to learn that the piggies found much in common between themselves and the hive queen. Let me tell you what the piggies said. They begged me to convince all the Hundred Worlds to end the rules that keep them isolated here. You see, the piggies don't think of the fence the way we do. We see it as a way of protecting their culture from human influence and corruption. They see it as a way of keeping them from learning all the wonderful secrets that we know. They imagine our ships going from star to star, colonizing them, filling them up. And five or ten thousand years from now, when they finally learn all that we refuse to teach them, they'll emerge into space to find all the worlds filled up. No place for them at all. They think of our fence as a form of species murder. We will keep them on Lusitania like animals in a zoo, while we go out and take all the rest of the universe.''

"That's nonsense," said Dom Cristão. "That isn't our intention at all.''

"Isn't it?" Ender retorted. "Why are we so anxious to keep them from any influence from our culture? It isn't just in the interest of science. It isn't just good xenological procedure. Remember, please, that our discovery of the ansible, of starflight, of partial gravity control, even of the weapon we used to destroy the buggers—all of them came as a *direct* result of our contact with the buggers. We learned most of the technology from the machines they left behind from their first foray into Earth's star system. We were using those machines long before we understood them. Some of them, like the philotic slope, we don't even understand now. We are in space precisely *because* of the impact of a devastatingly superior culture. And yet in only a few generations, we took their machines, surpassed them, and destroyed them. That's what our fence means—we're afraid the piggies will do the same to us. And they know that's what it means. They know it, and they hate it.''

"We aren't afraid of them," said the Bishop. "They're—savages, for heaven's sake—"

"That's how we looked to the buggers, too," said Ender. "But to Pipo and Libo and Ouanda and Miro, the piggies have never looked like savages. They're different from us, yes, far more different than framlings. But they're still *people*. Ramen, not varelse. So when Libo saw that the piggies were in danger of starving, that they were preparing to go to war in order to cut down the population, he didn't act like a scientist. He didn't observe their war and take notes on the death and suffering. He acted like a Christian. He got experimental amaranth that Novinha had rejected for human use because it was too closely akin to Lusitanian biochemistry, and he taught the piggies how to plant it and harvest it and prepare it as food. I have no doubt that the rise in piggy population and the fields of amaranth are what the Starways Congress saw. Not a willful violation of the law, but an act of compassion and love."

"How can you call such disobedience a Christian act?" said the Bishop.

"What man of you is there, when his son asks for bread, will give him a stone?"

"The devil can quote scripture to suit his own purpose," said the Bishop.

"I'm not the devil," said Ender, "and neither are the piggies. Their babies were dying of hunger, and Libo gave them food and saved their lives."

"And look what they did to *him!*"

"Yes, let's look what they did to him. They put him to death. Exactly the way they put to death their own most honored citizens. Shouldn't that have told us something?"

"It told us that they're dangerous and have no conscience," said the Bishop.

"It told us that death means something completely different to them. If you really believed that someone was perfect in heart, Bishop, so righteous that to live another day could only cause them to be less perfect, then wouldn't it be a good thing for them if they were killed and taken directly into heaven?"

"You mock us. You don't believe in heaven."

"But you do! What about the martyrs, Bishop Peregrino? Weren't they caught up joyfully into heaven?"

"Of course they were. But the men who killed them were beasts. Murdering saints didn't sanctify them, it damned their souls to hell forever."

"But what if the dead don't go to heaven? What if the dead are transformed into new life, right before your eyes? What if when a piggy dies, if they lay out his body just so, it takes root and turns into something else? What if it turns into a tree that lives fifty or a hundred or five hundred years more?"

"What are you talking about?" demanded the Bishop.

"Are you telling us that the piggies somehow metamorphose from animal to plant?" asked Dom Cristão. "Basic biology suggests that this isn't likely."

"It's practically impossible," said Ender. "That's why there are only a handful of species on Lusitania that survived the Descolada. Because only a few of them were able to make the transformation. When the piggies kill one of their people, he is transformed into a tree. And the tree retains at least some of its intelligence. Because today I saw the piggies sing to a tree, and without a single tool touching it, the tree severed its own roots, fell over, and split itself into exactly the shapes and forms of wood and bark that the piggies needed. It wasn't a dream. Miro and Ouanda and I all saw it with our own eyes, and heard the song, and touched the wood, and prayed for the soul of the dead.''

"What does this have to do with our decision?" demanded Bosquinha. "So the forests are made up of dead piggies. That's a matter for scientists.''

"I'm telling you that when the piggies killed Pipo and Libo they thought they were helping them transform into the next stage of their existence. They weren't beasts, they were ramen, giving the highest honor to the men who had served them so well.''

"Another moral transformation, is that it?" asked the Bishop. "Just as you did today in your Speaking, making us see Marcos Ribeira again and again, each time in a new light, now you want us to think the piggies are noble? Very well, they're noble. But I won't rebel against Congress, with all the suffering such a thing would cause, just so our scientists can teach the piggies how to make refrigerators.''

"Please," said Novinha.

They looked at her expectantly.

"You say that they stripped our files? They read them all?''

"Yes," said Bosquinha.

"Then they know everything that I have in my files. About the Descolada.''

"Yes," said Bosquinha.

Novinha folded her hands in her lap. "There won't be any evacuation.''

"I didn't think so," said Ender. "That's why I asked Ela to bring you.''

"Why won't there be an evacuation?" asked Bosquinha.

"Because of the Descolada."

"Nonsense," said the Bishop. "Your parents found a cure for that."

"They didn't cure it," said Novinha. "They controlled it. They stopped it from becoming active."

"That's right," said Bosquinha. "That's why we put the additives in the water. The Colador."

"Every human being on Lusitania, except perhaps the Speaker, who may not have caught it yet, is a carrier of the Descolada."

"The additive isn't expensive," said the Bishop. "But perhaps they might isolate us. I can see that they might do that."

"There's nowhere isolated enough," said Novinha. "The Descolada is infinitely variable. It attacks any kind of genetic material. The additive can be given to humans. But can they give additives to every blade of grass? To every bird? To every fish? To every bit of plankton in the sea?"

"They can all catch it?" asked Bosquinha. "I didn't know that."

"I didn't tell anybody," said Novinha. "But I built the protection into every plant that I developed. The amaranth, the potatoes, everything—the challenge wasn't making the protein usable, the challenge was to get the organisms to produce their own Descolada blockers."

Bosquinha was appalled. "So anywhere we go—"

"We can trigger the complete destruction of the biosphere."

"And you kept this a *secret*?" asked Dom Cristão.

"There was no need to tell it." Novinha looked at her hands in her lap. "Something in the information had caused the piggies to kill Pipo. I kept it secret so no one else would know. But now, what Ela has learned over the last few years, and what the Speaker has said tonight—now I know what it was that Pipo learned. The Descolada doesn't just split the genetic molecules and prevent them from reforming or dupli-

cating. It also encourages them to bond with completely
foreign genetic molecules. Ela did the work on this against
my will. All the native life on Lusitania thrives in plant-and-
animal pairs. The cabra with the capim. The watersnakes
with the grama. The suckflies with the reeds. The xingadora
bird with the tropeço vines. And the piggies with the trees of
the forest.''

"You're saying that one *becomes* the other?'' Dom Cristão
was at once fascinated and repelled.

"The piggies may be unique in that, in transforming from
the corpse of a piggy into a tree,'' said Novinha. "But
perhaps the cabras become fertilized from the pollen of the
capim. Perhaps the flies are hatched from the tassels of the
river reeds. It should be studied. I should have been studying
it all these years.''

"And now they'll know this?'' asked Dom Cristão. "From
your files?''

"Not right away. But sometime in the next twenty or thirty
years. Before any other framlings get here, they'll know,''
said Novinha.

"I'm not a scientist,'' said the Bishop. "Everyone else
seems to understand except me. What does this have to do
with the evacuation?''

Bosquinha fidgeted with her hands. "They can't take us
off Lusitania,'' she said. "Anywhere they took us, we'd
carry the Descolada with us, and it would kill everything.
There aren't enough xenobiologists in the Hundred Worlds to
save even a single planet from devastation. By the time they
get here, they'll know that we can't leave.''

"Well, then,'' said the Bishop. "That solves our problem.
If we tell them now, they won't even send a fleet to evacuate
us.''

"No,'' said Ender. "Bishop Peregrino, once they know
what the Descolada will do, they'll see to it that no one
leaves this planet, ever.''

The Bishop scoffed. "What, do you think they'll blow up

the planet? Come now, Speaker, there are no more Enders among the human race. The worst they might do is quarantine us here—''

"In which case," said Dom Cristão, "why should we submit to their control at all? We could send them a message telling them about the Descolada, informing them that we will not leave the planet and they should not come here, and that's it.''

Bosquinha shook her head. "Do you think that none of them will say, 'The Lusitanians, just by visiting another world, can destroy it. They have a starship, they have a known propensity for rebelliousness, they have the murderous piggies. Their existence is a threat.' ''

"Who would say that?" said the Bishop.

"No one in the Vatican," said Ender. "But Congress isn't in the business of saving souls.''

"And maybe they'd be right," said the Bishop. "You said yourself that the piggies want starflight. And yet wherever they might go, they'll have this same effect. Even uninhabited worlds, isn't that right? What will they do, endlessly duplicate this bleak landscape—forests of a single tree, prairies of a single grass, with only the cabra to graze it and only the xingadora to fly above it?''

"Maybe someday we could find a way to get the Descolada under control," said Ela.

"We can't stake our future on such a thin chance," said the Bishop.

"That's why we have to rebel," said Ender. "Because Congress will think exactly that way. Just as they did three thousand years ago, in the Xenocide. Everybody condemns the Xenocide because it destroyed an alien species that turned out to be harmless in its intentions. But as long as it seemed that the buggers were determined to destroy humankind, the leaders of humanity had no choice but to fight back with all their strength. We are presenting them with the same dilemma again. They're already afraid of the piggies. And once they understand the Descolada, all the pretense of trying to protect the piggies will be done with. For the sake of humanity's survival, they'll destroy us. Probably not the whole planet. As you said, there are no Enders today. But they'll certainly obliterate Milagre and remove any trace of human contact. Including killing all the piggies who know us. Then they'll set a watch over this planet to keep the piggies from ever emerging from their primitive state. If you knew what they know, wouldn't you do the same?''

"A Speaker for the Dead says this?" said Dom Cristão.

"You were there," said the Bishop. "You were there the first time, weren't you. When the buggers were destroyed."

"Last time we had no way of talking to the buggers, no way of knowing they were ramen and not varelse. This time *we're here*. We know that we won't go out and destroy other worlds. We know that we'll stay here on Lusitania until we can go out safely, the Descolada neutralized. *This* time," said Ender, "we can keep the ramen alive, so that whoever writes the piggies' story won't have to be a Speaker for the Dead."

The secretary opened the door abruptly, and Ouanda burst in. "Bishop," she said. "Mayor. You have to come. Novinha—"

"What is it?" said the Bishop.

"Ouanda, I have to arrest you," said Bosquinha.

"Arrest me later," she said. "It's Miro. He climbed over the fence."

"He can't do that," said Novinha. "It might kill him—" Then, in horror, she realized what she had said. "Take me to him—"

"Get Navio," said Dona Cristã.

"You don't understand," said Ouanda. "We can't get to him. He's on the other side of the fence."

"Then what can we do?" asked Bosquinha.

"Turn the fence off," said Ouanda.

Bosquinha looked helplessly at the others. "I can't do that.

The Committee controls that now. By ansible. They'd never turn it off.''

"Then Miro's as good as dead," said Ouanda.

"No," said Novinha.

Behind her, another figure came into the room. Small, fur-covered. None of them but Ender had ever before seen a piggy in the flesh, but they knew at once what the creature was. "Excuse me," said the piggy. "Does this mean we should plant him now?"

No one bothered to ask how the piggy got over the fence. They were too busy realizing what he meant by *planting* Miro.

"No!" screamed Novinha.

Mandachuva looked at her in surprise. "No?"

"I think," said Ender, "that you shouldn't plant any more humans."

Mandachuva stood absolutely still.

"What do you mean?" said Ouanda. "You're making him upset."

"I expect he'll be more upset before this day is over," said Ender. "Come, Ouanda, take us to the fence where Miro is."

"What good will it do if we can't get over the fence?" asked Bosquinha.

"Call for Navio," said Ender.

"I'll go get him," said Dona Cristã. "You forget that no one can call anybody."

"I said, what good will it do?" demanded Bosquinha.

"I told you before," said Ender. "If you decide to rebel, we can sever the ansible connection. And then we can turn off the fence."

"Are you trying to use Miro's plight to force my hand?" asked the Bishop.

"Yes," said Ender. "He's one of your flock, isn't he? So leave the ninety-nine, shepherd, and come with us to save the one that's lost."

"What's happening?" asked Mandachuva.

"You're leading us to the fence," said Ender. "Hurry, please."

They filed down the stairs from the Bishop's chambers to the Cathedral below. Ender could hear the Bishop behind him, grumbling about perverting scripture to serve private ends.

They passed down the aisle of the Cathedral, Mandachuva leading the way. Ender noticed that the Bishop paused near the altar, watching the small furred creature as the humans trooped after him. Outside the Cathedral, the Bishop caught up with him. "Tell me, Speaker," he said, "just as a matter of opinion, if the fence came down, if we rebelled against Starways Congress, would *all* the rules about contact with the piggies be ended?"

"I hope so," said Ender. "I hope that there'll be no more unnatural barriers between us and them."

"Then," said the Bishop, "we'd be able to teach the gospel of Jesus Christ to the Little Ones, wouldn't we? There'd be no rule against it."

"That's right," said Ender. "They might not be converted, but there'd be no rule against trying."

"I have to think about this," said the Bishop. "But perhaps, my dear infidel, your rebellion will open the door to the conversion of a great nation. Perhaps God led you here after all."

By the time the Bishop, Dom Cristão, and Ender reached the fence, Mandachuva and the women had already been there for some time. Ender could tell by the way Ela was standing between her mother and the fence, and the way Novinha was holding her hands out in front of her face, that Novinha had already tried to climb over the fence to reach her son. She was crying now and shouting at him. "Miro! Miro, how could you do this, how could you climb it—" while Ela tried to talk to her, to calm her.

On the other side of the fence, four piggies stood watching, amazed.

Ouanda was trembling with fear for Miro's life, but she had enough presence of mind to tell Ender what she knew he could not see for himself. "That's Cups, and Arrow, and Human, and Leaf-eater. Leaf-eater's trying to get the others to plant him. I think I know what that means, but we're all right. Human and Mandachuva have convinced them not to do it."

"But it still doesn't get us any closer," said Ender. "Why did Miro do something so stupid?"

"Mandachuva explained on the way here. The piggies chew capim and it has an anesthetic effect. They can climb the fence whenever they want. Apparently they've been doing it for years. They thought we didn't do it because we were so obedient to law. Now they know that capim doesn't have the same effect on us."

Ender walked to the fence. "Human," he said.

Human stepped forward.

"There's a chance that we can turn off the fence. But if we do it, we're at war with all the humans on every other world. Do you understand that? The humans of Lusitania and the piggies, together, at war against all the other humans."

"Oh," said Human.

"Will we win?" asked Arrow.

"We might," said Ender. "And we might not."

"Will you give us the hive queen?" asked Human.

"First I have to meet with the wives," said Ender.

The piggies stiffened.

"What are you talking about?" asked the Bishop.

"I have to meet with the wives," said Ender to the piggies, "because we have to make a treaty. An agreement. A set of rules between us. Do you understand me? Humans can't live by your laws, and you can't live by ours, but if we're to live in peace, with no fence between us, and if I'm to let the hive queen live with you and help you and teach you, then you have to make us some promises, and keep them. Do you understand?''

"I understand," said Human. "But you don't know what you're asking for, to deal with the wives. They're not smart the way that the brothers are smart."

"They make all the decisions, don't they?''

"Of course," said Human. "They're the keepers of the mothers, aren't they? But I warn you, it's dangerous to speak to the wives. Especially for you, because they honor you so much."

"If the fence comes down, I have to speak to the wives. If I can't speak to them, then the fence stays up, and Miro dies, and we'll have to obey the Congressional Order that all the humans of Lusitania must leave here." Ender did not tell them that the humans might well be killed. He always told the truth, but he didn't always tell it all.

"I'll take you to the wives," said Human.

Leaf-eater walked up to him and ran his hand derisively across Human's belly. "They named you right," he said. "You *are* a human, not one of us." Leaf-eater started to run away, but Arrow and Cups held him.

"I'll take you," said Human. "Now, stop the fence and save Miro's life."

Ender turned to the Bishop.

"It's not my decision," said the Bishop. "It's Bosquinha's."

"My oath is to the Starways Congress," said Bosquinha, "but I'll perjure myself this minute to save the lives of my people. I say the fence comes down and we try to make the most of our rebellion."

"If we can preach to the piggies," said the Bishop.

"I'll ask them when I meet with the wives," said Ender. "I can't promise more than that."

"Bishop!" cried Novinha. "Pipo and Libo already died beyond that fence!"

"Bring it down," said the Bishop. "I don't want to see this colony end with God's work here still untouched." He smiled grimly. "But Os Venerados had better be made saints pretty soon. We'll need their help."

"Jane," murmured Ender.

"That's why I love you," said Jane. "You can do anything, as long as I set up the circumstances just right."

"Cut off the ansible and turn off the fence, please," said Ender.

"Done," she said.

Ender ran for the fence, climbed over it. With the piggies' help he lifted Miro to the top and let his rigid body drop into the waiting arms of the Bishop, the Mayor, Dom Cristão, and Novinha. Navio was jogging down the slope right behind Dona Cristã. Whatever they could do to help Miro would be done.

Ouanda was climbing the fence.

"Go back," said Ender. "We've already got him over."

"If you're going to see the wives," said Ouanda, "I'm going with you. You need my help."

Ender had no answer to that. She dropped down and came to Ender.

Navio was kneeling by Miro's body. "He climbed the *fence*?" he said. "There's nothing in the books for that. It isn't possible. Nobody can bear enough pain to get his head right through the field."

"Will he live?" demanded Novinha.

"How should I know?" said Navio, impatiently stripping away Miro's clothing and attaching sensors to him. "Nobody covered this in medical school."

Ender noticed that the fence was shaking again. Ela was climbing over. "I don't need *your* help," Ender said.

"It's about time somebody who knows something about xenobiology got to see what's going on," she retorted.

"Stay and look after your brother," said Ouanda.

Ela looked at her defiantly. "He's your brother, too," she said. "Now let's both see to it that if he dies, he didn't die for nothing."

The three of them followed Human and the other piggies into the forest.

Bosquinha and the Bishop watched them go. "When I woke up this morning," Bosquinha said, "I didn't expect to be a rebel before I went to bed."

"Nor did I ever imagine that the Speaker would be our ambassador to the piggies," said the Bishop.

"The question is," said Dom Cristão, "will we ever be forgiven for it."

"Do you think we're making a mistake?" snapped the Bishop.

"Not at all," said Dom Cristão. "I think we've taken a step toward something truly magnificent. But humankind almost never forgives true greatness."

"Fortunately," said the Bishop, "humankind isn't the judge that matters. And now I intend to pray for this boy, since medical science has obviously reached the boundary of its competence."

Chapter 17
The Wives

*F*ind out how word got out that the Evacuation Fleet is armed with the Little Doctor. That is HIGHEST PRIORITY. Then find out who this so-called Demosthenes is. Calling the Evacuation Fleet a Second Xenocide is definitely a violation of the treason laws under the Code and if CSA can't find this voice and put a stop to it, I can't think of any good reason for CSA to continue to exist.

In the meantime, continue your evaluation of the files retrieved from Lusitania. It's completely irrational for them to rebel just because we want to arrest two errant xenologers. There was nothing in the Mayor's background to suggest this was possible. If there's a chance that there was a revolution, I want to find out who the leaders of that revolution might be.

Pyotr, I know you're doing your best. So am I. So is everybody. So are the people on Lusitania, probably. But my responsibility is the safety and integrity of the Hundred Worlds. I have a hundred times the responsibility of Peter the Hegemon and about a tenth of his power. Not to mention the fact that I'm far from being the genius he was. No doubt you and everybody else would be happier if Peter were still available. I'm just afraid that by the time this thing is over, we may need another Ender. Nobody wants Xenocide, but if it happens, I want to make sure it's the other guys that disappear. When it comes to war, human is human and alien is alien. All that raman business goes up in smoke when we're talking about survival.

Does that satisfy you? Do you believe me when I tell you that I'm not being soft? Now see to it you're not soft, either. See to it you get me results, fast. Now. Love and kisses, Bawa.

—Gobawa Ekimbo, Chmn Xen Ovst Comm, to Pyotr Martinov, Dir Cgrs Sec Agc, Memo 44:1970:5:4:2; cit. Demosthenes, *The Second Xenocide*, 87:1972:1:1:1

Human led the way through the forest. The piggies scrambled easily up and down slopes, across a stream, through thick underbrush. Human, though, seemed to make a dance of it, running partway up certain trees, touching and speaking to others. The other piggies were much more restrained, only occasionally joining him in his antics. Only Mandachuva hung back with the human beings.

"Why does he do that?" asked Ender quietly.

Mandachuva was baffled for a moment. Ouanda explained what Ender meant. "Why does Human climb the trees, or touch them and sing?"

"He sings to them about the third life," said Mandachuva. "It's very bad manners for him to do that. He has always been selfish and stupid."

Ouanda looked at Ender in surprise, then back at Mandachuva. "I thought everybody liked Human," she said.

"Great honor," said Mandachuva. "A wise one." Then Mandachuva poked Ender in the hip. "But he's a fool in one thing. He thinks you'll do him honor. He thinks you'll take him to the third life."

"What's the third life?" asked Ender.

"The gift that Pipo kept for himself," said Mandachuva. Then he walked faster, caught up with the other piggies.

"Did any of that make sense to you?" Ender asked Ouanda.

"I still can't get used to the way you ask them direct questions."

"I don't get much in the way of answers, do I?"

"Mandachuva is angry, that's something. And he's angry at Pipo, that's another. The third life—a gift that Pipo kept for himself. It will all make sense."

"When?"

"In twenty years. Or twenty minutes. That's what makes xenology so fun."

Ela was touching the trees, too, and looking from time to time at the bushes. "All the same species of tree. And the bushes, too, just alike. And that vine, climbing most of the trees. Have you ever seen any other plant species here in the forest, Ouanda?"

"Not that I noticed. I never looked for that. The vine is called merdona. The macios seem to feed on it, and the piggies eat the macios. The merdona root, *we* taught the piggies how to make it edible. Before the amaranth. So they're eating lower on the food chain now."

"Look," said Ender.

The piggies were all stopped, their backs to the humans, facing a clearing. In a moment Ender, Ouanda, and Ela caught up with them and looked over them into the moonlit glen. It was quite a large space, and the ground was beaten bare. Several log houses lined the edges of the clearing, but the middle was empty except for a single huge tree, the largest they had seen in the forest.

The trunk seemed to be moving. "It's crawling with macios," said Ouanda.

"Not macios," said Human.

"Three hundred twenty," said Mandachuva.

"Little brothers," said Arrow.

"And little mothers," added Cups.

"And if you harm them," said Leaf-eater, "we will kill you unplanted and knock down your tree."

"We won't harm them," said Ender.

The piggies did not take a single step into the clearing. They waited and waited, until finally there was some movement near the largest of the log houses, almost directly opposite them. It was a piggy. But larger than any of the piggies they had seen before.

"A wife," murmured Mandachuva.

"What's her name?" asked Ender.

The piggies turned to him and stared. "*They* don't tell *us* their names," said Leaf-eater.

"If they even *have* names," added Cups.

Human reached up and drew Ender down to where he could whisper in his ear. "We always call her Shouter. But never where a wife can hear."

The female looked at them, and then sang—there was no other way to describe the mellifluous flow of her voice—a sentence or two in Wives' Language.

"It's for you to go," said Mandachuva. "Speaker. You."

"Alone?" asked Ender. "I'd rather bring Ouanda and Ela with me."

Mandachuva spoke loudly in Wives' Language; it sounded like gargling compared to the beauty of the female's voice. Shouter answered, again singing only briefly.

"She says of course they can come," Mandachuva reported. "She says they're females, aren't they? She's not very sophisticated about the differences between humans and little ones."

"One more thing," said Ender. "At least one of you, as an interpreter. Or can she speak Stark?"

Mandachuva relayed Ender's request. The answer was brief, and Mandachuva didn't like it. He refused to translate it. It was Human who explained. "She says that you may have any interpreter you like, as long as it's me."

"Then we'd like to have you as our interpreter," said Ender.

"You must enter the birthing place first," said Human. "You are the invited one."

Ender stepped out into the open and strode into the moonlight. He could hear Ela and Ouanda following him, and Human padding along behind. Now he could see that Shouter was not the only female here. Several faces were in every doorway. "How many are there?" asked Ender.

Human didn't answer. Ender turned to face him. "How many wives are there?" Ender repeated.

Human still did not answer. Not until Shouter sang again, more loudly and commandingly. Only then did Human translate. "In the birthing place, Speaker, it is only to speak when a wife asks you a question."

Ender nodded gravely, then walked back to where the other males waited at the edge of the clearing. Ouanda and Ela followed him. He could hear Shouter singing behind him, and now he understood why the males referred to her by that name—her voice was enough to make the trees shake. Human caught up with Ender and tugged at his clothing. "She says why are you going, you haven't been given permission to go. Speaker, this is a very bad thing, she's very angry."

"Tell her that I did not come to give instructions or to receive instructions. If she won't treat me as an equal, I won't treat her as an equal."

"I can't tell her that," said Human.

"Then she'll always wonder why I left, won't she?"

"This is a great honor, to be called among the wives!"

"It is also a great honor for the Speaker of the Dead to come and visit them."

Human stood still for a few moments, rigid with anxiety. Then he turned and spoke to Shouter.

She in turn fell silent. There was not a sound in the glen.

"I hope you know what you're doing, Speaker," murmured Ouanda.

"I'm improvising," said Ender. "How do you think it's going?"

She didn't answer.

Shouter went back into the large log house. Ender turned around and again headed for the forest. Almost immediately Shouter's voice rang out again.

"She commands you to wait," said Human.

Ender did not break stride, and in a moment he was on the other side of the piggy males. "If she asks me to return, I may come back. But you must tell her, Human, that I did not come to command or to be commanded."

"I can't say that," said Human.

"Why not?" asked Ender.

"Let me," said Ouanda. "Human, do you mean you can't say it because you're afraid, or because there are no words for it?"

"No words. For a brother to speak to a wife about him commanding her, and her petitioning him, those words can't be said in that direction."

Ouanda smiled at Ender. "Not mores, here, Speaker. Language."

"Don't they understand *your* language, Human?" asked Ender.

"Males' Language can't be spoken in the birthing place," said Human.

"Tell her that my words can't be spoken in Wives' Language, but only in Males' Language, and tell her that I—petition—that you be allowed to translate my words in Males' Language."

"You are a lot of trouble, Speaker," said Human. He turned and spoke again to Shouter.

Suddenly the glen was full of the sound of Wives' Language, a dozen different songs, like a choir warming up.

"Speaker," said Ouanda, "you have now violated just about every rule of good anthropological practice."

"Which ones did I miss?"

"The only one I can think of is that you haven't killed any of them yet."

"What you're forgetting," said Ender, "is that I'm not here as a scientist to study them. I'm here as an ambassador to make a treaty with them."

Just as quickly as they started, the wives fell silent. Shouter emerged from her house and walked to the middle of the clearing to stand very near to the huge central tree. She sang.

Human answered her—in Brothers' Language. Ouanda murmured a rough translation. "He's telling her what you said, about coming as equals."

Again the wives erupted in cacophonous song.

"How do you think they'll respond?" asked Ela.

"How could I know?" asked Ouanda. "I've been here exactly as often as you."

"I think they'll understand it and let me in on those terms," said Ender.

"Why do you think that?" asked Ouanda.

"Because I came out of the sky. Because I'm the Speaker for the Dead."

"Don't start thinking you're a great white god," said Ouanda. "It usually doesn't work out very well."

"I'm not Pizarro," said Ender.

In his ear Jane murmured, "I'm beginning to make some sense out of the Wives' Language. The basics of the Males' Language were in Pipo's and Libo's notes. Human's translations are very helpful. The Wives' Language is closely related to Males' Language, except that it seems more archaic—closer to the roots, more old forms—and all the female-to-male forms are in the imperative voice, while the male-to-female forms are in the supplicative. The female word for *the brothers* seems to be related to the male word for *macio*, the tree worm. If this is the language of love, it's a wonder they manage to reproduce at all."

Ender smiled. It was good to hear Jane speak to him again, good to know he would have her help.

He realized that Mandachuva had been asking Ouanda a

question, for now he heard her whispered answer. "He's listening to the jewel in his ear."

"Is it the hive queen?" asked Mandachuva.

"No," said Ouanda. "It's a . . ." She struggled to find a word. "It's a computer. A machine with a voice."

"Can I have one?" asked Mandachuva.

"Someday," Ender answered, saving Ouanda the trouble of trying to figure out how to answer.

The wives fell silent, and again Shouter's voice was alone. Immediately the males became agitated, bouncing up and down on their toes.

Jane whispered in his ear. "She's speaking Males' Language herself," she said.

"Very great day," said Arrow quietly. "The wives speaking Males' Language in this place. Never happened before."

"She invites you to come in," said Human. "As a sister to a brother she invites you."

Immediately Ender walked into the clearing and approached her directly. Even though she was taller than the males, she was still a good fifty centimeters shorter than Ender, so he fell to his knees at once. They were eye to eye.

"I am grateful for your kindness to me," said Ender.

"I could say *that* in Wives' Language," Human said.

"Say it in *your* language anyway," said Ender.

He did. Shouter reached out a hand and touched the smooth skin of his forehead, the rough stubble of his jaw; she pressed a finger against his lip, and he closed his eyes but did not flinch as she laid a delicate finger on his eyelid.

She spoke. "You are the holy Speaker?" translated Human. Jane corrected the translation. "He added the word *holy*."

Ender looked Human in the eye. "I am not holy," he said. Human went rigid.

"Tell her."

He was in turmoil for a moment; then he apparently decided that Ender was the less dangerous of the two. "She didn't say holy."

"Tell me what she says, as exactly as you can," said Ender.

"If you aren't holy," said Human, "how did you know what she really said?"

"Please," said Ender, "be truthful between her and me."

"To you I'll be truthful," said Human. "But when I speak to her, it's *my* voice she hears saying your words. I have to say them—carefully."

"Be truthful," said Ender. "Don't be afraid. It's important that she knows exactly what I said. Tell her this. Say that I ask her to forgive you for speaking to her rudely, but I am a rude framling and you must say exactly what I say."

Human rolled his eyes, but turned to Shouter and spoke.

She answered briefly. Human translated. "She says her head is not carved from merdona root. Of course she understands that."

"Tell her that we humans have never seen such a great tree before. Ask her to explain to us what she and the other wives do with this tree."

Ouanda was aghast. "You certainly get straight to the point, don't you?"

But when Human translated Ender's words, Shouter immediately went to the tree, touched it, and began to sing.

Now, gathered closer to the tree, they could see the mass of creatures squirming on the bark. Most of them were no more than four or five centimeters long. They looked vaguely fetal, though a thin haze of dark fur covered their pinkish bodies. Their eyes were open. They climbed over each other, struggling to win a place at one of the smears of drying dough that dotted the bark.

"Amaranth mash," said Ouanda.

"Babies," said Ela.

"Not babies," said Human. "These are almost grown enough to walk."

Ender stepped to the tree, reached out his hand. Shouter abruptly stopped her song. But Ender did not stop his movement. He touched his fingers to the bark near a young piggy. In its climbing, it touched him, climbed over his hand, clung to him. "Do you know this one by name?" asked Ender.

Frightened, Human hastily translated. And gave back Shouter's answer. "That one is a brother of mine," he said. "He won't get a name until he can walk on two legs. His father is Rooter."

"And his mother?" asked Ender.

"Oh, the little mothers never have names," said Human. "Ask her."

Human asked her. She answered. "She says his mother was very strong and very courageous. She made herself fat in bearing her five children." Human touched his forehead. "Five children is a very good number. And she was fat enough to feed them all."

"Does his mother bring the mash that feeds him?"

Human looked horrified. "Speaker, I can't say that. Not in any language."

"Why not?"

"I told you. She was fat enough to feed all five of her little ones. Put back that little brother, and let the wife sing to the tree."

Ender put his hand near the trunk again and the little brother squirmed away. Shouter resumed her song. Ouanda glared at Ender for his impetuousness. But Ela seemed excited. "Don't you see? The newborns feed on their mother's body."

Ender drew away, repelled.

"How can you say that?" asked Ouanda.

"Look at them squirming on the trees, just like little macios. They and the macios must have been competitors." Ela pointed toward a part of the tree unstained by amaranth mash. "The tree leaks sap. Here in the cracks. Back before the Descolada there must have been insects that fed on the

sap, and the macios and the infant piggies competed to eat
them. That's why the piggies were able to mingle their
genetic molecules with these trees. Not only did the infants
live here, the adults constantly had to climb the trees to keep
the macios away. Even when there were plenty of other food
sources, they were still tied to these trees throughout their life
cycles. Long before they ever *became* trees."

"We're studying piggy society," said Ouanda impatiently.
"Not the distant evolutionary past."

"I'm conducting delicate negotiations," said Ender. "So
please be quiet and learn what you can without conducting a
seminar."

The singing reached a climax; a crack appeared in the side
of the tree.

"They're not going to knock down *this* tree for us, are
they?" asked Ouanda, horrified.

"She is asking the tree to open her heart." Human touched
his forehead. "This is the mothertree, and it is the only one
in all our forest. No harm may come to this tree, or all our
children will come from other trees, and our fathers all will
die."

All the other wives' voices joined Shouter's now, and soon
a hole gaped wide in the trunk of the mothertree. Immediately Ender moved to stand directly in front of the hole. It
was too dark inside for him to see.

Ela took her nightstick from her belt and held it out to him.
Ouanda's hand flew out and seized Ela's wrist. "A machine!" she said. "You can't bring that here."

Ender gently took the nightstick out of Ela's hand. "The
fence is off," said Ender, "and we all can engage in Questionable Activities now." He pointed the barrel of the nightstick at the ground and pressed it on, then slid his finger
quickly along the barrel to soften the light and spread it. The
wives murmured, and Shouter touched Human on the belly.

"I told them you could make little moons at night," he
said. "I told them you carried them with you."

"Will it hurt anything if I let this light into the heart of the mothertree?"

Human asked Shouter, and Shouter reached for the nightstick. Then, holding it in trembling hands, she sang softly and tilted it slightly so that a sliver of the light passed through the hole. Almost at once she recoiled and pointed the nightstick the other direction. "The brightness blinds them," Human said.

In Ender's ear, Jane whispered, "The sound of her voice is echoing from the inside of the tree. When the light went in, the echo modulated, causing a high overtone and a shaping of the sound. The tree was answering, using the sound of Shouter's own voice."

"Can you see?" Ender said softly.

"Kneel down and get me close enough, and then move me across the opening." Ender obeyed, letting his head move slowly in front of the hole, giving the jeweled ear a clear angle toward the interior. Jane described what she saw. Ender knelt there for a long time, not moving. Then he turned to the others. "The little mothers," said Ender. "There are little mothers in there, pregnant ones. Not more than four centimeters long. One of them is giving birth."

"You see with your jewel?" asked Ela.

Ouanda knelt beside him, trying to see inside and failing. "Incredible sexual dimorphism. The females come to sexual maturity in their infancy, give birth, and die." She asked Human, "All of these little ones on the outside of the tree, they're all brothers?"

Human repeated the question to Shouter. The wife reached up to a place near the aperture in the trunk and took down one fairly large infant. She sang a few words of explanation. "That one is a young wife," Human translated. "She will join the other wives in caring for the children, when she's old enough."

"Is there only one?" asked Ela.

Ender shuddered and stood up. "That one is sterile, or else

they never let her mate. She couldn't possibly have had children.''

"Why not?" asked Ouanda.

"There's no birth canal," said Ender. "The babies eat their way out."

Ouanda muttered a prayer.

Ela, however, was more curious than ever. "Fascinating," she said. "But if they're so small, how do they mate?"

"We carry them to the fathers, of course," said Human. "How do you think? The father's can't come *here*, can they?"

"The fathers," said Ouanda. "That's what they call the most revered trees."

"That's right," said Human. "The fathers are ripe on the bark. They put their dust on the bark, in the sap. We carry the little mother to the father the wives have chosen. She crawls on the bark, and the dust on the sap gets into her belly and fills it up with little ones."

Ouanda wordlessly pointed to the small protuberances on Human's belly.

"Yes," Human said. "These are the carries. The honored brother puts the little mother on one of his carries, and she holds very tight all the way to the father." He touched his belly. "It is the greatest joy we have in our second life. We would carry the little mothers every night if we could."

Shouter sang, long and loud, and the hole in the mothertree began to close again.

"All those females, all the little mothers," asked Ela. "Are they sentient?"

It was a word that Human didn't know.

"Are they awake?" asked Ender.

"Of course," said Human.

"What he means," explained Ouanda, "is can the little mothers think? Do they understand language?"

"Them?" asked Human. "No, they're no smarter than the cabras. And only a little smarter than the macios. They only do three things. Eat, crawl, and cling to the carry. The ones on the outside of the tree, now—they're beginning to learn. I can remember climbing on the face of the mothertree. So I had memory then. But I'm one of the very few that remember so far back.''

Tears came unbidden to Ouanda's eyes. "All the mothers, they're born, they mate, they give birth and die, all in their infancy. They never even know they were alive.''

"It's sexual dimorphism carried to a ridiculous extreme," said Ela. "The females reach sexual maturity early, but the males reach it late. It's ironic, isn't it, that the dominant female adults are all sterile. They govern the whole tribe, and yet their own genes can't be passed on—"

"Ela," said Ouanda, "what if we could develop a way to let the little mothers bear their children without being devoured. A caesarean section. With a protein-rich nutrient substitute for the little mother's corpse. Could the females survive to adulthood?''

Ela didn't have a chance to answer. Ender took them both by the arms and pulled them away. "How dare you!" he whispered. "What if *they* could find a way to let infant human girls conceive and bear children, which would feed on their mother's tiny corpse?''

"What are you talking about!" said Ouanda.

"That's sick," said Ela.

"We didn't come here to attack them at the root of their lives," said Ender. "We came here to find a way to share a world with them. In a hundred years or five hundred years, when they've learned enough to make changes for themselves, then *they* can decide whether to alter the way that their children are conceived and born. But we can't begin to guess what it would do to them if suddenly as many females as males came to maturity. To do what? They can't bear more children, can they? They can't compete with the males to become fathers, can they? What are they *for*?''

"But they're dying without ever being alive—"

"They are what they are," said Ender. "They decide what changes they'll make, not you, not from your blindly human perspective, trying to make them have full and happy lives, just like us."

"You're right," said Ela. "Of course, you're right, I'm sorry."

To Ela, the piggies weren't people, they were strange alien fauna, and Ela was used to discovering that other animals had inhuman life patterns. But Ender could see that Ouanda was still upset. She had made the raman transition: She thought of piggies as *us* instead of *them*. She accepted the strange behavior that she knew about, even the murder of her father, as within an acceptable range of alienness. This meant she was actually more tolerant and accepting of the piggies than Ela could possibly be; yet it also made her more vulnerable to the discovery of cruel, bestial behaviors among her friends.

Ender noticed, too, that after years of association with the piggies, Ouanda had one of their habits: At a moment of extreme anxiety, her whole body became rigid. So he reminded her of her humanity by taking her shoulder in a fatherly gesture, drawing her close under his arm.

At his touch Ouanda melted a little, laughed nervously, her voice low. "Do you know what I keep thinking?" she said. "That the little mothers have all their children and die unbaptized."

"If Bishop Peregrino converts them," said Ender, "maybe they'll let us sprinkle the inside of the mothertree and say the words."

"Don't mock me," Ouanda whispered.

"I wasn't. For now, though, we'll ask them to change enough that we can live with them, and no more. We'll change ourselves only enough that they can bear to live with us. Agree to that, or the fence goes up again, because then we truly would be a threat to their survival."

Ela nodded her agreement, but Ouanda had gone rigid again. Ender's fingers suddenly dug harshly into Ouanda's shoulder. Frightened, she nodded her agreement. He relaxed his grip. "I'm sorry," he said. "But they are what they are. If you want, they are what God made them. So don't try to remake them in your own image."

He returned to the mothertree. Shouter and Human were waiting.

"Please excuse the interruption," said Ender.

"It's all right," said Human. "I told her what you were doing."

Ender felt himself sink inside. "What did you tell her we were doing?"

"I said that they wanted to do something to the little mothers that would make us all more like humans, but you said they never could do that or you'd put back the fence. I told her that you said we must remain Little Ones, and you must remain humans."

Ender smiled. His translation was strictly true, but he had the sense not to get into specifics. It was conceivable that the wives might actually want the little mothers to survive child-birth, without realizing how vast the consequences of such a simple-seeming, humanitarian change might be. Human was an excellent diplomat; he told the truth and yet avoided the whole issue.

"Well," said Ender. "Now that we've all met each other, it's time to begin serious talking."

Ender sat down on the bare earth. Shouter squatted on the ground directly opposite him. She sang a few words.

"She says you must teach us everything you know, take us out to the stars, bring us the hive queen and give her the lightstick that this new human brought with you, or in the dark of night she'll send all the brothers of this forest to kill all the humans in your sleep and hang you high above the ground so you get no third life at all." Seeing the humans' alarm, Human reached out his hand and touched Ender's chest. "No, no, you must understand. That means nothing. That's the way we always begin when we're talking to another tribe. Do you think we're crazy? We'd never kill you! You gave us amaranth, pottery, the Hive Queen and the Hegemon."

"Tell her to withdraw that threat or we'll never give her anything else."

"I told you, Speaker, it doesn't mean—"

"She said the words, and I won't talk to her as long as those words stand."

Human spoke to her.

Shouter jumped to her feet and walked all the way around the mothertree, her hands raised high, singing loudly.

Human leaned to Ender. "She's complaining to the great mother and to all the wives that you're a brother who doesn't know his place. She's saying that you're rude and impossible to deal with."

Ender nodded. "Yes, that's exactly right. Now we're getting somewhere."

Again Shouter squatted across from Ender. She spoke in Males' Language.

"She says she'll never kill any human or let any of the brothers or wives kill any of you. She says for you to remember that you're twice as tall as any of us and you know everything and we know nothing. Now has she humiliated herself enough that you'll talk to her?"

Shouter watched him, glumly waiting for his response.

"Yes," said Ender. "Now we can begin."

Novinha knelt on the floor beside Miro's bed. Quim and Olhado stood behind her. Dom Cristão was putting Quara and Grego to bed in their room. The sound of his off-tune lullaby was barely audible behind the tortured sound of Miro's breathing.

Miro's eyes opened.

"Miro," said Novinha.

Miro groaned.

"Miro, you're home in bed. You went over the fence while it was on. Now Dr. Navio says that your brain has been damaged. We don't know whether the damage is permanent or not. You may be partially paralyzed. But you're alive, Miro, and Navio says that he can do many things to help you compensate for what you may have lost. Do you understand? I'm telling you the truth. It may be very bad for a while, but it's worth trying."

He moaned softly. But it was not a sound of pain. It was as if he were trying to talk, and couldn't.

"Can you move your jaw, Miro?" asked Quim.

Slowly Miro's mouth opened and closed.

Olhado held his hand a meter above Miro's head and moved it. "Can you make your eyes follow the movement of my hand?"

Miro's eyes followed. Novinha squeezed Miro's hand. "Did you feel me squeeze your hand?"

Miro moaned again.

"Close your mouth for *no*," said Quim, "and open your mouth for *yes*."

Miro closed his mouth and said, "Mm."

Novinha could not help herself; despite her encouraging words, this was the most terrible thing that had happened to any of her children. She had thought when Lauro lost his eyes and became Olhado—she hated the nickname, but now used it herself—that nothing worse could happen. But Miro, paralyzed, helpless, so he couldn't even feel the touch of her hand, that could not be borne. She had felt one kind of grief when Pipo died, and another kind when Libo died, and a terrible regret at Marcão's death. She even remembered the aching emptiness she felt as she watched them lower her mother and father into the ground. But there was no pain worse than to watch her child suffer and be unable to help.

She stood up to leave. For his sake, she would do her crying silently, and in another room.

"Mm. Mm. Mm."

"He doesn't want you to go," said Quim.

"I'll stay if you want," said Novinha. "But you should sleep again. Navio said that the more you sleep for a while—"

"Mm. Mm. Mm."

"Doesn't want to sleep, either," said Quim.

Novinha stifled her immediate response, to snap at Quim and tell him that she could hear his answers perfectly well for herself. This was no time for quarreling. Besides, it was Quim who had worked out the system that Miro was using to communicate. He had a right to take pride in it, to pretend that he was Miro's voice. It was his way of affirming that he was part of the family. That he was not quitting because of what he learned in the praça today. It was his way of forgiving her, so she held her tongue.

"Maybe he wants to tell us something," said Olhado.

"Mm."

"Or ask a question?" said Quim.

"Ma. Aa."

"That's great," said Quim. "If he can't move his hands, he can't write."

"Sem problema," said Olhado. "Scanning. He can scan. If we bring him in by the terminal, I can make it scan the letters and he just says *yes* when it hits the letters he wants."

"That'll take forever," said Quim.

"Do you want to try that, Miro?" asked Novinha.

He wanted to.

The three of them carried him to the front room and laid him on the bed there. Olhado oriented the terminal so it displayed all the letters of the alphabet, facing so Miro could see them. He wrote a short program that caused each letter to light up in turn for a fraction of a second. It took a few trial runs for the speed to be right—slow enough that Miro could make a sound that meant *this letter* before the light moved on to the next one.

Miro, in turn, kept things moving faster yet by deliberately abbreviating his words.

P-I-G.

"Piggies," said Olhado.

"Yes," said Novinha. "Why were you crossing the fence with the piggies?"

"Mmmmm!"

"He's asking a question, Mother," said Quim. "He doesn't want to answer any."

"Aa."

"Do you want to know about the piggies that were with you when you crossed the fence?" asked Novinha. He did. "They've gone back into the forest. With Ouanda and Ela and the Speaker for the Dead." Quickly she told him about the meeting in the Bishop's chambers, what they had learned about the piggies, and above all what they had decided to do. "When they turned off the fence to save you, Miro, it was a decision to rebel against Congress. Do you understand? The Committee's rules are finished. The fence is nothing but wires now. The gate will stand open."

Tears came to Miro's eyes.

"Is that all you wanted to know?" asked Novinha. "You should sleep."

No, he said. No no no no.

"Wait till his eyes are clear," said Quim. "And then we'll scan some more."

D-I-G-A F-A-L—

"Diga ao Falante pelos Mortos," said Olhado.

"What should we tell the Speaker?" asked Quim.

"You should sleep now and tell us later," said Novinha. "He won't be back for hours. He's negotiating a set of rules to govern relations between the piggies and us. To stop them from killing any more of us, the way they killed Pipo and L—and your father."

But Miro refused to sleep. He continued spelling out his message as the terminal scanned. Together the three of them worked out what he was trying to get them to tell the Speaker. And they understood that he wanted them to go now, before the negotiations ended.

So Novinha left Dom Cristão and Dona Cristã to watch over the house and the little children. On the way out of the house she stopped beside her oldest son. The exertion had worn him out; his eyes were closed and his breathing was regular. She touched his hand, held it, squeezed it; he couldn't feel her touch, she knew, but then it was herself she was comforting, not him.

He opened his eyes. And, ever so gently, she felt his fingers tighten on hers. "I felt it," she whispered to him. "You'll be all right."

He shut his eyes against his tears. She got up and walked blindly to the door. "I have something in my eye," she told Olhado. "Lead me for a few minutes until I can see for myself."

Quim was already at the fence. "The gate's too far!" he shouted. "Can you climb over, Mother?"

She could, but it wasn't easy. "No doubt about it," she said. "Bosquinha's going to have to let us install another gate right here."

It was late now, past midnight, and both Ouanda and Ela was getting sleepy. Ender was not. He had been on edge for hours in his bargaining with Shouter; his body chemistry had responded, and even if he had gone home right now it would have been hours before he was capable of sleep.

He now knew far more about what the piggies wanted and needed. Their forest was their home, their nation; it was all the definition of property they had ever needed. Now, however, the amaranth fields had caused them to see that the prairie was also useful land, which they needed to control. Yet they had little concept of land measurement. How many hectares did they need to keep under cultivation? How much land could the humans use? Since the piggies themselves barely understood their needs, it was hard for Ender to pin them down.

Harder still was the concept of law and government. The wives ruled: to the piggies, it was that simple. But Ender had finally got them to understand that humans made their laws differently, and that human laws applied to human problems. To make them understand why humans needed their own laws, Ender had to explain to them human mating patterns. He was amused to note that Shouter was appalled at the notion of *adults* mating with each other, and of men having an equal voice with women in the making of the laws. The idea of family and kinship separate from the tribe was "brother blindness" to her. It was all right for Human to take pride in his father's many matings, but as far as the wives were concerned, they chose fathers solely on the basis of what was good for the tribe. The tribe and the individual—they were the only entities the wives respected.

Finally, though, they understood that human laws must apply within the borders of human settlements, and piggy laws must apply within the piggy tribes. Where the borders should be was entirely a different matter. Now, after three hours, they had finally agreed to one thing and one thing only: Piggy law applied within the forest, and all humans who came within the forest were subject to it. Human law applied within the fence, and all piggies who came there were subject to human government. All the rest of the planet would be divided up later. It was a very small triumph, but at least there was some agreement.

"You must understand," Ender told her, "that humans will need a lot of open land. But we're only the beginning of the problem. You want the hive queen to teach you, to help you mine ore and smelt metals and make tools. But she'll also need land. And in a very short time she'll be far stronger than either humans or Little Ones." Every one of her buggers, he explained, was perfectly obedient and infinitely hardworking. They would quickly outstrip the humans in their productivity and power. Once she was restored to life on Lusitania, she would have to be reckoned with at every turn.

"Rooter says she can be trusted," said Human. And, translating for Shouter, he said, "The mothertree also gives the hive queen her trust."

"Do you give her your *land*?" Ender insisted.

"The world is big," Human translated for Shouter. "She can use all the forests of the other tribes. So can you. We give them to you freely."

Ender looked at Ouanda and Ela. "That's all very good," said Ela, "but are those forests theirs to give?"

"Definitely not," said Ouanda. "They even have wars with the other tribes."

"We'll kill them for you if they give you trouble," offered Human. "We're very strong now. Three hundred twenty babies. In ten years no tribe can stand against us."

"Human," said Ender, "tell Shouter that we are dealing with this tribe now. We'll deal with other tribes later."

Human translated quickly, his words tumbling over each other, and quickly had Shouter's response. "No no no no no."

"What is she objecting to?" asked Ender.

"You *won't* deal with our enemies. You came to *us*. If you go to them, then you are the enemy, too."

It was at that moment that the lights appeared in the forest behind them, and Arrow and Leaf-eater led Novinha, Quim, and Olhado into the wives' clearing.

"Miro sent us," Olhado explained.

"How is he?" asked Ouanda.

"Paralyzed," said Quim bluntly. It saved Novinha the effort of explaining it gently.

"Nossa Senhora," whispered Ouanda.

"But much of it is temporary," said Novinha. "Before I left, I squeezed his hand. He felt it, and squeezed me back.

Just a little, but the nerve connections aren't dead, not all of them, anyway."

"Excuse me," said Ender, "but that's a conversation you can carry on back in Milagre. I have another matter to attend to here."

"Sorry," Novinha said. "Miro's message. He couldn't speak, but he gave it to us letter by letter, and we figured out what went in the cracks. The piggies are planning war. Using the advantages they've gained from us. Arrows, their greater numbers—they'd be irresistible. As I understand it, though, Miro says that their warfare isn't just a matter of conquest of territory. It's an opportunity for genetic mixing. Male exogamy. The winning tribe gets the use of the trees that grow from the bodies of the war dead."

Ender looked at Human, Leaf-eater, Arrow. "It's true," said Arrow. "Of course it's true. We are the wisest of tribes now. All of us will make better fathers than any of the other piggies."

"I see," said Ender.

"That's why Miro wanted us to come to you now, tonight," said Novinha. "While the negotiations still aren't final. That has to end."

Human stood up, bounced up and down as if he were about to take off and fly. "I won't translate that," said Human.

"*I* will," said Leaf-eater.

"Stop!" shouted Ender. His voice was far louder than he had ever let it be heard before. Immediately everyone fell silent; the echo of his shout seemed to linger among the trees. "Leaf-eater," said Ender, "I will have no interpreter but Human."

"Who are you to tell me that I may not speak to the wives? I am a piggy, and you are nothing."

"Human," said Ender, "tell Shouter that if she lets Leaf-eater translate words that we humans have said among ourselves, then he is a spy. And if she lets him spy on us, we will go home now and you will have nothing from us. I'll take the hive queen to another world to restore her. Do you understand?''

Of course he understood. Ender also knew that Human was pleased. Leaf-eater was trying to usurp Human's role and discredit him—along with Ender. When Human finished translating Ender's words, Shouter sang at Leaf-eater. Abashed, he quickly retreated to the woods to watch with the other piggies.

But Human was by no means a puppet. He gave no sign that he was grateful. He looked Ender in the eye. "You said you wouldn't try to change us.''

"I said I wouldn't try to change you more than is necessary.''

"Why is this necessary? It's between us and the other piggies.''

"Careful,'' said Ouanda. "He's very upset.''

Before he could hope to persuade Shouter, he had to convince Human. "You are our first friends among the piggies. You have our trust and our love. We will never do anything to harm you, or to give any other piggies an advantage over you. But we didn't come just to you. We represent all of humankind, and we've come to teach all we can to all of the piggies. Regardless of tribe.''

"You don't represent all humankind. You're about to fight a war with other humans. So how can you say that *our* wars are evil and your wars are good?''

Surely Pizarro, for all his shortcomings, had an easier time of it with Atahualpa. "We're trying *not* to fight a war with other humans,'' said Ender. "And if we fight one, it won't be *our* war, trying to gain an advantage over them. It will be *your* war, trying to win you the right to travel among the stars.'' Ender held up his open hand. "We have set aside our humanness to become ramen with you.'' He closed his hand into a fist. "Human and piggy and hive queen, here on Lusitania, will be one. *All* humans. *All* buggers. *All* piggies.''

Human sat in silence, digesting this.

"Speaker," he finally said. "This is very hard. Until you humans came, other piggies were—always to be killed, and their third life was to be slaves to us in forests that we kept. This forest was once a battlefield, and the most ancient trees are the warriors who died in battle. Our oldest fathers are the heroes of that war, and our houses are made of the cowards. All our lives we prepare to win battles with our enemies, so that our wives can make a mothertree in a new battle forest, and make us mighty and great. These last ten years we have learned to use arrows to kill from far off. Pots and cabra skins to carry water across the drylands. Amaranth and merdona root so we can be many and strong and carry food with us far from the macios of our home forest. We rejoiced in this because it meant that we would always be victorious in war. We would carry our wives, our little mothers, our heroes to every corner of the great world, and finally one day out into the stars. This is our dream, Speaker, and you tell me now that you want us to lose it like wind in the sky."

It was a powerful speech. None of the others offered Ender any suggestions about what to say in answer. Human had half-convinced them.

"You dream is a good one," said Ender. "It's the dream of every living creature. The desire that is the very root of life itself: To grow until all the space you can see is part of you, under your control. It's the desire for greatness. There are two ways, though, to fulfil it. One way is to kill anything that is not yourself, to swallow it up or destroy it, until nothing is left to oppose you. But that way is evil. You say to all the universe, Only I will be great, and to make room for me the rest of you must give up even what you already have, and become nothing. Do you understand, Human, that if we humans felt this way, acted this way, we could kill every piggy in Lusitania and make this place our home. How much of your dream would be left, if we were evil?"

Human was trying hard to understand. "I see that you gave us great gifts, when you could have taken from us even the little that we had. But why did you give us the gifts, if we can't use them to become great?"

"We want you to grow, to travel among the stars. Here on Lusitania we want you to be strong and powerful, with hundreds and thousands of brothers and wives. We want to teach you to grow many kinds of plants and raise many different animals. Ela and Novinha, these two women, will work all the days of their lives to develop more plants that can live here in Lusitania, and every good thing that they make, they'll give to you. So you can grow. But why does a single piggy in any other forest have to die, just so you can have these gifts? And why would it hurt you in any way, if we also gave the same gifts to *them*?"

"If they become just as strong as we are, then what have we gained?"

What am I expecting this brother to do, thought Ender. His people have always measured themselves against the other tribes. Their forest isn't fifty hectares or five hundred—it's either larger or smaller than the forest of the tribe to the west or the south. What I have to do now is the work of a generation: I have to teach him a new way of conceiving the stature of his own people. "Is Rooter great?" asked Ender.

"I say he is," said Human. "He's my father. His tree isn't the oldest or thickest, but no father that we remember has ever had so many children so quickly after he was planted."

"So in a way, all the children that he fathered are still part of him. The more children he fathers, the greater he becomes." Human nodded slowly. "And the more you accomplish in your life, the greater you make your father, is that true?"

"If his children do well, then yes, it's a great honor to the fathertree."

"Do you have to kill all the other great trees in order for your father to be great?"

"That's different," said Human. "All the other great trees

are fathers of the tribe. And the lesser trees are still brothers.'' Yet Ender could see that Human was uncertain now. He was resisting Ender's ideas because they were strange, not because they were wrong or incomprehensible. He was beginning to understand.

"Look at the wives," said Ender. "They have no children. They can never be great the way that your father is great."

"Speaker, you know that they're the greatest of all. The whole tribe obeys them. When they rule us well, the tribe prospers; when the tribe becomes many, then the wives are also made strong—"

"Even though not a single one of you is their own child."

"How could we be?" asked Human.

"And yet you add to their greatness. Even though they aren't your mother or your father, they still grow when you grow."

"We're all the same tribe . . ."

"But *why* are you the same tribe? You have different fathers, different mothers."

"Because we *are* the tribe! We live here in the forest, we—"

"If another piggy came here from another tribe, and asked you to let him stay and be a brother—"

"We would never make him a fathertree!"

"But you tried to make Pipo and Libo fathertrees."

Human was breathing heavily. "I see," he said. "They were part of the tribe. From the sky, but we made them brothers and tried to make them fathers. The tribe is whatever we believe it is. If we say the tribe is all the Little Ones in the forest, and all the trees, then that is what the tribe is. Even though some of the oldest trees here came from warriors of two different tribes, fallen in battle. We become one tribe because we *say* we're one tribe."

Ender marveled at his mind, this small raman. How few humans were able to grasp this idea, or let it extend beyond the narrow confines of their tribe, their family, their nation.

Human walked behind Ender, leaned against him, the weight of the young piggy pressed against his back. Ender felt Human's breath on his cheek, and then their cheeks were pressed together, both of them looking in the same direction. All at once Ender understood: "You see what I see," said Ender.

"You humans grow by making us part of you, humans and piggies and buggers, ramen together. Then we are one tribe, and our greatness is your greatness, and yours is ours." Ender could feel Human's body trembling with the strength of the idea. "You say to us, we must see all other tribes the same way. As one tribe, our tribe all together, so that we grow by making them grow."

"You could send teachers," said Ender. "Brothers to the other tribes, who could pass into their third life in the other forests and have children there."

"This is a strange and difficult thing to ask of the wives," said Human. "Maybe an impossible thing. Their minds don't work the way a brother's mind works. A brother can think of many different things. But a wife thinks of only one thing: what is good for the tribe, and at the root of that, what is good for the children and the little mothers."

"Can you make them understand this?" asked Ender.

"Better than you could," said Human. "But probably not. Probably I'll fail."

"I don't think you'll fail," said Ender.

"You came here tonight to make a covenant between us, the piggies of this tribe, and you, the humans who live on this world. The humans outside Lusitania won't care about our covenant, and the piggies outside ths forest won't care about it."

"We want to make the same covenant with all of them."

"And in this covenant, you humans promise to teach us everything."

"As quickly as you can understand it."

"Any question we ask."

"If we know the answer."

"When! If! These aren't words in a covenant! Give me straight answers now, Speaker for the Dead." Human stood up, pushed away from Ender, walked around in front of him, bent down a little to look at Ender from above. "Promise to teach us everything that you know!"

"We promise that."

"And you also promise to restore the hive queen to help us."

"I'll restore the hive queen. You'll have to make your own covenant with her. She doesn't obey human law."

"You promise to restore the hive queen, whether she helps us or not."

"Yes."

"You promise to obey our law when you come into our forest. And you agree that the prairie land that we need will also be under our law."

"Yes."

"And you will go to war against all the other humans in all the stars of the sky to protect us and let us also travel in the stars?"

"We already have."

Human relaxed, stepped back, squatted in his old position. He drew with his finger in the dirt. "Now, what you want from us," said Human. "We will obey human law in your city, and also in the prairie land that you need."

"Yes," said Ender.

"And you don't want us to go to war," said Human.

"That's right."

"And that's all?"

"One more thing," said Ender.

"What you ask is already impossible," said Human. "You might as well ask more."

"The third life," said Ender. "When does it begin?

When you kill a piggy and he grows into a tree, is that right?''

"The first life is within the mothertree, where we never see the light, and where we eat blindly the meat of our mother's body and the sap of the mothertree. The second life is when we live in the shade of the forest, the half-light, running and walking and climbing, seeing and singing and talking, making with our hands. The third life is when we reach and drink from the sun, in the full light at last, never moving except in the wind; only to think, and on those certain days when the brothers drum on your trunk, to speak to them. Yes, that's the third life.''

"Humans don't have the third life.''

Human looked at him, puzzled.

"When we die, even if you plant us, nothing grows. There's no tree. We never drink from the sun. When we die, we're dead.''

Human looked at Ouanda. "But the other book you gave us. It talked all the time about living after death and being born again.''

"Not as a tree," said Ender. "Not as anything you can touch or feel. Or talk to. Or get answers from.''

"I don't believe you," said Human. "If that's true, why did Pipo and Libo make us plant them?''

Novinha knelt down beside Ender, touching him—no, leaning on him—so she could hear more clearly.

"How did they make you plant them?" said Ender.

"They made the great gift, won the great honor. The human and the piggy together. Pipo and Mandachuva. Libo and Leaf-eater. Mandachuva and Leaf-eater both thought that they would win the third life, but each time, Pipo and Libo would not. They insisted on keeping the gift for themselves. Why would they do that, if humans have no third life?''

Novinha's voice came then, husky and emotional. "What did they have to do, to give the third life to Mandachuva or Leaf-eater?''

"Plant them, of course," said Human. "The same as today."

"The same as *what* today?" asked Ender.

"You and me," said Human. "Human and the Speaker for the Dead. If we make this covenant so that the wives and the humans agree together, then this is a great, a noble day. So either you will give me the third life, or I will give it to you."

"With my own hand?"

"Of course," said Human. "If you won't give me the honor, then I must give it to you."

Ender remembered the picture he had first seen only two weeks ago, of Pipo dismembered and disemboweled, his body parts stretched and spread. Planted. "Human," said Ender, "the worst crime that a human being can commit is murder. And one of the worst ways to do it is to take a living person and cut him and hurt him so badly that he dies."

Again Human squatted for a while, trying to make sense of this. "Speaker," he said at last, "my mind keeps seeing this two ways. If humans don't have a third life, then planting is killing, forever. In our eyes, Libo and Pipo were keeping the honor to themselves, and leaving Mandachuva and Leaf-eater as you see them, to die without honor for their accomplishments. In our eyes, you humans came out of the fence to the hillside and tore them from the ground before their roots could grow. In our eyes, it was you who committed murder, when you carried Pipo and Libo away. But now I see it another way. Pipo and Libo wouldn't take Mandachuva and Leaf-eater into the third life, because to them it would be murder. So they willingly allowed their own death, just so they wouldn't have to kill any of us."

"Yes," said Novinha.

"But if that's so, then when you humans saw them on the hillside, why didn't you come into the forest and kill us all? Why didn't you make a great fire and consume all our fathers, and the great mothertree herself?"

Leaf-eater cried out from the edge of the forest, a terrible keening cry, an unbearable grief.

"If you had cut one of our trees," said Human. "If you had murdered a single tree, we would have come upon you in the night and killed you, every one of you. And even if some of you survived, our messengers would have told the story to every other tribe, and none of you would ever have left this land alive. Why didn't you kill *us*, for murdering Pipo and Libo?"

Mandachuva suddenly appeared behind Human, panting heavily. He flung himself to the ground, his hands outstretched toward Ender. "I cut him with these hands," he cried. "I tried to honor him, and I killed his tree forever!"

"No," said Ender. He took Mandachuva's hands, held them. "You both thought you were saving each other's life. He hurt you, and you—hurt him, yes, killed him, but you both believed you were doing good. That's enough, until now. Now you know the truth, and so do we. We know that you didn't mean murder. And you know that when you take a knife to a human being, we die forever. That's the last term in the covenant, Human. Never take another human being to the third life, because we don't know how to go."

"When I tell this story to the wives," said Human, "you'll hear grief so terrible that it will sound like the breaking of trees in a thunderstorm."

He turned and stood before Shouter, and spoke to her for a few moments. Then he returned to Ender. "Go now," he said.

"We have no covenant yet," said Ender.

"I have to speak to all the wives. They'll never do that while you're here, in the shade of the mothertree, with no one to protect the little ones. Arrow will lead you back out of the forest. Wait for me on the hillside, where Rooter keeps watch over the gate. Sleep if you can. I'll present the covenant to the wives and try to make them understand that we must deal as kindly with the other tribes as you have dealt with us.''

Impulsively, Human reached out a hand and touched Ender firmly on the belly. ''I make my own covenant,'' he said to Ender. ''I will honor you forever, but I will never kill you.''

Ender put out his hand and laid his palm against Human's warm abdomen. The protuberances under his hand were hot to the touch. ''I will also honor you forever,'' said Ender.

''And if we make this convenant between your tribe and ours,'' said Human, ''will you give me the honor of the third life? Will you let me rise up and drink the light?''

''Can we do it quickly? Not the slow and terrible way that—''

''And make me one of the silent trees? Never fathering? Without honor, except to feed my sap to the filthy macios and give my wood to the brothers when they sing to me?''

''Isn't there someone else who can do it?'' asked Ender. ''One of the brothers, who knows your way of life and death?''

''You don't understand,'' said Human. ''This is how the whole tribe knows that the truth has been spoken. Either you must take me into the third life, or I must take you, or there's no covenant. I won't kill *you,* Speaker, and we both want a treaty.''

''I'll do it,'' said Ender.

Human nodded, withdrew his hand, and returned to Shouter.

''Ó Deus,'' whispered Ouanda. ''How will you have the heart?''

Ender had no answer. He merely followed silently behind Arrow as he led them to the woods. Novinha gave him her own nightstick to lead the way; Arrow played with it like a child, making the light small and large, making it hover and swoop like a suckfly among the trees and bushes. He was as happy and playful as Ender had ever seen a piggy be.

But behind them, they could hear the voices of the wives, singing a terrible and cacophonous song. Human had told them the truth about Pipo and Libo, that they died the final death, and in pain, all so that they would not have to do to Mandachuva and Leaf-eater what they thought was murder. Only when they had gone far enough that the sound of the wives' keening was softer than their own footfalls and the wind in the trees did any of the humans speak.

"That was the mass for my father's soul," said Ouanda softly.

"And for mine," answered Novinha; they all knew that she spoke of Pipo, not the long-dead Venerado, Gusto.

But Ender was not part of their conversation; he had not known Libo and Pipo, and did not belong to their memory of grief. All he could think of was the trees of the forest. They had once been living, breathing piggies, every one of them. The piggies could sing to them, talk to them, even, somehow, understand their speech. But Ender couldn't. To Ender the trees were not *people*, could never be people. If he took the knife to Human, it might not be murder in the piggies' eyes, but to Ender himself he would be taking away the only part of Human's life that Ender understood. As a piggy, Human was a true raman, a brother. As a tree he would be little more than a gravestone, as far as Ender could understand, as far as he could really believe.

Once again, he thought, I must kill, though I promised that I never would again.

He felt Novinha's hand take him by the crook of the arm. She leaned on him. "Help me," she said. "I'm almost blind in the darkness."

"I have good night vision," Olhado offered cheerfully from behind her.

"Shut up, stupid," Ela whispered fiercely. "Mother wants to walk with him."

Both Novinha and Ender heard her clearly, and both could feel each other's silent laughter. Novinha drew closer to him as they walked. "I think you have the heart for what you have to do," she said softly, so that only he could hear.

"Cold and ruthless?" he asked. His voice hinted at wry humor, but the words tasted sour and truthful in his mouth.

"Compassionate enough," she said, "to put the hot iron into the wound when that's the only way to heal it."

As one who had felt his burning iron cauterize her deepest wounds, she had the right to speak; and he believed her, and it eased his heart for the bloody work ahead.

Ender hadn't thought it would be possible to sleep, knowing what was ahead of him. But now he woke up, Novinha's voice soft in his ear. He realized that he was outside, lying in the capim, his head resting on Novinha's lap. It was still dark.

"They're coming," said Novinha softly.

Ender sat up. Once, as a child, he would have come awake fully, instantly; but he was trained as a soldier then. Now it took a moment to orient himself. Ouanda, Ela, both awake and watching; Olhado asleep; Quim just stirring. The tall tree of Rooter's third life rising only a few meters away. And in the near distance, beyond the fence at the bottom of the little valley, the first houses of Milagre rising up the slopes; the Cathedral and the monastery atop the highest and nearest of the hills.

In the other direction, the forest, and coming down from the trees, Human, Mandachuva, Leaf-eater, Arrow, Cups, Calendar, Worm, Bark-dancer, several other brothers whose names Ouanda didn't know. "I've never seen them," she said. "They must come from other brother-houses."

Do we have a covenant? said Ender silently. That's all I care about. Did Human make the wives understand a new way of conceiving of the world?

Human was carrying something. Wrapped in leaves. The piggies wordlessly laid it before Ender; Human unwrapped it carefully. It was a computer printout.

"The Hive Queen and the Hegemon," said Ouanda softly. "The copy Miro gave them."

"The covenant," said Human.

Only then did they realize that the printout was upside down, on the blank side of the paper. And there, in the light of a nightstick, they saw faint hand-printed letters. They were large and awkwardly formed. Ouanda was in awe. "We never taught them to make ink," she said. "We never taught them to write."

"Calendar learned to make the letters," said Human. "Writing with sticks in the dirt. And Worm made the ink from cabra dung and dried macios. This is how you make treaties, isn't it?"

"Yes," said Ender.

"If we didn't write it on paper, then we would remember it differently."

"That's right," said Ender. "You did well to write it down."

"We made some changes. The wives wanted some changes, and I thought you would accept them." Human pointed them out. "You humans can make this covenant with other piggies, but you can't make a *different* covenant. You can't teach any other piggies things you haven't taught us. Can you accept that?"

"Of course," said Ender.

"That was the easy one. Now, what if we disagree about what the rules are? What if we disagree about where your prairie land ends and ours begins? So Shouter said, Let the hive queen judge between humans and Little Ones. Let the humans judge between the Little Ones and the hive queen. And let Little Ones judge between the hive queen and the humans."

Ender wondered how easy that would be. He remembered, as no other living human did, how terrifying the buggers were three thousand years ago. Their insectlike bodies were the nightmares of humanity's childhood. How easily would the people of Milagre accept their judgment?

So it's hard. It's no harder than what we've asked the piggies to do. "Yes," said Ender. "We can accept that, too. It's a good plan."

"And another change," said Human. He looked up at Ender and grinned. It looked ghastly, since piggy faces weren't designed for that human expression. "This is why it took so long. All these changes."

Ender smiled back.

"If a tribe of piggies won't sign the covenant with humans, and if that tribe attacks one of the tribes that *has* signed the covenant, *then* we can go to war against them."

"What do you mean by attack?" asked Ender. If they could take a mere insult as an attack, then this clause would reduce the prohibition of war to nothing.

"Attack," said Human. "It begins when they come into our lands and kill the brothers or the wives. It is not attack when they present themselves for war, or offer an agreement to begin a war. It *is* attack when they start to fight without an agreement. Since we will never agree to a war, an attack by another tribe is the only way war could begin. I knew you'd ask."

He pointed to the words of the covenant, and indeed the treaty carefully defined what constituted an attack.

"That is also acceptable," said Ender. It meant that the possibility of war would not be removed for many generations, perhaps for centuries, since it would take a long time to bring this covenant to every tribe of piggies in the world. But long before the last tribe joined the covenant, Ender thought, the benefits of peaceful exogamy would be made plain, and few would want to be warriors anymore.

"Now the last change," said Human. "The wives meant this to punish you for making this covenant so difficult. But I think you will believe it is no punishment. Since we are forbidden to take you into the third life, after this covenant is in effect humans are also forbidden to take brothers into the third life.''

For a moment Ender thought it meant his reprieve; he would not have to do the thing that Libo and Pipo had both refused.

"*After* the covenant," said Human. "You will be the first and last human to give this gift."

"I wish . . ." said Ender.

"I know what you wish, my friend Speaker," said Human. "To you it feels like murder. But to me—when a brother is given the right to pass into the third life as a father, then he chooses his greatest rival or his truest friend to give him the passage. You. Speaker—ever since I first learned Stark and read the Hive Queen and the Hegemon, I waited for you. I said many times to my father, Rooter, of all humans he is the one who will understand us. Then Rooter told me when your starship came, that it was you and the hive queen aboard that ship, and I knew then that you had come to give me passage, if only I did well."

"You did well, Human," said Ender.

"Here," he said. "See? We signed the covenant in the human way."

At the bottom of the last page of the covenant two words were crudely, laboriously shaped. "Human," Ender read aloud. The other word he could not read.

"It's Shouter's true name," said Human. "Star-looker. She wasn't good with the writing stick—the wives don't use tools very often, since the brothers do that kind of work. So she wanted me to tell you what her name is. And to tell you that she got it because she was always looking in the sky. She says that she didn't know it then, but she was watching for you to come."

So many people had so much hope in me, thought Ender. In the end, though, everything depended on them. On Novinha, Miro, Ela, who called for me; on Human and Star-looker. And on the ones who feared my coming, too.

Worm carried the cup of ink; Calendar carried the pen. It was a thin strip of wood with a slit in it and a narrow well that held a little ink when he dipped it in the cup. He had to dip it five times in order to sign his name. "Five," said Arrow. Ender remembered then that the number five was portentous to the piggies. It had been an accident, but if they chose to see it as a good omen, so much the better.

"I'll take the covenant to our Governor and the Bishop," said Ender.

"Of all the documents that were ever treasured in the history of mankind . . ." said Ouanda. No one needed her to finish the sentence. Human, Leaf-eater, and Mandachuva carefully wrapped the book again in leaves and handed it, not to Ender, but to Ouanda. Ender knew at once, with terrible certainty, what that meant. The piggies still had work for him to do, work that would require that his hands be free.

"Now the covenant is made the human way," said Human. "You must make it true for the Little Ones as well."

"Can't the signing be enough?" asked Ender.

"From now on the signing is enough," said Human. "But only because the same hand that signed for the humans also took the covenant in our way, too."

"Then I will," said Ender, "as I promised you I would."

Human reached out and stroked Ender from the throat to the belly. "The brother's word is not just in his mouth," he said. "The brother's word is in his life." He turned to the other piggies. "Let me speak to my father one last time before I stand beside him."

Two of the strange brothers came forward with their small clubs in their hands. They walked with Human to Rooter's tree and began to beat on it and sing in the Fathers' Language. Almost at once the trunk split open. The tree was still fairly young, and not so very much thicker in the trunk than Human's own body; it was a struggle for him to get inside. But he fit, and the trunk closed up after him. The drumming changed rhythm, but did not let up for a moment.

Jane whispered in Ender's ear. "I can hear the resonance of the drumming change inside the tree," she said. "The tree is slowly shaping the sound, to turn the drumming into language."

The other piggies set to work clearing ground for Human's tree. Ender noticed that he would be planted so that, from the gate, Rooter would seem to stand on the left hand, and Human on the right. Pulling up the capim by the root was hard work for the piggies; soon Quim was helping them, and then Olhado, and then Ouanda and Ela.

Ouanda gave the covenant to Novinha to hold while she helped dig capim. Novinha, in turn, carried it to Ender, stood before him, looked at him steadily. "You signed it Ender Wiggin," she said. "Ender."

The name sounded ugly even to his own ears. He had heard it too often as an epithet. "I'm older than I look," said Ender. "That was the name I was known by when I blasted the buggers' home world out of existence. Maybe the presence of that name on the first treaty ever signed between humans and ramen will do something to change the meaning of the name."

"Ender," she whispered. She reached toward him, the bundled treaty in her hands, and held it against his chest; it was heavy, since it contained all the pages of the Hive Queen and the Hegemon, on the other sides of pages where the covenant was written. "I never went to the priests to confess," she said, "because I knew they would despise me for my sin. Yet when you named all my sins today, I could bear it because I knew you didn't despise me. I couldn't understand *why*, though, till now."

"I'm not one to despise other people for their sins," said Ender. "I haven't found one yet, that I didn't say inside myself, I've done worse than this."

"All these years you've borne the burden of humanity's guilt."

"Yes, well, it's nothing mystical," said Ender. "I think of

it as being like the mark of Cain. You don't make many friends, but nobody hurts you much, either.''

The ground was clear. Mandachuva spoke in Tree Language to the piggies beating on the trunk; their rhythm changed, and again the aperture in the tree came open. Human slid out as if he were an infant being born. Then he walked to the center of the cleared ground. Leaf-eater and Mandachuva each handed him a knife. As he took the knives, Human spoke to them—in Portuguese, so the humans could understand, and so it would carry great force. ''I told Shouter that you lost your passage to the third life because of a great misunderstanding by Pipo and Libo. She said that before another hand of hands of days, you both would grow upward into the light.''

Leaf-eater and Mandachuva both let go of their knives, touched Human gently on the belly, and stepped back to the edge of the cleared ground.

Human held out the knives to Ender. They were both made of thin wood. Ender could not imagine a tool that could polish wood to be at once so fine and sharp, and yet so strong. But of course no tool had polished these. They had come thus perfectly shaped from the heart of a living tree, given as a gift to help a brother into the third life.

It was one thing to know with his mind that Human would not really die. It was another thing to believe it. Ender did not take the knives at first. Instead he reached past the blades and took Human by the wrists. ''To you it doesn't feel like death. But to me—I only saw you for the first time yesterday, and tonight I know you are my brother as surely as if Rooter were my father, too. And yet when the sun rises in the morning, I'll never be able to talk to you again. It feels like death to me, Human, how ever it feels to you.''

''Come and sit in my shade,'' said Human, ''and see the sunlight through my leaves, and rest your back against my trunk. And do this, also. Add another story to the Hive

Queen and the Hegemon. Call it the Life of Human. Tell all the humans how I was conceived on the bark of my father's tree, and born in darkness, eating my mother's flesh. Tell them how I left the life of darkness behind and came into the half-light of my second life, to learn language from the wives and then come forth to learn all the miracles that Libo and Miro and Ouanda came to teach. Tell them how on the last day of my second life, my true brother came from above the sky, and together we made this covenant so that humans and piggies would be one tribe, not a human tribe or a piggy tribe, but a tribe of ramen. And then my friend gave me passage to the third life, to the full light, so that I could rise into the sky and give life to ten thousand children before I die."

"I'll tell your story," said Ender.

"Then I will truly live forever."

Ender took the knives. Human lay down upon the ground.

"Olhado," said Novinha. "Quim. Go back to the gate. Ela, you too."

"I'm going to see this, Mother," said Ela. "I'm a scientist."

"You forget my eyes," said Olhado. "I'm recording everything. We can show humans everywhere that the treaty was signed. And we can show piggies that the Speaker took the covenant in their way, too."

"I'm not going, either," said Quim. "Even the Blessed Virgin stood at the foot of the cross."

"You can stay," said Novinha softly. And she also stayed.

Human's mouth was filled with capim, but he didn't chew it very much. "More," said Ender, "so you don't feel anything."

"That's not right," said Mandachuva. "These are the last moments of his second life. It's good to feel something of the pains of this body, to remember when you're in the third life, and beyond pain."

Mandachuva and Leaf-eater told Ender where and how to cut. It had to be done quickly, they told him, and their hands reached into the steaming body to point out organs that must go here or there. Ender's hands were quick and sure, his body calm, but even though he could only rarely spare a glance away from the surgery, he knew that above his bloody work, Human's eyes were watching him, watching him, filled with gratitude and love, filled with agony and death.

It happened under his hands, so quickly that for the first few minutes they could watch it grow. Several large organs shriveled as roots shot out of them; tendrils reached from place to place within the body; Human's eyes went wide with the final agony; and out of his spine a sprout burst upward, two leaves, four leaves—

And then stopped. The body was dead; its last spasm of strength had gone to making the tree that rooted in Human's spine. Ender had seen the rootlets and tendrils reaching through the body. The memories, the soul of Human had been transferred into the cells of the newly sprouted tree. It was done. His third life had begun. And when the sun rose in the morning, not long from now, the leaves would taste the light for the first time.

The other piggies were rejoicing, dancing. Leaf-eater and Mandachuva took the knives from Ender's hands and jammed them into the ground on either side of Human's head. Ender could not join their celebration. He was covered with blood and reeked with the stench of the body he had butchered. On all fours he crawled from the body, up the hill to a place where he didn't have to see it. Novinha followed him. Exhausted, spent, all of them, from the work and the emotions of the day. They said nothing, did nothing, but fell into the thick capim, each one leaning or lying on someone else, seeking relief at last in sleep, as the piggies danced away up the hill into the woods.

Bosquinha and Bishop Peregrino made their way to the gate before the sun was up, to watch for the Speaker's return from the forest. They were there a full ten minutes before they saw a movement much nearer than the forest's edge. It was a boy, sleepily voiding his bladder into a bush.

"Olhado!" called the Mayor.

The boy turned, waved, then hastily fastened his trousers and began waking others who slept in the tall grass. Bosquinha and the Bishop opened the gate and walked out to meet them.

"Foolish, isn't it," said Bosquinha, "but this is the moment when our rebellion seems most real. When I first walk beyond the fence."

"Why did they spend the night out of doors?" Peregrino wondered aloud. "The gate was open, they could have gone home."

Bosquinha took a quick census of the group outside the gates. Ouanda and Ela, arm in arm like sisters. Olhado and Quim. Novinha. And there, yes, the Speaker, sitting down, Novinha behind him, resting her hands on his shoulders. They all waited expectantly, saying nothing. Until Ender looked up at them. "We have the treaty," he said. "It's a good one."

Novinha held up a bundle wrapped in leaves. "They wrote it down," she said. "For you to sign."

Bosquinha took the bundle. "All the files were restored before midnight," she said. "Not just the ones we saved in your message queue. Whoever your friend is, Speaker, he's very good."

"She," said the Speaker. "Her name is Jane."

Now, though, the Bishop and Bosquinha could see what lay on the cleared earth just down the hill from where the Speaker had slept. Now they understood the dark stains on the Speaker's hands and arms, the spatter marks on his face.

"I would rather have no treaty," said Bosquinha, "than one you had to kill to get."

"Wait before you judge," said the Bishop. "I think the night's work was more than just what we see before us."

"Very wise, Father Peregrino," said the Speaker softly.

"I'll explain it to you if you want," said Ouanda. "Ela and I understand it as well as anyone."

"It was like a sacrament," said Olhado.

Bosquinha looked at Novinha, uncomprehending. "You let him watch?"

Olhado tapped his eyes. "All the piggies will see it, someday, through my eyes."

"It wasn't death," said Quim. "It was resurrection."

The Bishop stepped near the tortured corpse and touched the seedling tree growing from the chest cavity. "His name is Human," said the Speaker.

"And so is yours," said the Bishop softly. He turned and looked around at the members of his little flock, who had already taken humanity a step further than it had ever gone before. Am I the shepherd, Peregrino asked himself, or the most confused and helpless of the sheep? "Come, all of you. Come with me to the Cathedral. The bells will soon ring for mass."

The children gathered and prepared to go. Novinha, too, stepped away from her place behind the Speaker. Then she stopped, turned back to him, looked at him with silent invitation in her eyes.

"Soon," he said. "A moment more."

She, too, followed the Bishop through the gate and up the hill into the Cathedral.

The mass had barely begun when Peregrino saw the Speaker enter at the back of the Cathedral. He paused a moment, then found Novinha and her family with his eyes. In only a few steps he had taken a place beside her. Where Marcão had sat, those rare times when the whole family came together.

The duties of the service took his attention; a few moments later, when Peregrino could look again, he saw that Grego was now sitting beside the Speaker. Peregrino thought of the terms of the treaty as the girls had explained it to him. Of the meaning of the death of the piggy called Human, and before him, of the deaths of Pipo and Libo. All things coming clear, all things coming together. The young man, Miro, lying paralyzed in bed, with his sister Ouanda tending him. Novinha, the lost one, now found. The fence, its shadow so dark in the minds of all who had lived within its bounds, now still and harmless, invisible, insubstantial.

It was the miracle of the wafer, turned into the flesh of God in his hands. How suddenly we find the flesh of God within us after all, when we thought that we were only made of dust.

Chapter 18
The Hive Queen

*E*volution gave his mother no birth canal and no breasts. So the small creature who would one day be named Human was given no exit from the womb except by the teeth of his mouth. He and his infant siblings devoured their mother's body. Because Human was strongest and most vigorous, he ate the most and so became even stronger.

Human lived in utter darkness. When his mother was gone, there was nothing to eat but the sweet liquid that flowed on the surface of his world. He did not know yet that the vertical surface was the inside of a great hollow tree, and that the liquid that he ate was the sap of the tree. Nor did he know that the warm creatures that were far larger than himself were older piggies, almost ready to leave the darkness of the tree, and that the smaller creatures were younger ones, more recently emerged than himself.

All he really cared about was to eat, to move, and to see the light. For now and then, in rhythms that he could not comprehend, a sudden light came into the darkness. It began each time with a sound, whose source he could not comprehend. Then the tree would shudder slightly; the sap would cease to flow; and all the tree's energy would be devoted to changing the shape of the trunk in one place, to make an opening that let the light inside. When the light was there, Human moved toward it. When the light was gone, Human lost his sense of direction, and wandered aimlessly in search of liquid to drink.

Until one day, when almost all the other creatures were smaller than himself, and none at all were larger, the light came and he was so strong and swift that he reached the opening before it closed. He bent his body around the curve of the wood of the tree, and for the first time felt the rasp of outer bark under his soft belly. He hardly noticed this new pain, because the light dazzled him. It was not just in one place, but everywhere, and it was not grey but vivid green and yellow. His rapture lasted many seconds. Then he was hungry again, and here on the outside of the mothertree the sap flowed only in the fissures of the bark, where it was hard to reach, and instead of all the other creatures being little ones that he could push aside, they all were larger than himself, and drove him away from the easy feeding places. This was a new thing, a new world, a new life, and he was afraid.

Later, when he learned language, he would remember the journey from darkness into light, and he would call it the passage from the first life to the second, from the life of darkness to the half-lit life.

—Speaker for the Dead, *The Life of Human,* 1:1–5

Miro decided to leave Lusitania. Take the Speaker's starship and go to Trondheim after all. Perhaps at his trial he could persuade the Hundred Worlds not to go to war against Lusitania. At worst, he could become a martyr, to stir people's hearts, to be remembered, to stand for something. Whatever happened to him, it would be better than staying here.

In the first few days after he climbed the fence, Miro recovered rapidly. He gained some control and feeling in his arms and legs. Enough to take shuffling steps, like an old man. Enough to move his arms and hands. Enough to end the humiliation of his mother having to clean his body. But then his progress slowed and stopped. "Here it is," said Navio. "We have reached the level of permanent damage. You are so lucky, Miro, you can walk, you can talk, you are a whole man. You are no more limited than, say, a very healthy man who is a hundred years old. I would rather tell you that your body would be as it was before you climbed the fence, that you would have all the vigor and control of a twenty-year-old. But I'm very glad that I *don't* have to tell you that you will be bedridden all your life, diapered and catheterized, able to do nothing more than listen to soft music and wonder where your body went."

So I'm grateful, Miro thought. As my fingers curl into a useless club on the ends of my arms, as I hear my own speech sounding thick and unintelligible, my voice unable to modulate properly, then I will be so glad that I am like a hundred-year-old man, that I can look forward to eighty more years of life as a centegenarian.

Once it was clear that he did not need constant attention, the family scattered and went about their business. These days were too exciting for them to stay home with a crippled brother, son, friend. He understood completely. He did not want them to stay home with him. He wanted to be with them. His work was unfinished. Now, at long last, all the fences, all the rules were gone. Now he could ask the piggies the questions that had so long puzzled him.

He tried at first to work through Ouanda. She came to him every morning and evening and made her reports on the terminal in the front room of the Ribeira house. He read her reports, asked her questions, listened to her stories. And she very seriously memorized the questions he wanted her to ask the piggies. After a few days of this, however, he noticed that in the evening she would indeed have the answers to Miro's questions. But there was no follow-up, no exploration of meaning. Her real attention was devoted to her own work.

And Miro stopped giving her questions to ask for him. He lied and told her that he was far more interested in what she was doing, that her avenues of exploration were the most important.

The truth was that he hated seeing Ouanda. For him, the revelation that she was his sister was painful, terrible, but he knew that if the decision were his alone, he would cast aside the incest tabu, marry her and live in the forest with the piggies if need be. Ouanda, however, was a believer, a belonger. She couldn't possibly violate the only universal human law. She grieved when she learned that Miro was her brother, but she immediately began to separate herself from him, to forget the touches, the kisses, the whispers, the promises, the teasing, the laughter . . .

Better if he forgot them, too. But he could not. Every time he saw her, it hurt him to see how reserved she was, how *polite* and *kind* she was. He was her brother, he was crippled, she would be good to him. But the love was gone.

Uncharitably, he compared Ouanda to his own mother, who had loved her lover regardless of the barriers between them. But Mother's lover had been a whole man, an able man, not this useless carcass.

So Miro stayed home and studied the file reports of everybody else's work. It was torture to know what they were doing, that he could not take part in it; but it was better than doing nothing, or watching the tedious vids on the terminal, or listening to music. He could type, slowly, by aiming his hand so the stiffest of his fingers, the index finger, touched exactly one key. It wasn't fast enough to enter any meaningful data, or even to write memos, but he could call up other people's public files and read what they were doing. He could maintain some connection with the vital work that had suddenly blossomed on Lusitania, with the opening of the gate.

Ouanda was working with the piggies on a lexicon of the Males' and Wives' Languages, complete with a phonological spelling system so they could write their language down. Quim was helping her, but Miro knew that he had his own purpose: He intended to be a missionary to the piggies in other tribes, taking them the Gospels before they ever saw the Hive Queen and the Hegemon; he intended to translate at least some of the scripture and speak to the piggies in their own language. All this work with piggy language and culture was very good, very important, preserve the past, prepare to communicate with other tribes, but Miro knew that it could easily be done by Dom Cristão's scholars, who now ventured forth in their monkish robes and quietly asked questions of the piggies and answered their questions ably and powerfully. Ouanda was allowing herself to become redundant, Miro believed.

The real work with the piggies, as Miro saw it, was being done by Ender and a few key technicians from Bosquinha's services department. They were laying pipe from the river to the mothertree's clearing, to bring water to them. They were setting up electricity and teaching the brothers how to use a computer terminal. In the meantime, they were teaching them very primitive means of agriculture and trying to domesticate cabras to pull plows. It was confusing, the different levels of technology that were coming to the piggies all at once, but Ender had discussed it with Miro, explaining that he wanted the piggies to see quick, dramatic, immediate results from their treaty. Running water, a computer connection with a holographic terminal that let them read anything in the library, electric lights at night. But all this was still magic, completely dependent on human society. At the same time, Ender was trying to keep them self-sufficient, inventive, resourceful. The dazzle of electricity would make myths that would spread through the world from tribe to tribe, but it would be no more than rumor for many, many years. It was the wooden plow, the scythe, the harrow, the amaranth seed that

would make the real changes, that would allow piggy population to increase tenfold wherever they went. And those could
be transmitted from place to place with a handful of seeds in
a cabra-skin pouch and the memory of how the work was
done.

This was the work that Miro longed to be part of. But what
good were his clubbed hands and shuffling step in the amaranth fields? Of what use was he sitting at a loom, weaving
cabra wool? He couldn't even talk well enough to teach.

Ela was working on developing new strains of Earthborn
plants and even small animals and insects, new species that
could resist the Descolada, even neutralize it. Mother was
helping her with advice, but little more, for she was working
on the most vital and secret project of them all. Again, it was
Ender who came to Miro and told him what only his family
and Ouanda knew: that the hive queen lived, that she was
being restored as soon as Novinha found a way for her to
resist the Descolada, her and all the buggers that would be
born to her. As soon as it was ready, the hive queen would
be revived.

And Miro would not be part of that, either. For the first
time, humans and two alien races, living together as ramen
on the same world, and Miro wasn't part of any of it. He was
less human than the piggies were. He couldn't speak or use
his hands half so well. He had stopped being a tool-using,
language-speaking animal. He was varelse now. They only
kept him as a pet.

He wanted to go away. Better yet, he wanted to disappear,
to go away even from himself.

But not right now. There was a new puzzle that only he
knew about, and so only he could solve. His terminal was
behaving very strangely.

He noticed it the first week after he recovered from total
paralysis. He was scanning some of Ouanda's files and realized that without doing anything special, he had accessed
confidential files. They were protected with several layers, he

had no idea what the passwords were, and yet a simple, routine scan had brought the information forward. It was her speculations on piggy evolution and their probable pre-Descolada society and life patterns. The sort of thing that as recently as two weeks ago she would have talked about, argued about with Miro. Now she kept it confidential and never discussed it with him at all.

Miro didn't tell her he had seen the files, but he did steer conversations toward the subject and drew her out; she talked about her ideas willingly enough, once Miro showed his interest. Sometimes it was almost like old times. Except that he would hear the sound of his own slurred voice and keep most of his opinions to himself, merely listening to her, letting things he would have argued with pass right by. Still, seeing her confidential files allowed him to penetrate to what she was really interested in.

But how had he seen them?

It happened again and again. Files of Ela's, Mother's, Dom Cristão's. As the piggies began to play with their new terminal, Miro was able to watch them in an echo mode that he had never seen the terminal use before—it enabled him to watch all their computer transactions and then make some suggestions, change things a little. He took particular delight in guessing what the piggies were really trying to do and helping them, surreptitiously, to do it. But how had he got such unorthodox, powerful access to the machine?

The terminal was learning to accommodate itself to him, too. Instead of long code sequences, he only had to begin a sequence and the machine would obey his instructions. Finally he did not even have to log on. He touched the keyboard and the terminal displayed a list of all the activities he usually engaged in, then scanned through them. He could touch a key and it would go directly to the activity he wanted, skipping dozens of preliminaries, saving him many painful minutes of typing one character at a time.

At first he thought that Olhado had created the new program for him, or perhaps someone in the Mayor's office. But Olhado only looked blankly at what the terminal was doing and said, "Bacâna," that's great. And when he sent a message to the Mayor, she never got it. Instead, the Speaker for the Dead came to visit him.

"So your terminal is being helpful," said Ender.

Miro didn't answer. He was too busy trying to think why the Mayor had sent the Speaker to answer his note.

"The Mayor didn't get your message," said Ender. "I did. And it's better if you don't mention to anybody else what your terminal is doing."

"Why?" asked Miro. That was one word he could say without slurring too much.

"Because it isn't a new program helping you. It's a person."

Miro laughed. No human being could be as quick as the program that was helping him. It was faster, in fact, than most programs he had worked with before, and very resourceful and intuitive; faster than a human, but smarter than a program.

"It's an old friend of mine, I think. At least, she was the one who told me about your message and suggested that I let you know that discretion was a good idea. You see, she's a bit shy. She doesn't make many friends."

"How many?"

"At the present moment, exactly two. For a few thousand years before now, exactly one."

"Not human," said Miro.

"Raman," said Ender. "More human than most humans. We've loved each other for a long time, helped each other, depended on each other. But in the last few weeks, since I got here, we've drifted apart. I'm—involved more in the lives of people around me. Your family."

"Mother."

"Yes. Your mother, your brothers and sisters, the work with the piggies, the work for the hive queen. My friend and I used to talk to each other constantly. I don't have time now.

We've hurt each other's feelings sometimes. She's lonely, and so I think she's chosen another companion.''

"Não quero." Don't want one.

"Yes you do," said Ender. "She's already helped you. Now that you know she exists, you'll find that she's—a good friend. You can't have a better one. More loyal. More helpful.''

"Puppy dog?''

"Don't be a jackass," said Ender. "I'm introducing you to a fourth alien species. You're supposed to be a xenologer, aren't you? She knows you, Miro. Your physical problems are nothing to her. She has no body at all. She exists among the philotic disturbances in the ansible communications of the Hundred Worlds. She's the most intelligent creature alive, and you're the second human being she's ever chosen to reveal herself to.''

"How?'' How did she come to be? How did she know me, to choose me?

"Ask her yourself." Ender touched the jewel in his ear. "Just a word of advice. Once she comes to trust you, keep her with you always. Keep no secrets from her. She once had a lover who switched her off. Only for an hour, but things were never the same between them after that. They became— just friends. Good friends, loyal friends, always until he dies. But all his life he will regret that one thoughtless act of disloyalty.''

Ender's eyes glistened, and Miro realized that whatever this creature was that lived in the computer, it was no phantom, it was part of this man's life. And he was passing it down to Miro, like father to son, the right to know this friend.

Ender left without another word, and Miro turned to the terminal. There was a holo of a woman there. She was small, sitting on a stool, leaning against a holographic wall. She was not beautiful. Not ugly, either. Her face had character. Her eyes were haunting, innocent, sad. Her mouth delicate, about to smile, about to weep. Her clothing seemed veil-like, insubstantial, and yet instead of being provocative, it revealed a sort of innocence, a girlish, small-breasted body, the hands clasped lightly in her lap, her legs childishly parted with the toes pointing inward. She could have been sitting on a teeter-totter in a playground. Or on the edge of her lover's bed.

"Bom dia," Miro said softly.

"Hi," she said. "I asked him to introduce us."

She was quiet, reserved, but it was Miro who felt shy. For so long, Ouanda had been the only woman in his life, besides the women of his family, and he had little confidence in the social graces. At the same time, he was aware that he was speaking to a hologram. A completely convincing one, but a midair laser projection all the same.

She reached up one hand and laid it gently on her breast. "Feels nothing," she said. "No nerves."

Tears came to his eyes. Self-pity, of course. That he would probably never have a woman more substantial than this one. If he tried to touch one, his caresses would be crude pawing. Sometimes, when he wasn't careful, he drooled and couldn't even feel it. What a lover.

"But I have eyes," she said. "And ears. I see everything in all the Hundred Worlds. I watch the sky through a thousand telescopes. I overhear a trillion conversations every day." She giggled a little. "I'm the best gossip in the universe."

Then, suddenly, she stood up, grew larger, closer, so that she only showed from the waist up, as if she had moved closer to an invisible camera. Her eyes burned with intensity as she stared right at him. "And you're a parochial schoolboy who's never seen anything but one town and one forest in his life."

"Don't get much chance to travel," he said.

"We'll see about that," she answered. "So. What do you want to do today?"

"What's your name?" he asked.

"You don't need my name," she said.

"How do I call you?"

"I'm here whenever you want me."

"But I want to know," he said.

She touched her ear. "When you like me well enough to take me with you wherever you go, then I'll tell you my name."

Impulsively, he told her what he had told no one else. "I want to leave this place," said Miro. "Can you take me away from Lusitania?"

She at once became coquettish, mocking. "And we only just met! Really, Mr. Ribeira, I'm not that sort of girl."

"Maybe when we get to know each other," Miro said, laughing.

She made a subtle, wonderful transition, and the woman on the screen was a lanky feline, sprawling sensuously on a tree limb. She purred noisily, stretched out a limb, groomed herself. "I can break your neck with a single blow from my paw," she whispered; her tone of voice suggested seduction; her claws promised murder. "When I get you alone, I can bite your throat out with a single kiss."

He laughed. Then he realized that in all this conversation, he had actually forgotten how slurred his speech was. She understood every word. She never said, "What? I didn't get that," or any of the other polite but infuriating things that people said. She understood him without any special effort at all.

"I want to understand everything," said Miro. "I want to know everything and put it all together to see what it means."

"Excellent project," she said. "It will look very good on your résumé."

Ender found that Olhado was a much better driver than he was. The boy's depth perception was better, and when he plugged his eye directly into the onboard computer, navigation practically took care of itself. Ender could devote his energies to looking.

The scenery seemed monotonous when they first began these exploratory flights. Endless prairies, huge herds of cabra, occasional forests in the distance—they never came close to those, of course, since they didn't want to attract the attention of the piggies that lived there. Besides, they were looking for a home for the hive queen, and it wouldn't do to put her too close to any tribe.

Today they headed west, on the other side of Rooter's Forest, and they followed a small river to its outlet. They stopped there on the beach, with breakers rolling gently to shore. Ender tasted the water. Salt. The sea.

Olhado got the onboard terminal to display a map of this region of Lusitania, pointing out their location, Rooter's Forest, and the other piggy settlements nearby. It was a good place, and in the back of his mind Ender could sense the hive queen's approval. Near the sea, plenty of water, sunny.

They skimmed over the water, traveling upstream a few hundred meters until the right bank rose to form a low cliff. "Any place to stop along here?" asked Ender.

Olhado found a place, fifty meters from the crown of the hill. They walked back along the river's edge, where the reeds gave way to the grama. Every river on Lusitania looked like this, of course. Ela had easily documented the genetic patterns, as soon as she had access to Novinha's files and permission to pursue the subject. Reeds that co-reproduced with suckflies. Grama that mated with watersnakes. And then the endless capim, which rubbed its pollen-rich tassels on the bellies of fertile cabra to germinate the next generation of manure-producing animals. Entwined in the roots and stems of the capim were the tropeços, long trailing vines that Ela proved had the same genes as the xingadora, the ground-nesting bird that used the living plant for its nest. The same sort of pairing continued in the forest: Macio worms that hatched from the seeds of merdona vines and then gave birth to merdona seed. Puladors, small insects that mated with the shiny-leafed bushes in the forest. And, above all, the piggies and the trees, both at the peak of their kingdoms, plant and animal merged into one long life.

That was the list, the whole list of surface animals and plants of Lusitania. Under water there were many, many more. But the Descolada had left Lusitania monotonous.

And yet even the monotony had a peculiar beauty. The geography was as varied as any other world—rivers, hills, mountains, deserts, oceans, islands. The carpet of capim and the patches of forest became background music to the symphony of landforms. The eye became sensitized to undulations, outcroppings, cliffs, pits, and, above all, the sparkle and rush of water in the sunlight. Lusitania, like Trondheim, was one of the rare worlds that was dominated by a single motif instead of displaying the whole symphony of possibility. With Trondheim, however, it was because the planet was on the bare edge of habitability, its climate only just able to support surface life. Lusitania's climate and soil cried out a welcome to the oncoming plow, the excavator's pick, the mason's trowel. Bring me to life, it said.

Ender did not understand that he loved this place because it was as devastated and barren as his own life, stripped and distorted in his childhood by events every bit as terrible, on a small scale, as the Descolada had been to this world. And yet it had thrived, had found a few threads strong enough to survive and continue to grow. Out of the challenge of the Descolada had come the three lives of the Little Ones. Out of the Battle School, out of years of isolation, had come Ender Wiggin. He fit this place as if he had planned it. The boy who walked beside him through the grama felt like his true son, as if he had known the boy from infancy. I know how it feels to have a metal wall between me and the world, Olhado. But here and now I have made the wall come down, and flesh touches earth, drinks water, gives comfort, takes love.

The earthen bank of the river rose in terraces, a dozen

meters from shore to crest. The soil was moist enough to dig
and hold its shape. The hive queen was a burrower; Ender
felt the desire in him to dig, and so he dug, Olhado beside
him. The ground gave way easily enough, and yet the roof of
their cavelet stayed firm.

<Yes. Here.>

And so it was decided.

"Here it is," said Ender aloud.

Olhado grinned. But it was really Jane that Ender was
talking to, and her answer that he heard. "Novinha thinks
they have it. The tests all came through negative—the
Descolada stayed inactive with the new Colador present in
the cloned bugger cells. Ela thinks that the daisies she's been
working with can be adapted to produce the Colador naturally. If that works, you'll only have to plant seeds here and
there and the buggers can keep the Descolada at bay by
sucking flowers."

Her tone was lively enough, but it was all business, no
fun. No fun at all. "Fine," Ender said. He felt a stab of
jealousy—Jane was no doubt talking far more easily with
Miro, teasing him, taunting him as she used to do with
Ender.

But it was easy enough to drive the feeling of jealousy
away. He put out a hand and rested it easily on Olhado's
shoulder; he momentarily pulled the boy close, and then
together they walked back to the waiting flyer. Olhado marked
the spot on the map and stored it. He laughed and made jokes
all the way home, and Ender laughed with him. The boy
wasn't Jane. But he *was* Olhado, and Ender loved him, and
Olhado needed Ender, and that was what a few million years
of evolution had decided Ender needed most. It was the
hunger that had gnawed at him through all those years with
Valentine, that had kept him moving from world to world.
This boy with metal eyes. His bright and devastatingly destructive little brother Grego. Quara's penetrating understanding, her innocence; Quim's utter self-control, asceticism,

faith; Ela's dependability, like a rock, and yet she knew when to move out and act; and Miro . . .

Miro. I have no consolation for Miro, not in this world, not at this time. His life's work was taken from him, his body, his hope for the future, and nothing I can say or do will give him a vital work to do. He lives in pain, his lover turned into his sister, his life among the piggies now impossible to him as they look to other humans for friendship and learning.

"Miro needs . . ." Ender said softly.

"Miro needs to leave Lusitania," said Olhado.

"Mm," said Ender.

"You've got a starship, haven't you?" said Olhado. "I remember reading a story once. Or maybe it was a vid. About an old-time hero in the Bugger Wars, Mazer Rackham. He saved Earth from destruction once, but they knew he'd be dead long before the next battle. So they sent him out in a starship at relativistic speeds, just sent him out and had him come back. A hundred years had gone by for the Earth, but only two years for him."

"You think Miro needs something as drastic as that?"

"There's a battle coming. There are decisions to make. Miro's the smartest person in Lusitania, and the best. He doesn't get mad, you know. Even in the worst of times with Father. Marcão. Sorry, I still call him Father."

"That's all right. In most ways he *was*."

"Miro would think, and he'd decide the best thing to do, and it always *was* the best thing. Mother depended on him to. The way I see it, we need Miro when Starways Congress sends its fleet against us. He'll study all the information, everything we've learned in the years that he was gone, put it all together, and tell us what to do."

Ender couldn't help himself. He laughed.

"So it's a dumb idea," said Olhado.

"You see better than anybody else I know," said Ender. "I've got to think about this, but you might be right."

They drove on in silence for a while.

"I was just talking," said Olhado. "When I said that about Miro. It was just something I thought, putting him together with that old story. It probably isn't even a true story."

"It's true," said Ender.

"How do you know?"

"I knew Mazer Rackham."

Olhado whistled. "You're old. You're older than any of the trees."

"I'm older than any of the human colonies. It doesn't make me wise, unfortunately."

"Are you really Ender? *The* Ender?"

"That's why it's my password."

"It's funny. Before you got here, the Bishop tried to tell us all that you were Satan. Quim's the only one in the family that took him seriously. But if the Bishop had told us you were *Ender,* we would have stoned you to death in the praça the day you arrived."

"Why don't you now?"

"We know you now. That makes all the difference, doesn't it? Even Quim doesn't hate you now. When you really know somebody, you can't hate them."

"Or maybe it's just that you can't really know them until you stop hating them."

"Is that a circular paradox? Dom Cristão says that most truth can only be expressed in circular paradoxes."

"I don't think it has anything to do with truth, Olhado. It's just cause and effect. We never can sort them out. Science refuses to admit any cause except first cause—knock down one domino, the one next to it also falls. But when it comes to human beings, the only type of cause that matters is final cause, the purpose. What a person had in mind. Once you understand what people really want, you can't hate them any-more. You can fear them, but you can't hate them, because you can always find the same desires in your own heart."

"Mother doesn't like it that you're Ender."

"I know."

"But she loves you anyway."

"I know."

"And Quim—it's really funny, but now that he knows you're Ender, he likes you *better* for it."

"That's because he's a crusader, and I got my bad reputation by winning a crusade."

"And me," said Olhado.

"Yes, you," said Ender.

"You killed more people than anybody in history."

"Be the best at whatever you do, that's what my mother always told me."

"But when you Spoke for Father, you made me feel sorry for him. You make people love each other and forgive each other. How could you kill all those millions of people in the Xenocide?"

"I thought I was playing games. I didn't know it was the real thing. But that's no excuse, Olhado. If I had known the battle was real, I would have done the same thing. We thought they wanted to kill us. We were wrong, but we had no way to know that." Ender shook his head. "Except that I knew better. I knew my enemy. That's how I beat her, the hive queen, I knew her so well that I loved her, or maybe I loved her so well that I knew her. I didn't want to fight her anymore. I wanted to quit. I wanted to go home. So I blew up her planet."

"And today we found the place to bring her back to life." Olhado was very serious. "Are you sure she won't try to get even? Are you sure she won't try to wipe out humankind, starting with you?"

"I'm as sure," said Ender, "as I am of anything."

"Not absolutely sure," said Olhado.

"Sure enough to bring her back to life," said Ender. "And that's as sure as we ever are of anything. We believe it enough to act as though it's true. When we're that sure, we call it knowledge. Facts. We bet our lives on it.''

"I guess that's what you're doing. Betting your life on her being what you think she is."

"I'm more arrogant than that. I'm betting *your* life, too, and everybody else's, and I'm not so much as asking anyone else's opinion.''

"Funny," said Olhado. "If I asked somebody whether they'd trust Ender with a decision that might affect the future of the human race, they'd say, of course not. But if I asked them whether they'd trust the Speaker for the Dead, they'd say yes, most of them. And they wouldn't even guess that they were the same person."

"Yeah," said Ender. "Funny."

Neither of them laughed. Then, after a long time, Olhado spoke again. His thoughts had wandered to a subject that mattered more. "I don't want Miro to go away for thirty years."

"Say twenty years."

"In twenty years I'll be thirty-two. But he'd come back the age he is now. Twenty. Twelve years younger than me. If there's ever a girl who wants to marry a guy with reflecting eyes, I might even be married and have kids then. He won't even know me. I won't be his little brother anymore." Olhado swallowed. "It'd be like him dying."

"No," said Ender. "It'd be like him passing from his second life to his third."

"That's like dying, too," said Olhado.

"It's also like being born," said Ender. "As long as you keep getting born, it's all right to die sometimes."

Valentine called the next day. Ender's fingers trembled as he keyed instructions into the terminal. It wasn't just a message, either. It was a call, a full ansible voice communication. Incredibly expensive, but that wasn't a problem. It was the fact that ansible communications with the Hundred

Worlds were supposedly cut off; for Jane to allow this call to come through meant that it was urgent. It occurred to Ender right away that Valentine might be in danger. That Starways Congress might have decided Ender was involved in the rebellion and traced his connection with her.

She was older. The hologram of her face showed weather lines from many windy days on the islands, floes, and boats of Trondheim. But her smile was the same, and her eyes danced with the same light. Ender was silenced at first by the changes the years had wrought in his sister; she, too, was silenced, by the fact that Ender seemed unchanged, a vision coming back to her out of her past.

"Ah, Ender," she sighed. "Was I ever so young?"

"And will I age so beautifully?"

She laughed. Then she cried. He did not; how could he? He had missed her for a couple of months. She had missed him for twenty-two years.

"I suppose you've heard," he said, "about our trouble getting along with Congress."

"I imagine that you were at the thick of it."

"Stumbled into the situation, really," said Ender. "But I'm glad I was here. I'm going to stay."

She nodded, drying her eyes. "Yes. I thought so. But I had to call and make sure. I didn't want to spend a couple of decades flying to meet you, and have you gone when I arrive."

"Meet me?" he said.

"I got much too excited about your revolution there, Ender. After twenty years of raising a family, teaching my students, loving my husband, living at peace with myself, I thought I'd never resurrect Demosthenes again. But then the story came about illegal contact with the piggies, and right away the news that Lusitania was in revolt, and suddenly people were saying the most ridiculous things, and I saw it was the beginning of the same old hate. Remember the videos about the buggers? How terrifying and awful they were? Suddenly we were seeing videos of the bodies they found, of the xenologers, I can't remember their names, but grisly pictures everywhere you looked, heating us up to war fever. And then stories about the Descolada, how if anyone ever went from Lusitania to another world it would destroy everything—the most hideous plague imaginable—"

"It's true," said Ender, "but we're working on it. Trying to find ways to keep the Descolada from spreading when we go to other worlds."

"True or not, Ender, it's all leading to war. I remember war—nobody else does. So I revived Demosthenes. I stumbled across some memos and reports. Their fleet is carrying the Little Doctor, Ender. If they decide to, they can blow Lusitania to bits. Just like—"

"Just like I did before. Poetic justice, do you think, for me to end the same way? He who lives by the sword—"

"Don't joke with me, Ender! I'm a middle-aged matron now, and I've lost my patience with silliness. At least for now. I wrote some very ugly truths about what Starways Congress is doing, and published them as Demosthenes. They're looking for me. Treason is what they're calling it."

"So you're coming here?"

"Not just me. Dear Jakt is turning the fleet over to his brothers and sisters. We've already bought a starship. There's apparently some kind of resistance movement that's helping us—someone named Jane has jimmied the computers to cover our tracks."

"I know Jane," said Ender.

"So you do have an organization here! I was shocked when I got a message that I could call you. Your ansible was supposedly blown up."

"We have powerful friends."

"Ender, Jakt and I are leaving today. We're bringing our three children."

"Your first one—"

"Yes, Syfte, the one who was making me fat when you

left, she's almost twenty-two now. A very lovely girl. And a good friend, the children's tutor, named Plikt."

"I have a student by that name," said Ender, thinking back to conversations only a couple of months ago.

"Oh, yes, well, that was twenty years ago, Ender. And we're bringing several of Jakt's best men and their families. Something of an ark. It's not an emergency—you have twenty-two years to prepare for me. Actually longer, more like thirty years. We're taking the voyage in several hops, the first few in the wrong direction, so that nobody can be sure we're going to Lusitania."

Coming here. Thirty years from now. I'll be older than she is now. Coming here. By then I'll have my family, too. Novinha's and my children, if we have any, all grown, like hers.

And then, thinking of Novinha, he remembered Miro, remembered what Olhado had suggested several days ago, the day they found the nesting place for the hive queen.

"Would you mind terribly," said Ender, "if I sent someone to meet you on the way?"

"Meet us? In deep space? No, don't send someone to do that, Ender—it's too terrible a sacrifice, to come so far when the computers can guide us in just fine—"

"It's not really for you, though I want him to meet you. He's one of the xenologers. He was badly injured in an accident. Some brain damage; like a bad stroke. He's—he's the smartest person in Lusitania, says someone whose judgment I trust, but he's lost all his connections with our life here. Yet we'll need him later. When you arrive. He's a very good man, Val. He can make the last week of your voyage very educational."

"Can your friend arrange to get us course information for such a rendezvous? We're navigators, but only on the sea."

"Jane will have the revised navigational information in your ship's computer when you leave."

"Ender—for you it'll be thirty years, but for me—I'll see you in only a few weeks." She started to cry.

"Maybe I'll come with Miro to meet you."

"Don't!" she said. "I want you to be as old and crabbed as possible when I arrive. I couldn't put up with you as the thirty-year-old brat I see on my terminal."

"Thirty-five."

"You'll be there when I arrive!" she demanded.

"I will," he said. "And Miro, the boy I'm sending to you. Think of him as my son."

She nodded gravely. "These are such dangerous times, Ender. I only wish we had Peter."

"I don't. If *he* were running our little rebellion, he'd end up Hegemon of all the Hundred Worlds. We just want them to leave us alone."

"It may not be possible to get the one without the other," said Val. "But we can quarrel about that later. Good-bye, my dear brother."

He didn't answer. Just looked at her and looked at her until she smiled wryly and switched off the connection.

Ender didn't have to ask Miro to go; Jane had already told him everything.

"Your sister is Demosthenes?" asked Miro. Ender was used to his slurred speech now. Or maybe his speech was clearing a little. It wasn't as hard to understand, anyway.

"We were a talented family," said Ender. "I hope you like her."

"I hope she likes me." Miro smiled, but he looked afraid.

"I told her," said Ender, "to think of you as my son."

Miro nodded. "I know," he said. And then, almost defiantly, "She showed me your conversation with her."

Ender felt cold inside.

Jane's voice came into his ear. "I should have asked you," she said. "But you know you would have said yes."

It wasn't the invasion of privacy that Ender minded. It was

the fact that Jane was so very close to Miro. Get used to it, he told himself. He's the one she's looking out for now.

"We'll miss you," said Ender.

"Those who will miss me, miss me already," said Miro, "because they already think of me as dead."

"We need you alive," said Ender.

"When I come back, I'll still be only nineteen. And brain-damaged."

"You'll still be Miro, and brilliant, and trusted, and loved. You started this rebellion, Miro. The fence came down for you. Not for some great cause, but for you. Don't let us down."

Miro smiled, but Ender couldn't tell if the twist in his smile was because of his paralysis, or because it was a bitter, poisonous smile.

"Tell me something," said Miro.

"If I won't," said Ender, "she will."

"It isn't hard. I just want to know what it was that Pipo and Libo died for. What it was the piggies honored them for."

Ender understood better than Miro knew: He understood why the boy cared so much about the question. Miro had learned that he was really Libo's son only hours before he crossed the fence and lost his future. Pipo, then Libo, then Miro; father, son, grandson; the three xenologers who had lost their futures for the piggies' sake. Miro hoped that in understanding why his forebears died, he might make more sense of his own sacrifice.

The trouble was that the truth might well leave Miro feeling that none of the sacrifices meant anything at all. So Ender answered with a question. "Don't you already know why?"

Miro spoke slowly and carefully, so that Ender could understand his slurred speech. "I know that the piggies thought they were doing them an honor. I know that Mandachuva and Leaf-eater could have died in their places.

With Libo, I even know the occasion. It was when the first amaranth harvest came, and there was plenty of food. They were rewarding him for that. Except why not earlier? Why not when we taught them to use merdona root? Why not when we taught them to make pots, or shoot arrows?''

"The truth?'' said Ender.

Miro knew from Ender's tone that the truth would not be easy. "Yes,'' he said.

"Neither Pipo nor Libo really deserved the honor. It wasn't the amaranth that the wives were rewarding. It was the fact that Leaf-eater had persuaded them to let a whole generation of infants be conceived and born even though there wasn't enough food for them to eat once they left the mothertree. It was a terrible risk to take, and if he had been wrong, that whole generation of young piggies would have died. Libo brought the harvest, but Leaf-eater was the one who had, in a sense, brought the population to a point where they needed the grain.''

Miro nodded. "Pipo?''

"Pipo told the piggies about his discovery. That the Descolada, which killed humans, was part of their normal physiology. That their bodies could handle transformations that killed us. Mandachuva told the wives that this meant that humans were not godlike and all-powerful. That in some ways we were even weaker than the Little Ones. That what made humans stronger than piggies was not something inherent in us—our size, our brains, our language—but rather the mere accident that we were a few thousand years ahead of them in learning. If they could acquire our knowledge, then we humans would have no more power over them. Mandachuva's discovery that piggies were potentially equal to humans—that was what they rewarded, not the information Pipo gave that led to that discovery.''

"So both of them—''

"The piggies didn't want to kill either Pipo or Libo. In both cases, the crucial achievement belonged to a piggy. The only reason Pipo and Libo died was because they couldn't bring themselves to take a knife and kill a friend.''

Miro must have seen the pain in Ender's face, despite his best effort to conceal it. Because it was Ender's bitterness that he answered. "You," said Miro, "you can kill anybody."

"It's a knack I was born with," said Ender.

"You killed Human because you knew it would make him live a new and better life," said Miro.

"Yes."

"And me," said Miro.

"Yes," said Ender. "Sending you away is very much like killing you."

"But will I live a new and better life?"

"I don't know. Already you get around better than a tree."

Miro laughed. "So I've got one thing on old Human, don't I—at least I'm ambulatory. And nobody has to hit me with a stick so I can talk." Then Miro's expression grew sour again. "Of course, now *he* can have a thousand children."

"Don't count on being celibate all your life," said Ender. "You may be disappointed."

"I hope so," said Miro.

And then, after a silence: "Speaker?"

"Call me Ender."

"Ender, did Pipo and Libo die for nothing, then?" Ender understood the real question: Am I also enduring this for nothing?

"There are worse reasons to die," Ender answered, "than to die because you cannot bear to kill."

"What about someone," said Miro, "who can't kill, and can't die, and can't live, either?"

"Don't deceive yourself," said Ender. "You'll do all three someday."

Miro left the next morning. There were tearful good-byes. For weeks afterward, it was hard for Novinha to spend any time in her own house, because Miro's absence was so painful to her. Even though she had agreed wholeheartedly with Ender that it was right for Miro to go, it was still unbearable to lose her child. It made Ender wonder if his own parents felt such pain when he was taken away. He suspected they had not. Nor had they hoped for his return. He already loved another man's children more than his parents had loved their own child. Well, he'd get fit revenge for their neglect of him. He'd show them, three thousand years later, how a father should behave. Bishop Peregrino married them in his chambers. By Novinha's calculations, she was still young enough to have another six children, if they hurried. They set at the task with a will.

Before the marriage, though, there were two days of note. On a day in summer, Ela, Ouanda, and Novinha presented him with the results of their research and speculation: as completely as possible, the life cycle and community structure of the piggies, male and female, and a likely reconstruction of their patterns of life before the Descolada bonded them forever to the trees that, till then, had been no more to them than habitat. Ender had reached his own understanding of who the piggies were, and especially who Human was before his passage to the life of light.

He lived with the piggies for a week while he wrote the Life of Human. Mandachuva and Leaf-eater read it carefully, discussed it with him; he revised and reshaped; finally it was ready. On that day he invited everyone who was working with the piggies—all the Ribeira family, Ouanda and her sisters, the many workmen who had brought technological miracles to the piggies, the scholar-monks of the Children of the Mind, Bishop Peregrino, Mayor Bosquinha—and read the book to them. It wasn't long, less than an hour to read. They had gathered on the hillside near where Human's seedling tree reached upward, now more than three meters high, and where Rooter overshadowed them in the afternoon sunlight. "Speaker," said the Bishop, "almost thou persuadest me to become a humanist." Others, less trained to eloquence, found no words to say, not then or ever. But they knew from that day forward who the piggies were, just as the readers of the Hive Queen had understood the buggers, and the readers of the Hegemon had understood humankind in its endless quest for greatness in a wilderness of separation and suspicion. "This was why I called you here," said Novinha. "I dreamed once of writing this book. But you had to write it."

"I played more of a role in the story than I would have chosen for myself," said Ender. "But you fulfilled your dream, Ivanova. It was your work that led to this book. And you and your children who made me whole enough to write it."

He signed it, as he had signed the others, The Speaker for the Dead.

Jane took the book and carried it by ansible across the lightyears to the Hundred Worlds. With it she brought the text of the Covenant and Olhado's pictures of its signing and of the passage of Human into the full light. She placed it here and there, in a score of places on each of the Hundred Worlds, giving it to people likely to read it and understand what it was. Copies were sent as messages from computer to computer; by the time Starways Congress knew of it, it was too widely distributed to be suppressed.

Instead they tried to discredit it as a fake. The pictures were a crude simulation. Textual analysis revealed that it could not possibly have the same author as the other two books. Ansible usage records revealed that it could not possibly have come from Lusitania, which had no ansible. Some people believed them. Most people didn't care. Many who did care enough to read the Life of Human hadn't the heart to accept the piggies as ramen.

Some did accept the piggies, and read the accusation that Demosthenes had written a few months before, and began to call the fleet that was already under way toward Lusitania "The Second Xenocide." It was a very ugly name. There weren't enough jails in the Hundred Worlds to hold all those who used it. The Starways Congress had thought the war would begin when their ships reached Lusitania forty years from then. Instead, the war was already begun, and it would be fierce. What the Speaker for the Dead wrote, many people believed; and many were ready to accept the piggies as ramen, and to think of anyone who sought their deaths as murderers.

Then, on a day in autumn, Ender took the carefully wrapped cocoon, and he and Novinha, Olhado, Quim, and Ela skimmed over the kilometers of capim till they came to the hill beside the river. The daisies they had planted were in furious bloom; the winter here would be mild, and the hive queen would be safe from the Descolada.

Ender carried the hive queen gingerly to the riverbank, and laid her in the chamber he and Olhado had prepared. They laid the carcass of a freshly killed cabra on the ground outside her chamber.

And then Olhado drove them back. Ender wept with the vast, uncontrollable ecstasy that the hive queen placed within his mind, her rejoicing too strong for a human heart to bear; Novinha held him, Quim quietly prayed, and Ela sang a jaunty folksong that once had been heard in the hill country of Minas Geráis, among the caipiras and mineiros of old Brazil. It was a good time, a good place to be, better than Ender had ever dreamed for himself in the sterile corridors of the Battle School when he was little, and fighting for his life.

"I can probably die now," said Ender. "All my life's work is done."

"Mine too," said Novinha. "But I think that means that it's time to start to live."

Behind them, in the dank and humid air of a shallow cave by a river, strong mandibles tore at the cocoon, and a limp and skeletal body struggled forth. Her wings only gradually spread out and dried in the sunlight; she struggled weakly to the riverbank and pulled strength and moisture into her desiccated body. She nibbled at the meat of the cabra. The un-hatched eggs she held within her cried out to be released; she laid the first dozen of them in the cabra's corpse, then ate the nearest daisies, trying to feel the changes in her body as she came alive at last.

The sunlight on her back, the breeze against her wings, the water cool under her feet, her eggs warming and maturing in the flesh of the cabra: Life, so long waited for, and not until today could she be sure that she would be, not the last of her tribe, but the first.

F
Car